Elaine Showalter was born in Cambridge, Massachusetts in 1941 and was educated at Bryn Mawr College and the University of California. From 1967 to 1984 she taught English and Women's Studies at Rutgers University, and she is now Professor of English at Princeton University. She is the author of *A Literature of Their Own: Women Writers from Charlotte Brontë to Doris Lessing* (Virago, 1978), *The Female Malady: Women, Madness and English Culture, 1830–1980* (Virago, 1987), *Sexual Anarchy: Gender and Culture at the Fin de Siècle* and editor of *The New Feminist Criticism: Essays on Women, Literature and Theory* (Virago, 1986). Her most recent books are *Inventing Herself: Claiming a Feminist Intellectual Heritage* (2001) and *Teaching Literature* (2002). *The Jury of Her Peers: American Women Writers 1650–2000* will be published by Virago in 2008.

Other works by Elaine Showalter
also published by Virago

A Literature of Their Own
The Female Malady
Sexual Anarchy
The New Feminist Criticism (editor)

DAUGHTERS
·OF·
DECADENCE

Women Writers of the *Fin de Siècle*

EDITED AND INTRODUCED BY

Elaine Showalter

Virago

VIRAGO

First published in Great Britain by Virago Press 1993

Reprinted 1995, 1996, 1998, 2000, 2002, 2005, 2006, 2007

A CIP catalogue record for this book is available from the British Library

ISBN 978-1-85381-590-4

Papers used by Virago are natural, recyclable products made from wood grown in sustainable forests and certified in accordance with the rules of the Forest Stewardship Council.

Printed and bound in Great Britain by Clays Ltd, St Ives plc
Paper supplied by Hellefoss AS, Norway

Virago Press
An imprint of
Little, Brown Book Group
100 Victoria Embankment
London EC4Y 0DY

An Hachette Livre UK Company

www.virago.co.uk

CONTENTS

Acknowledgements		vi
Introduction		vii
Kate Chopin	'An Egyptian Cigarette'	1
Victoria Cross	'Theodora: A Fragment'	6
Ada Leverson	'Suggestion'	38
George Egerton	'A Cross Line'	47
'Borgia Smudgiton'	'She-Notes'	69
George Fleming	'By Accident'	74
Olive Schreiner	'The Buddhist Priest's Wife'	84
Charlotte Perkins Gilman	'The Yellow Wallpaper'	98
Charlotte Mew	'A White Night'	118
Mabel E. Wotton	'The Fifth Edition'	139
Constance Fenimore Woolson	'Miss Grief'	165
Vernon Lee	'Lady Tal'	192
Sarah Grand	'The Undefinable: A Fantasia'	262
Edith Wharton	'The Muse's Tragedy'	288
Kate Chopin	'Emancipation: A Life Fable'	306
Olive Schreiner	'Three Dreams in a Desert'	308
Olive Schreiner	'Life's Gifts'	317
Edith Wharton	'The Valley of Childish Things'	318
Biographical Notes		320

ACKNOWLEDGEMENTS

I owe special thanks to Jennie Kassanoff, who helped compile the bibliographies of these women writers. The original sources of the stories are the following: Kate Chopin, 'An Egyptian Cigarette', *Vogue* 15 (19 April, 1900) pp. 252–54; 'Emancipation: A Life Fable', from Per Seyersted (ed.) *The Complete Works of Kate Chopin*, (Baton Rouge: Louisiana State University, 1969); Victoria Cross, 'Theodora: A Fragment', *The Yellow Book* v (1895); Ada Leverson, 'Suggestion', *The Yellow Book* v (April 1895); George Egerton, 'A Cross Line', from *Keynotes*, (London: John Lane, 1893); 'Borgia Smudgiton' (Owen Seaman), 'She–Notes', *Punch*, cvi (10 March, 1884) p. 109, and cvi (17 March, 1894) p. 129, with illustrations by 'Mortarthurio Whiskersley' (Edward Tennyson Reed); 'George Fleming' (Julia Constance Fletcher), 'By Accident', from *Little Stories About Women*, (London: John Lane, 1898); Charlotte Perkins Gilman, 'The Yellow Wallpaper', *The New England Magazine* (May 1892); Sarah Grand, 'The Undefinable: A Fantasia', from *Emotional Moments* (London: Hurst and Blackett, 1908), pp. 303–58; Vernon Lee, 'Lady Tal', from *Vanities* (London: William Heinemann, 1896); Charlotte Mew, 'A White Night', from *Temple Bar* cxxvii (May 1903); Olive Shreiner, 'The Buddhist Priest's Wife', from *Stories, Dreams and Allegories*, intro. S.C. Cronwright–Schreiner (London: Unwin, 1923); 'Three Dreams in a Desert' and 'Life's Gift', from *Dreams* (London: Unwin, 1890); Edith Wharton, 'The Valley of Childish Things', *The Century Magazine LII* (1896) p. 467 and 'The Muse's Tragedy', from *The Greater Inclination* (New York: Scribner's, 1899); Constance Fenimore Woolson, 'Miss Grief', *Lippincott's* 25 (May 1880); and Mabel E. Wotton, 'The Fifth Edition', from *Day-Books* (London: John Lane, 1896).

INTRODUCTION

When we think of the literature of the *fin de siècle*, the writers who come most readily to mind are men. Whether they are the aesthetes and decadents who drank absinthe on the Wilde side, or strolled down Piccadilly with lilies in their hands; the adventurers who described the search for King Solomon's mines or the journey into an exotic heart of darkness; the essayists who contemplated modern life from the windows of the Savile Club; or the visionaries who championed sexual freedom, the celebrated artists of the 1890s do not include women. Yet for feminist thinkers and writers, the *fin de siècle* was also a period of exploration and experiment. Recalling the first London production of Ibsen's *A Doll's House* in 1889, Edith Lees described how women in the audience, including Olive Schreiner and Eleanor Marx, lingered after the play, 'breathless with excitement . . . We were restive and impetuous and almost savage in our arguments. This was either the end of the world or the beginning of a new world for women. What did it mean? Was there hope or despair in the banging of that door? Was it life or death for women? Was it joy or sorrow for men? Was it revelation or disaster?'[1]

Not only as heroines of drama, but also as competitors in the marketplace, women *were* a major presence in the new literary world of the 1880s and 1890s. They were writing with unprecedented candour about female sexuality, marital discontent, and their own aesthetic theories and aspirations; and speaking to – and about – the New Women of the *fin de siècle*. Famous, even notorious, in their own day, these women writers have been overshadowed not only by such distinguished male contemporaries as Conrad and Wilde, but also by minor novelists like Haggard and Stoker. Their contributions to the evolution of women's writing, the fiction of the *fin de siècle*, and the genealogy of modernism have been neglected or forgotten; and this collection attempts to reverse that trend by bringing together for the first time a group of remarkable stories by English and American women at the turn of the nineteenth century. These stories offer a feminist point of view on issues of sexuality, aesthetics, 'decadence', and quest. They are the missing links between the great women writers of the Victorian novel and the modern fiction of Mansfield, Woolf, and Stein.

One reason that the women writers of this period have been overlooked is that many of them were more interested in the short story than in the full-length novel, publishing their work in avant-garde magazines such as *The Savoy* and *The Yellow Book*, where they made up over one-third of the contributors. For men too, as H.G. Wells observed, the 1890s were 'a good and stimulating period for a short story writer . . . Short stories broke out everywhere'. With changes in the economics of publishing in the 1890s, the traditional three-volume novel disappeared. New periodicals on both sides of the Atlantic created a market for short fiction, and writers were influenced by the psychological realism of Flaubert and Maupassant, by the Scandinavian naturalists like Ibsen and Hamsun, and by the newly translated fiction of Turgenev and Tolstoy.

For late-nineteenth-century women writers in particular, the short story offered flexibility and freedom from the traditional plots of the three-decker Victorian novel, plots which invariably ended in the heroine's marriage or her death. In contrast to the sprawling three-decker, the short story emphasised psychological intensity and formal innovation. As Edith Wharton explained in *The Writing of Fiction*, in the hands of French and Russian writers, the short story had achieved 'a great closeness of texture with profundity of form. Instead of a loose web spread over the surface of life, they have made it, at its best, a shaft driven straight into the heart of experience'. The short story could vary in length and in form, from long novellas like Vernon Lee's 'Lady Tal', to brief fables like Olive Schreiner's 'Life's Gifts'. Some stories were naturalistic slice-of-life accounts of poor women in the city; others were impressionistic fragments dealing with a single epiphany or revery. The German feminist Laura Marholm Hansson found the women writers of the 1890s 'a new race of women' whose 'ego burst forth with such power that it ignored all outer circumstances; it pressed forward and crystallized itself into an artistic shape'. Seeking to tell a new story, the New Woman writer 'needs an artistic mode of expression; she flings aside the old forms and searches for new'.[2]

Hansson thought the New Women were 'women such as the new men require'. Yet to many outraged male reviewers, the New Women writers were threatening daughters of decadence. They saw connections between New Women and decadent men, as members of an avant garde attacking marriage and reproduction. As one modern critic notes, 'To most late Victorians, the decadent was new and the New Woman was decadent'.[3] *Punch* never wearied of the chance to caricature New Women in cartoons, or to parody their fiction. In dozens of reviews, women writers were labelled 'literary degenerates'. 'Emancipated woman in particular', one critic wrote in 1895, 'loves to show her independence by dealing freely with the relations of the sexes. Hence the prating of passion, animalism, "the natural workings of sex", and so forth, with which we are nauseated. Most of the characters in these books seem to be erotomaniacs'.[4] New Women and decadent artists were linked together as twin monsters of a degenerate age, sexual anarchists who blurred the boundaries of gender. Thus decadent art was unmanly and effeminate, while New Women's writing was unwomanly and perverse. Aubrey Beardsley's drawings adorned the covers of George Egerton's *Keynotes* and *Discords*, just as they graced the pages of Wilde's *Salome*.

Yet the decadent artist was invariably male, and decadence, as a hyper-aesthetic movement, defined itself against the feminine and biological creativity of women. 'My dear boy,' Wilde's Henry Wotton tells Dorian Gray, 'no woman is a genius. Women are the decorative sex. They are charmingly artificial, but they have no sense of art.' Decadent artists like Huysmans and Baudelaire were notoriously contemptuous of women, and anti-feminism, according to the French critic Jean Pierrot, was 'widespread in artistic and literary circles during the decadent era'. The anti-feminist stance in decadence stressed women's 'profound incapacity to achieve access to spiritual and artistic realms. Viewed like this, woman becomes the ball and chain preventing the artist from escaping the triviality of the everyday world'.[5] In decadent writing, women are seen as bound to Nature and the material world because they are more physical than men, more body than spirit. They appear as objects of value only when they are aestheticised as corpses or phallicised as *femmes fatales*.

New Women writers needed to purge aestheticism and decadence of their misogyny and to rewrite the myths of art that denigrated women. In her correspondence with the men of the London avant-garde, as well as in her stories and allegories, Olive Schreiner addressed both the possibilities and the dangers of the aesthetic sensibility. 'The most degraded type of the human creature I have ever known,' she wrote to Karl Pearson, 'is also one of the most aesthetic. A man who will send a little child quivering and crying out of a room because she has on a dress whose colour does not please him, who will get up and leave a table because there is some dish that offends him, who holds it impossible that an ugly woman or a deformed man should ever be loved by a person of the opposite sex; such a man is so immersed in the lower forms of aesthetic feeling that one knows the higher must be forever shut off from him.'[6]

Women writers needed to rescue female sexuality from the decadents' images of romantically doomed prostitutes or devouring Venus flytraps, and represent female desire as a creative force in artistic imagination as well as in biological reproduction. Numerous stories of the 1890s, such as Kate Chopin's 'An Egyptian Cigarette', deal with women's sexual fantasies of seduction, cross-dressing, and androgyny. Although she lived in St. Louis, Chopin subscribed to *The Yellow Book*, and published some of her own work in *Vogue* – a daring new magazine of the 1890s. Her heroine describes an erotic hallucination brought on by smoking a yellow opium cigarette, in which she is rejected by a dashing sheik named 'Bardja' – an image of the romantic poet. In 'Theodora: A Fragment', Victoria Cross uses a male narrative persona to create an atmosphere of ambiguous sexuality. Her sultry heroine tries on the narrator's Turkish robes, while he has pictures of both a handsome young Sikh and a beautiful Turkish woman in his photograph album. Building to an instant of 'hot, clear, blinding' passion between the protagonists, the story is a fragment both because Cross has taken her imagination to its limits, and because she hints that women's sexual narratives are unfinished.

Another New Woman who often wrote from a male point of view was Ada Leverson, who was part of Oscar Wilde's circle. Leverson's main weapons were satire and wit; she parodied Cross's hot-blooded story in *Punch* as 'Tooralorra: A Fragment', and imagined a domestic Princess Salome praising the refreshments at a party in Wildean language: 'Is that mayonnaise? . . . I am sure it is mayonnaise. It is the mayonnaise of salmon, pink as a branch of coral which fishermen find in the twilight of the sea, and which they keep for the King. It is pinker than the pink roses that bloom in the Queen's garden. The pink roses that bloom in the garden of the Queen of Arabia are not so pink.'[7] She presented a much more pointed critique of Wilde's decadent narratives in 'Suggestion', which dissects the sexual cruelty beneath the vanity and wounded narcissism of an effeminate young man.

In many respects, the paradigmatic figure among the New Women writers was George Egerton (Mary Chavelita Dunne, 1859–1945), whose first book of stories, *Keynotes* (1893), lent its name to an important series in which many other women writers made their debut. Egerton was seen as one of the most sexually-charged of the New Women writers. *Keynotes*, the *Athenaeum* remarked, is notable 'chiefly on account of the hysterical frankness of its amatory abandonment'.[8] The title of her book came from her praise of woman's 'eternal wildness, the untamed primitive savage temperament that lurks in the mildest, best woman . . . the keynote of woman's witchcraft and woman's strength'.

Egerton saw in the short story the chance to explore feminine psychology: 'I realised that in literature, everything had been better done by man than woman could hope to emulate. There was only one small plot left for her to tell: the *terra incognita* of herself, as she knew herself to be, not as man liked to imagine her – in a word, to give herself away, as man had given himself in his writings.' She set out to invent a new literary form for the feminine unconscious; 'If I did not know the technical jargon current today of Freud and his psycho-analysts, I did know something of complexes and inhibitions, repressions and the subconscious impulses that determine actions and reactions. I used them in my stories.' In addition, she attempted to break away from masculine models and plot conventions, and to write boldly about woman's 'nature', which she saw as intuitive and wild: 'I would use situations or conflicts as I saw them, with a total disregard of man's opinions. I would unlock a closed door with a key of my own fashioning.'[9] Egerton's stories form a counterpart to Freud's case studies of hysterical women, which were also being written in the 1890s. Where Freud makes his analytic technique a 'picklock' by which to penetrate the sexual secrets of Dora and other women patients, Egerton's key is her impressionistic technique of literary notation, including ellipses, dream-sequences, and symbolic abstraction, used to depict the consciousness of her enigmatic heroines.

'A Cross Line' was one of Egerton's most celebrated stories. It begins with a man and woman meeting as they fly-fish. As Martha Vicinus points out, in Egerton's fiction the outdoors is 'a freeing agent, providing the space and climate for personal growth', and 'men and women who fish meet as comrades-in-arms, recognising and appreciating each other's skill'.[10] But even if their fishing lines are straight, men and women speak to each other in crossed lines because their psyches are so dissimilar. Egerton sees humour in some of the missed communication. When her heroine, Gipsy, romantically asks her dreamy-eyed husband what he is thinking, he replies that he is thinking of fishing lures. But on a more serious note, he cannot imagine *her* thoughts, which range, with vivid images and metaphors, from theories of evolution to sympathy for women's oppression to fantasies of herself as Salome dancing before an audience of admiring men. The story dramatises Egerton's belief in an essential female nature which is most fully expressed in maternity; when she realises she is pregnant, Gipsy's dreams of infidelity and wanderlust are overwhelmed by the maternal instinct.

The clever *Punch* parody, 'She-Notes', by 'Borgia Smudgiton', included in this volume, gives a good sense of the ways Egerton's view of feminine nature shocked and startled readers of the 1890s. 'How can the dense brute male read the enigma of the Female Idea? They think us innocent! not we! but we all keep up the deception and lie courageously. They will never know that we are really primitive, untamable, ineradicable animalculae.' The accompanying illustrations by 'Mortarthurio Whiskersly' parodied Beardsley's 'keynote' design for the original series, and his famous drawings for *Salome*.

The most successful New Woman novels, including Mona Caird's *The Daughters of Danaus* (1894), Sarah Grand's *The Beth Book* (1894), and Mary Cholmondeley's *Red Pottage* (1899), described the obstacles that would face a female genius, and the obligations, jealousies, and malice that would undermine her art. Similarly, many of the best New Woman stories reflect upon the literary competition between men and women. In 'The Fifth Edition', Mabel Wotton draws a sardonic portrait of the exploitative male novelist Franklin Leyden, who appropriates and cheapens the autobiographical novel that the author, Miss Suttaby, too willingly gives him. As Margaret Stetz comments, it is tempting 'to see in this tale of the usurping of a woman's art and experience an allegory about the fate of the 'New Woman' novel in the mid-Nineties', in which even commercial writers like Grant Allen who took up the Woman Question have been remembered, while the work of Wotton and other women writers is virtually unknown.[11]

Male novelists of the period, like Oscar Wilde and Henry James, frequently satirised women writers in their work; and women writers returned the compliment. Two of the stories focus on a male novelist very much like Henry James. Vernon Lee (whose real name was Violet Paget, 1856–1935), met James in 1884, and dedicated her first novel *Miss Brown*, a satire of the aesthetic movement, to him, much to his discomfort. As James wrote to her, 'You take the aesthetic business too seriously', and 'with too great an implication of sexual motives'.[12] In *Lady Tal*, the methodical and repressed novelist Jervase Marion, 'an inmate of the world of Henry James and a kind of Henry James', finds himself assisting an aristocratic bohemian to write *her* novel, a relationship which reawakens his long-dormant emotions. James regarded the story as an act of 'treachery to private relations', and never forgave her for turning him into a character.[13]

Constance Fenimore Woolson (1840–1894) met James in Florence in the spring of 1880, the year she wrote 'Miss Grief', and they remained friends until her death – a probable suicide – in Venice fourteen years later. The narrator of 'Miss Grief' is a successful young man of letters who is asked to read 'Armor', the manuscript of an unpublished woman of genius. In attempting to edit out its peculiarities and flaws, he discovers that all he can do is destroy its originality and power. In many ways, the story reflects Woolson's ambivalence about her own work, and her half-admiring, half-hostile view of James's lofty superiority. To be his friend, even his muse, was not enough for a woman with artistic ambitions of her own.

The problem of the muse was obviously central for women artists. To become muses themselves, to have their lives appropriated and simplified in the interest of another's art, seemed a tragic fate. Edith Wharton's 'The Muse's Tragedy' rewrites James's *The Tragic Muse* to tell the story of a woman who is celebrated as the inspiration for a great poet, yet knows that he has never loved her and that she has given up her own chances of love for the image he has created of her in art. Yet the strong utopian impulses of the period led also to stories which reimagined the roles of artist and muse. In 'The Undefinable: A Fantasia', by Sarah Grand (Frances McFall, 1862–1943), a painter whose work has become sterile and conventional is visited and then deserted by an inspiring muse: 'a free woman, a new creature, a source of inspiration the like of which no man has even imagined in art or literature'. Her effect on his painting is so electrifying that he dedicates himself to rediscovering her.

On the whole, however, New Women writers were pessimistic about their chances of finding New Men to share their lives. In 'By Accident', George Fleming (Julia Constance Fletcher, 1853–1938) writes about a woman's marital unhappiness and secret passion for another man, revealed to her husband only at her death. Olive Schreiner's 'The Buddhist Priest's Wife', which she wrote during three months in 1892, was Schreiner's favourite among her own stories. It described her disillusioned realisation that Karl Pearson, the London intellectual who eagerly sought her ideas about the future development of relations between men and women, could not return her love, and would choose to marry a much more conventional woman. In the story, Schreiner identifies her characters generically as 'the woman' and 'the man'. Her heroine's New Womanhood is made evident by her silver cigarette case, and her London lodgings. The subject of their conversation, the taboos that prevent women from taking the sexual initiative or confessing their emotions, is an ironic counterpart to her unrequited love for the male intellectual who will go off to find a compliant wife while she goes off to work and die alone. 'Was she really so strong as she looked?' the narrator asks. 'Did she never wake up in the night crying for that which she could not have?'

Probably the most famous woman's story of the 1890s is Charlotte Perkins Gilman's 'The Yellow Wallpaper', a tale that has become a feminist classic in our own *fin de siècle*. Gilman (1860–1935) was a great admirer of Olive Schreiner, and shared Schreiner's commitment to work and self-sacrifice for future generations. She claimed to have written the story to warn other women against the dangers of the rest cure practised by Dr. Silas Weir Mitchell, whose treatment of her post-partum depression had nearly driven her mad. But the text is a horror story that taps a wide range of feminine anxieties about the confinement of marriage, the burdens of motherhood, and the demands of the body.

Even more frightening than 'The Yellow Wallpaper', and indeed the darkest of all these stories, 'A White Night' by Charlotte Mew (1869–1928), is a feminist counterpart of Conrad's apocalyptic *Heart of Darkness*. In Mew's story, the heroine Ella – She – is on a 'discursive honeymoon' with her husband, King, and her brother, Cameron. Ella is initially daring and robust, a New Woman who can rough it with the men. Yet on the trip which marks her entrance into adult sexuality, she and the men are accidentally trapped in the cloister of a Spanish convent, where they witness the ritual burying alive of a veiled woman, the act of horror at the heart of whiteness. The title of the story is ambiguous and suggestive. At one level, 'A White Night' refers punningly to the knight of chivalry, the Galahad who should – but does not – come forward to rescue the woman from sacrifice. On another level, it is a translation of the French *nuit blanche*, a sleepless night, a twilight zone of consciousness in which Ella and the men witness a performance of primal sexual difference. The ritual seems like a warning of female destiny in the contexts of patriarchy. At one moment, the faces of the individual chanting monks merge into 'one face – the face of nothing human – of a system, of a rule'. The effect on Ella is to reduce her to speechlessness and hysteria. Afterwards, 'the horror of those hours' continues to haunt her and to visit her dreams.

Yet to the voyeuristic Cameron, a photographic presence, a camera eye who voyeuristically watches events, 'the woman didn't really count'. She is only a spectacle. Why does Mew choose Cameron as the narrator of the story? Like Conrad's Marlow or the narrators of Henry James, he is a detached bachelor observer. For him, the terrible fate of the woman is both a 'spectacle' and 'a rather splendid crime'. Reading the story through his eyes emphasises the crucial differences for the *fin de siècle* between male and female forms of experience and story-telling.

Yet while male artists in the *fin de siècle* saw the prospects of a coming apocalypse, and feared the death of familiar structures, even the death of literature, women writers had less to lose in the disappearance of old cultural forms and much to hope for in the birth of a new century. They described their sense of transition in feminist allegories which acknowledge the failures of the present and the dangers of the future, but refuse to turn back. The lion in Chopin's fable, 'Emancipation', will not return to its cage, no matter how painful the emancipated life may be. Wharton's heroine cannot find a male partner to help her build bridges, drain swamps, and cut roads through the jungle; but she has outgrown forever the valley of childish things. The woman in Schreiner's 'Life's Gifts' must refuse the gift of love and choose freedom, but she laughs in her sleep. Reading Schreiner's stories aloud in prison a few years later, the suffragettes saw themselves as fortunate rather than doomed. As one feminist leader wrote to a friend, 'We shall send out stronger and stronger thoughts that will change the course of the world's life. Dear, in spite of all, we are more to be envied than any people living.'[14] A century later, the utopian dreams of *fin-de-siècle* feminists have yet to be fully realised, but reading their stories we can take heart from their talent and their courage to look with hope to the new century, and to another beginning of a new world for women.

NOTES

1. Edith Lees, 'Olive Schreiner and Her Relation to the Woman Movement', *Book News Monthly*, New York, Vol. 33 (February 1915).
2. Laura Marholm Hansson, *Modern Women*, (trans. Hermione Ramsden), London, 1896, pp. 78–9.
3. Linda Dowling, 'The Decadent and the New Woman', *Nineteenth-Century Fiction*, 33 (1979), p.136.
4. Hugh Stutfield, 'Tommyrotics', *Blackwood's Magazine*, 157 (June 1895), p. 836.
5. Jean Pierrot, *The Decadent Imagination 1880–1900*, (trans. Derek Coltman), Chicago: University of Chicago Press, 1981, p. 126.
6. *Olive Schreiner Letters*, 6 July 1886, (ed. Richard Rive), London: Oxford University Press, 1985, I:88.
7. 'An Afternoon Party', *Punch*, CIV (15 July 1893), p. 13.
8. 'The Year in Review', *Athenaeum*, (6 January 1894), p. 18.
9. George Egerton, 'A Keynote to *Keynotes*', in *Ten Contemporaries: Notes Toward their Definitive Bibliography*, (ed. 'John Gawsworth' [Terence Armstrong]), London, 1932.
10. Martha Vicinus, 'Introduction', George Egerton, *Keynotes & Discords*, London: Virago, 1983, p. xi.
11. Margaret Stetz, 'Turning Points: Mabel E. Wotton', *Turn-of-the-Century Women* III (Winter 1886), 3.
12. *Henry James Letters*, (ed. Leon Edel), Vol. III, Cambridge: Harvard University Press, 1980, p. 87. See also Adeline Tintner, 'Fiction is

the Best Revenge: Portraits of Henry James by Four Women Writers', *Turn-of-the Century Women*, II (Winter 1985), pp. 42–9.
13. See Leon Edel, *Henry James: The Middle Years*, Philadelphia: J.B. Lippincott, 1962, pp. 332–3.
14. Mrs. F.W. Pethick Lawrence to Dora Marsden (6 October 1909), Dora Marsden Collection, Firestone Library, Princeton University. Published with permission of the Manuscripts Division, Department of Rare Books and Special Collection, Princeton University Libraries.

KATE CHOPIN

AN EGYPTIAN CIGARETTE

MY friend, the Architect, who is something of a traveller, was showing us various curios which he had gathered during a visit to the Orient.

'Here is something for you,' he said, picking up a small box and turning it over in his hand. 'You are a cigarette-smoker; take this home with you. It was given to me in Cairo by a species of fakir, who fancied I had done him a good turn.'

The box was covered with glazed, yellow paper, so skilfully gummed as to appear to be all one piece. It bore no label, no stamp – nothing to indicate its contents.

'How do you know they are cigarettes?' I asked, taking the box and turning it stupidly around as one turns a sealed letter and speculates before opening it.

'I only know what he told me,' replied the Architect, 'but it is easy enough to determine the question of his integrity.' He handed me a sharp, pointed paper-cutter, and with it I opened the lid as carefully as possible.

The box contained six cigarettes, evidently hand-made. The wrappers were of pale-yellow paper, and the tobacco was almost the same colour. It was of finer cut than the Turkish or ordinary Egyptian, and threads of it stuck out at either end.

'Will you try one now, Madam?' asked the Architect, offering to strike a match.

'Not now and not here,' I replied, 'after the coffee, if you will permit me to slip into your smoking-den. Some of the women here detest the odour of cigarettes.'

The smoking-room lay at the end of a short, curved passage. Its appointments were exclusively oriental. A broad, low window opened out upon a balcony that overhung the garden. From the divan upon which I reclined, only the swaying treetops could be seen. The maple leaves glistened in the afternoon sun. Beside the divan was a low stand which contained the complete paraphernalia of a smoker. I was feeling quite comfortable, and congratulated myself upon having escaped for a while the incessant chatter of the women that reached me faintly.

I took a cigarette and lit it, placing the box upon the stand just as the tiny clock, which was there, chimed in silvery strokes the hour of five.

I took one long inspiration of the Egyptian cigarette. The grey-green smoke arose in a small puffy column that spread and broadened, that seemed to fill the room. I could see the maple leaves dimly, as if they were veiled in a shimmer of moonlight. A subtle, disturbing current passed through my whole body and went to my head like the fumes of disturbing wine. I took another deep inhalation of the cigarette.

'Ah! the sand has blistered my cheek! I have lain here all day with my face in the sand. Tonight, when the everlasting stars are burning, I shall drag myself to the river.'

He will never come back.

Thus far I followed him; with flying feet; with stumbling feet; with hands and knees, crawling; and outstretched arms, and here I have fallen in the sand.

The sand has blistered my cheek; it has blistered all my body, and the sun is crushing me with hot torture. There is shade beneath yonder cluster of palms.

I shall stay here in the sand till the hour and the night comes.

I laughed at the oracles and scoffed at the stars when they told that after the rapture of life I would open my arms inviting death, and the waters would envelop me.

Oh! how the sand blisters my cheek! and I have no tears to quench the fire. The river is cool and the night is not far distant.

I turned from the gods and said: 'There is but one; Bardja is my god.' That was when I decked myself with lilies and wove flowers into a garland and held him close in the frail, sweet fetters.

He will never come back. He turned upon his camel as he rode away. He turned and looked at me crouching here and laughed, showing his gleaming white teeth.

Whenever he kissed me and went away he always came back again. Whenever he flamed with fierce anger and left me with stinging words, he always came back. But to-day he neither kissed me nor was he angry. He only said:

'Oh! I am tired of fetters, and kisses, and you. I am going away. You will never see me again. I am going to the great city where men swarm like bees. I am going beyond, where the monster stones are rising heavenward in a monument for the unborn ages. Oh! I am tired. You will see me no more.'

And he rode away on his camel. He smiled and showed his cruel white teeth as he turned to look at me crouching here.

How slow the hours drag! It seems to me that I have lain here for days in the sand, feeding upon despair. Despair is bitter and it nourishes resolve.

I hear the wings of a bird flapping above my head, flying low, in circles.

The sun is gone.

The sand has crept between my lips and teeth and under my parched tongue.

If I raise my head, perhaps I shall see the evening star.

Oh! the pain in my arms and legs! My body is sore and bruised as if broken. Why can I not rise and run as I did this morning? Why must I drag myself thus like a wounded serpent, twisting and writhing?

The river is near at hand. I hear it – I see it – Oh! the sand! Oh! the shine! How cool! how cold!

The water! the water! In my eyes, my ears, my throat! It strangles me! Help! will the gods not help me?

Oh! the sweet rapture of rest! There is music in the Temple. And here is fruit to taste. Bardja came with the music – The moon shines and the breeze is soft – A garland of flowers – let us go into the King's garden and look at the blue lily, Bardja.

The maple leaves looked as if a silvery shimmer enveloped them. The grey-green smoke no longer filled the room. I could hardly lift the lids of my eyes. The weight of centuries seemed to suffocate my soul that struggled to escape, to free itself and breathe.

I had tasted the depths of human despair.

The little clock upon the stand pointed to a quarter past five. The cigarettes still reposed in the yellow box. Only the stub of the one I had smoked remained. I had laid it in the ash tray.

As I looked at the cigarettes in their pale wrappers, I wondered what other visions they might hold for me; what might I not find in their mystic fumes? Perhaps a vision of celestial peace; a dream of hopes fulfilled; a taste of rapture, such as had not entered into my mind to conceive.

I took the cigarettes and crumpled them between my hands. I walked to the window and spread my palms wide. The light breeze caught up the golden threads and bore them writhing and dancing far out among the maple leaves.

My friend, the Architect, lifted the curtain and entered, bringing me a second cup of coffee.

'How pale you are!' he exclaimed, solicitously. 'Are you not feeling well?'

'A little the worse for a dream,' I told him.

VICTORIA CROSS

THEODORA: A FRAGMENT

I did not turn out of bed till ten o'clock the next morning, and I was still in dressing-gown and slippers, sitting by the fire, looking over a map, when Digby came in upon me.

'Hullo, Ray, only just up, eh? as usual?' was his first exclamation as he entered, his ulster buttoned to his chin, and the snow thick upon his boots. 'What a fellow you are! I can't understand anybody lying in bed till ten o'clock in the morning.'

'And I can't understand anybody driving up at seven,' I said, smiling, and stirring my coffee idly. I had laid down the map with resignation. I knew Digby had come round to jaw for the next hour at least. 'Can I offer you some breakfast?'

'Breakfast!' returned Digby contemptuously. 'No, thanks. I had mine hours ago. Well, what do you think of her?'

'Of whom? – this Theodora?'

'Oh, it's Theodora already, is it?' said Digby, looking at me. 'Well, never mind: go on. Yes, what do you think of her?'

'She seems rather clever, I think.'

'Do you?' returned Digby, with a distinct accent of regret, as if I had told him I thought she squinted. 'I never noticed it. But her looks, I mean?'

'She is very peculiar,' I said, merely.

'But you like everything extraordinary. I should have

thought her very peculiarity was just what would have attracted you.'

'So it does,' I admitted; 'so much so, that I am going to take the trouble of calling this afternoon expressly to see her again.'

Digby stared hard at me for a minute, and then burst out laughing. 'By Jove! You've made good use of your time. Did she ask you?'

'She did,' I said.

'This looks as if it would be a case,' remarked Digby lightly, and then added, 'I'd have given anything to have had her myself. But if it's not to be for me, I'd rather you should be the lucky man than any one else.'

'Don't you think all that is a little "previous"?' I asked satirically, looking at him over the coffee, which stood on the map of Mesopotamia.

'Well, I don't know. You must marry some time, Cecil.'

'Really!' I said, raising my eyebrows and regarding him with increased amusement. 'I think I have heard of men remaining celibates before now, especially men with my tastes.'

'Yes,' said Digby, becoming suddenly as serious and thoughtful as if he were being called upon to consider some weighty problem, and of which the solution must be found in the next ten minutes. 'I don't know how you would agree. She is an awfully religious girl.'

'Indeed?' I said with a laugh. 'How do you know?'

Digby thought hard.

'She is,' he said with conviction, at last. 'I see her at church every Sunday.'

'Oh then, of course she must be – proof conclusive,' I answered.

Digby looked at me and then grumbled, 'Confounded sneering fellow you are. Has she been telling you she is not?'

I remembered suddenly that I had promised Theodora not to repeat her opinions, so I only said, 'I really don't know what she is; she may be most devout for all I know – or care.'

'Of course you can profess to be quite indifferent,' said Digby ungraciously. 'But all I can say is, it doesn't look like it – your going there this afternoon; and anyway, she is not indifferent to you. She said all sorts of flattering things about you.'

'Very kind, I am sure,' I murmured derisively.

'And she sent round to my rooms this morning a thundering box of Havannahs in recognition of my having won the bet about your looks.'

I laughed outright. 'That's rather good biz for you! The least you can do is to let me help in the smoking of them, I think.'

'Of course I will. But it shows what she thinks of you, doesn't it?'

'Oh, most convincingly,' I said with mock earnestness. 'Havannahs are expensive things.'

'But you know how awfully rich she is, don't you?' asked Digby, looking at me as if he wanted to find out whether I were really ignorant or affecting to be so.

'My dear Charlie, you know I know nothing whatever about her except what you tell me – or do you suppose she showed me her banking account between the dances?'

'Don't know, I am sure,' Digby grumbled back. 'You sat in that passage long enough to be going through a banking account, and balancing it too, for that matter! However, the point is, she is rich – tons of money, over six thousand a year.'

'Really?' I said, to say something.

'Yes, but she loses every penny on her marriage. Seems such a funny way to leave money to a girl, doesn't it? Some old pig of a maiden aunt tied it up in that way. Nasty thing to do, I think; don't you?'

'Very immoral of the old lady, it seems. A girl like that, if she can't marry, will probably forego nothing but the ceremony.'

'She runs the risk of losing her money, though, if anything were known. She only has it *dum casta manet*, just like a separation allowance.'

'Hard lines,' I murmured sympathetically.

'And so of course her people are anxious she should make a good match – take some man, I mean, with an income equal to what she has now of her own, so that she would not feel any loss. Otherwise, you see, if she married a poor man, it would be rather a severe drop for her.'

'Conditions calculated to prevent any fellow but a millionaire proposing to her, I should think,' I said.

'Yes, except that she is a girl who does not care about money. She has been out now three seasons, and had one or two good chances and not taken them. Now myself, for instance, if she wanted money and position and so on, she could hardly do better, could she? And my family and the rest of it are all right; but she couldn't get over my red hair – I know it was that. She's mad upon looks – I know she is; she let it out to me once, and I bet you anything, she'd take you and chuck over her money and everything else, if you gave her the chance.'

'I am certainly not likely to,' I answered. 'All this you've just told me alone would be enough to choke me off. I have always thought I could never love a decent woman unselfishly enough, even if she gave up nothing for me; and, great heavens! I should be sorry to value myself, at – what do you say she has? – six thousand a year?'

'Leave the woman who falls in love with the cut of your nose to do the valuation. You'll be surprised at the figure!'

said Digby with a touch of resentful bitterness, and getting up abruptly. 'I'll look round in the evening,' he added, buttoning up his overcoat. 'Going to be in?'

'As far as I know,' I answered, and he left.

I got up and dressed leisurely, thinking over what he had said, and those words 'six thousand' repeating themselves unpleasantly in my brain.

The time was in accordance with strict formality when I found myself on her steps. The room I was shown into was large, much too large to be comfortable on such a day; and I had to thread my way through a perfect maze of gilt-legged tables and statuette-bearing tripods before I reached the hearth. Here burnt a small, quiet, chaste-looking fire, a sort of Vestal flame, whose heat was lost upon the tesselated tiles, white marble, and polished brass about it. I stood looking down at it absently for a few minutes, and then Theodora came in.

She was very simply dressed in some dark stuff that fitted closely to her, and let me see the harmonious lines of her figure as she came up to me. The plain, small collar of the dress opened at the neck, and a delicious, solid, white throat rose from the dull stuff like an almond bursting from its husk. On the pale, well-cut face and small head great care had evidently been bestowed. The eyes were darkened, as last night, and the hair arranged with infinite pains on the forehead and rolled into one massive coil at the back of her neck.

She shook hands with a smile – a smile that failed to dispel the air of fatigue and fashionable dissipation that seemed to cling to her; and then wheeled a chair as near to the fender as she could get it.

As she sat down, I thought I had never seen such splendid shoulders combined with so slight a hip before.

'Now I hope no one else will come to interrupt us,' she

said simply. 'And don't let's bother to exchange comments on the weather nor last night's dance. I have done that six times over this morning with other callers. Don't let's talk for the sake of getting through a certain number of words. Let us talk because we are interested in what we are saying.'

'I should be interested in anything if you said it,' I answered.

Theodora laughed. 'Tell me something about the East, will you? That is a nice warm subject, and I feel so cold.'

And she shot out towards the blaze two well-made feet and ankles.

'Yes, in three weeks' time I shall be in a considerably warmer climate than this,' I answered, drawing my chair as close to hers as fashion permits.

Theodora looked at me with a perceptibly startled expression as I spoke.

'Are you really going out so soon?' she said.

'I am, really,' I said with a smile.

'Oh, I am so sorry!'

'Why?' I asked merely.

'Because I was thinking I should have the pleasure of meeting you lots more times at different functions.'

'And would that be a pleasure?'

'Yes, very great,' said Theodora, with a smile lighting her eyes and parting faintly the soft scarlet lips.

She looked at me, a seducing softness melting all her face and swimming in the liquid darkness of the eyes she raised to mine. A delicious intimacy seemed established between us by that smile. We seemed nearer to each other after it than before, by many degrees. A month or two of time and ordinary intercourse may be balanced against the seconds of such a smile as this.

A faint feeling of surprise mingled with my thoughts, that she should show her own attitude of mind so clearly, but

I believe she felt instinctively my attraction towards her, and also undoubtedly she belonged, and had always been accustomed, to a fast set. I was not the sort of man to find fault with her for that, and probably she had already been conscious of this, and felt all the more at ease with me. The opening-primrose type of woman, the girl who does or wishes to suggest the modest violet unfolding beneath the rural hedge, had never had a charm for me. I do not profess to admire the simple violet; I infinitely prefer a well-trained hothouse gardenia. And this girl, about whom there was nothing of the humble, crooked-neck violet – in whom there was a dash of virility, a hint at dissipation, a suggestion of a certain decorous looseness of morals and fastness of manners – could stimulate me with a keen sense of pleasure, as our eyes or hands met.

'Why would it be a pleasure to meet me?' I asked, holding her eyes with mine, and wondering whether things would so turn out that I should ever kiss those parting lips before me.

Theodora laughed gently.

'For a good many reasons that it would make you too conceited to hear,' she answered. 'But one is because you are more interesting to talk to than the majority of people I meet every day. The castor of your chair has come upon my dress. Will you move it back a little, please?'

I pushed my chair back immediately and apologised.

'Are you going alone?' resumed Theodora.

'Quite alone.'

'Is that nice?'

'No. I should have been very glad to find some fellow to go with me, but it's rather difficult. It is not everybody that one meets whom one would care to make such an exclusive companion of, as a life like that out there necessitates.

Still, there's no doubt I shall be dull unless I can find some chum there.'

'Some Englishman, I suppose?'

'Possibly; but they are mostly snobs who are out there.'

Theodora made a faint sign of assent, and we both sat silent, staring into the fire.

'Does the heat suit you?' Theodora asked, after a pause.

'Yes, I like it.'

'So do I.'

'I don't think any woman would like the climate I am going to now, or could stand it,' I said.

Theodora said nothing, but I had my eyes on her face, which was turned towards the light of the fire, and I saw a tinge of mockery come over it.

We had neither said anything farther, when the sound of a knock reached us, muffled, owing to the distance the sound had to travel to reach us by the drawing-room fire at all, but distinct in the silence between us.

Theodora looked at me sharply.

'There is somebody else. Do you want to leave yet?' she asked, and then added in a persuasive tone, 'Come into my own study, where we shan't be disturbed, and stay and have tea with me, will you?'

She got up as she spoke.

The room had darkened considerably while we had been sitting there, and only a dull light came from the leaden, snow-laden sky beyond the panes, but the firelight fell strongly across her figure as she stood, glancing and playing up it towards the slight waist, and throwing scarlet upon the white throat and under-part of the full chin. In the strong shadow on her face I could see merely the two seducing eyes. Easily excitable where once a usually hypercritical or rather hyperfanciful eye has been attracted, I felt a keen sense of pleasure stir me as I watched her rise and stand, that sense of pleasure which is nothing more than an assurance to the roused and unquiet instincts within one, of future satisfaction or gratification, with, from, or at the expense of the object creating the sensation. Unconsciously a certainty of possession of Theodora to-day, to-morrow, or next year, filled me for the moment as completely as if I had just made her my wife. The instinct that demanded her was immediately answered by a mechanical process of the brain, not with doubt or fear, but simple confidence. 'This is a pleasant and delightful object to you – as others have been. Later it will be a source of enjoyment to you – as others have been.' And the lulling of this painful instinct is what we know as pleasure. And this instinct and its answer are exactly that which we should not feel within us for any beloved object. It is this that tends inevitably to degrade the loved one, and to debase our own passion. If the object is worthy and lovely in any sense, we should be ready to love it as being such, for itself, as moralists preach to us of Virtue, as theologians preach to us of the Deity. To love or at least to strive to love an object for the object's sake, and not our own sake, to love it in its relation to *its* pleasure and not in its relation to our own pleasure, is to feel the only love which is worthy of offering to a fellow human being, the one which elevates – and the only one – both giver and receiver. If we ever learn this lesson, we learn it late. I had not learnt it yet.

I murmured a prescribed 'I shall be delighted,' and followed Theodora behind a huge red tapestry screen that reached half-way up to the ceiling.

We were then face to face with a door which she opened, and we both passed over the threshold together.

She had called the room her own, so I glanced round it with a certain curiosity. A room is always some faint index to the character of its occupier, and as I looked a smile came to my face. This room suggested everywhere, as I should have expected, an intellectual but careless and independent spirit. There were two or three tables, in the window, heaped up with books and strewn over with papers. The centre-table had been pushed away, to leave a clearer space by the grate, and an armchair, seemingly of unfathomable depths, and a sofa, dragged forward in its place. Within the grate roared a tremendous fire, banked up half way to the chimney, and a short poker was thrust into it between the bars. The red light leapt over the whole room and made it brilliant, and glanced over a rug, and some tumbled cushions on the floor in front of the fender, evidently where she had been lying. Now, however, she picked up the cushions, and tossed them into the corner of the couch, and sat down herself in the other corner.

'Do you prefer the floor generally?' I asked, taking the armchair as she indicated it to me.

'Yes, one feels quite free and at ease lying on the floor, whereas on a couch its limits are narrow, and one has the constraint and bother of taking care one does not go to sleep and roll off.'

'But suppose you did, you would then but be upon the floor.'

'Quite so; but I should have the pain of falling.'

Our eyes met across the red flare of the firelight.

Theodora went on jestingly: 'Now, these are the ethics of the couch and the floor. I lay myself voluntarily on the floor, knowing it thoroughly as a trifle low, but undeceptive and favourable to the condition of sleep which will probably arise, and suitable to my requirements of ease and space. I avoid the restricted and uncertain couch, recognising that if I fall to sleep on that raised level, and the desire to stretch myself should come, I shall awake with pain and shock to feel the ground, and see above me the couch from which I fell – do you see?'

She spoke lightly, and with a smile, and I listened with one. But her eyes told me that these ethics of the couch and floor covered the ethics of life.

'No, you must accept the necessity of the floor, I think, unless you like to forego your sleep and have the trouble of taking care to stick upon your couch; and for me the difference of level between the two is not worth the additional bother.'

She laughed, and I joined her.

'What do you think?' she asked.

I looked at her as she sat opposite me, the firelight playing all over her, from the turn of her knee just marked beneath her skirt to her splendid shoulders, and the smooth soft hand and wrist supporting the distinguished little head. I did not tell her what I was thinking; what I said was: 'You are very logical. I am quite convinced there's no place like the ground for a siesta.'

Theodora laughed, and laid her hand on the bell.

A second or two after, a door, other than the one we had entered by, opened, and a maid appeared.

'Bring tea and pegs,' said Theodora, and the door shut again.

'I ordered pegs for you because I know men hate tea,' she said. 'That's my own maid. I never let any of the servants answer this bell except her, she has my confidence, as far as one ever gives confidence to a servant. I think she likes me. I like making myself loved,' she added impulsively.

'You've never found the least difficulty in it, I should think,' I answered, perhaps a shade more warmly than I ought, for the colour came into her cheek and a slight confusion into her eyes.

The servant's re-entry saved her from replying.

'Now tell me how you like your peg made, and I'll make

it,' said Theodora, getting up and crossing to the table when the servant had gone.

I got up, too, and protested against this arrangement.

Theodora turned round and looked up at me, leaning one hand on the table.

'Now, how ridiculous and conventional you are!' she said. 'You would think nothing of letting me make you a cup of tea, and yet I must by no means mix you a peg!'

She looked so like a young fellow of nineteen as she spoke that half the sense of informality between us was lost, and there was a keen, subtle pleasure in this superficial familiarity with her that I had never felt with far prettier women. The half of nearly every desire is curiosity, a vague, undefined curiosity, of which we are hardly conscious; and it was this that Theodora so violently stimulated, while her beauty was sufficient to nurse the other half. This feeling of curiosity arises, of course, for any woman who may be new to us, and who has the power to move us at all. But generally, if it cannot be gratified for the particular one, it is more or less satisfied by the general knowledge applying to them all; but here, as Theodora differed so much from the ordinary feminine type, even this instinctive sort of consolation was denied me. I looked down at her with a smile.

'We shan't be able to reconcile Fashion and Logic, so it's no use,' I said. 'Make the peg, then, and I'll try and remain in the fashion by assuming it's tea.'

'Great Scott! I hope you won't fancy it's tea while you are drinking it!' returned Theodora laughing.

She handed me the glass, and I declared nectar wasn't in it with that peg, and then she made her own tea and came and sat down to drink it, in not at all an indecorous, but still informal proximity.

'Did you collect anything in the East?' she asked me, after a minute or two.

'Yes; a good many idols and relics and curiosities of sorts,' I answered. 'Would you like to see them?'

'Very much,' Theodora answered. 'Where are they?'

'Well, not in my pocket,' I said smiling. 'At my chambers. Could you and Mrs. Long spare an afternoon and honour me with a visit there?'

'I should like it immensely. I know Helen will come if I ask her.'

'When you have seen them I must pack them up, and send them to my agents. One can't travel about with those things.'

A sort of tremor passed over Theodora's face as I spoke, and her glance met mine, full of demands and questionings, and a very distinct assertion of distress. It said distinctly, 'I am so sorry you are going.' The sorrow in her eyes touched my vanity deeply, which is the most responsive quality we have. It is difficult to reach our hearts or our sympathies, but our vanity is always available. I felt inclined to throw my arm round that supple-looking waist – and it was close to me – and say, 'Don't be sorry; come too.' I don't know whether my looks were as plain as hers, but Theodora rose carelessly, apparently to set her teacup down, and then did not resume her seat by me, but went back to the sofa on the other side of the rug. This, in the state of feeling into which I had drifted, produced an irritated sensation, and I was rather pleased than not when a gong sounded somewhere in the house and gave me a graceful opening to rise.

'May I hope to hear from you, then, which day you will like to come?' I asked, as I held out my hand.

Now this was the moment I had been expecting, practically, ever since her hand had left mine last night, the moment when it should touch it again. I do not mean consciously, but there are a million slight, vague physical experiences and sensations within us of which the mind remains unconscious. Theodora's white right hand rested on her hip, the light from above struck upon it, and I noted that all the rings had been stripped from it; her left was crowded with them, so that the hand sparkled at each movement, but not one remained on her right. I coloured violently for the minute as I recollected my last night's pressure, and the idea flashed upon me at once that she had removed them expressly to avoid the pain of having them ground into her flesh.

The next second Theodora had laid her hand confidently in mine. My mind, annoyed at the thought that had just shot through it, bade me take her hand loosely and let it go, but Theodora raised her eyes to me, full of a soft disappointment which seemed to say, 'Are you not going to press it, then, after all, when I have taken off all the rings entirely that you may?' That look seemed to push away, walk over, ignore my reason, and appeal directly to the eager physical nerves and muscles. Spontaneously, whether I would or not, they responded to it, and my fingers laced themselves tightly round this morsel of velvet-covered fire.

We forgot in those few seconds to say the orthodox good-byes; she forgot to answer my question. That which we were both saying to each other, though our lips did not open, was, 'So I should like to hold and embrace you;' and she, 'So I should like to be held and embraced.'

Then she withdrew her hand, and I went out by way of the drawing-room where we had entered.

In the hall her footman showed me out with extra obsequiousness. My three-hours' stay raised me, I suppose, to the rank of more than an ordinary caller.

It was dark now in the streets, and the temperature must have been somewhere about zero. I turned my collar up and started to walk sharply in the direction of my chambers. Walking always induces in me a tendency to reflection and retrospection, and now, removed from the excitement of Theodora's actual presence, my thoughts lapped quietly over the whole interview, going through it backwards, like the calming waves of a receding tide, leaving lingeringly the sand. There was no doubt that this girl attracted me very strongly, that the passion born yesterday was nearing adolescence; and there was no doubt, either, that I ought to strangle it now before it reached maturity. My thoughts, however, turned impatiently from this question, and kept closing and centring round the object itself, with maddening persistency. I laughed to myself as Schopenhauer's theory shot across me that all impulse to love is merely the impulse of the genius of the genus to select a fitting object which will help in producing a Third Life. Certainly the genius of the genus in me was weaker than the genius of my own individuality, in this instance, for Theodora was as unfitted, according to the philosopher's views, to become a co-worker with me in carrying out Nature's aim, as she was fitted to give me as an individual the strongest personal pleasure.

I remember Schopenhauer does admit that this instinct in man to choose some object which will best fulfil the duty of the race, is apt to be led astray, and it is fortunate he did not forget to make this admission, if his theory is to be generally applied, considering how very particularly often we are led astray, and that our strongest, fiercest passions and keenest pleasures are constantly not those suitable to, nor in accordance with, the ends of Nature. The sharpest, most violent stimulus, we may say, the true essence of pleasure, lies in some gratification which has no claim whatever, in any sense, to be beneficial or useful, or to have any ulterior motive, conscious or instinctive, or any lasting result, or any fulfilment of any object, but which is simple gratification and dies naturally in its own excess.

As we admit of works of pure genius that they cannot

claim utility, or motive, or purpose, but simply that they exist as joy-giving and beautiful objects of delight, so must we have done with utility, motive, purpose, and the aims of Nature, before we can reach the most absolute degree of positive pleasure. To choose an admissible instance, a naturally hungry man, given a slice of bread, will he or will he not devour it with as great a pleasure as the craving drunkard feels in swallowing a draught of raw brandy?

In the first case a simple natural desire is gratified, and the aim of Nature satisfied; but the individual's longing and subsequent pleasure cannot be said to equal the furious craving of the drunkard, and his delirious sense of gratification as the brandy burns his throat.

My inclination towards Theodora could hardly be the simple, natural instinct, guided by natural selection, for then surely I should have been swayed towards some more womanly individual, some more vigorous and at the same time more feminine physique. In me, it was the mind that had first suggested to the senses, and the senses that had answered in a dizzy pleasure, that this passionate, sensitive frame, with its tensely-strung nerves and excitable pulses, promised the height of satisfaction to a lover. Surely to Nature it promised a poor if possible mother, and a still poorer nurse. And these desires and passions that spring from that border-land between mind and sense, and are nourished by the suggestions of the one and the stimulus of the other, have a stronger grip upon our organisation, because they offer an acuter pleasure, than those simple and purely physical ones in which Nature is striving after her own ends and using us simply as her instruments.

I thought on in a desultory sort of way, more or less about Theodora, and mostly about the state of my own feelings, until I reached my chambers. There I found Digby, and in his society, with his chaff and gabble in my ears, all reflection and philosophy fled, without leaving me any definite decision made.

The next afternoon but one found myself and Digby standing at the windows of my chambers awaiting Theodora's arrival. I had invited him to help me entertain the two women, and also to help me unearth and dust my store of idols and curiosities, and range them on the tables for inspection. There were crowds of knick-knacks picked up in the crooked streets and odd corners of Benares, presents made to me, trifles bought in the Cairo bazaars, and vases and coins discovered below the soil in the regions of the Tigris. Concerning several of the most typical objects Digby and I had had considerable difference of opinion. One highly interesting bronze model of the monkey-god at Benares he had declared I could not exhibit on account of its too pronounced realism and insufficient attention to the sartorial art. I had insisted that the god's deficiencies in this respect were not more striking than the objects in flesh-tints, hung at the Academy, that Theodora viewed every season.

'Perhaps not,' he answered. 'But this is *not* in pink and white, and hung on the Academy walls for the public to stare at, and therefore you can't let her see it.'

This was unanswerable. I yielded, and the monkey-god was wheeled under a side-table out of view.

Every shelf and stand and table had been pressed into the service, and my rooms had the appearance of a corner in an Egyptian bazaar, now when we had finished our preparations.

'There they are,' said Digby, as Mrs. Long's victoria came in sight.

Theodora was leaning back beside her sister, and it struck me then how representative she looked, as it were, of herself and her position. From where we stood we could see down into the victoria, as it drew up at our door. Her knees were crossed under the blue carriage-rug, on the edge of which rested her two small pale-gloved hands. A velvet jacket, that fitted her as its skin fits the grape, showed us her magnificent shoulders, and the long easy slope of her figure to the small waist. On her head, in the least turn of which lay the acme of distinction, amongst the black glossy masses of her hair, sat a small hat in vermilion velvet, made to resemble the Turkish fez. As the carriage stopped, she glanced up; and a brilliant smile swept over her face, as she bowed slightly to us at the window. The handsome painted eyes, the naturally scarlet lips, the pallor of the oval face, and each well-trained movement of the distinguished figure, as she rose and stepped from the carriage, were noted and watched by our four critical eyes.

'A typical product of our nineteenth-century civilisation,' I said, with a faint smile, as Theodora let her fur-edged skirt draw over the snowy pavement, and we heard her clear cultivated tones, with the fashionable drag in them, ordering the coachman not to let the horses get cold.

'But she's a splendid sort of creature, don't you think?' asked Digby. 'Happy the man who – eh?'

I nodded. 'Yes,' I assented. 'But how much that man should have to offer, old chap, that's the point; that six thousand of hers seems an invulnerable protection.'

'I suppose so,' said Digby with a nervous yawn. 'And to think I have more than double that and yet – It's a pity. Funny it will be if my looks and your poverty prevent either of us having her.'

'My own case is settled,' I said decisively. 'My position and hers decide it for me.'

'I'd change places with you this minute if I could,' muttered Digby moodily, as steps came down to our door, and we went forward to meet the women as they entered.

It seemed to arrange itself naturally that Digby should be occupied in the first few seconds with Mrs. Long, and that I should be free to receive Theodora.

Of all the lesser emotions, there is hardly any one greater than that subtle sense of pleasure felt when a woman we love crosses for the first time our own threshold. We may have met her a hundred times in her house, or on public ground, but the sensation her presence then creates is altogether different from that instinctive, involuntary, momentary and delightful sense of ownership that rises when she enters any room essentially our own.

It is the very illusion of possession.

With this hatefully egoistic satisfaction infused through me, I drew forward for her my own favourite chair, and Theodora sank into it, and her tiny, exquisitely-formed feet sought my fender-rail. At a murmured invitation from me, she unfastened and laid aside her jacket. Beneath, she revealed some purplish, silk-like material, that seemed shot with different colours as the firelight fell upon it. It was strained tight and smooth upon her, and the swell of a low bosom was distinctly defined below it. There was no excessive development, quite the contrary, but in the very slightness there was an indescribably sensuous curve, and a depression, rising and falling, that seemed as if it might be the very home itself of passion. It was a breast with little suggestion of the duties or powers of Nature, but with infinite seduction for a lover.

'What a marvellous collection you have here,' she said throwing her glance round the room. 'What made you bring home all these things?'

'The majority were gifts to me – presents made by the different natives whom I visited or came into connection with in various ways. A native is never happy, if he likes you at all, until he has made you some valuable present.'

'You must be very popular with them indeed,' returned Theodora, glancing from a brilliant Persian carpet, suspended on the wall, to a gold and ivory model of a temple, on the console by her side.

'Well, when one stays with a fellow as his guest, as I have done with some of these small rajahs and people, of course one tries to make oneself amiable.'

'The fact is, Miss Dudley,' interrupted Digby, 'Ray admires these fellows, and that is why they like him. Just look at this sketch-book of his – what trouble he has taken to make portraits of them.'

And he stretched out a limp-covered pocket-album of mine.

I reddened slightly and tried to intercept his hand.

'Nonsense, Digby. Give the book to me,' I said; but Theodora had already taken it, and she looked at me as I spoke with one of those delicious looks of hers that could speak so clearly. Now it seemed to say, 'If you are going to love me, you must have no secrets from me.' She opened the book and I was subdued and let her. I did not much care, except that it was some time now since I had looked at it, and I did not know what she might find in it. However, Theodora was so different from girls generally, that it did not greatly matter.

'Perhaps these are portraits of your different conquests amongst the Ranees, are they?' she said. 'I don't see "my victims", though, written across the outside as the Frenchmen write on their albums.'

'No,' I said, with a smile, 'I think these are only portraits of men whose appearance struck me. The great difficulty is to persuade any Mohammedan to let you draw him.'

The very first leaf she turned seemed to give the lie to my words. Against a background of yellow sand and blue sky, stood out a slight figure in white, bending a little backward, and holding in its hands, extended on either side, the masses of its black hair that fell through them, till they touched the sand by its feet. Theodora threw a side-glance full of derision on me, as she raised her eyes from the page.

'I swear it isn't,' I said hastily, colouring, for I saw she thought it was a woman. 'It's a young Sikh I bribed to let me paint him.'

'Oh, a young Sikh, is it?' said Theodora, bending over the book again. 'Well it's a lovely face; and what beautiful hair!'

'Yes, almost as beautiful as yours,' I murmured, in safety, for the others were wholly occupied in testing the limits of the flexibility of the soapstone.

Not for any consideration in this world could I have restrained the irresistible desire to say the words, looking at her sitting sideways to me, noting that shining weight of hair lying on the white neck, and that curious masculine shade upon the upper lip. A faint liquid smile came to her face.

'Mine is not so long as that when you see it undone,' she said, looking at me.

'How long is it?' I asked mechanically, turning over the leaves of the sketch-book, and thinking in a crazy sort of way what I would not give to see her with that hair unloosed, and have the right to lift a single strand of it.

'It would not touch the ground,' she answered, 'it must be about eight inches off it, I think.'

'A marvellous length for a European,' I answered in a conventional tone, though it was a difficulty to summon it.

Within my brain all the dizzy thoughts seemed reeling together till they left me hardly conscious of anything but an acute painful sense of her proximity.

'Find me the head of a Persian, will you?' came her voice next.

'A Persian?' I repeated mechanically.

Theodora looked at me wonderingly and I recalled myself.

'Oh, yes,' I answered, 'I'll find you one. Give me the book.'

I took the book and turned over the leaves towards the end. As I did so, some of the intermediate pages caught her eyes, and she tried to arrest the turning leaves.

'What is that? Let me see.'

'It is nothing,' I said, passing them over. 'Allow me to find you the one you want.'

Theodora did not insist, but her glance said: 'I will be revenged for this resistance to my wishes!'

When I had found her the portrait, I laid the open book back upon her knees. Theodora bent over it with an unaffected exclamation of delight. 'How exquisite! and how well you have done it! What a talent you must have!'

'Oh no, no talent,' I said hastily. 'It's easy to do a thing like that when your heart is in it.'

Theodora looked up at me and said simply, 'This is a woman.'

And I looked back in her eyes and said as simply, 'Yes, it is a woman.'

Theodora was silent, gazing at the open leaf, absorbed. And half-unconsciously my eyes followed hers and rested with hers on the page.

Many months had gone by since I had opened the book; and many, many cigars, that according to Tolstoi deaden every mental feeling, and many, many pints of brandy that do the same thing, only more so, had been consumed, since I had last looked upon that face. And now I saw it over the shoulder of this woman. And the old pain revived and surged through me, but it was dull – dull as every emotion must be in the near neighbourhood of a new object of desire – every emotion except one.

'Really it is a very beautiful face, isn't it?' she said at last, with a tender and sympathetic accent, and as she raised her head our eyes met.

I looked at her and answered, 'I should say yes, if we were not looking at it together, but you know beauty is entirely a question of comparison.'

Her face was really not one-tenth so handsome as the mere shadowed, inanimate representation of the Persian girl, beneath our hands. I knew it and so did she. Theodora herself would have been the first to admit it. But nevertheless the words were ethically true. True in the sense that underlay the society compliment, for no beauty of the dead can compare with that of the living. Such are we, that as we love all objects in their relation to our own pleasure from them, so even in our admiration, the greatest beauty, when absolutely useless to us, cannot move us as a far lesser degree has power to do, from which it is possible to hope, however vaguely, for some personal gratification. And to this my words would come if translated. And I think Theodora understood the translation rather than the conventional form of them, for she did not take the trouble to deprecate the flattery.

I got up, and, to change the subject, said, 'Let me wheel up that little table of idols. Some of them are rather curious.'

I moved the tripod up to the arm of her chair.

Theodora closed the sketch-book and put it beside her, and looked over the miniature bronze gods with interest. Then she stretched out her arm to lift and move several of them, and her soft finger seemed to lie caressingly – as they did on everything they touched – on the heads and shoulders of the images. I watched her, envying those senseless little blocks of brass.

'This is the Hindu equivalent of the Greek Aphrodite,' I said, lifting forward a small, unutterably hideous, squat female figure, with the face of a monkey, and two closed wings of a dragon on its shoulders.

'Oh, Venus,' said Theodora. 'We must certainly crown her amongst them, though hardly, I think, in this particular case, for her beauty!'

And she laughingly slipped off a diamond half-hoop from her middle finger, and slipped the ring on to the model's head. It fitted exactly round the repulsive brows of the deformed and stunted image, and the goddess stood crowned in the centre of the table, amongst the other figures, with the circlet of brilliants, flashing brightly in the firelight, on her head. As Theodora passed the ring from her own warm white finger on to the forehead of the misshapen idol, she looked at me. The look, coupled with the action, in my state, went home to those very inner cells of the brain where are the springs themselves of passion. At the same instant the laughter and irresponsible gaiety and light pleasure on the face before me, the contrast between the delicate hand and the repellent monstrosity it had crowned – the sinister, allegorical significance – struck me like a blow. An unexplained feeling of rage filled me. Was it against her, myself, her action, or my own desires? It seemed for the moment to burn against them all. On the spur of it, I dragged forward to myself another of the images from behind the Astarte, slipped off my own signet-ring, and put it on the head of the idol.

'This is the only one for me to crown,' I said bitterly, with a laugh, feeling myself whiten with the stress and strain of a host of inexplicable sensations that crowded in upon me, as I met Theodora's lovely inquiring glance.

There was a shade of apprehensiveness in her voice as she said, 'What is that one?'

'Shiva,' I said curtly, looking her straight in the eyes. 'The god of self-denial.'

I saw the colour die suddenly out of her face, and I knew I had hurt her. But I could not help it. With her glance she had summoned me to approve or second her jesting act. It was a challenge I could not pass over. I must in some correspondingly joking way either accept or reject her coronation. And to reject it was all I could do, since this woman must be nothing to me. There was a second's blank pause of strained silence. But, superficially, we had not strayed off the legitimate ground of mere society nothings, whatever we might feel lay beneath them. And Theodora was trained thoroughly in the ways of fashion.

The next second she leant back in her chair, saying lightly, 'A false, absurd, and unnatural god; it is the greatest error to strive after the impossible; it merely prevents you accomplishing the possible. Gods like these,' and she indicated the abominable squint-eyed Venus, 'are merely natural instincts personified, and one may well call them gods since they are invincible. Don't you remember the fearful punishments that the Greeks represented as overtaking mortals who dared to resist nature's laws, that they chose to individualise as their gods? You remember the fate of Hippolytus who tried to disdain Venus, of Pentheus who tried to subdue Bacchus? These two plays teach the immortal lesson that if you have the presumption to try to be greater than nature she will in the end take a terrible revenge. The most we can do is to guide her. You can never be her conqueror. Consider yourself fortunate if she allows you to be her charioteer.'

It was all said very lightly and jestingly, but at the last phrase there was a flash in her eye, directed upon me – yes, me – as if she read down into my inner soul, and it sent the blood to my face.

As the last word left her lips, she stretched out her hand and deliberately took my ring from the head of Shiva, put it above her own diamonds on the other idol, and laid the god I had chosen, the god of austerity and mortification, prostrate on its face, at the feet of the leering Venus.

Then, without troubling to find a transition phrase, she

got up and said, 'I am going to look at that Persian carpet.'

It had all taken but a few seconds; the next minute we were over by the carpet, standing in front of it and admiring its hues in the most orthodox terms. The images were left as she had placed them. I could do nothing less, of course, than yield to a woman and my guest. The jest had not gone towards calming my feelings, nor had those two glances of hers – the first so tender and appealing as she had crowned the Venus, the second so virile and mocking as she had discrowned the Shiva. There was a strange mingling of extremes in her. At one moment she seemed will-less, deliciously weak, a thing only made to be taken in one's arms and kissed. The next, she was full of independent uncontrollable determination and opinion. Most men would have found it hard to be indifferent to her. When beside her you must either have been attracted or repelled. For me, she was the very worst woman that could have crossed my path.

As I stood beside her now, her shoulder only a little below my own, her neck and the line of her breast just visible to the side vision of my eye, and heard her talking of the carpet, I felt there was no price I would not have paid to have stood for one half-hour in intimate confidence with her, and been able to tear the veils from this irritating character.

From the carpet we passed on to a table of Cashmere work and next to a pile of Mohammedan garments. These had been packed with my own personal luggage, and I should not have thought of bringing them forth for inspection. It was Digby who, having seen them by chance in my portmanteau, had insisted that they would add interest to the general collection of Eastern trifles. 'Clothes, my dear fellow, clothes; why, they will probably please her more than anything else.'

Theodora advanced to the heap of stuffs and lifted them.

'What is the history of these?' she said laughing. 'These were not presents to you!'

'No,' I murmured. 'Bought in the native bazaars.'

'Some perhaps,' returned Theodora, throwing her glance over them. 'But a great many are not new.'

It struck me that she would not be a woman very easy to deceive. Some men value a woman in proportion to the ease with which they can impose upon her, but to me it is too much trouble to deceive at all, so that the absence of that amiable quality did not disquiet me. On the contrary, the comprehensive, cynical, and at the same time indulgent smile that came so readily to Theodora's lips charmed me more, because it was the promise of even less trouble than a real or professed obtuseness.

'No,' I assented merely.

'Well, then?' asked Theodora, but without troubling to seek a reply. 'How pretty they are and how curious! this one, for instance.' And she took up a blue silk zouave, covered with gold embroidery, and worth perhaps about thirty pounds. 'This has been a good deal worn. It is a souvenir, I suppose?'

I nodded. With any other woman I was similarly anxious to please I should have denied it, but with her I felt it did not matter.

'Too sacred perhaps, then, for me to put on?' she asked with her hand in the collar, and smiling derisively.

'Oh dear no!' I said, 'not at all. Put it on by all means.'

'Nothing is sacred to you, eh? I see. Hold it then.'

She gave me the zouave and turned for me to put it on her. A glimpse of the back of her white neck, as she bent her head forward, a convulsion of her adorable shoulders as she drew on the jacket, and the zouave was fitted on. Two seconds perhaps, but my self-control wrapped round me had lost one of its skins.

'Now I must find a turban or fez,' she said, turning over gently, but without any ceremony, the pile. 'Oh, here's one!' She drew out a white fez, also embroidered in gold, and, removing her hat, put it on very much to one side, amongst her black hair, with evident care lest one of those silken inflected waves should be disturbed; and then affecting an undulating gait, she walked over to the fire.

'How do you like me in Eastern dress, Helen?' she said, addressing her sister, for whom Digby was deciphering some old coins. Digby and I confessed afterwards to each other the impulse that moved us both to suggest it was not at all complete without the trousers. I did offer her a cigarette, to enhance the effect.

'Quite passable, really,' said Mrs. Long, leaning back and surveying her languidly.

Theodora took the cigarette with a laugh, lighted and smoked it, and it was then, as she leant against the mantelpiece with her eyes full of laughter, a glow on her pale skin, and an indolent relaxation in the long, supple figure, that I first said, or rather an involuntary, unrecognised voice within me said, 'It is no good; whatever happens I must have you.'

'Do you know that it is past six, Theo?' said Mrs. Long.

'You will let me give you a cup of tea before you go?' I said.

'Tea!' repeated Theodora. 'I thought you were going to say haschisch or opium, at the least, after such an Indian afternoon.'

'I have both,' I answered, 'would you like some?' thinking, 'By Jove, I should like to see you after the haschisch.'

'No,' replied Theodora, 'I make it a rule not to get intoxicated in public.'

When the women rose to go, Theodora, to my regret, divested herself of the zouave without my aid, and declined it also for putting on her own cloak. As they stood drawing on their gloves I asked if they thought there was anything worthy of their acceptance amongst these curiosities. Mrs. Long chose from the table near her an ivory model of the Taj, and Digby took it up to carry for her to the door. As he did so his eye caught the table of images.

'This is your ring, Miss Dudley, I believe,' he said.

I saw him grin horridly as he noted the arrangement of the figures. Doubtless he thought it was mine.

I took up my signet-ring again, and Theodora said carelessly, without the faintest tinge of colour rising in her cheek, 'Oh, yes, I had forgotten it. Thanks.'

She took it from him and replaced it.

I asked her if she would honour me as her sister had done.

'There is one thing in this room that I covet immensely,' she said, meeting my gaze.

'It is yours, of course, then,' I answered. 'What is it?'

Theodora stretched out her open hand. 'Your sketch-book.'

For a second I felt the blood dye suddenly all my face. The request took me by surprise, for one thing; and immediately after the surprise followed the vexatious and embarrassing thought that she had asked for the one thing in the room that I certainly did not wish her to have. The book contained a hundred thousand memories, embodied in writing, sketching, and painting, of those years in the East. There was not a page in it that did not reflect the emotions of the time when it had been filled in, and give a chronicle of the life lived at the date inscribed on it. It was a sort of diary in cipher, and to turn over its leaves was to re-live the hours they represented. For my own personal pleasure I liked the book and wanted to keep it, but there were other reasons too why I disliked the idea of surrendering it. It flashed through me, the question as to what her object was in possessing herself of it. Was it jealousy of the faces or any face within it that prompted her, and would she amuse herself, when she had it, by tearing out the leaves or burning it? To give over these portraits merely to be sacrificed to a petty feminine spite and malice, jarred upon me. Involuntarily I looked hard into her eyes to try and read her intentions, and I felt I had wronged her. The eyes were full of the softest, tenderest light. It was impossible to imagine them vindictive. She had seen my hesitation and she smiled faintly.

'Poor Herod with your daughter of Herodias,' she said, softly. 'Never mind, I will not take it.'

The others who had been standing with her saw there was some embarrassment that they did not understand, and Mrs. Long turned to go slowly down the corridor. Digby had to follow. Theodora was left standing alone before me, her seductive figure framed in the open doorway. Of course she was irresistible. Was she not the new object of my desires?

I seized the sketch-book from the chair. What did anything matter?

'Yes,' I said hastily, putting it into that soft, small hand before it could draw back. 'Forgive me the hesitation. You know I would give you anything.'

If she answered or thanked me, I forget it. I was sensible of nothing at the moment but that the blood seemed flowing to my brain, and thundering through it, in ponderous waves. Then I knew we were walking down the passage, and in a few minutes more we should have said good-bye, and she would be gone.

An acute and yet vague realisation came upon me that the corridor was dark, and that the others had gone on in front, a confused recollection of the way she had lauded Nature and its domination a short time back, and then all these were lost again in the eddying torrent of an overwhelming desire to take her in my arms and hold her, control her, assert my will over hers, this exasperating object who had been pleasing and seducing every sense for the last three hours, and now was leaving them all unsatisfied. That impulse towards some physical demonstration, that craving for physical contact, which attacks us suddenly with its terrific impetus, and chokes and stifles us, ourselves, beneath it, blinding us to all except itself, rushed upon me then, walking beside her in the dark passage; and at that instant Theodora sighed.

'I am tired,' she said languidly. 'May I take your arm?' and her hand touched me.

I did not offer her my arm, I flung it round her neck, bending back her head upon it, so that her lips were just beneath my own as I leant over her, and I pressed mine on them in a delirium of passion.

Everything that should have been remembered I forgot.

Knowledge was lost of all, except those passive, burning lips under my own. As I touched them, a current of madness seemed to mingle with my blood, and pass flaming through all my veins.

I heard her moan, but for that instant I was beyond the reach of pity or reason, I only leant harder on her lips in a wild, unheeding, unsparing frenzy. It was a moment of ecstasy that I would have bought with years of my life. One moment, the next I released her, and so suddenly, that she reeled against the wall of the passage. I caught her wrist to steady her. We dared neither of us speak, for the others were but little ahead of us; but I sought her eyes in the dusk.

They met mine, and rested on them, gleaming through the darkness. There was no confusion nor embarrassment in them, they were full of the hot, clear, blinding light of passion; and I knew there would be no need to crave forgiveness.

The next moment had brought us up to the others, and to the end of the passage.

Mrs. Long turned round, and held out her hand to me.

'Good-bye,' she said. 'We have had a most interesting afternoon.'

It was with an effort that I made some conventional remark.

Theodora, with perfect outward calm, shook hands with myself and Digby, with her sweetest smile, and passed out.

I lingered some few minutes with Digby, talking; and then he went off to his own diggings, and I returned slowly down the passage to my rooms.

My blood and pulses seemed beating as they do in fever, my ears seemed full of sounds, and that kiss burnt like the brand of hot iron on my lips. When I reached my rooms, I locked the door and flung both the windows open to the snowy night. The white powder on the ledge crumbled and drifted in.

ADA LEVERSON

SUGGESTION

IF Lady Winthrop had not spoken of me as 'that intolerable, effeminate boy,' she might have had some chance of marrying my father. She was a middle-aged widow; prosaic, fond of domineering, and an alarmingly excellent housekeeper; the serious work of her life was paying visits; in her lighter moments she collected autographs. She was highly suitable and altogether insupportable; and this unfortunate remark about me was, as people say, the last straw. Some encouragement from father Lady Winthrop must, I think, have received; for she took to calling at odd hours, asking my sister Marjorie sudden abrupt questions, and being generally impossible. A tradition existed that her advice was of use to our father in his household, and when, last year, he married his daughter's school-friend, a beautiful girl of twenty, it surprised every one except Marjorie and myself.

The whole thing was done, in fact, by suggestion. I shall never forget that summer evening when father first realised, with regard to Laura Egerton, the possible. He was giving a little dinner of eighteen people. *Through a mistake of Marjorie's* (my idea) Lady Winthrop did not receive her invitation till the very last minute. Of course she accepted – we knew she would – but unknowing that it was a dinner party, she came without putting on evening-dress.

Nothing could be more trying to the average woman than

such a *contretemps*: and Lady Winthrop was not one to rise, sublimely, and laughing, above the situation. I can see her now, in a plaid blouse and a vile temper, displaying herself, mentally and physically, to the utmost disadvantage, while Marjorie apologised the whole evening, in pale blue crèpe-de-chine; and Laura, in yellow, with mauve orchids, sat – an adorable contrast – on my father's other side, with a slightly conscious air that was perfectly fascinating. It is quite extraordinary what trifles have their little effect in these matters. *I* had sent Laura the orchids, anonymously; I could not help it if she chose to think they were from my father. Also, I had hinted of his secret affection for her, and lent her Verlaine. I said I had found it in his study, turned down at her favourite page. Laura has, like myself, the artistic temperament; she is cultured, rather romantic, and in search of the *au-delà*. My father has at times – never to me – rather charming manners; also he is still handsome, with that look of having suffered that comes from enjoying oneself too much. That evening his really sham melancholy and apparently hollow gaiety were delightful for a son to witness, and appealed evidently to her heart. Yes, strange as it may seem, while the world said that pretty Miss Egerton married old Carington for his money, she was really in love, or thought herself in love, with our father. Poor girl! She little knew what an irritating, ill-tempered, absent-minded person he is in private life; and at times I have pangs of remorse.

A fortnight after the wedding, father forgot he was married, and began again treating Laura with a sort of *distrait* gallantry as Marjorie's friend, or else ignoring her altogether. When, from time to time, he remembers she is his wife, he scolds her about the housekeeping in a fitful, perfunctory way, for he does not know that Marjorie does it still. Laura bears the rebukes like an angel; indeed, rather than take the slightest practical trouble she would prefer to listen to the strongest language in my father's vocabulary.

But she is sensitive; and when father, speedily resuming his bachelor manners, recommenced his visits to an old friend who lives in one of the little houses opposite the Oratory, she seemed quite vexed. Father is horribly careless, and Laura found a letter. They had a rather serious explanation, and for a little time after, Laura seemed depressed. She soon tried to rouse herself, and is at times cheerful enough with Marjorie and myself, but I fear she has had a disillusion. They never quarrel now, and I think we all three dislike father about equally, though Laura never owns it, and is gracefully attentive to him in a gentle, filial sort of way.

We are fond of going to parties – not father – and Laura is a very nice chaperone for Marjorie. They are both perfectly devoted to me. 'Cecil knows everything,' they are always saying, and they do nothing – not even choosing a hat – without asking my advice.

Since I left Eton I am supposed to be reading with a tutor, but as a matter of fact I have plenty of leisure; and am very glad to be of use to the girls, of whom I'm, by the way, quite proud. They are rather a sweet contrast; Marjorie has the sort of fresh rosy prettiness you see in the park and on the river. She is tall, and slim as a punt-pole, and if she were not very careful how she dresses, she would look like a drawing by Pilotelle in the *Lady's Pictorial*. She is practical and lively, she rides and drives and dances; skates, and goes to some mysterious haunt called *The Stores*, and is, in her own way, quite a modern English type.

Laura has that exotic beauty so much admired by Philistines; dreamy dark eyes, and a wonderful white complexion. She loves music and poetry and pictures and admiration in a lofty sort of way; she has a morbid fondness for mental gymnastics, and a dislike to physical exertion, and never takes any exercise except waving her hair. Sometimes she looks bored, and I have heard her sigh.

'Cissy,' Marjorie said, coming one day into my study, 'I want to speak to you about Laura.'

'Do you have pangs of conscience too?' I asked, lighting a cigarette.

'Dear, we took a great responsibility. Poor girl! Oh, couldn't we make Papa more –'

'Impossible,' I said; 'no one has any influence with him. He can't bear even me, though if he had a shade of decency he would dash away an unbidden tear every time I look at him with my mother's blue eyes.'

My poor mother was a great beauty, and I am supposed to be her living image.

'Laura has no object in life,' said Marjorie. 'I have, all girls have, I suppose. By the way, Cissy, I am quite sure Charlie Winthrop is serious.'

'How sweet of him! I am so glad. I got father off my hands last season.'

'Must I really marry him, Cissy? He bores me.'

'What has that to do with it? Certainly you must. You are not a beauty, and I doubt your ever having a better chance.'

Marjorie rose and looked at herself in the long pier-glass that stands opposite my writing-table. I could not resist the temptation to go and stand beside her.

'I am just the style that is admired now,' said Marjorie, dispassionately.

'So am I,' I said reflectively. 'But *you* will soon be out of date.'

Every one says I am strangely like my mother. Her face was of that pure and perfect oval one so seldom sees, with delicate features, rosebud mouth, and soft flaxen hair. A blondness without insipidity, for the dark-blue eyes are fringed with dark lashes, and from their languorous depths looks out a soft mockery. I have a curious ideal devotion to my mother; she died when I was quite young – only two months old – and I often spend hours thinking of her, as I gaze at myself in the mirror.

'Do come down from the clouds,' said Marjorie impatiently, for I had sunk into a reverie. 'I came to ask you to think of something to amuse Laura – to interest her.'

'We ought to make it up to her in some way. Haven't you tried anything?'

'Only palmistry; and Mrs. Wilkinson prophesied her all that she detests, and depressed her dreadfully.'

'What do you think she really needs most?' I asked.

Our eyes met.

'Really, Cissy, you're too disgraceful,' said Marjorie. There was a pause.

'And so I'm to accept Charlie?'

'What man do you like better?' I asked.

'I don't know what you mean,' said Marjorie, colouring.

'*I* thought Adrian Grant would have been more sympathetic to Laura than to you. I have just had a note from him, asking me to tea at his studio to-day.' I threw it to her. 'He says I'm to bring you both. Would that amuse Laura?'

'Oh,' cried Marjorie, enchanted, 'of course we'll go. I wonder what he thinks of me,' she added wistfully.

'He didn't say. He is going to send Laura his verses, "Hearts-ease and Heliotrope."'

She sighed. Then she said, 'Father was complaining again to-day of your laziness.'

'I, lazy! Why, I've been swinging the censer in Laura's boudoir because she wants to encourage the religious temperament, and I've designed your dress for the Clives' fancy ball.'

'Where's the design?'

'In my head. You're not to wear white; Miss Clive must wear white.'

'I wonder you don't marry her,' said Marjorie, 'you admire her so much.'

'I never marry. Besides, I know she's pretty, but that furtive Slade-school manner of hers gets on my nerves. You don't know how dreadfully I suffer from my nerves.'

She lingered a little, asking me what I advised her to choose for a birthday present for herself – an American organ, a black poodle, or an *édition de luxe* of Browning. I advised the last, as being least noisy. Then I told her I felt sure that in spite of her admiration for Adrian, she was far too good-natured to interfere with Laura's prospects. She said I was incorrigible, and left the room with a smile of resignation.

And I returned to my reading. On my last birthday – I was seventeen – my father – who has his gleams of dry humour – gave me *Robinson Crusoe!* I prefer Pierre Loti, and intend to have an onyx-paved bath-room, with soft apricot-coloured light shimmering through the blue-lined green curtains in my chambers, as soon as I get Marjorie married, and Laura more – settled down.

I met Adrian Grant first at a luncheon party at the Clives'. I seemed to amuse him; he came to see me, and became at once obviously enamoured of my step-mother. He is rather an impressionable impressionist, and a delightful creature, tall and graceful and beautiful, and altogether most interesting. Every one admits he's fascinating; he is very popular and very much disliked. He is by way of being a painter; he has a little money of his own – enough for his telegrams, but not enough for his buttonholes – and nothing could be more incongruous than the idea of his marrying. I have never seen Marjorie so much attracted. But she is a good loyal girl, and will accept Charlie Winthrop, who is a dear person, good-natured and ridiculously rich – just the sort of man for a brother-in-law. It will annoy my old enemy Lady Winthrop – he is her nephew, and she wants him to marry that little Miss Clive. Dorothy Clive has her failings, but she could not – to do her justice – be happy with Charlie Winthrop.

Adrian's gorgeous studio gives one the complex impression of being at once the calm retreat of a mediaeval saint and the luxurious abode of a modern Pagan. One feels that everything could be done there, everything from praying to flirting – everything except painting. The tea-party amused me, I was pretending to listen to a brown person who was talking absurd worn-out literary clichés – as that the New Humour is not funny, or that Bourget understood women, when I overheard this fragment of conversation.

'But don't you like Society?' Adrian was saying.

'I get rather tired of it. People are so much alike. They all say the same things,' said Laura.

'Of course they all say the same things to *you*,' murmured Adrian, as he affected to point out a rather curious old silver crucifix.

'That,' said Laura, 'is one of the things they say.'

About three weeks later I found myself dining alone with Adrian Grant, at one of the two restaurants in London. (The cooking is better at the other, this one is the more becoming.) I had lilies-of-the-valley in my buttonhole, Adrian was wearing a red carnation. Several people glanced at us. Of course he is very well known in Society. Also, I was looking rather nice, and I could not help hoping, while Adrian gazed rather absently over my head, that the shaded candles were staining to a richer rose the waking wonder of my face.

Adrian was charming of course, but he seemed worried and a little preoccupied, and drank a good deal of champagne.

Towards the end of dinner, he said – almost abruptly for him – 'Carington.'

'Cecil,' I interrupted. He smiled.

'Cissy . . . it seems an odd thing to say to you, but though you are so young, I think you know everything. I am sure you know everything. You know about me. I am in love. I am quite miserable. What on earth am I to do!' He drank more champagne. 'Tell me,' he said, 'what to do.' For a few minutes, while we listened to that interminable hackneyed *Intermezzo*, I reflected; asking myself by what strange phases I had risen to the extraordinary position of giving advice to Adrian on such a subject?

Laura was not happy with our father. From a selfish motive, Marjorie and I had practically arranged that monstrous marriage. That very day he had been disagreeable, asking me with a clumsy sarcasm to raise his allowance, so that he could afford my favourite cigarettes. If Adrian were free, Marjorie might refuse Charlie Winthrop. I don't want her to refuse him. Adrian has treated me as a friend. I like him – I like him enormously. I am quite devoted to him. And how can I rid myself of the feeling of responsibility, the sense that I owe some compensation to poor beautiful Laura?

We spoke of various matters. Just before we left the table, I said, with what seemed, but was not, irrelevance, 'Dear Adrian, Mrs. Carington –'

'Go on, Cissy.'

'She is one of those who must be appealed to, at first, by her imagination. She married our father because she thought he was lonely and misunderstood.'

'*I* am lonely and misunderstood,' said Adrian, his eyes flashing with delight.

'Ah, not twice! She doesn't like that now.'

I finished my coffee slowly, and then I said, 'Go to the Clives' fancy-ball as Tristan.'

Adrian pressed my hand . . . .

At the door of the restaurant we parted, and I drove

home through the cool April night, wondering, wondering. Suddenly I thought of my mother – my beautiful sainted mother, who would have loved me, I am convinced, had she lived, with an extraordinary devotion. What would she have said to all this? What would she have thought? I know not why, but a mad reaction seized me. I felt recklessly conscientious. My father! After all, he was my father. I was possessed by passionate scruples. If I went back now to Adrian – if I went back and implored him, supplicated him never to see Laura again!

I felt I could persuade him. I have sufficient personal magnetism to do that, if I make up my mind. After one glance in the looking-glass, I put up my stick and stopped the hansom. I had taken a resolution. I told the man to drive to Adrian's rooms.

He turned round with a sharp jerk. In another second a brougham passed us – a swift little brougham that I knew. It slackened – it stopped – we passed it – I saw my father. He was getting out at one of the little houses opposite the Brompton Oratory.

'Turn round again,' I shouted to the cabman. And he drove me straight home.

GEORGE EGERTON

A CROSS LINE

THE rather flat notes of a man's voice float out into the clear air, singing the refrain of a popular music-hall ditty. There is something incongruous between the melody and the surroundings. It seems profane, indelicate, to bring this slangy, vulgar tune, and with it the mental picture of footlight flare and fantastic dance into the lovely freshness of this perfect spring day.

A woman sitting on a felled tree turns her head to meet its coming, and an expression flits across her face in which disgust and humorous appreciation are subtly blended. Her mind is nothing if not picturesque; her busy brain, with all its capabilities choked by a thousand vagrant fancies, is always producing pictures and finding associations between the most unlikely objects. She has been reading a little sketch written in the daintiest language of a fountain scene in Tanagra, and her vivid imagination has made it real to her. The slim, graceful maids grouped around it filling their exquisitely-formed earthen jars, the dainty poise of their classic heads, and the flowing folds of their draperies have been actually present with her; and now? – why, it is like the entrance of a half-tipsy vagabond player bedizened in tawdry finery – the picture is blurred. She rests her head against the trunk of a pine tree behind her, and awaits the singer. She is sitting on an incline in the midst of a wilderness of trees;

some have blown down, some have been cut down, and the lopped branches lie about; moss and bracken and trailing bramble, fir-cones, wild rose bushes, and speckled red 'fairy hats' fight for life in wild confusion. A disused quarry to the left is an ideal haunt of pike, and to the right a little river rushes along in haste to join a greater sister that is fighting a troubled way to the sea. A row of stepping-stones crosses it, and if you were to stand on one you would see shoals of restless stone loach 'Beardies' darting from side to side. The tails of several ducks can be seen above the water, and the paddle of their balancing feet, and the gurgling suction of their bills as they search for larvae can be heard distinctly between the hum of insect, twitter of bird, and rustle of stream and leaf. The singer has changed his lay to a whistle, and presently he comes down the path a cool, neat, grey-clad figure, with a fishing creel slung across his back, and a trout rod held on his shoulder. The air ceases abruptly, and his cold grey eyes scan the seated figure with its gipsy ease of attitude, a scarlet shawl that has fallen from her shoulders forming an accentuative background to the slim roundness of her waist.

Persistent study, coupled with a varied experience of the female animal, has given the owner of the grey eyes some facility in classing her, although it has not supplied him with any definite data as to what any one of the species may do in a given circumstance. To put it in his own words, in answer to a friend who chaffed him on his untiring pursuit of women as an interesting problem:

'If a fellow has had much experience of his fellow-man he may divide him into types, and, given a certain number of men and a certain number of circumstances, he is pretty safe on hitting on the line of action each type will strike; 't aint so with woman. You may always look out for the unexpected, she generally upsets a fellow's calculations, and you are never safe in laying odds on her. Tell you what, old chappie, we may talk about superior intellect; but, if a woman wasn't handicapped by her affection, or need of it, the cleverest chap in Christendom would be just a bit of putty in her hands. I find them more fascinating as problems than anything going. Never let an opportunity slip to get new data – never!'

He did not now. He met the frank, unembarrassed gaze of eyes that would have looked with just the same bright inquiry at the advent of a hare, or a toad, or any other object that might cross her path, and raised his hat with respectful courtesy, saying, in the drawling tone habitual with him –

'I hope I am not trespassing?'

'I can't say; you may be, so may I, but no one has ever told me so!'

A pause. His quick glance has noted the thick wedding ring on her slim brown hand, and the flash of a diamond in its keeper. A lady decidedly. Fast? perhaps. Original? undoubtedly. Worth knowing? rather.

'I am looking for a trout stream, but the directions I got were rather vague; might I –'

'It's straight ahead, but you won't catch anything now, at least not here, sun's too glaring and water too low, a mile up you may, in an hour's time.'

'Oh, thanks awfully for the tip. You fish then?'

'Yes, sometimes.'

'Trout run big here?' (what odd eyes the woman has, kind of magnetic.)

'No, seldom over a pound, but they are very game.'

'Rare good sport isn't it, whipping a stream? There is so much besides the mere catching of fish. The river and the trees and the quiet sets a fellow thinking – kind of sermon – makes a chap feel good, don't it?'

She smiles assentingly. And yet what the devil is she

amused at he queries mentally. An inspiration. He acts upon it, and says eagerly:

'I wonder – I don't half like to ask – but fishing puts people on a common footing, don't it? You knowing the stream, you know, would you tell me what are the best flies to use?'

'I tie my own, but –'

'Do you? how clever of you! wish I could,' and sitting down on the other end of the tree, he takes out his flybook, 'but I interrupted you, you were going to say?'

'Only,' stretching out her hand (of a perfect shape but decidedly brown) for the book, 'that you might give the local fly-tyer a trial, he'll tell you.'

'Later on, end of next month, or perhaps later, you might try the oak-fly, the natural fly you know; a horn is the best thing to hold them in, they get out of anything else – and put two on at a time.'

'By Jove, I must try that dodge!'

He watches her as she handles his book and examines the contents critically, turning aside some with a glance, fingering others almost tenderly, holding them daintily and noting the cock of wings and the hint of tinsel, with her head on one side; a trick of hers he thinks.

'Which do you like most, wet or dry fly?' (she is looking at some dry flies.)

'Oh,' with that rare smile, 'at the time I swear by whichever happens to catch most fish. Perhaps, really, dry fly. I fancy most of these flies are better for Scotland or England. Up to this March-brown has been the most killing thing. But you might try an "orange-grouse", that's always good here; with perhaps a "hare's ear" for a change – and put on a "coachman" for the evenings. My husband (he steals a side look at her) brought home some beauties yesterday evening.'

'Lucky fellow!'

She returns the book. There is a tone in his voice as he says this that jars on her, sensitive as she is to every inflection of a voice, with an intuition that is almost second sight. She gathers up her shawl. She has a cream-coloured woollen gown on, and her skin looks duskily foreign by contrast. She is on her feet before he can regain his, and says, with a cool little bend of her head: 'Good afternoon, I wish you a full basket!'

Before he can raise his cap she is down the slope, gliding with easy steps that have a strange grace, and then springing lightly from stone to stone across the stream. He feels small, snubbed someway, and he sits down on the spot where she sat and, lighting his pipe, says 'check!'

She is walking slowly up the garden path. A man in his shirt sleeves is stooping amongst the tender young peas. A bundle of stakes lies next him, and he whistles softly and all out of tune as he twines the little tendrils round each new support. She looks at his broad shoulders and narrow flanks; his back is too long for great strength, she thinks. He hears her step, and smiles up at her from under the shadow of his broad-leafed hat.

'How do you feel now, old woman?'

'Beastly. I've got that horrid qualmish feeling again. I can't get rid of it.'

He has spread his coat on the side of the path and pats it for her to sit down.

'What is it' (anxiously)? 'if you were a mare I'd know what to do for you. Have a nip of whisky?'

He strides off without waiting for her reply and comes back with it and a biscuit, kneels down and holds the glass to her lips.

'Poor little woman, buck up! You'll see that'll fix you. Then you go by-and-by and have a shy at the fish.'

She is about to say something when a fresh qualm attacks her and she does not.

He goes back to his tying.

'By Jove!' he says suddenly, 'I forgot. Got something to show you!'

After a few minutes he returns carrying a basket covered with a piece of sacking. A dishevelled-looking hen, with spread wings trailing and her breast bare from sitting on her eggs, screeches after him. He puts it carefully down and uncovers it, disclosing seven little balls of yellow fluff splashed with olive green. They look up sideways with bright round eyes, and their little spoon bills look disproportionately large.

'Aren't they beauties (enthusiastically)? This one is just out,' taking up an egg, 'mustn't let it get chilled.' There is a chip out of it and a piece of hanging skin. 'Isn't it funny?' he asks, showing her how it is curled in the shell, with its paddles flattened and its bill breaking through the chip, and the slimy feathers sticking to its violet skin.

She suppresses an exclamation of disgust, and looks at his fresh-tinted skin instead. He is covering basket, hen, and all –

'How you love young things!' she says.

'Some. I had a filly once, she turned out a lovely mare! I cried when I had to sell her, I wouldn't have let any one in God's world mount her.'

'Yes, you would!'

'Who?' with a quick look of resentment.

'Me!'

'I wouldn't!'

'What! you wouldn't?'

'I wouldn't!'

'I think you would if I wanted to!' with a flash out of the tail of her eye.

'No, I wouldn't!'

'Then you would care more for her than for me. I would give you your choice (passionately), her or me!'

'What nonsense!'

'May be (concentrated), but it's lucky she isn't here to make deadly sense of it.' A humble-bee buzzes close to her ear, and she is roused to a sense of facts, and laughs to think how nearly they have quarrelled over a mare that was sold before she knew him.

Some evenings later, she is stretched motionless in a chair, and yet she conveys an impression of restlessness; a sensitively nervous person would feel it. She is gazing at her husband, her brows are drawn together, and make three little lines. He is reading, reading quietly, without moving his eyes quickly from side to side of the page as she does when she reads, and he pulls away at a big pipe with steady enjoyment. Her eyes turn from him to the window, and follow the course of two clouds, then they close for a few seconds, then open to watch him again. He looks up and smiles.

'Finished your book?'

There is a singular soft monotony in his voice; the organ with which she replies is capable of more varied expression.

'Yes, it is a book makes one think. It would be a greater book if he were not an Englishman. He's afraid of shocking the big middle class. You wouldn't care about it.'

'Finished your smoke?'

'No, it went out, too much fag to light up again! No (protestingly), never you mind, old boy, why do you?'

He has drawn his long length out of his chair, and, kneeling down beside her, guards a lighted match from the incoming evening air. She draws in the smoke contentedly, and her eyes smile back with a general vague tenderness.

'Thank you, dear old man!'

'Going out again?' negative head shake.

'Back aching?' affirmative nod, accompanied by a steadily aimed puff of smoke, that she has been carefully inhaling, into his eyes.

'Scamp! Have your booties off?'

'Oh, don't you bother, Lizzie will do it!'

He has seized a foot from under the rocker, and, sitting on his heels, holds it on his knee, whilst he unlaces the boot; then he loosens the stocking under her toes, and strokes her foot gently.

'Now, the other!' Then he drops both boots outside the door, and fetching a little pair of slippers, past their first smartness, from the bedroom, puts one on. He examines the left foot; it is a little swollen round the ankle, and he presses his broad fingers gently round it as one sees a man do to a horse with windgalls. Then he pulls the rocker nearer to his chair and rests the slipperless foot on his thigh. He relights his pipe, takes up his book, and rubs softly from ankle to toes as he reads.

She smokes and watches him, diverting herself by imagining him in the hats of different periods. His is a delicate-skinned face with regular features; the eyes are fine, in colour and shape with the luminous clearness of a child's; his pointed beard is soft and curly. She looks at his hand, – a broad strong hand with capable fingers, – the hand of a craftsman, a contradiction to the face with its distinguished delicacy. She holds her own up with a cigarette poised between the first and second fingers, idly pleased with its beauty of form and delicate nervous slightness. One speculation chases the other in her quick brain; odd questions as to race arise; she dives into theories as to the why and wherefore of their distinctive natures, and holds a mental debate in which she takes both sides of the question impartially. He has finished his pipe, laid down his book, and is gazing dreamily, with his eyes darkened by their long lashes, and a look of tender melancholy in their clear depths, into space.

'What are you thinking of?' There is a look of expectation in her quivering nervous little face.

He turns to her, chafing her ankle again.

'I was wondering if lob-worms would do for –'

He stops. A strange look of disappointment flits across her face and is lost in an hysterical peal of laughter.

'You are the best emotional check I ever knew,' she gasps.

He stares at her in utter bewilderment, and then a slow smile creeps to his eyes and curves the thin lips under his moustache, a smile at her.

'You seem amused, Gipsy!'

She springs out of her chair and seizes book and pipe; he follows the latter anxiously with his eyes until he sees it laid safely on the table. Then she perches herself, resting her knees against one of his legs, whilst she hooks her feet back under the other –

'Now I am all up, don't I look small?'

He smiles his slow smile. 'Yes, I believe you are made of gutta percha.'

She is stroking out all the lines in his face with the tip of her finger; then she runs it through his hair. He twists his head half impatiently, she desists.

'I divide all the people in the world,' she says, 'into those who like their hair played with, and those who don't. Having my hair brushed gives me more pleasure than anything else; it's delicious. I'd *purr* if I knew how. I notice (meditatively) I am never in sympathy with those who don't like it; I am with those who do. I always get on with them.'

'You are a queer little devil!'

'Am I? I shouldn't have thought you would have found out

I was the latter at all. I wish I were a man! I believe if I were a man, I'd be a disgrace to my family.'

'Why?'

'I'd go on a jolly old spree!'

He laughs: 'Poor little woman, is it so dull?'

There is a gleam of devilry in her eyes, and she whispers solemnly –

'Begin with a D,' and she traces imaginary letters across his forehead, and ending with a flick over his ear, says, 'and that is the tail of the y!'

After a short silence she queries –

'Are you fond of me?' She is rubbing her chin up and down his face.

'Of course I am, don't you know it?'

'Yes, perhaps I do,' impatiently; 'but I want to be told it. A woman doesn't care a fig for a love as deep as the death-sea and as silent, she wants something that tells her it in little waves all the time. It isn't the love, you know, it's the being loved; it isn't really the man, it's his loving!'

'By Jove, you're a rum un!'

'I wish I wasn't then. I wish I was as commonplace as –. You don't tell me anything about myself (a fierce little kiss), you might, even if it were lies. Other men who cared for me told me things about my eyes, my hands, anything. I don't believe you notice.'

'Yes I *do*, little one, only I think it.'

'Yes, but I don't care a bit for your thinking; if I can't see what's in your head what good is it to me?'

'I wish I could understand you, dear!'

'I wish to God you could. Perhaps if you were badder and I were gooder we'd meet half way. *You* are an awfully good old chap; it's just men like you send women like me to the devil!'

'But you are good (kissing her), a real good chum! You

understand a fellow's weak points. You don't blow him up if he gets on a bit. Why (enthusiastically), being married to you is like chumming with a chap! Why (admiringly), do you remember before we were married, when I let that card fall out of my pocket? Why, I couldn't have told another girl about her. She wouldn't have believed that I *was* straight. She'd have thrown me over. And you sent her a quid because she was sick. You are a great little woman!'

'Don't see it! (she is biting his ear). Perhaps I was a man last time, and some hereditary memories are cropping up in this incarnation!'

He looks so utterly at sea that she has to laugh again, and, kneeling up, shuts his eyes with kisses, and bites his chin and shakes it like a terrier in her strong little teeth.

'You imp! was there ever such a woman!'

Catching her wrists, he parts his knees and drops her on to the rug. Then, perhaps the subtle magnetism that is in her affects him, for he stoops and snatches her up and carries her up and down, and then over to the window and lets the fading light with its glimmer of moonshine play on her odd face with its tantalising changes. His eyes dilate and his colour deepens as he crushes her soft little body to him and carries her off to her room.

Summer is waning and the harvest is ripe for ingathering, and the voice of the reaping machine is loud in the land. She is stretched on her back on the short heather-mixed moss at the side of a bog stream. Rod and creel are flung aside, and the wanton breeze, with the breath of coolness it has gathered in its passage over the murky dykes of black bog water, is playing with the tail fly, tossing it to and fro with a half threat to fasten it to a prickly spine of golden gorse. Bunches of bog wool nod their fluffy heads, and through the myriad indefinite sounds comes the regular scrape of a strickle on the scythe of a reaper in a neighbouring meadow. Overhead a flotilla of clouds is steering from the south in a north-easterly direction. Her eyes follow them. Old time galleons, she thinks, with their wealth of snowy sail spread, riding breast to breast up a wide blue fjord after victory. The sails of the last are rose flushed, with a silver edge. Somehow she thinks of Cleopatra sailing down to meet Antony, and a great longing fills her soul to sail off somewhere too – away from the daily need of dinner-getting and the recurring Monday with its washing; life with its tame duties and virtuous monotony. She fancies herself in Arabia on the back of a swift steed. Flashing eyes set in dark faces surround her, and she can see the clouds of sand swirl, and feel the swing under her of his rushing stride. Her thoughts shape themselves into a wild song, a song to her steed of flowing mane and satin skin; an uncouth rhythmical jingle with a feverish beat; a song to the untamed spirit that dwells in her. Then she fancies she is on the stage of an ancient theatre out in the open air, with hundreds of faces upturned towards her. She is gauze-clad in a cobweb garment of wondrous tissue. Her arms are clasped by jewelled snakes, and one with quivering diamond fangs coils round her hips. Her hair floats loosely, and her feet are sandal-clad, and the delicate breath of vines and the salt freshness of an incoming sea seems to fill her nostrils. She bounds forward and dances, bends her lissom waist, and curves her slender arms, and gives to the soul of each man what he craves, be it good or evil. And she can feel now, lying here in the shade of Irish hills with her head resting on her scarlet shawl and her eyes closed, the grand intoxicating power of swaying all these human souls to wonder and applause. She can see herself with parted lips and panting, rounded breasts, and a dancing devil in each glowing eye, sway voluptuously to the wild music that rises, now slow, now fast, now deliriously wild, seductive, intoxicating, with a human note of passion in its strain. She can feel the answering shiver of feeling that quivers up to her from the dense audience, spellbound by the motion of her glancing feet, and she flies swifter and swifter, and lighter and lighter, till the very serpents seem alive with jewelled scintillations. One quivering, gleaming, daring bound, and she stands with outstretched arms and passion-filled eyes, poised on one slender foot, asking a supreme note to finish her dream of motion. And the men rise to a man and answer her, and cheer, cheer till the echoes shout from the surrounding hills and tumble wildly down the crags. The clouds have sailed away, leaving long feathery streaks in their wake. Her eyes have an inseeing look, and she is tremulous with excitement. She can hear yet that last grand shout, and the strain of that old-time music that she has never heard in this life of hers, save as an inner accompaniment to the memory of hidden things, born with her, not of this time.

And her thoughts go to other women she has known, women good and bad, school friends, casual acquaintances, women workers – joyless machines for grinding daily corn, unwilling maids grown old in the endeavour to get settled, patient wives who bear little ones to indifferent husbands until they wear out – a long array. She busies herself with questioning. Have they, too, this thirst for excitement, for change, this restless craving for sun and love and motion? Stray words, half confidences, glimpses through soul-chinks of suppressed fires, actual outbreaks, domestic catastrophes, how the ghosts dance in the cells of her memory! And she laughs, laughs softly to herself because the denseness of man, his chivalrous conservative devotion to the female idea he has created blinds him, perhaps happily, to the problems of her complex nature. Ay, she mutters musingly, the wisest of them can only say we are enigmas. Each one of them sets about solving the riddle of the *ewig weibliche* – and well it is that the workings of our hearts are closed to them, that we are cunning enough or *great* enough to seem to be what they would have us, rather than be what we are. But few of them have had the insight to find out the key to our seeming contradictions. The why a refined, physically fragile woman will mate with a brute, a mere male animal with primitive passions – and love him – the why strength and beauty appeal more often than the more subtly fine qualities of mind or heart – the why women (and not the innocent ones) will condone sins that men find hard to forgive in their fellows. They have all overlooked the eternal wildness, the untamed primitive savage temperament that lurks in the mildest, best woman. Deep in through ages of convention this primeval trait burns, an untameable quantity that may be concealed but is never eradicated by culture – the keynote of woman's witchcraft and woman's strength. But it is there, sure enough, and each woman is conscious of it in her truth-telling hours of quiet self-scrutiny – and each woman in God's wide world will deny it, and each woman will help another to conceal it – for the woman who tells the truth and is not a liar about these things is untrue to her sex and abhorrent to man, for he has fashioned a model on imaginary lines, and he has said, 'so I would have you', and every woman is an unconscious liar, for so man loves her. And when a Strindberg or a Nietzsche arises and peers into the recesses of her nature and dissects her ruthlessly, the men shriek out louder than the women, because the truth is at all times unpalatable, and the gods they have set up are dear to them . . .'

'Dreaming, or speering into futurity? You have the look of a seer. I believe you are half a witch!'

And he drops his grey-clad figure on the turf. He has dropped his drawl long ago, in midsummer.

'Is not every woman that? Let us hope I'm, for my friends, a white one.'

'A-ah! Have you many friends?'

'That is a query! If you mean many correspondents, many persons who send me Christmas cards, or remember my birthday, or figure in my address-book? No.'

'Well, grant I don't mean that!'

'Well, perhaps, yes. Scattered over the world, if my death were belled out, many women would give me a tear, and some a prayer. And many men would turn back a page in their memory and give me a kind thought, perhaps a regret, and go back to their work with a feeling of having lost something – that they never possessed. I am a creature of moments. Women have told me that I came into their lives just when they needed me. Men had no need to tell me, I felt it. People have needed me more than I them. I have given freely whatever they craved from me in the way of understanding or love. I have touched sore places they showed me and healed them, but they never got at me. I have been for myself, and helped myself, and borne the burden of my own mistakes. Some have chafed at my self-sufficiency and have called me fickle – not understanding that they gave me nothing, and that when I had served them, their moment was ended, and I was to pass on. I read people easily, I am written in black letter to most –'

'To your husband!'

'He (quickly) – we will not speak of him; it is not loyal.'

'Do not I understand you a little?'

'You do not misunderstand me.'

'That is something.'

'It is much!'

'Is it? (searching her face). It is not one grain of sand in the desert that stretches between you and me, and you are as impenetrable as a sphinx at the end of it. This (passionately) is my moment, and what have you given me?'

'Perhaps less than other men I have known; but you want

less. You are a little like me, you can stand alone. And yet (her voice is shaking), have I given you nothing?'

He laughs, and she winces – and they sit silent, and they both feel as if the earth between them is laid with infinitesimal electric threads vibrating with a common pain. Her eyes are filled with tears that burn but don't fall, and she can see his somehow through her closed lids, see their cool greyness troubled by sudden fire, and she rolls her handkerchief into a moist cambric ball between her cold palms.

'You have given me something – something to carry away with me – an infernal want. You ought to be satisfied. I am infernally miserable.'

'You (nearer) have the most tantalising mouth in the world when your lips tremble like that. I . . . What! can you cry? You?'

'Yes, even I can cry!'

'You dear woman! (pause) And I can't help you!'

'You can't help me. No man can. Don't think it is because you are you I cry, but because you probe a little nearer into the real me that I feel so.'

'Was it necessary to say that? (reproachfully). Do you think I don't know it? I can't for the life of me think how you, with that free gipsy nature of yours, could bind yourself to a monotonous country life, with no excitement, no change. I wish I could offer you my yacht. Do you like the sea?'

'I love it, it answers one's moods.'

'Well, let us play pretending, as the children say. Grant that I could, I would hang your cabin with your own colours; fill it with books, all those I have heard you say you care for; make it a nest as rare as the bird it would shelter. You would reign supreme; when your highness would deign to honour her servant I would come and humour your every whim. If you were glad, you could clap your hands and order music, and we would dance on the white deck, and we would skim through the sunshine of Southern seas on a spice-scented breeze. You make me poetical. And if you were angry you could vent your feelings on me, and I would give in and bow my head to your mood. And we would drop anchor and stroll through strange cities, go far inland and glean folklore out of the beaten track of everyday tourists. And at night when the harbour slept we would sail out through the moonlight over silver seas. You are smiling, you look so different when you smile; do you like my picture?'

'Some of it!'

'What not?'

'You!'

'Thank you.'

'You asked me. Can't you understand where the spell lies? It is the freedom, the freshness, the vague danger, the unknown that has a witchery for me, ay, for every woman!'

'Are you incapable of affection, then?'

'Of course not, I share' (bitterly) 'that crowning disability of my sex. But not willingly, I chafe under it. My God, if it were not for that, we women would master the world. I tell you men would be no match for us. At heart we care nothing for laws, nothing for systems. All your elaborately reasoned codes for controlling morals or man do not weigh a jot with us against an impulse, an instinct. We learn those things from you, you tamed, amenable animals; they are not natural to us. It is a wise disposition of providence that this untameableness of ours is corrected by our affections. We forge our own chains in a moment of softness, and then' (bitterly) 'we may as well wear them with a good grace. Perhaps many of our seeming contradictions are only the outward evidences of inward chafing. Bah! the qualities that go to make a Napoleon – superstition, want of honour, disregard of opinion and the eternal I – are oftener to be found in a woman than a man. Lucky for the world perhaps that all these attributes weigh as nothing in the balance with the need to love if she be a good woman, to be loved if she is of a coarser fibre.'

'I never met any one like you, you are a strange woman!'

'No, I am merely a truthful one. Women talk to me – why, I can't say – but always they come, strip their hearts and souls naked, and let me see the hidden folds of their natures. The greatest tragedies I have ever read are child's play to those I have seen acted in the inner life of outwardly commonplace women. A woman must beware of speaking the truth to a man; he loves her the less for it. It is the elusive spirit in her that he divines but cannot seize, that fascinates and keeps him.'

There is a long silence, the sun is waning and the scythes are silent, and overhead the crows are circling, a croaking irregular army, homeward bound from a long day's pillage.

She has made no sign, yet so subtly is the air charged with her that he feels but a few moments remain to him. He goes over and kneels beside her and fixes his eyes on her odd dark face. They both tremble, yet neither speaks. His breath is coming quickly, and the bistre stains about her eyes seem to have deepened, perhaps by contrast as she has paled.

'Look at me!'

She turns her head right round and gazes straight into his face. A few drops of sweat glisten on his forehead.

'You witch woman! what am I to do with myself? Is my moment ended?'

'I think so.'

'Lord, what a mouth!'

'Don't, oh don't!'

'No, I won't. But do you mean it? Am I, who understand your every mood, your restless spirit, to vanish out of your life? You can't mean it. Listen; are you listening to me? I can't see your face; take down your hands. Go back over every chance meeting you and I have had together since I met you first by the river, and judge them fairly. To-day is Monday; Wednesday afternoon I shall pass your gate, and if – if my moment is ended, and you mean to send me away, to let me go with this weary aching . . .'

'A-ah!' she stretches out one brown hand appealingly, but he does not touch it.

'Hang something white on the lilac bush!'

She gathers up creel and rod, and he takes her shawl, and, wrapping it round her, holds her a moment in it, and looks searchingly into her eyes, then stands back and raises his hat, and she glides away through the reedy grass.

Wednesday morning she lies watching the clouds sail by. A late rose spray nods into the open window, and the petals fall every time. A big bee buzzes in and fills the room with his bass note, and then dances out again. She can hear his footstep on the gravel. Presently he looks in over the half window.

'Get up and come out, 'twill do you good. Have a brisk walk!'

She shakes her head languidly, and he throws a great soft dewy rose with sure aim on her breast.

'Shall I go in and lift you out and put you, "nighty" and all, into your tub?'

'No (impatiently). I'll get up just now.'

The head disappears, and she rises wearily and gets through her dressing slowly, stopped every moment by a feeling of faintness. He finds her presently rocking slowly to and fro with closed eyes, and drops a leaf with three plums in it on to her lap.

'I have been watching four for the last week, but a bird, greedy beggar, got one this morning early – try them. Don't you mind, old girl, I'll pour out my own tea!'

She bites into one and tries to finish it, but cannot.

'You are a good old man!' she says, and the tears come

unbidden to her eyes, and trickle down her cheeks, dropping on to the plums, streaking their delicate bloom. He looks uneasily at her, but doesn't know what to do, and when he has finished his breakfast he stoops over her chair and strokes her hair, saying, as he leaves a kiss on the top of her head –

'Come out into the air, little woman; do you a world of good!' And presently she hears the sharp thrust of his spade above the bee's hum, leaf rustle, and the myriad late summer sounds that thrill through the air. It irritates her almost to screaming point. There is a practical non-sympathy about it, she can distinguish the regular one, two, three, the thrust, interval, then pat, pat, on the upturned sod. To-day she wants some one, and her thoughts wander to the grey-eyed man who never misunderstands her, and she wonders what he would say to her. Oh, she wants some one so badly to soothe her. And she yearns for the little mother who is twenty years under the daisies. The little mother who is a faint memory strengthened by a daguerreotype in which she sits with silk-mittened hands primly crossed on the lap of her moiré gown, a diamond brooch fastening the black velvet ribbon crossed so stiffly over her lace collar, the shining tender eyes looking steadily out, and her hair in the fashion of fifty-six. How that spade dominates over every sound! And what a sickening pain she has; an odd pain, she never felt it before. Supposing she were to die, she tries to fancy how she would look. They would be sure to plaster her curls down. He might be digging her grave – no, it is the patch where the early peas grew; the peas that were eaten with the twelve weeks' ducklings; she remembers them, little fluffy golden balls with waxen bills, and such dainty paddles. Remembers holding an egg to her ear and listening to it cheep inside before even there was a chip in the shell. Strange how things come to life. What! she sits bolt upright and holds tightly to the chair, and a questioning, awesome look comes over her face. Then the quick blood creeps up through her olive skin right up to her temples, and she buries her face in her hands and sits so a long time.

The maid comes in and watches her curiously, and moves softly about. The look in her eyes is the look of a faithful dog, and she loves her with the same rare fidelity. She hesitates, then goes into the bedroom and stands thoughtfully, with her hands clasped over her breast.

She is a tall, thin, flat-waisted woman, with misty blue eyes and a receding chin. Her hair is pretty.

She turns as her mistress comes in, with an expectant look on her face. She has taken up a nightgown, but holds it idly.

'Lizzie, had you ever a child?'

The girl's long left hand is ringless, yet she asks it with a quiet insistence as if she knew what the answer would be, and the odd eyes read her face with an almost cruel steadiness. The girl flushes painfully and then whitens, her very eyes seem to pale, and her under lip twitches as she jerks out huskily –

'Yes!'

'What happened it?'

'It died, Ma'm.'

'Poor thing! Poor old Liz!'

She pats the girl's hand softly, and the latter stands dumbly and looks down at both hands, as if fearful to break the wonder of a caress. She whispers hesitatingly –

'Have you, have you any little things left?'

And she laughs such a soft, cooing little laugh, like the churring of a ring-dove, and nods shyly back in reply to the tall maid's questioning look. The latter goes out, and comes back with a flat, red-painted deal box and unlocks it. It does not hold very much, and the tiny garments are not of costly material, but the two women pore over them as a gem collector over a rare stone. She has a glimpse of thick crested paper as the girl unties a packet of letters, and looks away until she says tenderly –

'Look, Ma'm!'

A little bit of hair inside a paper heart. It is almost white, so silky, and so fine, that it is more like a thread of bog wool than a baby's hair. And the mistress, who is a wife, puts her arms round the tall maid, who has never had more than a moral claim to the name, and kisses her in her quick way.

The afternoon is drawing on; she is kneeling before an open trunk with flushed cheeks and sparkling eyes. A heap of unused, dainty lace trimmed ribbon-decked cambric garments is scattered around her. She holds the soft scented web to her cheek and smiles musingly. Then she rouses herself and sets to work, sorting out the finest, with the narrowest lace and tiniest ribbon, and puckers her swarthy brows, and measures lengths along her middle finger. Then she gets slowly up, as if careful of herself as a precious thing, and half afraid.

'Lizzie!'

'Yes, Ma'm!'

'Wasn't it lucky they were too fine for every day? They will be so pretty. Look at this one with the tiny valenciennes edging. Why, one nightgown will make a dozen little shirts – such elfin-shirts as they are too – and Lizzie!'

'Yes, Ma'm!'

'Just hang it out on the lilac bush; mind, the lilac bush!'

'Yes, Ma'm.'

'Or Lizzie, wait – I'll do it myself!'

'BORGIA SMUDGITON'

SHE-NOTES

'My Soozie! My Toozie! My Soozie!'

IT is the voice of a man, and he sings. He has grey eyes, and wears a grey Norfolk-broad. They accentuate one another; the pine-trees also accentuate his fishing-rod. His hum blends with the bleating of the *Bufo rulgaris* and the cooing of *Coleoptera*.

Beside a fallen pine lies a woman (*genus*, in fact, *muliebre*). Where the tree fell there she lies. Her fresh animal instinct sniffs the music-hall refrain; the footlights of the Pavillon Rouge mix rather weirdly with a vision, just rudely interrupted, of terra-cottas from Tanagra. Not every woman thinks of these things in a wood.

The male is a student of the Eternal Femininity. Already, while still out of gunshot, he has noticed her wedding-ring and the diamond keeper. 'Talking of keepers,' he begins with the affected drawl now sufficiently familiar to the reader, 'are we trespassing here?' She replies in her frank unembarrassed way. 'Better ask a p'leeceman,' she says. (A lady, obviously! Worth cultivating? Bet your braces!)

'After trout, you know. Any local tips in flies?' A rare smile comes with her ready answer. '"Pick-me-ups" after a heavy night; "Henry Clays" after lunch; "spotted cocktails" for the evening. Like a "coachman" myself; sometimes find them quite killing!' 'Happy coachman!'

A chill comes over the sylvan scene with these reckless words. She has gathered her cream-coloured mittens about her wrists; the contrast at once strikes him; in the subdued evening light he can see that her hands are unwashed. She bows coolly, and is off across the stream like a water-snake.

She is lounging nervously on the edge of the parlour-grate. There are two (an acute observer would say three) furrows on her forehead. 'Off your pipe, old chappie? Feel a bit cheap?' (It is her husband who speaks in this way.) 'Yes, beastly, thanks, old man!' 'Try a nip o' whisky. No soda; soda for boys. There, that's right! Buck up! What's your book?' 'Oh! one of WILDE's little things. I like WILDE; he shocks the middle classes. Only the middle classes are so easily shocked!' He smiles a gentle, dull smile. There is a long pause; he cannot follow her swift eternally feminine fancy. 'What's it now, old buffer? A brass for your thoughts!' 'I was thinking, little woman, of a filly foal I once had. She grew up to be a mare. I never would have let anyone on God's beautiful earth ride her.' 'I'd have ridden her!' 'No, you wouldn't!' 'Yes, I would!' (passionately and concentratedly). 'Well, I sold her anyway. Lucky the beast isn't here now to spoil our conjugal unity!' The crisis had past. Another moment and she might have left him for ever lonely and forlorn! But in a twinkling her wild, free instinct doubles at a tangent. With a supple bound she is on his shoulders curling her lithe fishing boots into one of his waistcoat pockets. Surely gipsy blood runs in her veins!

'Oh! I wish I were a devil' (it is the lady speaking); 'yes, a d-e-v-i-l!' 'But you *are*, old woman, you *are!* and such a dear little devil!' 'Say it again, old man!' (kissing him fiercely in the left eye and worrying his ear like a ferret), 'I love to hear you call me that. We women yearn for praise!' 'You're a rare brick, old dear; and you're never jealous. Look at that photo of the other girl! Some women would have cut up rough about it. But *you* – why, you sent her a quid when she was peckish, and she chewed it for a week! Was there ever such a little chip?'

PART II

She is lying on her back in a bog-stream. Strangely enough there are white clouds waltzing along the sky. To her fancy, which is nothing if not picturesque, they are a troop of fairy geese on their way to Michaelmas. No? well then, plainly they are ANTONY and CLEOPATRA. And oh! the dalliance, the wild free life of Egypt! No dinners to order; very little washing on Mondays.

Presto! In imagination she is on a stage. She is a *Tableau Vivant!* All the fauteuils have their glasses up. She has pink overalls, with a cestus round her neck. Her lissom limbs scintillate; she dances slightly. KILANYI says she must try and keep still. A moment more and there is a lovely cat-call from the gallery; she can still hear it above the orchestra, as the next tableau is being wheeled on. It *was* a supreme keynote!

And the other women? Crushed, joyless, machines – misunderstood! How can the dense brute male read the enigma of the Female Idea? They think us innocent! not we! but we all keep up the deception and lie courageously. They will never know that we are really primitive, untameable, ineradicable animalculae.

'Got the blue devils, little witch?' (It is the grey man. He has dropped his drawl and his flybook. They have been getting on nicely, thank you, since we saw them last.)

'Yes, we are all witches, we women. We can read men

but they can't read us.' 'Can't *I* read you?' 'Me, the real ineffable *me?* Yes, perhaps just a little. You have a dash of the Everlasting Female in you.' As she speaks she rolls up her shawl into an infinitesimal pellet.

'Well, look here' (desperately). 'What do you say to a trip in my yacht? Southern seas! Venice! Constantinople! Olympia! And then, when the winds are hushed and the steam is shut off for the night, we would fly with no visible means of locomotion over the silvery deep! You smile? Where is the pain?' 'Oh! if I could only have the yacht without you in it!' (He winces.) 'Yes, I say, give us women freedom and we would all go one better than NAPOLEON. NELSON knew nothing of the eternal I! Bah! and he was blind in the other.' 'You strange creature!' 'No, not strange; only true. Were I more elusive I might be more fascinating.'

A long silence broken only by the chirp of a grasshopper. The air is charged like a battery. It seems that a submarine cable connects these two souls. Nevertheless, she distinctly observes that the grasshopper has strained his Achilles-tendon. Curious that at such a climax the minutest detail should not escape her. Am I right in thinking that no novelist has as yet detected this remarkable phenomenon? He comes nearer (I mean the grey man). His skin beneath his collar blushes a rich cobalt. 'Is my little moment up?' he gasps. (His stop-watch is in his trembling hand.) 'Lord! what a cheek you have!' 'Don't, oh, don't say that!' 'Very well, I withdraw it.' 'But listen!' (she is dropping asleep); 'listen, I say!' (she will be snoring directly); 'if my moment is really ended – and my stop-watch points to the fact – and if you mean to send me away, *hang something white on the gooseberry-bush* (our *gooseberry-bush) to-morrow about the ninth hour*!' She rises and is gone like a water-snake.

It is to-morrow about the eighth hour. She is still in bed.

There is a nod at the window. It is all right; only a blushing sweet-william. On the mantel-piece is a daguerreotype of her late aunt, in a velvet bodice and other things. But it is not *that* which drives her crazy. It is her husband's cheery pick-axe in the garden. Is he really digging her grave? Why, surely, no; he is simply arranging the onion-bed. Yet what an interesting corpse she would make! The pity is that one can never see one's own corpse in the glass. Stay, is that BETSY? 'Oh! BETSY' (the young cook enters demurely for orders), 'I wonder had you ever a lover?' 'Well, Ma'm, what do *you* think?'

Say, what happened him, anyway?' 'Why, he left me, Ma'm, left me for Another; and' (regretfully) 'we might have married, and had such *heavenly* twins; and, oh! he *had* such a beautiful crest on his writing-paper!'

A moment's tension follows; the next sees the lady feeling for a coin in her dress-pocket. She spins it deftly. 'Heads, he stays: tails, he goes! Tails! by all that is virtuous.'

'BETSY!' (Her voice is firm, like a quickset hedge.) 'BETSY! I cannot spare my "nighty" just now, but your white apron will do as well. You *do* love me, don't you?' (Kisses her.) 'Then for *my* sake go and hang yourself for a little while on the gooseberry-bush. Mind! the *gooseberry*-bush!' 'Yes, Ma'm.'

A rare fidelity! And so few men could have understood or even spelt the why in BETSY!

Two hours later she wakes up and remembers the faithful girl! Perhaps it is even now too late! She hurries through her toilet. The daguerreotype shows no sign. Threads of bog wool float persistently in the summer air. She is by the gooseberry-bush with a stout pair of scissors. Too late! The girl is gone! Another hand, a hand that held a stop-watch, has cut her down, and BETSY is by this time a free and unfettered woman, on her way to a yacht.

The grey man, after all, had his consolation.

GEORGE FLEMING

BY ACCIDENT

'Nous sommes tous dans un désert. Personne ne comprend personne.' *

IT was one of those rough, common street accidents which smash through every decorum of a delicate life. As the carriage, a slight, daintily built victoria, a mere plaything of a carriage – as her carriage came swinging around the corner of Duke Street into Oxford Street, something frightened the horses, who swerved, first half way up across the sidewalk, and then backed, plunging furiously, into an omnibus and a brewer's dray. One of the grooms was driving her that morning – her own coachman was down in the country having his summer holiday – and this lad, who was a sober, steady young fellow too, went nervous all over at the first *rip, rip, ri-ip* of the breaking panels, and lost his head.

'I see'd Beauty there – 'er as 'as cut 'er knee so bad – give a plunge; an' I sez, 'old hup! Old *hup*, you devil, for Gawd's sake, I sez; an' s'elp me, the next thing was all the bones of my body bein' drawn out o' me like teeth. An' then *you* was a-wipin' of my face, constable. An' – an' – that's 'ow it

* The epigraph is from Flaubert's letters: 'We are all of us in a waste place. No one person understands another.'

'appened. S'elp me Gawd, it did,' the young groom went on repeating hysterically.

The blood from his cut head soaked through his thick sandy hair and ran down his cheek from under the extemporised bandages. His shaking hands were all smeared with it, and the glass, which some quick-witted sympathiser in the crowd had run to fetch from the nearest public.

'*You* was a-wipin' o' my face. An' my lady is killed; or worse. An' Beauty, there. Oh, *here's* a nice show! An' –'

'Drink,' said the big policeman encouragingly, and held the reddened glass to the other man's twitching lips, while the crowd looked on with interest and approved. Then a dozen men piled up the broken wheels together, and made a heap of the cushions and the shiny varnished panels of the wreck, while some one else led away the cowed and limping horses; they went meekly enough now, with heads drooped and eyes full of terror. And the latest arrived omnibus drove off, the people on the roof all standing up to stare back at the nasty splash by the curbstone that a man from the nearest shop was already washing away with floods of soapy water dashed down out of a pail.

'And Mother av God, but it's meself that saw her, the crathur. Mercy be upon us, woman dear, but 'tis I saw her. One minute sittin' up there, in her own illigant carriage, like a little white bird on a goulden throne, and with a smile on the pretty face of her to show she was thinkin' of just nothin' at all. And the nex' minute – the nex' –. Mother av God, ah! merciful Mother av God, but it was just one wisp o' black disthruction,' the little old apple-woman at the corner repeated, beginning on the same story for the fiftieth time, since already the original crowd of eye-witnesses was all dispersed, swept off by every kind of occupation and errand, along the hurrying indifferent street. The affair had made a stoppage of four minutes in the traffic.

All this took place some time between ten and eleven in the morning, but it was nearer eight o'clock before her husband saw her. He had been out shooting when the telegram arrived at the country house where he was expecting her to join him. Time had been wasted; he had missed the quick up-train.

'Yes, yes, quite so. I feel for you, my dear Sir Edward. Believe me, I *feel* for you. But she is conscious still. She has seen her children, poor lady – poor lady. She is entirely conscious, yes. But naturally she experiences a certain difficulty in speaking,' the doctor said, meeting him in the passage, at the door of her room.

All the rest of the house was dismantled, swathed in foldings of paper and brown holland, with severest reference to a finished season; but in Her room everything was precisely the same as he had always known it. There was the same impression of a great deal of space and a great deal of pretty extravagance; the old smell of flowers, the look – Her look – of exquisite order, of luxury, of a great deal of money spent. She was lying in bed, very pale, all rolled in spotless white bandages, but she lifted one hand a little as he came and stood close beside her. Her face was not in the least disfigured – that was the first thing he noticed. Then he laid his own hand on hers, and she smiled, quite naturally and cheerfully. He bent over the bed to kiss her.

'Well. I'm – finished, you see,' she said, speaking very weakly, but otherwise exactly in her own every-day indifferent little voice.

For the last six hours he had been sitting in trains, in carriages – hurrying, hurrying on – with the familiar world he knew falling to pieces all about him. But nothing had changed her. Nothing ever did affect her. His narrow, furrowed brow twitched with an old, old feeling of baffled disapproval as he stood looking down at her bed. She had always been inclined to underestimate the importance of things which seemed to him intensely serious. She had done it for years, ever since their marriage, in spite of all his attempts to impress her. And now she was lying there – like that, and smiling – like that – on her death-bed. If it had been any one but herself he felt it would have been proper to allude to it as a Death-Bed. But with her – !

'I was – I am deeply, inexpressibly shocked and grieved,' he began, in his solemn, measured way. Then he bent over and kissed the little white face on the pillow a second time. 'I was out when the telegram came. I – I came to you as soon as I could, dear,' he said, huskily. And under his close-cropped grey moustache the muscles of his mouth twisted all to one side.

'Yes,' she answered, calmly.

As the doctor said, she was perfectly conscious; but it seemed to take a certain time before words conveyed to her their common meaning, for it was two or three minutes before she added:

'Yes; telegrams always are – a bother – at Cecilia's. It's the worst of living – so far in the country. I've told her so – often,' said the weak little voice.

She was his wife, and that was the way they had been in the habit of talking to one another, day after day, for years. They had lived together, always on excellent terms; gone out to dinner together; accepted the same invitations together; known very nearly the same people, and shared one another's daily habits, until they were familiar with each other's idiosyncrasies down to the smallest particular. Only, somehow, they had never seemed nearer together than this.

'You – you have seen the children, dear, Davis tells me,' he murmured suggestively; and he pulled up a chair, and sat down by her bedside, still without letting go of the small, apathetic hand.

'The children?' she repeated softly. 'Oh, yes. The baby and little Ju. I sent them out again – with nurse. Ju has on a new frock; she made me look – look at all the ribbons. Little monkey! She – she looked – so pretty,' said the mother with her weak, amused smile.

'Gone out again? Dear, dear!' Sir Edward tapped his knee with the fingers of his other hand with an expression of grave displeasure. 'I am astonished, I confess I am astonished, at nurse. When you are – When she knows you are – When she must have understood! I regret I was not here in time to prevent this. The children's place is – with their mother,' he said; and his wife's blue eyes turned and rested upon his face with a faint, half-mocking curiosity.

'Poor little Ju! She is – very little. Only three. I don't think – she would have understood much – about it – if you shut her up all the afternoon in the nursery,' she said softly. 'And if very little children – *can't* really mind things – why – why make them pretend? Besides – you couldn't make them – even if you try to, Edward.'

That was precisely the sort of speech which always annoyed him coming from her; always. It cost him an effort of remembrance, even now, not to slacken his hold of her irresponsive fingers. But he mastered his rising sense of irritation. It was impossible to admit that one could feel irritated by a fellow-creature, dying.

'Is there any one? – It is most painful that all our friends should be out of town: but, naturally, at this time of year – But is there any person, anywhere, I could send for – wire to?' He cleared his throat, which had suddenly grown husky. 'My dear child, is there any one in the world you would like to see?'

The doctor and the white-capped hospital nurse had come back into the room while he was still speaking. The doctor looked quickly across at the bed, and then came closer and felt with professional interest for the soft, slackening beat of her pulse.

'My dear lady, if there were any one, as Sir Edward suggests, it would be a satisfaction to you to send for?' he murmured sympathetically; and she gazed back at him with the fixed disquieting eyes of the dying. People had always admired her blue eyes; there were ugly rings under them now. They travelled slowly, curiously, from one sober, middle-aged face to the other.

'You look – you both look – as if you would go on living for ever. And you will go to such – hundreds of dinner-parties,' she said suddenly. Then she laughed. It was weak, hysterical laughter, but it shocked and affected and humiliated Sir Edward where he felt most keenly and in a manner quite indescribable. The doctor called it feverishness. It was to be expected. No doubt it was a trifle increased by the excitement of an interview with one so near and dear to her.

'Nurse knows exactly what to do in my absence if – if there should be any change,' he said, with a little bow to Sir Edward.

So they left him to sit with her in the pale long twilight of the hot London night. The little silver carriage clock ticked on the small table by the open window, and she lay very quietly, with those wide-open eyes staring, staring at the big, shadowy sheet of looking-glass which covered nearly one side of the wall. She had stood before that same mirror so often – hundreds and hundreds of times – to look at herself, at all hours of the day and night, and in every kind and variety of dress! Now, all she could see in it from her bed was a pale, gleaming reflection of the empty evening sky.

'It is – as if I were gone – already. Quite gone. It looks – as if there were no more Me – in the world; no more – anywhere,' she said out loud, as the thought struck her. But her husband punctiliously refrained from answering; the doctor said she was to be kept quiet. And presently – quite soon – she forgot to think about him again.

Now she was trying to recall, in every detail, the exact appearance of the person who interested her the most in all the world; very differently and very much more than any other man, woman, or child in all the hundreds of people of her acquaintance. It was months – months and months – nearly a year now, since she had first recognised this fact; but whether he was aware of it or not – ah! that was a different question. Sometimes, especially of late, she had fancied he did know, and was giving her to understand that he knew; but really, she had not troubled much about it. For herself, to go on meeting him constantly, almost daily, as she had been in the habit of doing; to talk to him, in peace, about whatever came into her head; to see him; to be for hours in the same room with him, was absolutely all she wanted. There was no capacity for strong passion in this woman; from first to last, there was no more chance of her 'going wrong', as she would have called it, than for little Ju. Only, this man satisfied her. 'Yes; he is my type,' she said once, speaking of him. And it was true. Possibly he appealed in her to some dumb, latent instincts of domesticity which no one else had ever come near awakening. In spite of her marriage, her children, all the social routine of her life, it is probable that she had never come so near to a feeling of home – and what a home means – as in her easy, joyous intercourse with this man, between whom and herself there could be no possible relationship.

But there was no touch of tragedy in her nature, nothing introspective, no rebellion before the Rules. Even at the present crisis she was clearly, humorously aware of all the difficulties, social and material, which prevented her from sending for him, as the one 'any one' her husband and the doctor spoke of so glibly. Think of the surprise, the scandal!

Her husband would do it for her certainly. Because she was dying, you know; and one doesn't – Edward wouldn't – refuse the request of a dying person. Only think – think of his face!

And then there was another thing. *He* was such a long, long way off; shooting, at a place she knew also, far up in the Highlands. Lying there, quite still, in her white bed, with all those horrible bandages about her, she could *see* the very look of the moorside where he must be walking now. She could see the hilly miles of bright heather, she felt the wind and the sun in her face. Her breath came quick, as breath quickens tramping up the clean, rough purple slopes. And hark! the guns. That was *his* gun now; and that smile on his face was because he was enjoying himself – always enjoying himself. He was so prosperous, and young, and well, and strong. He had such years and years of life before him – such a long time in which to be alive in the sun and air, and feel things, and care for them, and know, and touch, and see – while she –

'Can I do anything for you, dear? Is the pain worse? Shall I send again for the doctor?' broke in Sir Edward's anxious, melancholy voice.

But she only made a petulant little movement of refusal with her free hand on the silken counterpane. *That* was not what she wanted; and those familiar measured tones had broken up all that beautiful purple world, where the heather grew and the people were happy. Now, she saw the empty, shining mirror again, shining darkly, like water in deep shadow, with nothing reflected in it: nothing of herself or her life; never – never any more. She moved her head a very little on the pillow. She could see her husband's face, looking grey and careworn in the half-light. His eyes were red at the rims. With one hand he was stroking down the bedclothes mechanically. She looked into his eyes, deep into them; not with any mockery now, not with indifference; only with the desperate instinctive animal craving for companionship; with the revolt of warm living flesh against extinction; the pitiful, horrible shrinking from the Outside and the Dark. She saw the two clear, living eyes, so close to her own, and she could not, she never could, penetrate one single inch beyond. What did she know of him? What did he know of her thought, this man, this husband, who was holding her by the hand? What help could he give her, even if she asked for it? Now, as he watched her and drew long breaths of sorrow, and sat with his sleek, grey head dejected, bowed upon his other hand, what was there in common between his sensations of the universe and hers? To-morrow would come for him. To-morrow he would still be moving about, alive and moving, warm and alive, in a world of living people; while she – Since that first sickening moment, when the carriage began to slowly swing over, that was what she felt most – the loneliness of it all. The loneliness of life, of death; the loneliness of every separate, isolated, incommunicable human experience.

'It is a pity – a pity to leave all the pleasant – all the pleasure. But I wish,' she muttered faintly, 'I wish you would telegraph to – to – to –'

Sir Edward started to his feet.

'Yes, dear, yes; to whom?' he said eagerly. And he dropped her hand without knowing it in the relief of some possible action. The nurse came forward too, noiselessly, out of her silent corner.

'To whom?' the weak voice repeated slowly. 'Oh, yes. But no scandal, Edward. Oh, no; no scandal. For *personne ne comprend personne*. I read that in a book once. In a book. – Yes. – You can look at the eyes, you know, but never behind them; oh, never behind. And each one is living inside there; shut away, all alone – alone! I'm tired of being alone now. And I want to live, you know,' she broke out with sudden sharp fretfulness. 'And – oh, dear me, I wish some one *would* tell me – if Jim – Jim Trafford – you know, Edward – has been out – out on the hills – shooting all to-day. And –'

'She has begun to wander in her mind now, poor lady. It's what had to be expected, sir,' said the nurse.

'What had to be – expected. But *I* wouldn't shoot if *you* were dying,' repeated the choked, wavering voice.

Then she died.

OLIVE SCHREINER

THE BUDDHIST PRIEST'S WIFE

COVER her up! How still it lies! You can see the outline under the white. You would think she was asleep. Let the sunshine come in; it loved it so. She that had travelled so far, in so many lands, and done so much and seen so much, how she must like rest now! Did she ever love anything absolutely, this woman whom so many men loved, and so many women; who gave so much sympathy and never asked for anything in return! did she ever need a love she could not have? Was she never obliged to unclasp her fingers from anything to which they clung? Was she really so strong as she looked? Did she never wake up in the night crying for that which she could not have? Were thought and travel enough for her? Did she go about for long days with a weight that crushed her to earth? Cover her up! I do not think she would have liked us to look at her. In one way she was alone all her life; she would have liked to be alone now! . . . Life must have been very beautiful to her, or she would not look so young now. Cover her up! Let us go!

Many years ago in a London room, up long flights of stairs, a fire burnt up in a grate. It showed the marks on the walls where pictures had been taken down, and the little blue flowers in the wallpaper and the blue felt carpet on the floor, and a woman sat by the fire in a chair at one side.

Presently the door opened, and the old woman came in who took care of the entrance hall downstairs.

'Do you not want anything to-night?' she said.

'No, I am only waiting for a visitor; when they have been, I shall go.'

'Have you got all your things taken away already?'

'Yes, only these I am leaving.'

The old woman went down again, but presently came up with a cup of tea in her hand.

'You must drink that; it's good for one. Nothing helps one like tea when one's been packing all day.'

The young woman at the fire did not thank her, but she ran her hand over the old woman's from the wrist to the fingers.

'I'll say good-bye to you when I go out.'

The woman poked the fire, put the last coals on, and went.

When she had gone the young one did not drink the tea, but drew her little silver cigarette case from her pocket and lighted a cigarette. For a while she sat smoking by the fire; then she stood up and walked the room.

When she had paced for a while she sat down again beside the fire. She threw the end of her cigarette away into the fire, and then began to walk again with her hands behind her. Then she went back to her seat and lit another cigarette, and paced again. Presently she sat down, and looked into the fire; she pressed the palms of her hands together, and then sat quietly staring into it.

Then there was a sound of feet on the stairs and someone knocked at the door.

She rose and threw the end into the fire and said without moving, 'Come in.'

The door opened and a man stood there in evening dress. He had a great-coat on, open in front.

'May I come in? I couldn't get rid of this downstairs; I didn't see where to leave it!' He took his coat off. 'How are you? This is a real bird's nest!'

She motioned to a chair.

'I hope you did not mind my asking you to come?'

'Oh no, I am delighted. I only found your note at my club twenty minutes ago.'

'So you really are going to India? How delightful! But what are you to do there? I think it was Grey told me six weeks ago you were going, but regarded it as one of those mythical stories which don't deserve credence. Yet I am sure I don't know! Why, nothing would surprise me.'

He looked at her in a half-amused, half-interested way.

'What a long time it is since we met! Six months, eight?'

'Seven,' she said.

'I really thought you were trying to avoid me. What have you been doing with yourself all this time?'

'Oh, been busy. Won't you have a cigarette?'

She held out the little case to him.

'Won't you take one yourself? I know you object to smoking with men, but you can make an exception in my case!'

'Thank you.' She lit her own and passed him the matches.

'But really what have you been doing with yourself all this time? You've entirely disappeared from civilised life. When I was down at the Grahams' in the spring, they said you were coming down there, and then at the last moment cried off. We were all quite disappointed. What is taking you to India now? Going to preach the doctrine of social and intellectual equality to the Hindu women and incite them to revolt? Marry some old Buddhist Priest, build a little cottage on the top of the Himalayas and live there, discuss philosophy and meditate? I believe that's what you'd like. I really shouldn't wonder if I heard you'd done it!'

She laughed and took out her cigarette case.

She smoked slowly.

'I've been here a long time, four years, and I want change. I was glad to see how well you succeeded in that election,' she said. 'You were much interested in it, were you not?'

'Oh, yes. We had a stiff fight. It tells in my favour, you know, though it was not exactly a personal matter. But it was a great worry.'

'Don't you think,' she said, 'you were wrong in sending that letter to the papers? It would have strengthened your position to have remained silent.'

'Yes, perhaps so; I think so now, but I did it under advice. However, we've won, so it's all right.' He leaned back in the chair.

'Are you pretty fit?'

'Oh, yes; pretty well; bored, you know. One doesn't know what all this working and striving is for sometimes.'

'Where are you going for your holiday this year?'

'Oh, Scotland, I suppose; I always do; the old quarters.'

'Why don't you go to Norway? It would be more change for you and rest you more. Did you get a book on sport in Norway?'

'Did you send it me? How kind of you! I read it with much interest. I was almost inclined to start off there and then. I suppose it is the kind of *vis inertiae* that creeps over one as one grows older that sends one back to the old place. A change would be much better.'

'There's a list at the end of the book,' she said, 'of exactly the things one needs to take. I thought it would save trouble; you could just give it to your man, and let him get them all. Have you still got him?'

'Oh, yes. He's as faithful to me as a dog. I think nothing would induce him to leave me. He won't allow me to go out hunting since I sprained my foot last autumn. I have to do it surreptitiously. He thinks I can't keep my seat with a sprained ankle; but he's a very good fellow; takes care of me like a mother.' He smoked quietly with the firelight glowing on his black coat. 'But what are you going to India for? Do you know anyone there?'

'No,' she said. 'I think it will be so splendid. I've always been a great deal interested in the East. It's a complex, interesting life.'

He turned and looked at her.

'Going to seek for more experience, you'll say, I suppose. I never knew a woman throw herself away as you do; a woman with your brilliant parts and attractions, to let the whole of life slip through your hands, and make nothing of it. You ought to be the most successful woman in London. Oh, yes; I know what you are going to say: "You don't care." That's just it; you don't. You are always going to get experience, going to get everything, and you never do. You are always going to write when you know enough, and you are never satisfied that you do. You ought to be making your two thousand a year, but you don't care. That's just it! Living, burying yourself here with a lot of old frumps. You will never do anything. You could have everything and you let it slip.'

'Oh, my life is very full,' she said. 'There are only two things that are absolute realities, love and knowledge, and you can't escape them.'

She had thrown her cigarette end away and was looking into the fire, smiling.

'I've let these rooms to a woman friend of mine.' She glanced round the room, smiling. 'She doesn't know I'm going to leave these things here for her. She'll like them because they were mine. The world's very beautiful, I think – delicious.'

'Oh, yes. But what do you do with it? What do you make of it? You ought to settle down and marry like other women, not go wandering about the world to India and China and

Italy, and God knows where. You are simply making a mess of your life. You're always surrounding yourself with all sorts of extraordinary people. If I hear any man or woman is a great friend of yours, I always say: 'What's the matter? Lost his money? Lost his character? Got an incurable disease?' I believe the only way in which anyone becomes interesting to you is by having some complaint of mind or body. I believe you worship rags. To come and shut yourself up in a place like this away from everybody and everything! It's a mistake; it's idiotic, you know.'

'I'm very happy,' she said. 'You see,' she said, leaning forwards towards the fire with hands on her knees, 'what matters is that something should need you. It isn't a question of love. What's the use of being near a thing if other people could serve it as well as you can. If they could serve it better, it's pure selfishness. It's the need of one thing for another that makes the organic bond of union. You love mountains and horses, but they don't need you; so what's the use of saying anything about it! I suppose the most absolutely delicious thing in life is to feel a thing needs you, and to give at the moment it needs. Things that don't need you, you must love from a distance.'

'Oh, but a woman like you ought to marry, ought to have children. You go squandering yourself on every old beggar or forlorn female or escaped criminal you meet; it may be very nice for them, but it's a mistake from your point of view.'

He touched the ash gently with the tip of his little finger and let it fall.

'I intend to marry. It's a curious thing,' he said, resuming his pose with an elbow on one knee and his head bent forward on one side, so that she saw the brown hair with its close curls a little tinged with grey at the sides, 'that when a man reaches a certain age he wants to marry. He doesn't fall in love; it's not that he definitely plans anything; but he has a feeling that he ought to have a home and a wife and children. I suppose it is the same kind of feeling that makes a bird build nests at certain times of the year. It's not love; it's something else. When I was a young man I used to despise men for getting married; wondered what they did it for; they had everything to lose and nothing to gain. But when a man gets to be six-and-thirty his feeling changes. It's not love, passion, he wants; it's a home; it's a wife and children. He may have a house and servants; it isn't the same thing. I should have thought a woman would have felt it too.'

She was quiet for a minute, holding a cigarette between her fingers; then she said slowly:

'Yes, at times a woman has a curious longing to have a child, especially when she gets near to thirty or over it. It's something distinct from love for any definite person. But it's a thing one has to get over. For a woman, marriage is much more serious than for a man. She might pass her life without meeting a man whom she could possibly love, and, if she met him, it might not be right or possible. Marriage has become very complex now it has become so largely intellectual. Won't you have another?'

She held out the case to him. 'You can light it from mine.' She bent forward for him to light it.

'You are a man who ought to marry. You've no absorbing mental work with which the woman would interfere; it would complete you.' She sat back, smoking serenely.

'Yes,' he said, 'but life is too busy; I never find time to look for one, and I haven't a fancy for the pink-and-white prettiness so common and that some men like so. I need something else. If I am to have a wife I shall have to go to America to look for one.'

'Yes, an American would suit you best.'

'Yes,' he said, 'I don't want a woman to look after; she must be self-sustaining and she mustn't bore you. You know what I mean. Life is too full of cares to have a helpless child added to them.'

'Yes,' she said, standing up and leaning with her elbow against the fireplace. 'The kind of woman you want would be young and strong; she need not be excessively beautiful, but she must be attractive; she must have energy, but not too strongly marked an individuality; she must be largely neutral; she need not give you too passionate or too deep a devotion, but she must second you in a thoroughly rational manner. She must have the same aims and tastes that you have. No woman has the right to marry a man if she has to bend herself out of shape for him. She might wish to, but she could never be to him with all her passionate endeavour what the other woman could be to him without trying. Character will dominate over all and will come out at last.'

She looked down into the fire.

'When you marry you mustn't marry a woman who flatters you too much. It is always a sign of falseness somewhere. If a woman absolutely loves you as herself, she will criticise and understand you as herself. Two people who are to live through life together must be able to look into each other's eyes and speak the truth. That helps one through life. You would find many such women in America,' she said: 'women who would help you to succeed, who would not drag you down.'

'Yes, that's my idea. But how am I to obtain the ideal woman?'

'Go and look for her. Go to America instead of Scotland this year. It is perfectly right. A man has a right to look for what he needs. With a woman it is different. That's one of the radical differences between men and women.'

She looked downwards into the fire.

'It's a law of her nature and of sex relationship. There's nothing arbitrary or conventional about it any more than there is in her having to bear her child while the male does not. Intellectually we may both be alike. I suppose if fifty men and fifty women had to solve a mathematical problem, they would all do it in the same way; the more abstract and intellectual, the more alike we are. The nearer you approach to the personal and sexual, the more different we are. If I were to represent men's and women's natures,' she said, 'by a diagram, I would take two circular discs; the right side of each I should paint bright red; then I would shade the red away till in a spot on the left edge it became blue in the one and green in the other. That spot represents sex, and the nearer you come to it, the more the two discs differ in colour. Well then, if you turn them so that the red sides touch, they seem to be exactly alike, but if you turn them so that the green and blue paint form their point of contact, they will seem to be entirely unlike. That's why you notice the brutal, sensual men invariably believe women are entirely different from men, another species of creature; and very cultured, intellectual men sometimes believe we are exactly alike. You see, sex love in its substance may be the same in both of us; in the form of its expression it must differ. It is not man's fault; it is nature's. If a man loves a woman, he has a right to try to make her love him because he can do it openly, directly, without bending. There need be no subtlety, no indirectness. With a woman it's not so; she can take no love that is not laid openly, simply, at her feet. Nature ordains that she should never show what she feels; the woman who had told a man she loved him would have put between them a barrier once and for ever that could not be crossed; and if she subtly drew him towards her, using the woman's means – silence, finesse, the dropped handkerchief, the surprise visit, the gentle assertion she had not thought to see him when she had come a long way to meet him, then she would be damned; she would hold the love, but she would have desecrated it by subtlety; it would have no value. Therefore she must always go with her arms folded sexually; only the love which lays itself down at her feet and implores of her to accept it is love she can ever rightly take up. That is the true difference between a man and a woman. You may seek for love because you can do it openly; we cannot because we must do it subtly. A woman should always walk with her arms folded. Of course friendship is different. You are on a perfect equality with man then; you can ask him to come and see you as I asked you. That's the beauty of the intellect and intellectual life to a woman, that she drops her shackles a little; and that is why she shrinks from sex so. If she were dying perhaps, or doing something equal to death, she might . . . Death means so much more to a woman than a man; when you knew you were dying, to look round on the world and feel the bond of sex that has broken and crushed you all your life gone, nothing but the human left, no woman any more, to meet everything on perfectly even ground. There's no reason why you shouldn't go to America and look for a wife perfectly deliberately. You will have to tell no lies. Look till you find a woman that you absolutely love, that you have not the smallest doubt suits you apart from love, and then ask her to marry you. You must have children; the life of an old childless man is very sad.'

'Yes, I should like to have children. I often feel now, what is it all for, this work, this striving, and no one to leave it to? It's a blank, suppose I succeed . . . ?'

'Suppose you get your title?'

'Yes; what is it all worth to me if I've no one to leave it to? That's my feeling. It's really very strange to be sitting and talking like this to you. But you are so different from other women. If all women were like you, all your theories of the equality of men and women would work. You're the only woman with whom I never realise that she is a woman.'

'Yes,' she said.

She stood looking down into the fire.

'How long will you stay in India?'

'Oh, I'm not coming back.'

'Not coming back! That's impossible. You will be breaking the hearts of half the people here if you don't. I never knew a woman who had such power of entrapping men's hearts as you have in spite of that philosophy of yours. I don't know,' he smiled, 'that I should not have fallen into the snare myself – three years ago I almost thought I should – if you hadn't always attacked me so incontinently and persistently on all and every point and on each and every occasion. A man doesn't like pain. A succession of slaps damps him. But it doesn't seem to have that effect on other men . . . There was that fellow down in the country when I was there last year, perfectly ridiculous. You know his name . . .' He moved his fingers to try and remember it – 'big, yellow moustache, a major, gone to the east coast of Africa now; the ladies unearthed it that he was always carrying about a photograph of yours in his pocket; and he used to take out little scraps of things you printed and show them to people mysteriously. He almost had a duel with a man one night after dinner because he mentioned you; he seemed to think there was something incongruous between your name and –'

'I do not like to talk of any man who has loved me,' she said. 'However small and poor his nature may be, he has given me his best. There is nothing ridiculous in love. I think a woman should feel that all the love men have given her which she has not been able to return is a kind of crown set up above her which she is always trying to grow tall enough to wear. I can't bear to think that all the love that has been given me has been wasted on something unworthy of it. Men have been very beautiful and greatly honoured me. I am grateful to them. If a man tells you he loves you,' she said, looking into the fire, 'with his breast uncovered before you for you to strike him if you will, the least you can do is to put out your hand and cover it up from other people's eyes. If I were a deer,' she said, 'and a stag got hurt following me, even though I could not have him for a companion, I would stand still and scrape the sand with my foot over the place where his blood had fallen; the rest of the herd should never know he had been hurt there following me. I would cover the blood up, if I were a deer,' she said, and then she was silent.

Presently she sat down in her chair and said, with her hand before her: 'Yet, you know, I have not the ordinary feeling about love. I think the one who is loved confers the benefit on the one who loves, it's been so great and beautiful that it should be loved. I think the man should be grateful to the woman or the woman to the man whom they have been able to love, whether they have been loved back or whether circumstances have divided them or not.' She stroked her knee softly with her hand.

'Well, really, I must go now.' He pulled out his watch. 'It's so fascinating sitting here talking that I could stay all night, but I've still two engagements.' He rose; she rose also and stood before him looking up at him for a moment.

'How well you look! I think you have found the secret of perpetual youth. You don't look a day older than when I first saw you just four years ago. You always look as if you were on fire and being burnt up, but you never are, you know.'

He looked down at her with a kind of amused face as one does at an interesting child or a big Newfoundland dog.

'When shall we see you back?'

'Oh, not at all!'

'Not at all! Oh, we must have you back; you belong here, you know. You'll get tired of your Buddhist and come back to us.'

'You didn't mind my asking you to come and say good-bye?' she said in a childish manner unlike her determinateness when she discussed anything impersonal. 'I wanted to say good-bye to everyone. If one hasn't said good-bye one feels restless and feels one would have to come back. If one has said good-bye to all one's friends, then one knows it is all ended.'

'Oh, this isn't a final farewell! You must come in ten years' time and we'll compare notes – you about your Buddhist Priest, I about my fair ideal American; and we'll see who succeeded best.'

She laughed.

'I shall always see your movements chronicled in the newspapers, so we shall not be quite sundered; and you will hear of me perhaps.'

'Yes, I hope you will be very successful.'

She was looking at him, with her eyes wide open, from head to foot. He turned to the chair where his coat hung.

'Can't I help you put it on?'

'Oh, no, thank you.'

He put it on.

'Button the throat,' she said, 'the room is warm.'

He turned to her in his great-coat and with his gloves. They were standing near the door.

'Well, good-bye. I hope you will have a very pleasant time.'

He stood looking down upon her, wrapped in his great-coat.

She put up one hand a little in the air. 'I want to ask you something,' she said quickly.

'Well, what is it?'

'Will you please kiss me?'

For a moment he looked down at her, then he bent over her.

In after years he could never tell certainly, but he always thought she put up her hand and rested it on the crown of his head, with a curious soft caress, something like a mother's touch when her child is asleep and she does not want to wake it. Then he looked round, and she was gone. The door had closed noiselessly. For a moment he stood motionless, then he walked to the fireplace and looked down into the fender at a little cigarette end lying there, then he walked quickly back to the door and opened it. The stairs were in darkness and silence. He rang the bell violently. The old woman came up. He asked her where the lady was. She said she had gone out, she had a cab waiting. He asked when she would be back. The old woman said, 'Not at all'; she had left. He asked where she had gone. The woman said she did not know; she had left orders that all her letters should be kept for six or eight months till she wrote and sent her address. He asked whether she had no idea where he might find her. The woman said no. He walked up to a space in the wall where a picture had hung and stood staring at it as though the picture were still hanging there. He drew his mouth as though he were emitting a long whistle, but no sound came. He gave the old woman ten shillings and went downstairs.

That was eight years ago.

How beautiful life must have been to it that it looks so young still!

CHARLOTTE PERKINS GILMAN

THE YELLOW WALLPAPER

IT is very seldom that mere ordinary people like John and myself secure ancestral halls for the summer.

A colonial mansion, a hereditary estate, I would say a haunted house, and reach the height of romantic felicity – but that would be asking too much of fate!

Still I will proudly declare that there is something queer about it.

Else, why should it be let so cheaply? And why have stood so long untenanted?

John laughs at me, of course, but one expects that in marriage.

John is practical in the extreme. He has no patience with faith, an intense horror of superstition, and he scoffs openly at any talk of things not to be felt and seen and put down in figures.

John is a physician, and *perhaps* – (I would not say it to a living soul, of course, but this is dead paper and a great relief to my mind) – *perhaps* that is one reason I do not get well faster.

You see he does not believe I am sick!

And what can one do?

If a physician of high standing, and one's own husband, assures friends and relatives that there is really nothing the matter with one but temporary nervous depression – a slight hysterical tendency – what is one to do?

My brother is also a physician, and also of high standing, and he says the same thing.

So I take phosphates or phosphites – whichever it is, and tonics, and journeys, and air, and exercise, and am absolutely forbidden to 'work' until I am well again.

Personally, I disagree with their ideas.

Personally, I believe that congenial work, with excitement and change, would do me good.

But what is one to do?

I did write for a while in spite of them; but it *does* exhaust me a good deal – having to be so sly about it, or else meet with heavy opposition.

I sometimes fancy that in my condition if I had less opposition and more society and stimulus – but John says the very worst thing I can do is to think about my condition, and I confess it always makes me feel bad.

So I will let it alone and talk about the house.

The most beautiful place! It is quite alone, standing well back from the road, quite three miles from the village. It makes me think of English places that you read about, for there are hedges and walls and gates that lock, and lots of separate little houses for the gardeners and people.

There is a *delicious* garden! I never saw such a garden – large and shady, full of box-bordered paths, and lined with long grape-covered arbors with seats under them.

There were greenhouses, too, but they are all broken now.

There was some legal trouble, I believe, something about the heirs and coheirs; anyhow, the place has been empty for years.

That spoils my ghostliness, I am afraid, but I don't care – there is something strange about the house – I can feel it.

I even said so to John one moonlight evening, but he said what I felt was a *draught*, and shut the window.

I get unreasonably angry with John sometimes. I'm sure I never used to be so sensitive. I think it is due to this nervous condition.

But John says if I feel so, I shall neglect proper self-control; so I take pains to control myself – before him, at least, and that makes me very tired.

I don't like our room a bit. I wanted one downstairs that opened on the piazza and had roses all over the window, and such pretty old-fashioned chintz hangings! but John would not hear of it.

He said there was only one window and not room for two beds, and no near room for him if he took another.

He is very careful and loving, and hardly lets me stir without special direction.

I have a schedule prescription for each hour in the day; he takes all care from me, and so I feel basely ungrateful not to value it more.

He said we came here solely on my account, that I was to have perfect rest and all the air I could get. 'Your exercise depends on your strength, my dear,' said he, 'and your food somewhat on your appetite; but air you can absorb all the time.' So we took the nursery at the top of the house.

It is a big, airy room, the whole floor nearly, with windows that look all ways, and air and sunshine galore. It was nursery first and then playroom and gymnasium, I should judge; for the windows are barred for little children, and there are rings and things in the walls.

The paint and paper look as if a boys' school had used it. It is stripped off – the paper – in great patches all around the head of my bed, about as far as I can reach, and in a great place on the other side of the room low down. I never saw a worse paper in my life.

One of those sprawling flamboyant patterns committing every artistic sin.

It is dull enough to confuse the eye in following, pronounced enough to constantly irritate and provoke study, and when you follow the lame uncertain curves for a little distance they suddenly commit suicide – plunge off at outrageous angles, destroy themselves in unheard of contradictions.

The colour is repellent, almost revolting; a smouldering unclean yellow, strangely faded by the slow-turning sunlight.

It is a dull yet lurid orange in some places, a sickly sulphur tint in others.

No wonder the children hated it! I should hate it myself if I had to live in this room long.

There comes John, and I must put this away, – he hates to have me write a word.

We have been here two weeks, and I haven't felt like writing before, since that first day.

I am sitting by the window now, up in this atrocious nursery, and there is nothing to hinder my writing as much as I please, save lack of strength.

John is away all day, and even some nights when his cases are serious.

I am glad my case is not serious!

But these nervous troubles are dreadfully depressing.

John does not know how much I really suffer. He knows there is no *reason* to suffer, and that satisfies him.

Of course it is only nervousness. It does weigh on me so not to do my duty in any way!

I meant to be such a help to John, such a real rest and comfort, and here I am a comparative burden already!

Nobody would believe what an effort it is to do what little I am able, – to dress and entertain, and order things.

It is fortunate Mary is so good with the baby. Such a dear baby!

And yet I *cannot* be with him, it makes me so nervous.

I suppose John never was nervous in his life. He laughs at me so about this wallpaper!

At first he meant to repaper the room, but afterwards he said that I was letting it get the better of me, and that nothing was worse for a nervous patient than to give way to such fancies.

He said that after the wallpaper was changed it would be the heavy bedstead, and then the barred windows, and then that gate at the head of the stairs, and so on.

'You know the place is doing you good,' he said, 'and really, dear, I don't care to renovate the house just for a three months' rental.'

'Then do let us go downstairs,' I said, 'there are such pretty rooms there.'

Then he took me in his arms and called me a blessed little goose, and said he would go down to the cellar, if I wished, and have it whitewashed into the bargain.

But he is right enough about the beds and windows and things.

It is an airy and comfortable room as any one need wish, and, of course, I would not be so silly as to make him uncomfortable just for a whim.

I'm really getting quite fond of the big room, all but that horrid paper.

Out of one window I can see the garden, those mysterious deepshaded arbors, the riotous old-fashioned flowers, and bushes and gnarly trees.

Out of another I get a lovely view of the bay and a little private wharf belonging to the estate. There is a beautiful shaded lane that runs down there from the house. I always fancy I see people walking in these numerous paths and arbors, but John has cautioned me not to give way to fancy in the least. He says that with my imaginative power and habit of story-making, a nervous weakness like mine is sure to lead to all manner of excited fancies, and that I ought to use my will and good sense to check the tendency. So I try.

I think sometimes that if I were only well enough to write a little it would relieve the press of ideas and rest me.

But I find I get pretty tired when I try.

It is so discouraging not to have any advice and companionship about my work. When I get really well, John says we will ask Cousin Henry and Julia down for a long visit; but he says he would as soon put fireworks in my pillow-case as to let me have those stimulating people about now.

I wish I could get well faster.

But I must not think about that. This paper looks to me as if it *knew* what a vicious influence it had!

There is a recurrent spot where the pattern lolls like a broken neck and two bulbous eyes stare at you upside down.

I get positively angry with the impertinence of it and the everlastingness. Up and down and sideways they crawl, and those absurd, unblinking eyes are everywhere. There is one place where two breadths didn't match, and the eyes go all up and down the line, one a little higher than the other.

I never saw so much expression in an inanimate thing before, and we all know how much expression they have! I used to lie awake as a child and get more entertainment and terror out of blank walls and plain furniture than most children could find in a toy-store.

I remember what a kindly wink the knobs of our big, old bureau used to have, and there was one chair that always seemed like a strong friend.

I used to feel that if any of the other things looked too fierce I could always hop into that chair and be safe.

The furniture in this room is no worse than inharmonious, however, for we had to bring it all from downstairs. I suppose when this was used as a playroom they had to take the nursery things out, and no wonder! I never saw such ravages as the children have made here.

The wallpaper, as I said before, is torn off in spots, and it sticketh closer than a brother – they must have had perserverance as well as hatred.

Then the floor is scratched and gouged and splintered, the plaster itself is dug out here and there, and this great heavy bed which is all we found in the room, looks as if it had been through the wars.

But I don't mind it a bit – only the paper.

There comes John's sister. Such a dear girl as she is, and so careful of me! I must not let her find me writing.

She is a perfect and enthusiastic housekeeper, and hopes for no better profession. I verily believe she thinks it is the writing which made me sick!

But I can write when she is out, and see her a long way off from these windows.

There is one that commands the road, a lovely shaded winding road, and one that just looks off over the country. A lovely country, too, full of great elms and velvet meadows.

This wallpaper has a kind of sub-pattern in a different shade, a particularly irritating one, for you can only see it in certain lights, and not clearly then.

But in the places where it isn't faded and where the sun is just so – I can see a strange, provoking, formless sort of figure, that seems to skulk about behind that silly and conspicuous front design.

There's sister on the stairs!

Well, the Fourth of July is over! The people are all gone and I am tired out. John thought it might do me good to see a little company, so we just had Mother and Nellie and the children down for a week.

Of course I didn't do a thing. Jennie sees to everything now.

But it tired me all the same.

John says if I don't pick up faster he shall send me to Weir Mitchell in the fall.

But I don't want to go there at all. I had a friend who was in his hands once, and she says he is just like John and my brother, only more so!

Besides, it is such an undertaking to go so far.

I don't feel as if it was worth while to turn my hand over for anything, and I'm getting dreadfully fretful and querulous.

I cry at nothing, and cry most of the time.

Of course I don't when John is here, or anybody else, but when I am alone.

And I am alone a good deal just now. John is kept in town very often by serious cases, and Jennie is good and lets me alone when I want her to.

So I walk a little in the garden or down that lovely lane, sit on the porch under the roses, and lie down up here a good deal.

I'm getting really fond of the room in spite of the wallpaper. Perhaps *because* of the wallpaper.

It dwells in my mind so!

I lie here on this great immovable bed – it is nailed down, I believe – and follow that pattern about by the hour. It is as good as gymnastics, I assure you. I start, we'll say, at the bottom, down in the corner over there where it has not been touched, and I determine for the thousandth time that I *will* follow that pointless pattern to some sort of a conclusion.

I know a little of the principle of design, and I know this thing was not arranged on any laws of radiation, or alternation, or repetition, or symmetry, or anything else that I ever heard of.

It is repeated, of course, by the breadths, but not otherwise.

Looked at in one way each breadth stands alone, the bloated curves and flourishes – a kind of 'debased Romanesque' with *delirium tremens* – go waddling up and down in isolated columns of fatuity.

But, on the other hand, they connect diagonally, and the sprawling outlines run off in great slanting waves of optic horror, like a lot of wallowing seaweeds in full chase.

The whole thing goes horizontally, too, at least it seems so, and I exhaust myself in trying to distinguish the order of its going in that direction.

They have used a horizontal breadth for a frieze, and that adds wonderfully to the confusion.

There is one end of the room where it is almost intact, and there, when the crosslights fade and the low sun shines directly upon it, I can almost fancy radiation after all, – the interminable grotesques seem to form around a common centre and rush off in headlong plunges of equal distraction.

It makes me tired to follow it. I will take a nap I guess.

I don't know why I should write this.

I don't want to.

I don't feel able.

And I know John would think it absurd. But I *must* say what I feel and think in some way – it is such a relief!

But the effort is getting to be greater than the relief.

Half the time now I am awfully lazy, and lie down ever so much.

John says I mustn't lose my strength, and has me take cod liver oil and lots of tonics and things, to say nothing of ale and wine and rare meat.

Dear John! He loves me very dearly, and hates to have me sick. I tried to have a real earnest reasonable talk with him the other day, and tell him how I wish he would let me go and make a visit to Cousin Henry and Julia.

But he said I wasn't able to go, nor able to stand it after I got there; and I did not make out a very good case for myself, for I was crying before I had finished.

It is getting to be a great effort for me to think straight. Just this nervous weakness I suppose.

And dear John gathered me up in his arms, and just carried me upstairs and laid me on the bed, and sat by me and read to me till it tired my head.

He said I was his darling and his comfort and all he had, and that I must take care of myself for his sake, and keep well.

He says no one but myself can help me out of it, that I must use my will and self-control and not let any silly fancies run away with me.

There's one comfort, the baby is well and happy, and does not have to occupy this nursery with the horried wallpaper.

If we had not used it, that blessed child would have! What a fortunate escape! Why, I wouldn't have a child of mine, an impressionable little thing, live in such a room for worlds.

I never thought of it before, but it is lucky that John kept me here after all, I can stand it so much easier than a baby, you see.

Of course I never mention it to them any more – I am too wise – but I keep watch of it all the same.

There are things in that paper that nobody knows but me, or ever will.

Behind that outside pattern the dim shapes get clearer every day.

It is always the same shape, only very numerous.

And it is like a woman stooping down and creeping about behind that pattern. I don't like it a bit. I wonder – I begin to think – I wish John would take me away from here!

It is so hard to talk with John about my case, because he is so wise, and because he loves me so.

But I tried it last night.

It was moonlight. The moon shines in all around just as the sun does.

I hate to see it sometimes, it creeps so slowly, and always comes in by one window or another.

John was asleep and I hated to waken him, so I kept still and watched the moonlight on that undulating wallpaper till I felt creepy.

The faint figure behind seemed to shake the pattern, just as if she wanted to get out.

I got up softly and went to feel and see if the paper *did* move, and when I came back John was awake.

'What is it, little girl?' he said. 'Don't go walking about like that – you'll get cold.'

I thought it was a good time to talk, so I told him that I really was not gaining here, and that I wished he would take me away.

'Why darling!' said he, 'our lease will be up in three weeks, and I can't see how to leave before.

'The repairs are not done at home, and I cannot possibly leave town just now. Of course if you were in any danger, I could and would, but you realy are better, dear, whether you can see it or not. I am a doctor, dear, and I know. You are gaining flesh and colour, your appetite is better, I feel really much easier about you.'

'I don't weigh a bit more,' said I, 'nor as much; and my appetite may be better in the evening when you are here, but it is worse in the morning when you are away!'

'Bless her little heart!' said he with a big hug, 'she shall be as sick as she pleases! But now let's improve the shining hours by going to sleep, and talk about it in the morning!'

'And you won't go away?' I asked gloomily.

'Why, how can I, dear? It is only three weeks more and then we will take a nice little trip of a few days while Jennie is getting the house ready. Really dear you are better!'

'Better in body perhaps –' I began, and stopped short, for he sat up straight and looked at me with such a stern, reproachful look that I could not say another word.

'My darling,' said he, 'I beg of you, for my sake and for our child's sake, as well as for your own, that you will never for one instant let that idea enter your mind! There is nothing so dangerous, so fascinating, to a temperament like yours. It is a false and foolish fancy. Can you not trust me as a physician when I tell you so?'

So of course I said no more on that score, and we went to sleep before long. He thought I was asleep first, but I wasn't, and lay there for hours trying to decide whether that front pattern and the back pattern really did move together or separately.

On a pattern like this, by daylight, there is a lack of sequence, a defiance of law, that is a constant irritant to a normal mind.

The colour is hideous enough, and unreliable enough, and infuriating enough, but the pattern is torturing.

You think you have mastered it, but just as you get well underway in following, it turns a back-somersault and there you are. It slaps you in the face, knocks you down, and tramples upon you. It is like a bad dream.

The outside pattern is a florid arabesque, reminding one of a fungus. If you can imagine a toadstool in joints, an interminable string of toadstools, budding and sprouting in endless convolutions – why, that is something like it.

That is, sometimes!

There is one marked peculiarity about this paper, a thing

nobody seems to notice but myself, and that is that it changes as the light changes.

When the sun shoots in through the east window – I always watch for that first long, straight ray – it changes so quickly that I never can quite believe it.

That is why I watch it always.

By moonlight – the moon shines in all night when there is a moon – I wouldn't know it was the same paper.

At night in any kind of light, in twilight, candle light, lamplight, and worst of all by moonlight, it becomes bars! The outside pattern I mean, and the woman behind it is as plain as can be.

I didn't realise for a long time what the thing was that showed behind, that dim sub-pattern, but now I am quite sure it is a woman.

By daylight she is subdued, quiet. I fancy it is the pattern that keeps her so still. It is so puzzling. It keeps me quiet by the hour.

I lie down ever so much now. John says it is good for me, and to sleep all I can.

Indeed he started the habit by making me lie down for an hour after each meal.

It is a very bad habit I am convinced, for you see I don't sleep.

And that cultivates deceit, for I don't tell them I'm awake – O no!

The fact is I am getting a little afraid of John.

He seems very queer sometimes, and even Jennie has an inexplicable look.

It strikes me occasionally, just as a scientific hypothesis, – that perhaps it is the paper!

I have watched John when he did not know I was looking, and come into the room suddenly on the most innocent excuses, and I've caught him several times *looking at the paper!* And Jennie too. I caught Jennie with her hand on it once.

She didn't know I was in the room, and when I asked her in a quiet, a very quiet voice, with the most restrained manner possible, what she was doing with the paper – she turned around as if she had been caught stealing, and looked quite angry – asked me why I should frighten her so!

Then she said that the paper stained everything it touched, that she had found yellow smooches on all my clothes and John's, and she wished we would be more careful!

Did not that sound innocent? But I know she was studying that pattern, and I am determined that nobody shall find it out but myself!

Life is very much more exciting now than it used to be. You see I have something more to expect, to look forward to, to watch. I really do eat better, and am more quiet than I was.

John is so pleased to see me improve! He laughed a little the other day, and said I seemed to be flourishing in spite of my wallpaper.

I turned it off with a laugh. I had no intention of telling him it was *because* of the wallpaper – he would make fun of me. He might even want to take me away.

I don't want to leave now until I have found it out. There is a week more, and I think that will be enough.

I'm feeling ever so much better! I don't sleep much at night, for it is so interesting to watch developments; but I sleep a good deal in the daytime.

In the daytime it is tiresome and perplexing.

There are always new shoots on the fungus, and new shades of yellow all over it. I cannot keep count of them, though I have tried conscientiously.

It is the strangest yellow, that wallpaper! It makes me think of all the yellow things I ever saw – not beautiful ones like buttercups, but old foul, bad yellow things.

But there is something else about that paper – the smell! I noticed it the moment we came into the room, but with so much air and sun it was not bad. Now we have had a week of fog and rain, and whether the windows are open or not, the smell is here.

It creeps all over the house.

I find it hovering in the dining-room, skulking in the parlour, hiding in the hall, lying in wait for me on the stairs.

It gets into my hair.

Even when I go to ride, if I turn my head suddenly and surprise it – there is that smell!

Such a peculiar odour, too! I have spent hours in trying to analyse it, to find what it smelled like.

It is not bad – at first, and very gentle, but quite the subtlest, most enduring odour I ever met.

In this damp weather it is awful, I wake up in the night and find it hanging over me.

It used to disturb me at first. I thought seriously of burning the house – to reach the smell.

But now I am used to it. The only thing I can think of that it is like is the *colour* of the paper! A yellow smell.

There is a very funny mark on this wall, low down, near the mopboard. A streak that runs round the room. It goes behind every piece of furniture, except the bed, a long, straight, even *smooch*, as if it had been rubbed over and over.

I wonder how it was done and who did it, and what they did it for. Round and round and round – round and round and round – it makes me dizzy!

*

I really have discovered something at last.

Through watching so much at night, when it changes so, I have finally found out.

The front pattern *does* move – and no wonder! The woman behind shakes it!

Sometimes I think there are a great many women behind, and sometimes only one, and she crawls around fast, and her crawling shakes it all over.

Then in the very bright spots she keeps still, and in the very shady spots she just takes hold of the bars and shakes them hard.

And she is all the time trying to climb through. But nobody could climb through that pattern – it strangles so; I think that is why it has so many heads.

They get through, and then the pattern strangles them off and turns them upside down, and makes their eyes white!

If those heads were covered or taken off it would not be half so bad.

I think that woman gets out in the daytime!

And I'll tell you why – privately – I've seen her!

I can see her out of every one of my windows!

It is the same woman, I know, for she is always creeping, and most women do not creep by daylight.

I see her on that long road under the trees, creeping along, and when a carriage comes she hides under the blackberry vines.

I don't blame her a bit. It must be very humiliating to be caught creeping by daylight!

I always lock the door when I creep by daylight. I can't do it at night, for I know John would suspect something at once.

And John is so queer now, that I don't want to irritate him. I wish he would take another room! Besides, I don't want anybody to get that woman out at night but myself.

I often wonder if I could see her out of all the windows at once.

But, turn as fast as I can, I can only see out of one at one time.

And though I always see her, she *may* be able to creep faster than I can turn!

I have watched her sometimes away off in the open country, creeping as fast as a cloud shadow in a high wind.

If only that top pattern could be gotten off from the under one! I mean to try it, little by little.

I have found out another funny thing, but I shan't tell it this time! It does not do to trust people too much.

There are only two more days to get this paper off, and I believe John is beginning to notice. I don't like the look in his eyes.

And I heard him ask Jennie a lot of professional questions about me. She had a very good report to give.

She said I slept a good deal in the daytime.

John knows I don't sleep very well at night, for all I'm so quiet!

He asked me all sorts of questions, too, and pretended to be very loving and kind.

As if I couldn't see through him!

Still, I don't wonder he acts so, sleeping under this paper for three months.

It only interests me, but I feel sure John and Jennie are secretly affected by it.

Hurrah! This is the last day, but it is enough. John to stay in town over night, and won't be out until this evening.

Jennie wanted to sleep with me – the sly thing! but I told her I should undoubtedly rest better for a night all alone.

That was clever, for really I wasn't alone a bit! As soon

as it was moonlight and that poor thing began to crawl and shake the pattern, I got up and ran to help her.

I pulled and she shook, I shook and she pulled, and before morning we had peeled off yards of that paper.

A strip about as high as my head and half around the room.

And then when the sun came and that awful pattern began to laugh at me, I declared I would finish it to-day!

We go away to-morrow, and they are moving all my furniture down again to leave things as they were before.

Jennie looked at the wall in amazement, but I told her merrily that I did it out of pure spite at the vicious thing.

She laughed and said she wouldn't mind doing it herself, but I must not get tired.

How she betrayed herself that time!

But I am here, and no person touches this paper but me, – not *alive*!

She tried to get me out of the room – it was too patent! But I said it was so quiet and empty and clean now that I believed I would lie down again and sleep all I could; and not to wake me even for dinner – I would call when I woke.

So now she is gone, and the servants are gone, and the things are gone, and there is nothing left but that great bedstead nailed down, with the canvas mattress we found on it.

We shall sleep downstairs to-night, and take the boat home to-morrow.

I quite enjoy the room, now it is bare again.

How those children did tear about here!

This bedstead is fairly gnawed!

But I must get to work.

I have locked the door and thrown the key down into the front path.

I don't want to go out, and I don't want to have anybody come in, till John comes.

I want to astonish him.

I've got a rope up here that even Jennie did not find. If that woman does get out, and tries to get away, I can tie her!

But I forgot I could not reach far without anything to stand on!

This bed will *not* move!

I tried to lift and push it until I was lame, and then I got so angry I bit off a little piece at one corner – but it hurt my teeth.

Then I peeled off all the paper I could reach standing on the floor. It sticks horribly and the pattern just enjoys it! All those strangled heads and bulbous eyes and waddling fungus growths just shriek with derision!

I am getting angry enough to do something desperate. To jump out of the window would be admirable exercise, but the bars are too strong even to try.

Besides I wouldn't do it. Of course not. I know well enough that a step like that is improper and might be misconstrued.

I don't like to *look* out of the windows even – there are so many of those creeping women, and they creep so fast.

I wonder if they all come out of that wallpaper as I did?

But I am securely fastened now by my well-hidden rope – you don't get *me* out in the road there!

I suppose I shall have to get back behind the pattern when it comes night, and that is hard!

It is so pleasant to be out in this great room and creep around as I please!

I don't want to go outside. I won't, even if Jennie asks me to.

For outside you have to creep on the ground, and everything is green instead of yellow.

But here I can creep smoothly on the floor, and my

shoulder just fits in that long smooch around the wall, so I cannot lose my way.

Why there's John at the door!

It is no use, young man, you can't open it!

How he does call and pound!

Now he's crying for an axe.

It would be a shame to break down that beautiful door!

'John dear!' said I in the gentlest voice, 'the key is down by the front steps, under a plantain leaf!'

That silenced him for a few moments.

Then he said – very quietly indeed, 'Open the door, my darling!'

'I can't,' said I. 'The key is down by the front door under a plantain leaf!'

And then I said it again, several times, very gently and slowly, and said it so often that he had to go and see, and he got it of course, and came in. He stopped short by the door.

'What is the matter?' he cried. 'For God's sake, what are you doing!'

I kept on creeping just the same, but I looked at him over my shoulder.

'I've got out at last,' said I, 'in spite of you and Jane. And I've pulled off most of the paper, so you can't put me back!'

Now why should that man have fainted? But he did, and right across my path by the wall, so that I had to creep over him every time!

CHARLOTTE MEW

A WHITE NIGHT

'THE incident', said Cameron, 'is spoiled inevitably in the telling, by its merely accidental quality of melodrama, its sensational machinery, which, to the view of anyone who didn't witness it, is apt to blur the finer outlines of the scene. The subtlety, or call it the significance, is missed, and unavoidably, as one attempts to put the thing before you, in a certain casual crudity, and inessential violence of fact. Make it a mediaeval matter – put it back some centuries – and the affair takes on its proper tone immediately, is tinctured with the sinister solemnity which actually enveloped it. But as it stands, a recollection, an experience, a picture, well, it doesn't reproduce; one must have the original if one is going to hang it on one's wall.'

In spite of which I took it down the night he told it and, thanks to a trick of accuracy, I believe you have the story as I heard it, almost word for word.

It was in the spring of 1876, a rainless spring, as I remember it, of white roads and brown crops and steely skies.

Sent out the year before on mining business, I had been then some eighteen months in Spain. My job was finished; I was leaving the Black Country, planning a vague look round, perhaps a little sport among the mountains, when a letter from my sister Ella laid the dust of doubtful schemes.

She was on a discursive honeymoon. They had come on from Florence to Madrid, and disappointed with the rank modernity of their last halt, wished to explore some of the least known towns of the interior: 'Something unique, untrodden, and uncivilised', she indicated modestly. Further, if I were free and amiable, and so on, they would join me anywhere in Andalusia. I was in fact to show them round.

I did 'my possible'; we roughed it pretty thoroughly, but the young person's passion for the strange bore her robustly through the risks and discomforts of those wilder districts which at best, perhaps, are hardly woman's ground.

King, on occasion nursed anxiety, and mourned his little luxuries; Ella accepted anything that befell, from dirt to danger, with a humorous composure dating back to nursery days – she had the instincts and the physique of a traveller, with a brilliancy of touch and a decision of attack on human instruments which told. She took our mule-drivers in hand with some success. Later, no doubt, their wretched beasts were made to smart for it, in the reaction from a lull in that habitual brutality which makes the animals of Spain a real blot upon the gay indifferentism of its people.

It pleased her to devise a lurid *Dies Irae* for these affable barbarians, a special process of reincarnation for the Spaniard generally, whereby the space of one dog's life at least should be ensured to him.

And on the day I'm coming to, a tedious, dislocating journey in a springless cart had brought her to the verge of quite unusual weariness, a weariness of spirit only, she protested, waving a hand toward our man who lashed and sang alternately, fetching at intervals a sunny smile for the poor lady's vain remonstrances before he lashed again.

The details of that day – our setting forth, our ride, and our arrival – all the minor episodes stand out with singular distinctness, forming a background in one's memory to the eventual, central scene.

We left our inn – a rough *posada* – about sunrise, and our road, washed to a track by winter rains, lay first through wide half-cultivated slopes, capped everywhere with orange trees and palm and olive patches, curiously bare of farms or villages, till one recalls the lawless state of those outlying regions and the absence of communication between them and town.

Abruptly, blotted in blue mist, vineyards and olives, with the groups of aloes marking off field boundaries, disappeared. We entered on a land of naked rock, peak after peak of it, cutting a jagged line against the clear intensity of the sky.

This passed again, with early afternoon our straight, white road grew featureless, a dusty stretch, save far ahead the sun-tipped ridge of a sierra, and the silver ribbon of the river twisting among the barren hills. Toward the end we passed one of the wooden crosses set up on these roads to mark some spot of violence or disaster. These are the only signposts one encounters, and as we came up with it, our beasts were goaded for the last ascent.

Irregular grey walls came into view; we skirted them and turned in through a Roman gateway and across a bridge into a maze of narrow stone-pitched streets, spanned here and there by Moorish arches, and execrably rough to rattle over.

A strong illusion of the Orient, extreme antiquity and dreamlike stillness marked the place.

Crossing the grey arcaded Plaza, just beginning at that hour to be splashed with blots of gaudy colour moving to the tinkling of the mule-bells, we were soon upon the outskirts of the town – the most untouched, remote and, I believe, the most remarkable that we had dropped upon.

In its neglect and singularity, it made a claim to something like supremacy of charm. There was the quality of diffidence belonging to unrecognised abandoned personalities in that appeal.

That's how it's docketed in memory – a city with a claim, which, as it happened, I was not to weigh.

Our inn, a long, one-storeyed building with caged windows, most of them unglazed, had been an old palacio; its broken fortunes hadn't robbed it of its character, its air.

The spacious place was practically empty, and the shuttered rooms, stone-flagged and cool, after our shadeless ride, invited one to a prolonged siesta; but Ella wasn't friendly to a pause. Her buoyancy survived our meal. She seemed even to face the morrow's repetition of that indescribable experience with serenity. We found her in the small paved garden, sipping chocolate and airing Spanish with our host, a man of some distinction, possibly of broken fortunes too.

The conversation, delicately edged with compliment on his side, was on hers a little blunted by a limited vocabulary, and left us both presumably a margin for imagination.

Si, la Señora, he explained as we came up, knew absolutely nothing of fatigue, and the impetuosity of the *Señora*, this attractive eagerness to make acquaintance with it, did great honour to his much forgotten, much neglected town. He spoke of it with rather touching ardour, as a place unvisited, but '*digno de renombre illustre*', worthy of high fame.

It has stood still, it was perhaps too stationary; innovation was repellent to the Spaniard, yet this conservatism, lack of enterprise, the virtue or the failing of his country – as we pleased – had its aesthetic value. Was there not, he would appeal to the *Señora*, '*una belleza de reposo*', a beauty of quiescence, a dignity above prosperity? '*Muy bien.*' Let the *Señora* judge, you had it there!

We struck out from the town, perhaps insensibly toward the landmark of a Calvary, planted a mile or so beyond the walls, its three black shafts above the mass of roofs and pinnacles, in sharp relief against the sky, against which suddenly a flock of vultures threw the first white cloud. With the descending sun, the clear persistence of the blue was losing permanence, a breeze sprang up and birds began to call.

The Spanish evening has unique effects and exquisite exhilarations: this one led us on some distance past the Calvary and the last group of scattered houses – many in complete decay – which straggle, thinning outwards from the city boundaries into the *campo*.

Standing alone, after a stretch of crumbling wall, a wretched little *venta*, like a stop to some meandering sentence, closed the broken line.

The place was windowless, but through the open door an oath or two – the common blend of sacrilege and vileness – with a smell of charcoal, frying oil-cakes and an odour of the stable, drifted out into the freshness of the evening air.

Immediately before us lay a dim expanse of treeless plain: behind, clear cut against a smokeless sky, the flat roof lines and towers of the city, seeming, as we looked back on them, less distant than in fact they were.

We took a road which finally confronted us with a huge block of buildings, an old church and convent, massed in the shadow of a hill and standing at the entrance to three cross-roads.

The convent, one of the few remaining in the south, not fallen into ruin, nor yet put, as far as one could judge, to worldly uses, was exceptionally large. We counted over thirty windows in a line upon the western side below the central tower with its pointed turret; the eastern wing, an evidently older part, was cut irregularly with a few square gratings.

The big, grey structure was impressive in its loneliness, its blank negation of the outside world, its stark expressionless detachment.

The church, of darker stone, was massive too; its only noticeable feature a small cloister with Romanesque arcades joining the nave on its south-western wall.

A group of peasant women coming out from vespers passed us and went chattering up the road, the last, an aged creature shuffling painfully some yards behind the rest still muttering her

Madre purisima,
Madre castisima,
Ruega por nosostros,

in a kind of automatic drone.

We looked in, as one does instinctively: the altar lights which hang like sickly stars in the profound obscurity of Spanish churches were being quickly blotted out.

We didn't enter then, but turned back to the convent gate, which stood half open, showing a side of the uncorniced cloisters, and a crowd of flowers, touched to an intensity of brilliance and fragrance by the twilight. Six or seven dogs, the sandy-coloured lurchers of the country, lean and wolfish-looking hounds, were sprawling round the gateway; save for this dejected crew, the place seemed resolutely lifeless; and this absence of a human note was just. One didn't want its solitude or silence touched, its really fine impersonality destroyed.

We hadn't meant – there wasn't light enough – to try the church again, but as we passed it, we turned into the small cloister. King, who had come to his last match, was seeking shelter from the breeze which had considerably freshened, and at the far end we came upon a little door, unlocked. I don't know why we tried it, but mechanically, as the conscientious tourist will, we drifted in and groped round.

Only the vaguest outlines were discernible; the lancets of the lantern at the transept crossing, and a large rose window at the western end seemed, at a glance, the only means of light, and this was failing, leaving fast the fading panes.

One half-detected, almost guessed, the blind triforium, but the enormous width of the great building made immediate mark. The darkness, masking as it did distinctive features, emphasised the sense of space, which, like the spirit of a shrouded form, gained force, intensity, from its material disguise.

We stayed not more than a few minutes, but on reaching the small door again we found it fast; bolted or locked undoubtedly in the short interval. Of course we put our backs to it and made a pretty violent outcry, hoping the worthy sacristan was hanging round or somewhere within call. Of course he wasn't. We tried two other doors; both barred, and there was nothing left for it but noise. We shouted, I suppose, for half an hour, intermittently, and King persisted hoarsely after I had given out.

The echo of the vast, dark, empty place caught up our cries, seeming to hold them in suspension for a second in the void invisibility of roof and arches, then to fling them down in hollow repetition with an accent of unearthly mimicry which struck a little grimly on one's ear; and when we paused the silence seemed alert, expectant, ready to repel the first recurrence of unholy clamour. Finally, we gave it up; the hope of a release before the dawn, at earliest, was too forlorn. King, explosive and solicitous, was solemnly perturbed, but Ella faced the situation with an admirable tranquillity. Some chocolate and a muff would certainly, for her, she said, have made it more engaging, but poor dear men, the really tragic element resolved itself into – No matches, no cigar!

Unluckily we hadn't even this poor means of temporary light. Our steps and voices sounded loud, almost aggressive, as we groped about; the darkness then was shutting down and shortly it grew absolute. We camped eventually in one of the side chapels on the south side of the chancel, and kept a conversation going for a time, but gradually it dropped. The temperature, the fixed obscurity, and possibly a curious oppression in the spiritual atmosphere relaxed and forced it down.

The scent of incense clung about; a biting chillness crept up through the aisles; it got intensely cold. The stillness too became insistent; it was literally deathlike, rigid, exclusive, even awfully remote. It shut us out and held aloof; our passive presences, our mere vitality, seemed almost a disturbance of it; quiet as we were, we breathed, but it was breathless, and as time went on, one's impulse was to fight the sort of shapeless personality it presently assumed, to talk, to walk about and make a definite attack on it. Its influence on the others was presumably more soothing, obviously they weren't that way inclined.

Five or six hours must have passed. Nothing had marked them, and they hadn't seemed to move. The darkness seemed to thicken, in a way, to muddle thought and filter through into one's brain, and waiting, cramped and cold for it to lift, the soundlessness again impressed itself unpleasantly – it was intense, unnatural, acute.

And then it stirred.

The break in it was vague but positive; it might have been that, scarcely audible, the wind outside was rising, and yet not precisely that. I barely caught, and couldn't localise the sound.

Ella and King were dozing, they had had some snatches of uncomfortable sleep; I, I suppose, was preternaturally awake. I heard a key turn, and the swing back of a door, rapidly followed by a wave of voices breaking in. I put my hand out and touched King and in a moment, both of them waked and started up.

I can't say how, but it at once occurred to us that quiet was our cue, that we were in for something singular.

The place was filling slowly with a chant, and then, emerging from the eastern end of the north aisle and travelling down just opposite, across the intervening dark, a line of light came into view, crossing the opening of the arches, cut by the massive piers, a moving, flickering line, advancing and advancing with the voices.

The outlines of the figures in the long procession weren't perceptible, the faces, palely lit and level with the tapers they were carrying, one rather felt than saw; but unmistakably the voices were men's voices, and the chant, the measured, reiterated cadences, prevailed over the wavering light.

Heavy and sombre as the stillness which it broke, vaguely akin to it, the chant swept in and gained upon the silence with a motion of the tide. It was a music neither of the senses, nor the spirit, but the mind, as set, as stately, almost as inanimate as the dark aisles through which it echoed; even, colourless and cold.

And then, quite suddenly, against its grave and passionless inflections something clashed, a piercing intermittent note, an awful discord, shrilling out and dying down and shrilling out again – a cry – a scream.

The chant went on; the light, from where we stood, was steadily retreating, and we ventured forward. Judging our whereabouts as best we could, we made towards the choir and stumbled up some steps, placing ourselves eventually behind one of the pillars of the apse. And from this point, the whole proceeding was apparent.

At the west end the line of light was turning; fifty or sixty monks (about – and at a venture) habited in brown and carrying tapers, walking two and two, were moving up the central aisle towards us, headed by three, one with the cross between two others bearing heavy silver candlesticks with tapers, larger than those carried by the rest.

Reaching the chancel steps, they paused; the three bearing the cross and candlesticks stood facing the altar, while those following diverged to right and left and lined the aisle. The first to take up this position were quite young, some almost boys; they were succeeded gradually by older men, those at the tail of the procession being obviously aged and infirm.

And then a figure, white and slight, erect – a woman's figure – struck a startling note at the far end of the brown line, a note as startling as the shrieks which jarred recurrently, were jarring still against the chant.

A pace or two behind her walked two priests in surplices, and after them another, vested in a cope. And on the whole impassive company her presence, her disturbance, made no mark. For them, in fact, she wasn't there.

Neither was she aware of them. I doubt if to her consciousness, or mine, as she approached, grew definite, there was a creature in the place besides herself.

She moved and uttered her successive cries as if both sound and motion were entirely mechanical – more like a person in some trance of terror or of anguish than a voluntary rebel; her cries bespoke a physical revulsion into which her spirit didn't enter; they were not her own – they were outside herself; there was no discomposure in her carriage, nor, when we presently saw it, in her face. Both were distinguished by a certain exquisite hauteur, and this detachment of her personality from her distress impressed one curiously. She wasn't altogether real, she didn't altogether live, and yet her presence there was the supreme reality of the unreal scene, and lent to it, at least as I was viewing it, its only element of life.

She had, one understood, her part to play; she wasn't, for the moment, quite prepared; she played it later with superb effect.

As she came up with the three priests, the monks closed in and formed a semi-circle round them, while the priests advanced and placed themselves behind the monks who bore the cross and candlesticks, immediately below the chancel steps, facing the altar. They left her standing some few paces back, in the half-ring of sickly light shed by the tapers.

Now one saw her face. It was of striking beauty, but its age? One couldn't say. It had the tints, the purity of youth – it might have been extremely young, matured merely by the moment; but for a veil of fine repression which only years, it seemed, could possibly have woven. And it was itself – this face – a mask, one of the loveliest that spirit ever wore. It kept the spirit's counsel. Though what stirred it then, in that unique emergency, one saw – to what had stirred it, or might stir it gave no clue. It threw one back on vain conjecture.

Put the match of passion to it – would it burn? Touch it with grief and would it cloud, contract? With joy – and could it find, or had it ever found, a smile? Again, one couldn't say.

Only, as she stood there, erect and motionless, it showed the faintest flicker of distaste, disgust, as if she shrank from some repellent contact. She was clad, I think I said, from head to foot in a white linen garment; head and ears were covered too, the oval of the face alone was visible, and this was slightly flushed. Her screams were changing into little cries or moans, like those of a spent animal, from whom the momentary pressure of attack has been removed. They broke from her at intervals, unnoticed, unsuppressed, and now on silence, for the monks had ceased their chanting.

As they did so one realised the presence of these men, who, up to now, had scarcely taken shape as actualities, been more than an accompaniment – a drone. They shifted from a mass of voices to a row of pallied faces, each one lit by its own taper, hung upon the dark, or thrown abruptly, as it were, upon a screen; all different; all, at first distinct, but linked together by a subtle likeness, stamped with that dye which blurs the print of individuality – the signet of the cloister.

Taking them singly, though one did it roughly, rapidly enough, it wasn't difficult at starting to detect varieties of natural and spiritual equipment. There they were, spread out for sorting, nonentities and saints and devils, side by side, and what was queerer, animated by one purpose, governed by one law.

Some of the faces touched upon divinity; some fell below humanity; some were, of course, merely a blotch of book and bell, and all were set impassively toward the woman standing there.

And then one lost the sense of their diversity in their resemblance; the similarity persisted and persisted till the row of faces seemed to merge into one face – the face of nothing human – of a system, of a rule. It framed the woman's and one felt the force of it: she wasn't in the hands of men.

There was a pause filled only by her cries, a space of silence which they hardly broke; and then one of the monks stepped forward, slid into the chancel and began to light up the high altar. The little yellow tongues of flame struggled and started up, till first one line and then another starred the gloom.

Her glance had followed him; her eyes were fixed upon that point of darkness growing to a blaze. There was for her, in that illumination, some intense significance, and as she gazed intently on the patch of brilliance, her cries were suddenly arrested – quelled. The light had lifted something, given back to her an unimpaired identity. She was at last in full possession of herself. The flicker of distaste had passed and left her face to its inflexible, inscrutable repose.

She drew herself to her full height and turned towards the men behind her with an air of proud surrender, of magnificent disdain. I think she made some sign.

Another monk stepped out, extinguished and laid down his taper, and approached her.

I was prepared for something singular, for something passably bizarre, but not for what immediately occurred. He touched her eyes and closed them; then her mouth, and made a feint of closing that, while one of the two priests threw over his short surplice a black stole and started audibly with a *Sub venite*. The monks responded. Here and there I caught the words or sense of a response. The prayers for the most part were unintelligible: it was no doubt the usual office for the dead, and if it was, no finer satire for the work in hand could well have been devised. Loudly and unexpectedly above his unctuous monotone a bell clanged out three times. An *Ave* followed, after which two bells together, this time muffled, sounded out again three times. The priest proceeded with a *Miserere*, during which they rang the bells alternately, and there was something curiously suggestive and determinate about this part of the performance. The real action had, one felt, begun.

At the first stroke of the first bell her eyelids fluttered, but she kept them down; it wasn't until later at one point in the response, '*Non intres in judicium cum ancilla tua Domine*', she yielded to an impulse of her lips, permitted them the shadow of a smile. But for this slip she looked the thing of death they reckoned to have made of her – detached herself, with an inspired touch, from all the living actors in the solemn farce, from all apparent apprehension of the scene. I, too, was quite incredibly outside it all.

I hadn't even asked myself precisely what was going to take place. Possibly I had caught the trick of her quiescence, acquiescence, and I went no further than she went; I waited – waited with her, as it were, to see it through. And I experienced a vague, almost resentful sense of interruption, incongruity, when King broke in to ask me what was up.

He brought me back to Ella's presence, to the consciousness that this, so far as the spectators were concerned, was not a woman's comedy.

I made it briefly plain to them, as I knew something of the place and people, that any movement on our side would probably prove more than rash, and turned again to what was going forward.

They were clumsily transforming the white figure. Two monks had robed her in a habit of their colour of her order, I suppose, and were now putting on the scapular and girdle. Finally they flung over her the long white-hooded cloak and awkwardly arranged the veil, leaving her face uncovered; then they joined her hands and placed between them a small cross.

This change of setting emphasised my first impression of her face; the mask was lovelier now and more complete.

Two voices started sonorously, '*Libera me, Domine*', the monks took up the chant, the whole assembly now began to move, the muffled bells to ring again at intervals, while the procession formed and filed into the choir. The monks proceeded to their stalls, the younger taking places in the rear. The two who had assisted at the robing led the passive figure to the centre of the chancel, where the three who bore the cross and candlesticks turned round and stood a short way off confronting her. Two others, carrying the censer and *bénitier*, stationed themselves immediately behind her with the priests and the officiant, who now, in a loud voice began his recitations.

They seemed, with variations, to be going through it all again. I caught the '*Non intres in judicium*' and the '*Sub venite*' recurring with the force of a refrain. It was a long elaborate affair. The grave deliberation of its detail heightened its effect. Not to be tedious, I give it you in brief. It lasted altogether possibly two hours.

The priest assisting the officiant, lifting the border of his cope, attended him when he proceeded first to sprinkle, then to incense the presumably dead figure, with the crucifix confronting it, held almost like a challenge to its sightless face. They made the usual inclinations to the image as they passed it, and repeated the performance of the incensing and sprinkling with extreme formality at intervals, in all, I think, three times.

There was no break in the continuous drone proceeding from the choir; they kept it going; none of them looked up – or none at least of whom I had a view – when four young monks slid out, and, kneeling down in the clear space between her and the crucifix, dislodged a stone which must have previously been loosened in the paving of the chancel, and disclosed a cavity, the depth of which I wasn't near enough to see.

For this I wasn't quite prepared, and yet I wasn't discomposed. I can't attempt to make it clear under what pressure I accepted this impossible *dénouement*, but I did accept it. More than that, I was exclusively absorbed in her reception of it. Though she couldn't, wouldn't see, she must have been aware of what was happening. But on the other hand, she was prepared, dispassionately ready, for the end.

All through the dragging length of the long offices, although she hadn't stirred or given any sign (except that one faint shadow of a smile) of consciousness, I felt the force of her intense vitality, the tension of its absolute impression. The life of those enclosing presences seemed to have passed into her presence, to be concentrated there. For to my view it was these men who held her in death's grip who didn't live, and she alone who was absorbently alive.

The candles, burning steadily on either side the crucifix, the soft illumination of innumerable altar lights confronting her, intensified the darkness which above her and behind her – everywhere beyond the narrow confines of the feeble light in which she stood – prevailed.

This setting lent to her the aspect of an unsubstantial, almost supernatural figure, suddenly arrested in its passage through the dark.

She stood compliantly and absolutely still. If she had swayed, or given any hint of wavering, of an appeal to God or man, I must have answered it magnetically. It was she who had the key to what I might have done but didn't do. Make what you will of it – we were inexplicably *en rapport*.

But failing failure I was backing her; it hadn't once occurred to me, without her sanction, to step in, to intervene; that I had anything to do with it beyond my recognition of her – of her part, her claim to play it as she pleased. And now it was – a thousand years too late!

They managed the illusion for themselves and me magnificently. She had come to be a thing of spirit only, not in any sort of clay. She was already in the world of shades; some power as sovereign and determinate as Death itself had lodged her there, past rescue or the profanation of recall.

King was in the act of springing forward; he had got out his revolver; meant, if possible, to shoot her before closing with the rest. It was the right and only workable idea. I held him back, using the first deterrent that occurred to me, reminding him of Ella, and the notion of her danger may have hovered on the outskirts of my mind. But it was not for her at all that I was consciously concerned. I was impelled to stand aside, to force him, too, to stand aside and see it through.

What followed, followed as such things occur in dreams; the senses seize, the mind, or what remains of it, accepts mechanically the natural or unnatural sequence of events.

I saw the grave surrounded by the priests and blessed; and then the woman and the grave repeatedly, alternately, incensed and sprinkled with deliberate solemnity; and heard, as if from a great distance, the recitations of the prayers, and chanting of interminable psalms.

At the last moment, with their hands upon her, standing for a second still erect, before she was committed to the darkness, she unclosed her eyes, sent one swift glance towards the light, a glance which caught it, flashed it back, recaptured it and kept it for the lighting of her tomb. And then her face was covered with her veil.

The final act was the supreme illusion of the whole. I watched the lowering of the passive figure as if I had been witnessing the actual entombment of the dead.

The grave was sprinkled and incensed again, the stone replaced and fastened down. A long sequence of prayers said over it succeeded, at the end of which, the monks put out their tapers, only one or two remaining lit with those beside the Crucifix.

The priests and the officiant at length approached the altar, kneeling and prostrating there some minutes and repeating '*Pater Nosters*', followed by the choir.

Finally in rising, the officiant pronounced alone and loudly '*Requiescat in pace.*' The monks responded sonorously, 'Amen'.

The altar lights were one by one extinguished; at a sign, preceded by the cross, the vague, almost invisible procession formed and travelled down the aisle, reciting quietly the '*De Profundis*' and guided now, by only, here and there, a solitary light. The quiet recitation, growing fainter, was a new and unfamiliar impression; I felt that I was missing something – what? I missed, in fact, the chanting; then quite suddenly and certainly I missed – the scream. In place of it there was this '*De Profundis*' and her silence. Out of her deep I realised it, dreamily, of course she would not call.

The door swung to; the church was dark and still again – immensely dark and still.

There was a pause, in which we didn't move or speak; in which I doubted for a second the reality of the incredibly remote, yet almost present scene, trying to reconstruct it in imagination, pit the dream against the fact, the fact against the dream.

'Good God!' said King at length, 'what are we going to do?'

His voice awoke me forcibly to something nearer daylight, to the human and inhuman elements in the remarkable affair, which hitherto had missed my mind; they struck against it now with a tremendous shock, and mentally I rubbed my eyes. I saw what King had all along been looking at, the sheer, unpicturesque barbarity. What *were* we going to do?

She breathed perhaps, perhaps she heard us – something of us – we were standing not more than a yard or so away; and if she did, she waited, that was the most poignant possibility, for our decision, our attack.

Ella was naturally unstrung: we left her crouching by the pillar; later I think she partially lost consciousness. It was as well – it left us free.

Striking, as nearly as we could, the centre of the altar, working from it, we made a guess at the position of the stone, and on our hands and knees felt blindly for some indication of its loosened edge. But everywhere the paving, to our touch, presented an uneveness of surface, and we picked at random, chiefly for the sake of doing something. In that intolerable darkness there was really nothing to be done but wait for dawn or listen for some guidance from below. For that we listened breathless and alert enough, but nothing stirred. The stillness had become again intense, acute, and now a grim significance attached to it.

The minutes, hours, dragged; time wasn't as it had been, stationary, but desperately, murderously slow.

Each moment of inaction counted – counted horribly, as

we stood straining ears and eyes for any hint of sound, of light.

At length the darkness lifted, almost imperceptibly at first; the big rose window to the west became a scarcely visible grey blot; the massive piers detached themselves from the dense mass of shadow and stood out, immense and vague; the windows of the lantern just above us showed a ring of slowly lightening panes; and with the dawn, we found the spot and set to work.

The implements we improvised we soon discovered to be practically useless. We loosened, but we couldn't move the stone.

At intervals we stopped and put our ears to the thin crevices. King thought, and still believes, he heard some sound or movement; but I didn't. I was somehow sure, for that, it was too late.

For everything it was too late, and we returned reluctantly to a consideration of our own predicament; we had, if possible, to get away unseen. And this time luck was on our side. The sacristan, who came in early by the cloister door which we had entered by, without perceiving us, proceeded to the sacristy.

We made a rapid and effectual escape.

We sketched out and elaborated, on our way back to the town, the little scheme of explanation to be offered to our host, which was to cover an announcement of abrupt departure. He received it with polite credulity, profound regret. He ventured to believe that the *Señora* was unfortunately missing a unique experience – cities, like men, had elements of beauty, or of greatness which escape the crowd; but the *Señora* was not of the crowd, and he had hoped she would be able to remain.

Nothing, however, would induce her to remain for more than a few hours. We must push on without delay and put the night's occurrences before the nearest British Consul. She made no comments and admitted no fatigue, but on this point she was persistent to perversity. She carried it.

The Consul proved hospitable and amiable. He heard the story and was suitably impressed. It was a truly horrible experience – remarkably dramatic – yes. He added it – we saw him doing it – to his collection of strange tales.

The country was, he said, extremely rich in tragic anecdote; and men in his position earned their reputation for romance. But as to *doing* anything in this case, as in others even more remarkable, why, there was absolutely nothing to be done!

The laws of Spain were theoretically admirable, but practically, well – the best that could be said of them was that they had their comic side.

And this was not a civil matter, where the wheels might often, certainly, be oiled. The wheel ecclesiastic was more intractable.

He asked if we were leaving Spain immediately. We said, 'Perhaps in a few days.' 'Take my advice,' said he, 'and make it a few hours.'

We did.

Ella would tell you that the horror of those hours hasn't ever altogether ceased to haunt her, that it visits her in dreams and poisons sleep.

She hasn't ever understood, or quite forgiven me my attitude of temporary detachment. She refuses to admit that, after all, what one is pleased to call reality is merely the intensity of one's illusion. My illusion was intense.

'Oh, for you,' she says, and with a touch of bitterness, 'it was a spectacle. The woman didn't really count.'

For me it was a spectacle, but more than that: it was an acquiescence in a rather splendid crime.

On looking back I see that, at the moment in my mind, the woman didn't really count. She saw herself she didn't. That's precisely what she made me see.

What counted chiefly with her, I suspect, was something infinitely greater to her vision than the terror of men's dreams.

She lies, one must remember, in the very centre of the sanctuary – has a place uniquely sacred to her order, the traditions of her kind. It was this honour, satisfying, as it did, some pride of spirit or of race, which bore her honourably through.

She had, one way or other, clogged the wheels of an inflexible machine. But for the speck of dust she knew herself to be, she was – oh horribly, I grant you! – yet not lightly, not dishonourably, swept away.

MABEL E. WOTTON

THE FIFTH EDITION

HIS afternoon had not been a success. Miss Elliott, whom he particularly wanted to see, had not been 'at home', which was the more vexing as she knew he intended to call; and an overzealous friend had posted him a paper containing a paragraph which had greatly annoyed him, and which otherwise he might not have seen. So when he bethought himself that he was near Maxwell's rooms, he instantly resolved to look him up, and see if the young actor could not give him a stall somewhere or other for that night. He had an intense hatred of even a passing discomfort, and he wanted something fresh to think about.

Maxwell's rooms were in Museum Street, and Leyden had been in them so often, that when he found the street door ajar, he unceremoniously pushed it open, and walked up to the second floor. Probably the small maid-of-all-work had gone to post a letter, or to a near shop, and it was useless ringing a bell which would not be answered.

Once in the room the first thing that struck him was that Maxwell must have been tidying-up, – the next, that the transformation was too complete to be so interpreted. The numberless photographs which, grimed with dust, were wont to adorn the mantelpiece and the top of the hanging book-shelf which was always guiltless of books, were now conspicuous by their absence. The stacks of newspapers, which Leyden used to complain made locomotion difficult, had wholly vanished, together with the pipe-racks and the tobacco jars. The familiar furniture seemed set at more convenient angles, a few good engravings had been hung on the walls, and a work-basket yawned on the windowsill. On the table was a pot of daffodils, and a book. It was evident that Maxwell had at last fulfilled his weekly threat, and had betaken himself and his chattels elsewhere. It was equally evident that the room was now the property of a woman.

The intruder looked about him with approving eyes. It was all very quiet and restful, he thought, and the place had acquired a certain self-respecting atmosphere which results from turning a lodging into a home.

Wondering idly what manner of woman she was, he had turned to go, when the whim seized him to glance at the name of the paper-covered volume she had been reading. *Franklyn Leyden* looked boldly up at him from the title-page. It was one of his own books.

Does one require to be abnormally vain to glean pleasure from so slight a matter? Leyden, at all events, being by temperament depressed or elated by trifles too insignificant to weigh with other men, was vastly pleased with his little discovery; and when, farthermore, he noticed that some of his especially pet passages has been singled out for marginal marking, the thin lips, which the annoyances of the afternoon had drawn into a straight line, relaxed into their ordinary curves of weak good-nature. He felt that something pleasant was about to happen, when he caught the soft rustle of a woman's gown in the adjoining room, and when the folding-doors opened, and Maxwell's successor came suddenly upon her unexpected guest, he feigned a momentary unconsciousness of her presence.

She, for her part, gave a gasp of surprise, possibly of fright, and Leyden turned round instantly, hat in one hand, book in the other.

'Pray forgive my intrusion,' he began, in his most dulcet tones, though the situation lost most of its charm so soon as he faced her. She was old enough to have mothered the girl he had unwittingly pictured. 'I came up unannounced to call on my friend Maxwell, who used to lodge here until quite recently. Can you tell me what has happened to him? I had no idea he had moved.'

She only stared at him instead of replying. Into her cheeks there came the slow-growing, lovely flush of a woman who has retained the pure colouring of her otherwise lost youth.

'You are . . . You must be . . . Forgive me, but surely you are Mr. Leyden?' she said, at last.

The tone hurried, then lagged, as the words stumbled over each other in her eagerness.

'I have seen pictures of you . . . every one has seen them . . . and I love . . . I reverence your work. Won't you . . . Won't you stop a little while? It is not my fault I am not Mr. Maxwell.'

The glorious colour still flooding her face, and the ill-chosen, stammering words, were more than incense to Franklyn Leyden. It was for this he worked, and wrote, and had his somewhat indiscriminating being; it was for the attempt to baulk him of what he had grown to consider his due, that he could have strangled the paragraphist of that afternoon; and it was for the sake of her genuine hero-worship that he now forgave this woman her forty years and the lines on her careworn face, and cheerfully consented to do her bidding.

'Not Maxwell? No; that is my good fortune,' he assured her. 'You will think me very impertinent if I tell you the truth, but I was so charmed with the peaceful little home into which I had wandered, that I was quite longing to see its owner. You are,' he turned to the fly-leaf of the novel, 'you are Miss Suttaby?'

'Yes, I am Janet Suttaby.' She still stood by the inner room where she had paused on first seeing him. 'I will make enquiries about your friend. I know some gentleman left here on Saturday, and I think that was the name.'

'We will find out presently,' Leyden returned. He put down what he was holding, and pulled forward a chair. 'Can't we have our talk first? It was curious, wasn't it, that you should recognise me? The pictures must be very like.'

She surveyed him gravely as he leaned back in his seat, a fair-haired giant with china-blue eyes, and large hands which were extraordinarily white and mobile. When they had nothing else to work upon, the left was habitually fingering the lappet of his coat.

'You are younger than I thought,' she told him.

She still looked at him as if he were some god who had dropped from another planet, but her nervousness was decreasing.

'What drew me first to your book was its deep knowledge of suffering. I thought you much older, to have lived through so much.'

'Perhaps I am, actually, if with Bailey you "count time by hearthrobs,"' he said gently, while inwardly he was cogitating as to 'what the deuce she meant.'

Nothing amazed him so much about 'Wrecked' as the number of times he had been told how he had suffered. He could only explain it as a fresh witness to the extreme faithfulness with which he had reproduced that poor chap in Algiers of whom he had made copy.

'Tell me the especial points. Ah, yes, do tell me. Has sorrow visited you too?'

From the exceeding diffidence with which she answered him, he gathered that she had seldom been asked so directly personal a question. This was quite easy to understand, he acknowledged, for, now that the flush had gone, it was undeniable that Miss Suttaby was really a plain person. She was also uninteresting, which was worse, or at least he knew she would be found uninteresting by most people; and he recalled Kingsley's contention that it takes a noble soul to see beauty in an ordinary careworn face. For his own part, Miss Suttaby did interest him, and he found the pale face attractive.

She told him a little of her life, – the barest outlines merely, and even these were dragged from her, not indeed unwillingly, but as from one who was unaccustomed to talk of herself at all. Possibly she had never had time for our modern employment of thinking herself out, and appraising and cataloguing herself; possibly no one had ever cared to listen.

She was the daughter of a well-to-do farmer, who dying had left a second family to her charge, young, and cursed with the seeds of the lung trouble their mother had bequeathed them. Her life had been spent on these youngsters, whom she had tended, and watched, and slaved for, only to lose them one after another as they grew out of their teens. Bertie had lingered the longest, and Bertie had died last year.

Undoubtedly Franklyn Leyden made an admirable audience. Your good things might bore him, but your sad ones never, averred his friends, and in their whole-hearted enthusiasm they rarely noticed that all his kindnesses and all his consideration were called forth by what he saw, by what affected him personally. His best friend might be dying, and he would give him a wide berth for fear of a heart-ache; but if he came upon a little child who had tripped in the street, it would be impossible for him to pass it without attempted consolation. The child's wailing would have worried him else.

So betrayed by his curiosity in connection with the book

into hearing something of the troubles of this stranger, he was speedily and very genuinely concerned about them.

'I am so sorry! So very heartily sorry!' was his comment, and Janet Suttaby found herself murmuring grateful thanks.

She had recognised the sincerity of the tone, and few of us, thank God! question that deeper sincerity, or the lack of it, which the tone may hide.

By the time he went away they both felt that they knew more about each other than a dozen mere ordinary meetings could have told them; and if on her side at least this impression was quite wrong, that did not detract at all from its pleasure.

'I shall come and see you again quite soon,' he said, as they shook hands.

If he had been parting from Miss Elliott he knew he should have added, 'if I may', but one soon catches the trick of how to bow from a pedestal, and with many men it is learned in an hour.

'Thursday or Friday. H'm. Yes. I will come in on Thursday.'

It chanced, however, that Thursday, when it came, brought a pleasanter engagement, and it was not until a day or two later that he went to Museum Street. The result of which alteration in dates was to teach him the means by which Miss Suttaby earned her livelihood. She wrote.

'But not what *you* would understand by writing. There is no art about it,' she said ingenuously, when he accused her of keeping the fact a secret. 'I just string things together for bread and butter, and they take them in little cheap-looking papers of which you have probably never heard. Here is the latest.'

She pulled a weekly paper from under the pile of manuscript. It was one of the many serious-minded publications where religion, as understood by the particular sect the proprietor favours, is made palatable to every one but his staff.

'They give me seven-and-six a thousand, and I generally have to alter one-third, while they cut out another.' Miss Suttaby explained. 'But I know it is foolish to mind, for if I were fit for the magazines I should be paid more of course.'

'Meanwhile, you should not buy daffodils.'

'I don't in meat weeks. Daffodils mean bread and coffee; but I would rather. I am very strong.'

Leyden picked up the paper.

'Do you mind if I have a cigarette? I will smoke and read this, and you shall get on with your work. You can't before me? Oh, nonsense! I am going to make myself quite comfortable and at home, and you'll get quite used to me in a minute or two.'

The story proved far better than he had expected. The plot was hardly worth the very inferior type in which it was printed; but there were delicate little touches here and there in the working out, and a fair amount of originality was shown in the depicting of an old farmer who was represented in the rather blurred woodcut as a London dandy in the prime of life. It was difficult to make the right amount of allowance for editorial restrictions, but if she were given a free hand she would do well, he decided. Possibly she might achieve something really fine.

Then, because the easy-chair was comfortable, and to turn to his companion would have necessitated shifting his position, he left her to her writing for a bit longer, and began to think about his own affairs.

The book, – that confounded book! – how on earth was he to get it written? Two years ago he had been one of that band of young men whose names and productions are apt to become indistinctly glorious under the generic title of that of 'our younger writers'. He had tried his 'prentice hand at some small plays preparatory to taking the dramatic world by storm when he should be in the vein; and he had turned out two books of verse which not only sold as poems, but sold well. His publisher, who had seen too many versifiers perhaps to be especially impressed by this one, always declared that the soft voice and the white gesticulating hands were more responsible for the success than were the lines themselves; but as he only aired these opinions in private no harm was done, and certainly it was no fault of Leyden's that his personality was a good advertisement. Added to these slender pillars was the solid background of press work.

This had been his modest position when he had written 'Wrecked', but the book had dragged him several rungs up the literary ladder, and he was now a person whom a certain set of aspiring nobodies used to point out to each other at first-nights and other society functions, and whom the real somebodies tolerated in a good-humoured fashion as a hanger-on who might speedily become one of themselves.

In other words, his first novel had contained such real promise that the majority were enthusiastic: the minority awaited fruition. They wanted to see what his second story would be like, said divers of the critics. If Mr. Franklyn Leyden were wise he would comprehend that 'Wrecked' could only make an ephemeral reputation. If he wanted it sustained he must follow it up with something more equally written, and of more strength.

With this verdict Franklyn Leyden perfectly agreed. Indeed, he went farther, and told himself precisely wherein lay his weakness. He could not create. No one seemed to have discovered this as yet, for his critical powers were good, and his receptivity enormous; but unless some such chance came to him as that which had come during his fortnight's stay in Algiers, he knew that the book the reviewers wanted would never get written. Of course, to use Miss Suttaby's phrase, he could 'string things together' to a required length, but he knew perfectly that if he could not improve upon 'Wrecked', it would be far better for him to leave well severely alone.

Recalling it all as he sat quietly smoking, and watching the opposite houses through half-closed lids, he felt as if he almost owed Ned Jermyn a grudge for having decoyed him into his present position. The poor fellow had been dying at the hotel, when a chance had brought the two together, and possibly because he was weak and companionless, but more probably because of the other's intense sympathy of manner, he had told Leyden his life.

'It is a bit tragic, isn't it?' he had asked, with the indifference which besets a man who knows he will soon have ended his difficulties. 'I started with the ten talents of the parable, but I've made an even bigger wreck of my life than the chap who had only one. You might do worse than tip me into one of your books some day, eh, Leyden?'

And Leyden, considering the wisdom of the self-mocking suggestion, had taken him at his word, and immediately upon his return to England, he had 'tipped' poor Ned Jermyn, with all his sins and sorrows, into manuscript, and from manuscript they had emerged into print as soon after Jermyn's death as could be conveniently arranged. He had written it at a white heat, and the follies and the repentances . . . 'People always talk as if repentance implied remorse,' said the sick man querulously. 'I don't regret what I've gone through. I am only sorry I did not pull it off better'; . . . the darkened room, with the glaring sunlight outside glinting through a broken bit in the wooden shutters; the weary voice, and the inert hands, lying open on the coverlet, had all found faithful reproduction. Jermyn had been a lonely man, and reticent, so he said; and it was extremely unlikely that anyone who knew one side of his character, or one part of his life, would know anything of any other. An alteration of names and places afforded an extra safety, though after all, if the truth were discovered, it could not possibly matter to him, Leyden told himself. He had the man's permission, and everything depended on the fashion of narration. He did not think one iota the less highly of himself that purely original work was beyond him. It did not happen to be his especial forte, that was all. Only, of course, the lack of it was awkward, when it came to the question of a second novel.

'Deucedly awkward!' he repeated, mentally, and turned round at last to survey Miss Suttaby.

'I am afraid you have finished some time ago. I seem to have missed the sound of your pen.'

'Yes; some little time. I did not want to disturb you.'

He looked at her gratefully. He had always understood that women of the class from which she sprang put on their best clothes in which to receive guests, and that being taken by surprise rendered them miserable. Yet here was Miss Suttaby in the painfully shabby serge she had worn when he had first seen her; and it did not appear to occur to her to deplore the fact, or to conceal the ink-stain on her finger. Unwilling to relinquish his pre-conceived theories, he settled in his own mind that her mother must have come of gentle blood, and have married beneath her; while aloud he thanked her warmly for allowing him to be happy in his own way.

'. . . This is quite a little haven of refuge. The restfulness of it makes me terribly selfish,' he added, and watched to see if such obvious underrating of himself would bring a show of that lovely colour which had gratified him the time before. That she uttered no verbal disclaimer to vulgarise it, added to his pleasure. 'You look tired,' he said, solicitously, wondering the while what other chord he could touch upon to obtain so instantaneous a response.

Every man knows the satisfaction of telling a good story when he can confidently count upon an appreciative laugh;

and this feeling, which is perhaps mentally akin to the physical experience of a successful hunter, had been abnormally developed by Franklyn Leyden. It interested him if he were shut into a railway carriage with a complete stranger, to imagine of what mirth, for instance, or of what anger the man were capable; and then he would back himself within a given time to test the aptness of his theorising. The result of which apparently harmless piece of vanity was that he had grown to look upon his fellow-beings as so many pegs on which to hang his own emotions through the skilful drawing out of theirs; and it was largely owing to the fact that Winifred Elliott had declined to be viewed in this light, that their friendship had recently betrayed a tendency towards friction. At one time he had had an idea of marrying her, since she was quite the nicest girl . . . as a rule that was, of course, not when she contradicted . . . whom he knew; and in his heart he was attracted as strongly towards the class of ritual and ease and plenty, as are many of that class to the denizens of Bohemia. That idea had not died, though it was not prominently to the fore just at present, but meanwhile Miss Suttaby's 'reverence' made a pleasing change, and it fortified him in his resolution to give his girl-friend time to miss him, and then to write and tell him of the miss.

When Miss Suttaby owned that he was right, and that she was very tired, he proposed they should go for a drive, and, growing keener as she demurred, finally gained his way, and went out to fetch a hansom.

'You are good enough to think highly of me, so you must let me do some little thing to live up to the position,' he said, gaily.

His spirits had risen. He threw off all thought of his own worries, and of the unwritten book, and devoted himself to his companion.

'Can we go straight along Oxford Street? Why, of course

we can! I feel that, too, that there is no point in driving towards Hampstead, because one never walks there. In Oxford Street you can feel every inch of the way, "Ah, how often I have trudged you!" and your cab becomes a coach and four by comparison . . . If you don't like the sunset glinting straight into your eyes, you must screw yourself into a sheltered angle . . . You do like it? I am so glad, for, do you know, so do I! It seems to me as wicked to shut out the sunshine as the sound of a little child's laughter. The day is sure to come when you will pine for them both.'

Miss Suttaby drew a long breath. She seemed literally to be drinking in the soft spring breezes.

'I – I think this is *lovely*,' she said. 'I had never seen a famous writer until I saw you, and – please don't laugh! – I have never been in a cab until this afternoon.'

'Never been in a cab?'

'Not a hansom. When Bertie and I first came to London we took a four-wheeler to our lodgings, because of the luggage, and since then it has always been omnibuses or walking.'

'Nor seen a writer?'

She shook her head.

'Except in the Reading-Room perhaps, but then I did not know who they were.'

'Well, I never!' Leyden's astonishment vented itself in a prolonged stare. 'Miss Suttaby, we must positively shake hands at once. You are more refreshing than April itself. I am glad that the cab, at all events, is a good specimen of its kind.'

She hardly heard him as she leaned forward in undisguised enjoyment.

'How mauve the pavements look against the road. I never noticed that before. And aren't there quantities of flower-sellers? I wish I could give them, or someone, a happy hour in return for the one you are giving me.'

'You shouldn't wish that. You should just enjoy it.'

She looked round at him with a little laugh. It was the first he had heard from her, and it was musical.

'You are joking. The cream of the pleasure is the passing it on. Tonight I shall go upstairs to a sick girl on the top storey, and tell her of the colouring, and the wind which blows to-day as it used to blow over our fields. And of how it feels to be in the streets, and yet not to be tired, and not to be intent on getting somewhere else.'

'And of me?' asked Franklyn Leyden. 'See! We are nearing the park. Shall you tell her of me?'

It seemed a trick of Miss Suttaby's that she seldom answered questions which patently answered themselves. Her candid eyes spoke instead.

Later on, by way of amusing her, he began to talk of his fellow-workers, but this was hardly a success, and Leyden instantly felt that it was so, and desisted. He did not want to set them also on little pinnacles in her estimation, or his own height might thereby be lessened; and he could not tell her anecdotes, which, though possibly true, hardly tended to present them in a heroic light, when she met the attempt with such hurt wonderment.

'But *you* could not think that. You must be quoting. You always see the best in everybody.'

He was nettled, albeit flattered.

'We may raise an altar to Art, Miss Suttaby, but neither you nor I can insist that only the worthiest shall be altar-servers. Many of them have shirked their apprenticeship, and the consequences are as disastrous as I tell you.'

He was not quite sure what he meant, though he thought it sounded well. But he had often found that women made a beautiful translation from a very imperfect original, and he waited for her answer, knowing it would furnish the keynote to what she believed she had discovered in him.

'Yes, I see,' she said thoughtfully. They were on their return journey by now; the sunlight had faded and the wind was growing chill. 'You mean that unless Life has taught you servitude at her other altars, – at those of duty and self-sacrifice, and conquered longings, perhaps especially, – one should not dare approach to the high altar of Art. Of necessity one would have no fruits to lay upon it. Yes, it is a beautiful idea, and I quite see what you mean.'

'Exactly,' said Franklyn Leyden.

After that he saw her continually, since one must have somewhere to spend odd hours, and the friendship grew apace. From the first she had interested him, and the interest deepened as he formed whimsical theories concerning her.

Physically, he knew she was ageing long before her time. For her there would be no Saint Martin's summer to her days, when the audacities of youth should mellow into a middle age, which to many is as captivating, and to all far more gracious. Here there would be no tender dalliance with Time, for pressing anxiety and sharp actual need were already drawing upon her those gifts of furrowed cheeks and full-veined hands which he usually holds in patient reserve.

Yet this was merely physical; while in startling contrast to it, there looked out at him through the steadfast eyes, with their environing network of wrinkles, the girlish soul which circumstance had never allowed to grow.

The fancy proved arrestive. She had never had a lover in her life, – she told him so simply when the subject in its generalities came up between them one day in talk, – and the amazing candour of her gaze confirmed this statement. No woman's eyes, or so Leyden complacently told himself, as one who was a past master on such matters, no woman's eyes could have retained such absolute simplicity if they had ever dealt in the coquettish glances of youth, or had ever tried, and failed, to meet their lover in the first shy stages of her wooing. Something of the old sweetness and the old pain would always linger, ran his silent communings, and memories would make them their abiding place.

Despite the stretch of years between them, the temptation assailed him to flash into those eyes the love-light their serenity had never known, but strong though it was, he resisted it, applauding himself immensely for his self-denial, and offering a pious thanksgiving that he 'was not blackguard enough' to initiate so absorbing a study. After all, his judgment may not have been so wrong, for when all is said and done, such a matter is probably one of degree, and being the man he was, that he still contrived to leave her peace undisturbed, may doubtless be counted unto him for righteousness.

On other points he held there was no need for scruple. There must be a multitude of tones in her voice which had never been brought out, and which corresponded to the capacities in her which lay dormant. There must be a whole gamut of delicious laughter which with her lay dumb, but which with other women stretches from the soft cooing of babyhood to the suppressed chuckle of quite old age. Had she ever laughed from a gleeful sense of pulsing blood? or because skies were blue and grass was green? She never seemed to have had any individual existence at all, since with her it had always been bound up with and dominated by 'the others'.

Leyden set himself to liberate the imprisoned powers, and was rewarded in a fashion which was quaintly refreshing. It was as if one should rescue withered roses of a bygone summer from between the pages of an old book, and placing them in water, should find them suddenly a-bloom with fragrance and beauty.

It was about this time that he asked her if she would care to show him any of her manuscripts. He might possibly be able to procure her better payment than she usually received.

At all events he could try. He made the offer in pure good nature, but was secretly dismayed and inclined to back out of it, when she handed him a tattered pile of foolscap with the remark that she had submitted it to all the papers for which she worked, but that they would not even accept it on the ordinary terms of cutting and scoring what they pleased, and merely paying for the mutilated remainder.

'I am afraid it is very long; but if they took it as it is, it would mean ten pounds, and . . .'

'I understand,' said Leyden, kindly. 'I'll try to read it to-night; and you must not feel depressed about it. You are so absurdly humble-minded that it is quite possible you have not soared high enough in your efforts to place it, and that that is the reason it always comes back. Good-bye, Miss Suttaby. I will let you know very soon.'

That he did not redeem his promise, or indeed go near her for the next week, was due in both cases to not knowing what to say. He had begun the reading with scant interest, and with his mind reverting to the old farmer whom the woodcut had transmogrified, but speedily his attention was enchained, and, though her hand was not easy to read, he did not put down the manuscript until he had arrived at the last page.

'There is no art about it,' Miss Suttaby had said long ago when describing her writing, and he recalled her words now as a peculiarly apt criticism.

There was no art about it at all. She had produced no book before, and probably, if he could judge aright, and he thought he could, she would never produce one again. She had simply obeyed a forgotten mandate, and with perfect literalness. She had looked into her own heart, and written of what she found there, and what she wrote of was a great loneliness.

Her heroine was a deserted wife whose baby had died, – a woman who had revelled in intense happiness, who had passed through the first anguish of its loss, and who then had gone on enduring a twilight sort of existence, in which neither the one nor the other could ever touch her poignantly again. Her warmest greeting was at arm's-length now, being just a friendly hand-clasp instead of the old wealth of kisses, and this was typical of the changed attitude of her world. Everything was at arm's-length and never came right up to her, not even Death.

It was a miserable book, and in the latter part of it there was no relief, except that which was afforded by delicate little descriptions of country, where the wind seemed to blow as invigoratingly as she had said it blew over certain fields near the old home. But in spite of this monotony, and of the poverty of its construction, sometimes even of its language, it was a powerful book, because it bore so plainly the impress of truth.

Leyden returned to it again and again.

At first he refused to own to himself that his long doubt as to where his second novel was to come from, was now practically solved. He locked the thing away from him, and spent a day in strenous efforts to forget it. With the evening he had an idea which he dignified to the height of an aspiration, since it allowed him to run riot on a line of thought which otherwise must have stayed debarred. He would have another look at the story, he decided, and amuse himself by arranging in his own mind what he would have done with it if Miss Suttaby had died and bequeathed it to him for his personal property. He would alter the position of the chapters for one thing, and work up two or three of the minor characters to something more imposing than their present shadowy condition. Towards the middle he might possibly interpolate that odd experience of his last year at the Hague; though he was not quite sure of this, since, though the book wanted lengthening, it must be done with the utmost delicacy. And certainly he would cut out one or two of the passages where the pathos of the loneliness of the woman was, to his thinking, much overstrained. For example, one could hardly ask one's readers to accept the notion of a woman who was otherwise sane taking a roll of baby clothes to bed with her in lieu of the dead child for whom she roused herself by feeling in her sleep; and though she might conceivably prefer to starve herself rather than omit the buying of certain flowers at certain given seasons in memory of birthdays and the like, did it not border upon the ridiculous to imagine she would always soil two cups in the solitary tea-drinking, rather than see only the one upon the board, and wash up only the one when the meal was over?

For the rest there was but little to suggest; and again reminding himself that the whole thing was farcical in the extreme, and a whimsical impossibility which he was concocting for his private amusement, he finally put down the manuscript and began devising imaginary reviews.

Naturally, what would strike the critics most would be his extraordinary versatility. Between 'Wrecked' and this story, which was as yet unnamed, but which he should entitle 'The Loneliness of a Woman', the difference of their style and treatment would be amazing. That had been largely incident, – Ned Jermyn's voice recurred to him, and the weak chuckle with which he had congratulated himself on the fullness with which he had packed his life: this was almost wholly introspective, for even the sins of the husband, of which much more might have been made, were touched upon very lightly, since to the woman's purity they were unknown, save for results.

There was only one quality which, the reviewers would point out, largely dominated both books; and that . . . a smile stole over Franklyn Leyden's lips, and his hand hugged the lappet of his opened coat . . . that was his enormous sympathy with suffering.

Heigh – o! He stretched out his arms, and rose with a sigh. What was the use of such roseate dreams? The manuscript which had so enthralled him was not his, but hers. She should . . . He hesitated a moment, disputing the word his imagination had supplied. Enthralled? Had it enthralled him? Was he not really enthralled of the book as he would have made it, rather than of the book as it actually was? Now he came to think of it, she would probably have great difficulty in getting it published. She was unknown, for one thing: those who had already seen it had rejected it: it was crude and unusual. It was highly probable no one would take it, and it was more than probable that if they did, she would never make a penny by the transaction. Whatever its merits, it was undeniably a book to enhance a reputation rather than make one.

He felt that the ground was a good deal cleared by the time he arrived at this conclusion. Naturally, he must think only of what was best for her; and it was very evident that to drop himself out of the matter would be very far from best for her. Yet, how to work it? He spent more than a week in indecision; but his thoughts were not occupied with how he was to make the story his own, and yet be enabled to repeat his thanksgiving anent blackguardism. They were solely concerned, he told himself daily, with the consideration of Miss Suttaby's interests.

'We must collaborate,' he told her, when at length he betook himself to the dingy rooms in Museum Street. 'Your story is much too good to be lost; and I should think . . .'

Miss Suttaby did not wait for him to finish his sentence.

'Collaborate?' She uttered a joyful, quivering cry. 'You and I! Oh, Mr. Leyden, you must be joking! Why, it is like . . . like . . .'

All kinds of impossible similies presented themselves. It was like the sun-god asking a buttercup to ally its yellow gleams to his own. It was like . . . Oh! she did not know. She threw up her hands helplessly. Her eyes lost their gravity, and shone in bewildered excitement.

'Why not?' said Leyden quietly.

It was a pity her voice should have failed her just then, since she had seemed on the brink of a gratifying compliment. How extraordinary it was with this woman that her emotions seemed constantly getting in her way.

She had not even an elementary idea of using them gracefully, and if she ever cried, he felt convinced that instead of tears 'like summer showers', she would blot and blur her face in a manner which would be quite sufficient to alienate sympathy.

'You don't think it would be to our mutual advantage?'

Miss Suttaby laughed.

'No, I don't,' she said bluntly. 'If you really think there is any good in it . . .'

'I really do.'

'. . . it must either go back to the drawer until I have time to polish it, or . . .'

'You musn't do that,' Leyden cried sharply. 'You would spoil it. It is perfect as it is.'

Then he remembered that this was not what he had intended to say, because, of course, he did not think it.

'I mean, it is its unconsciousness which is its charm. You would only bungle it if you attempted improvement. But what is the alternative? "Or," you said.'

'Or you must take it,' said Miss Suttaby, quietly.

Leyden brought both his hands sharply down upon the table.

'Take it? What do you mean?'

'I mean, if there is anything worthy of your acceptance, please accept it.'

Leyden's charm of manner was somewhat apt to evaporate

when one came to know him well. When he had taken a friend's soundings, or believed he had taken them, and when in consequence his interest was upon the wane, quite unwittingly he saved himself for newer work. But those demurely spoken words brought it back with redoubled intensity.

'Miss Suttaby!' He leaned across the narrow table, and took one of the fast-ageing hands in both his own smooth ones. 'This is one of the most beautiful gifts I ever had in my life. The thought, I mean, not the story itself, for of course I would never take that. How good of you! How infinitely gracious! I – I really don't know what to say to you, you kindest of friends. You have robbed me of words.'

His warmth made her uncomfortable. She tried to withdraw her hand, and uneasily shifted her chair an inch or two.

'Robbed me of words!' murmured Leyden.

He wished she had not robbed herself of words as well. He would have liked her to look up at him with eyes becomingly humid, and tell him – what was indeed the truth – that he had done more for her, both in his book and in his friendship, than she could ever hope to repay. But as she said nothing of this, he was again obliged to break into ecstasy, grateful that he, at least, formed an appreciative audience to himself.

'Your generosity will make one of the red-letter days of my life. Your sweet sympathy . . .'

He paused. One cannot talk of sympathy to a woman who apparently does not want to listen. He released her hand.

'Miss Suttaby, let us strike a bargain. You say you are averse from collaboration. Probably you feel as I do, that it is not quite honest work. But let me strike a bargain with you. Let me buy this story from you out and out, and put it to what use I like. I think you said you might get ten pounds for it. I will give you thirty.'

'That would buy a head-stone,' Miss Suttaby said irrelevantly. She was oblivious of the fact that it would also buy bread and butter. 'I promised Bertie. He thought that just a grass mound looked like a labourer's at our home. Mr. Leyden, I know it is too much, but since you will not take it as a gift, why . . . Bertie . . .'

Leyden was as kindly as ever. He talked away her scruples, and shared her tremulous delight, and it was only when he was upon his feet, and saying good-bye, that he referred to the tale.

'I must cut a good deal, I am afraid. Now Huldah cuddling those baby-clothes in bed, weren't you drawing a *little* too much on your imagination, eh, Miss Suttaby?'

She did not answer him at once, and accustomed as he had grown to her unaccountable fits of confusion, he could not but be struck by the paling cheeks and downcast eyes.

'One gets worked-up, and forgets probabilities, I find. But frankly it did not strike me as reading quite sanely, you know.'

'I . . . I think a woman might, if her arms felt *very* empty,' said Miss Suttaby.

Her voice sounded oddly muffled.

'Good-bye,' said Leyden suddenly. 'Write to me if I can ever be of the slightest use to you, won't you? You promise? That's right! Good-bye.'

So it was she who had done that thing which he had branded in his own mind as preposterous! To women of her temperament, at least, it would read as supremely natural, and he was bound to confess that she had so amazed him that for aught he knew to the contrary they might form the generality. From that choked tone he had gathered much. Undoubtedly it was she, too, who had resorted to the ghastly fashion of preparing the solitary meal as if it were for two. He had been stupid, indeed, to think she could have evolved these and similar passages, when he knew her imagination to be so strictly limited. He would not cut a single line.

Next day he sent her ten pounds, with a promise of the remainder when the book should be out. He told her candidly he could not afford the whole of the amount at one fell swoop; and since he was invariably thoughtful in such matters, he tore up the cheque which she might have had some difficulty in cashing, and sent her notes instead.

Then he set to work in good earnest. Huldah should be no mere book-heroine, she should live. So far as he knew, the portrayal of a woman had never been done before in the only way in which fidelity is likely to be secured. She had never been drawn first by one who has suffered the actual suffering, and enjoyed the actual joys, and then by a second who has noted the visible results. She had never been the joint work of a woman dealing with the subtleties a man could not divine, and of a man writing of what a woman never notices.

He built upon Miss Suttaby's foundations, and for the purpose of keeping the work all of a piece and devoid of scrappiness, his material was Miss Suttaby herself. The narrowness and the pathos of the narrowness, the arrested growth of the gentle soul, her simplicities of movement and talk, – nothing of what he had observed escaped transmittal. He told himself she would never recognise her own portrait, and probably in this he was right, since people are mostly 'unexplored Africas' to themselves. Ask any ordinary person how he cuts the loaf at breakfast, and he will gape in speechless ignorance. He has not the faintest idea if he jumps to his feet and saws away energetically, if he produces dainty symmetrical slices, or attacks the first corner that presents itself. All that makes the homely act individual to the onlooker, has never struck the actor at all.

No, no, he would be quite safe, or he would not risk

wounding her for the world. And with all the reverence of which he was capable he went steadily on his way, until 'her book' grew into 'the book', and then to 'mine'. The last stage naturally saw its completion.

The following autumn and early winter found one man, at all events, blissfully content. Franklyn Leyden's new book had scored an immediate success, and the incense of adulation enveloped him in its clouds. It included, amongst other items, better business terms than he had expected, and a widely-advertised engagement to Lady Elliott's daughter, with whom he had long ago smoothed over old differences.

Once only had he heard from Miss Suttaby. She then wrote to tell him she had been ill, and unable to work. Would it be inconvenient to him to let her have at least a little of the money he had so generously promised? She gave a fresh address; two rooms were beyond her means.

Leyden was touched, and wrote back effusively, enclosing a couple of sovereigns. These were nothing to do with the sum she mentioned, he explained, but just a token of sincere friendship, which he begged her to accept in the spirit in which it was offered. In regard to what she asked, most certainly. He was only waiting until his royalties should have accumulated to allow of sending her a good round sum. It was all nonsense to refer to the paltry amount they had arranged: fifty pounds would be far nearer the mark. He could never forget the gift she had wished to make him, and was exactly as grateful as if he had thought it right to accept it – Remaining, 'ever faithfully', hers.

He found it such an expensive matter to be even contemplating marriage, that the carrying out of these benevolent intentions was unavoidably delayed; and when one day the post brought him a second appeal, he felt deservedly provoked. To worry him at such a time, after all he had done, and was still doing, for her, surely showed a lamentable lack of consideration.

So he left the pencil-written note severely unanswered, fixing in his own mind the publication of the fifth edition of the book as a suitable time for writing again to his whilom acquaintance, and for settling the matter once and for all. It would be out in a week or two.

He kept his word on the very day of its appearance, and went to call on her personally, remembering what pleasure it would give her to see him again, and wondering if she would greet him with that lovely slow-growing flush.

The month was April, and the sight of the flower-sellers in Oxford Street reminded him of how she had once longed to share with them her own exceeding happiness, and what an important event she had made of a cab drive. He must see how the time went, but if he could possibly manage it, he would ask her to come out with him for another drive today. Such trifles pleased her.

He had so vividly pictured the delighted surprise with which she would recognise her visitor, that on reaching his destination he was considerably taken aback at being informed she had 'gone away'.

Yes, she had gone away from London altogether. And, no, she had left no address. On these two points the grim-visaged woman was certain, and as she was the 'missus' of the house, as she carefully stated several times, who should be certain if not she herself? she ''ud like ter know'. She eyed him suspiciously the while, wondering what on earth he wanted with 'that Miss Suttaby'; wondering, too, if he took her to be 'flat enough' to admit to her lodger having died, especially when the alleged cause of 'practical starvation' was so humiliating for any respectable landlady.

'I wish I could 'elp you, sir, but I can't.'

Leyden thanked her courteously, and went away much

crestfallen. The saving to his pocket he did not weigh for one moment against the hurt to his feelings. That she should have gone and not told him! He could not understand it.

Presently his mortification faded into a kindly pity. She was piqued, he supposed, that he had not instantly replied, and had therefore adopted this extraordinary method of punishing him, heedless of the fact that she was also punishing herself. Well! well! How like a woman!

Here a passing carriage distracted his attention. By the time he reached home he was full of other thoughts. The whole episode had been too insignificant, and the heroine of it too homely to cut an enduring niche in his memory. Clearly it was no fault of his that she had chosen to drift out of his life.

So he simply forgot her.

It is probable that this is exactly what Miss Suttaby would have wished.

CONSTANCE FENIMORE WOOLSON

'MISS GRIEF'

'A conceited fool' is a not uncommon expression. Now, I know that I am not a fool, but I also know that I am conceited. But, candidly, can it be helped if one happens to be young, well and strong, passably good looking with some money that one has inherited and more that one has earned – in all, enough to make life comfortable – and if upon this foundation rests also the pleasant superstructure of a literary success? The success is deserved, I think: certainly it was not lightly gained. Yet even with this I fully appreciate its rarity. Thus, I find myself very well entertained in life: I have all I wish in the way of society, and a deep, though of course carefully concealed, satisfaction in my own little fame; which fame I foster by a gentle system of non-interference. I know that I am spoken of as 'that quiet young fellow who writes those delightful little studies of society, you know'; and I live up to that definition.

A year ago I was in Rome, and enjoying life particularly. I had a large number of my acquaintances there, both American and English, and no day passed without its invitation. Of course I understood it: it is seldom that you find a literary man who is good tempered, well dressed, sufficiently provided with money, and amiably obedient to all the rules and requirements of 'society'. 'When found, make a note of it'; and the note was generally an invitation.

One evening, upon returning to my lodgings, my man Simpson informed me that a person had called in the afternoon, and upon learning that I was absent had left not a card, but her name – 'Miss Grief'. The title lingered – Miss Grief! 'Grief has not so far visited me here,' I said to myself, dismissing Simpson and seeking my little balcony for a final smoke, 'and she shall not now. I shall take care to be 'not at home' to her if she continues to call.' And then I fell to thinking of Isabel Abercrombie, in whose society I had spent that and many evenings: they were golden thoughts.

The next day there was an excursion; it was late when I reached my rooms, and again Simpson informed me that Miss Grief had called.

'Is she coming continously?' I said, half to myself.

'Yes, sir: she mentioned that she should call again.'

'How does she look?'

'Well, sir, a lady, but not so prosperous as she was, I should say,' answered Simpson, discreetly.

'Young?'

'No, sir.'

'Alone?'

'A maid with her, sir.'

But once outside in my little high-up balcony with my cigar, I again forgot Miss Grief and whatever she might represent. Who would not forget in that moonlight, with Isabel Abercrombie's face to remember?

The stranger came a third time, and I was absent; then she let two days pass, and began again. It grew to be a regular dialogue between Simpson and myself when I came in at night: 'Grief today?'

'Yes, sir.'

'What time?'

'Four, sir.'

'Happy the man,' I thought, 'who can keep her confined to a particular hour!'

But I should not have treated my visitor so cavalierly if I had not felt sure that she was eccentric and unconventional – qualities extremely tiresome in a woman no longer young or attractive. If she were not eccentric, she would not have persisted in coming to my door day after day in this silent way, without stating her errand, leaving a note, or presenting her credentials in any shape. I made up my mind that she had something to sell – a bit of carving or some intaglio supposed to be antique. It was known that I had a fancy for oddities. I said to myself, 'She has read or heard of my "Old Gold" story, or else "The Buried God", and she thinks me an idealising ignoramus upon whom she can impose. Her sepulchral name is at least not Italian; probably she is a sharp countrywoman of mine, turning, by means of the present aesthetic craze, an honest penny when she can.'

She had called seven times during a period of two weeks without seeing me, when one day I happened to be at home in the afternoon, owing to a pouring rain and a fit of doubt concerning Miss Abercrombie. For I had constructed a careful theory of that young lady's characteristics in my own mind, and she had lived up to it delightfully until the previous evening, when with one word she had blown it to atoms and taken flight, leaving me standing, as it were, on a desolate shore, with nothing but a handful of mistaken inductions wherewith to console myself. I do not know a more exasperating frame of mind, at least for a constructor of theories. I could not write, and so I took up a French novel (I model myself a little on Balzac). I had been turning over its pages but a few moments when Simpson knocked, and, entering softly, said, with just a shadow of a smile on his well-trained face, 'Miss Grief'. I briefly consigned Miss Grief to all the Furies, and then, as he still lingered – perhaps not knowing where they resided – I asked where the visitor was.

'Outside, sir – in the hall. I told her I would see if you were at home.'

'She must be unpleasantly wet if she had no carriage.'

'No carriage, sir: they always come on foot. I think she *is* a little damp, sir.'

'Well, let her in; but I don't want the maid. I may as well see her now, I suppose, and end the affair.'

'Yes, sir.'

I did not put down my book. My visitor should have a hearing, but not much more: she had sacrificed her womanly claims by her persistent attacks upon my door. Presently Simpson ushered her in. 'Miss Grief,' he said, and then went out, closing the curtain behind him.

A woman – yes, a lady – but shabby, unattractive, and more than middle-aged.

I rose, bowed slightly, and then dropped into my chair again, still keeping the book in my hand. 'Miss Grief?' I said interrogatively as I indicated a seat with my eyebrows.

'Not Grief,' she answered – 'Crief: my name is Crief.'

She sat down, and I saw that she held a small flat box.

'Not carving, then,' I thought – 'probably old lace, something that belonged to Tullia or Lucrezia Borgia.' But, as she did not speak, I found myself obliged to begin: 'You have been here, I think, once or twice before?'

'Seven times; this is the eighth.'

A silence.

'I am often out; indeed, I may say that I am never in,' I remarked carelessly.

'Yes; you have many friends.'

'– Who will perhaps buy old lace,' I mentally added. But this time I too remained silent; why should I trouble myself to draw her out? She had sought me; let her advance her idea, whatever it was, now that entrance was gained.

But Miss Grief (I preferred to call her so) did not look as though she could advance anything: her black gown, damp with rain, seemed to retreat fearfully to her thin self, while her thin self retreated as far as possible from me, from the chair, from everything. Her eyes were cast down; an old-fashioned lace veil with a heavy border shaded her face. She looked at the floor, and I looked at her.

I grew a little impatient, but I made up my mind that I would continue silent and see how long a time she would consider necessary to give due effect to her little pantomime. Comedy? Or was it tragedy? I suppose full five minutes passed thus in our double silence; and that is a long time when two persons are sitting opposite each other alone in a small still room.

At last my visitor, without raising her eyes, said slowly, 'You are very happy, are you not, with youth, health, friends, riches, fame?'

It was a singular beginning. Her voice was clear, low, and very sweet as she thus enumerated my advantages one by one in a list. I was attracted by it, but repelled by her words, which seemed to me flattery both dull and bold.

'Thanks,' I said, 'for your kindness, but I fear it is undeserved. I seldom discuss myself even when with my friends.'

'I am your friend,' replied Miss Grief. Then, after a moment, she added slowly, 'I have read every word you have written.'

I curled the edges of my book indifferently; I am not a fop, I hope, but – others have said the same.

'What is more, I know much of it by heart,' continued my visitor. 'Wait: I will show you'; and then, without pause, she began to repeat something of mine word for word, just as I had written it. On she went, and I – listened. I intended interrupting her after a moment, but I did not, because she was reciting so well, and also because I felt a desire gaining upon me to see what she would make of a certain conversation which I knew was coming – a conversation between two of my characters which was, to say the least, sphinx-like, and somewhat incandescent as well. What won me a little, too, was the fact that the scene she was reciting (it was hardly more than that, though called a story) was secretly my favourite among all the sketches from my pen which a gracious public has received with favour. I never said so, but it was; and I had always felt a wondering annoyance that the aforesaid public, while kindly praising beyond their worth other attempts of mine, had never noticed the higher purpose of this little shaft, aimed not at the balconies and lighted windows of society, but straight up toward the distant stars. So she went on, and presently reached the conversation: my two people began to talk. She had raised her eyes now, and was looking at me soberly as she gave the words of the woman, quiet, gentle, cold, and the replies of the man, bitter, hot, and scathing. Her very voice changed, and took, though always sweetly, the different tones required, while no point of meaning, however small, no breath of delicate emphasis which I had meant, but which the dull types could not give, escaped an appreciative and full, almost overfull, recognition which startled me. For she had understood me – understood me almost better than I had understood myself. It seemed to me that while I had laboured to interpret, partially, a psychological riddle, she, coming after, had comprehended its bearings better than I had, though confining herself strictly to my own words and emphasis. The scene ended (and it ended rather suddenly), she dropped her eyes, and moved her hand nervously to and fro over the box she held; her gloves were old and shabby, her hands small.

I was secretly much surprised by what I had heard, but my ill humour was deep-seated that day, and I still felt sure, beside, that the box contained something which I was expected to buy.

'You recite remarkably well,' I said carelessly, 'and I am much flattered also by your appreciation of my attempt. But it is not, I presume, to that alone that I owe the pleasure of this visit?'

'Yes,' she answered, still looking down, 'it is, for if you had not written that scene I should not have sought you. Your other sketches are interiors – exquisitely painted and delicately finished, but of small scope. *This* is a sketch in a few bold, masterly lines – work of entirely different spirit and purpose.'

I was nettled by her insight. 'You have bestowed so much of your kind attention upon me that I feel your debtor,' I said, conventionally. 'It may be that there is something I can do for you – connected, possibly, with that little box?'

It was impertinent, but it was true; for she answered, 'Yes.'

I smiled, but her eyes were cast down and she did not see the smile.

'What I have to show you is a manuscript,' she said after a pause which I did not break; 'it is a drama. I thought that perhaps you would read it.'

'An authoress! This is worse than old lace,' I said to myself in dismay. – Then, aloud, 'My opinion would be worth nothing, Miss Crief.'

'Not in a business way, I know. But it might be – an assistance personally.' Her voice had sunk to a whisper; outside, the rain was pouring steadily down. She was a very depressing object to me as she sat there with her box.

'I hardly think I have the time at present –' I began.

She had raised her eyes and was looking at me; then, when

I paused, she rose and came suddenly toward my chair. 'Yes, you will read it,' she said with her hand on my arm – 'you will read it. Look at this room; look at yourself; look at all you have. Then look at me, and have pity.'

I had risen, for she held my arm, and her damp skirt was brushing my knees.

Her large dark eyes looked intently into mine as she went on: 'I have no shame in asking. Why should I have? It is my last endeavour; but a calm and well-considered one. If you refuse I shall go away, knowing that Fate has willed it so. And I shall be content.'

'She is mad,' I thought. But she did not look so, and she had spoken quietly, even gently. 'Sit down,' I said, moving away from her. I felt as if I had been magnetized; but it was only the nearness of her eyes to mine, and their intensity. I drew forward a chair, but she remained standing.

'I cannot,' she said in the same sweet, gentle tone, 'unless you promise.'

'Very well, I promise; only sit down.'

As I took her arm to lead her to the chair, I perceived that she was trembling, but her face continued unmoved.

'You do not, of course, wish me to look at your manuscript now?' I said, temporising; 'it would be much better to leave it. Give me your address, and I will return it to you with my written opinion; though, I repeat, the latter will be of no use to you. It is the opinion of an editor or publisher that you want.'

'It shall be as you please. And I will go in a moment,' said Miss Grief, pressing her palms together, as if trying to control the tremor that had seized her slight frame.

She looked so pallid that I thought of offering her a glass of wine; then I remembered that if I did it might be a bait to bring her here again, and this I was desirous to prevent. She rose while the thought was passing through my mind.

Her pasteboard box lay on the chair she had first occupied; she took it, wrote an address on the cover, laid it down, and then, bowing with a little air of formality, drew her black shawl round her shoulders and turned toward the door.

I followed, after touching the bell. 'You will hear from me by letter,' I said.

Simpson opened the door, and I caught a glimpse of the maid, who was waiting in the anteroom. She was an old woman, shorter than her mistress, equally thin, and dressed like her in rusty black. As the door opened she turned toward it a pair of small, dim, blue eyes with a look of furtive suspense. Simpson dropped the curtain, shutting me into the inner room; he had no intention of allowing me to accompany my visitor further. But I had the curiosity to go to a bay window in an angle from whence I could command the street door, and presently I saw them issue forth in the rain and walk away side by side, the mistress, being the taller, holding the umbrella: probably there was not much difference in rank between persons so poor and forlorn as these.

It grew dark. I was invited out for the evening, and I knew that if I should go I should meet Miss Abercrombie. I said to myself that I would not go. I got out my paper for writing, I made my preparations for a quiet evening at home with myself; but it was of no use. It all ended slavishly in my going. At the last allowable moment I presented myself, and – as a punishment for my vacillation, I suppose – I never passed a more disagreeable evening. I drove homeward in a murky temper; it was foggy without, and very foggy within. What Isabel really was, now that she had broken through my elaborately built theories, I was not able to decide. There was, to tell the truth, a certain young Englishman – But that is apart from this story.

I reached home, went up to my rooms, and had a supper. It was to console myself; I am obliged to console myself scientifically once in a while. I was walking up and down afterward, smoking and feeling somewhat better, when my eye fell upon the paste-board box. I took it up; on the cover was written an address which showed that my visitor must have walked a long distance in order to see me: 'A. Crief.' – 'A Grief,' I thought; 'and so she is. I positively believe she has brought all this trouble upon me: she has the evil eye.' I took out the manuscript and looked at it. It was in the form of a little volume, and clearly written; on the cover was the word 'Armor' in German text, and, underneath, a pen-and-ink sketch of a helmet, breastplate, and shield.

'Grief certainly needs armor,' I said to myself, sitting down by the table and turning over the pages. 'I may as well look over the thing now; I could not be in a worse mood.' And then I began to read.

Early the next morning Simpson took a note from me to the given address, returning with the following reply: 'No; I prefer to come to you; at four; A.. CRIEF.' These words, with their three semicolons, were written in pencil upon a piece of coarse printing paper, but the handwriting was as clear and delicate as that of the manuscript in ink.

'What sort of a place was it, Simpson?'

'Very poor, sir, but I did not go all the way up. The elder person came down, sir, took the note, and requested me to wait where I was.'

'You had no chance, then, to make inquiries?' I said, knowing full well that he had emptied the entire neighbourhood of any information it might possess concerning these two lodgers.

'Well, sir, you know how these foreigners will talk, whether one wants to hear or not. But it seems that these two persons have been there but a few weeks; they live alone, and are uncommonly silent and reserved. The people round there call them something that signifies 'the Madames American, thin and dumb.'"

At four the 'Madames American' arrived; it was raining again, and they came on foot under their old umbrella. The maid waited in the anteroom, and Miss Grief was ushered into my bachelor's parlour. I had thought that I should meet her with great deference; but she looked so forlorn that my deference changed to pity. It was the woman that impressed me then, more than the writer – the fragile, nerveless body more than the inspired mind. For it was inspired; I had sat up half the night over her drama, and had felt thrilled through and through more than once by its earnestness, passion, and power.

No one could have been more surprised than I was to find myself thus enthusiastic. I thought I had outgrown that sort of thing. And one would have supposed, too (I myself should have supposed so the day before), that the faults of the drama, which were many and prominent, would have chilled any liking I might have felt, I being a writer myself, and therefore critical; for writers are as apt to make much of the 'how', rather than the 'what', as painters, who, it is well known, prefer an exquisitely rendered representation of a commonplace theme to an imperfectly executed picture of even the most striking subject. But in this case, on the contrary, the scattered rays of splendour in Miss Grief's drama had made me forget the dark spots, which were numerous and disfiguring; or, rather, the splendour had made me anxious to have the spots removed. And this also was a philanthropic state very unusual with me. Regarding unsuccessful writers, my motto had been 'Vae victis!'

My visitor took a seat and folded her hands; I could see, in spite of her quiet manner, that she was in breathless suspense. It seemed so pitiful that she should be trembling there before me – a woman so much older than I was, a woman who possessed the divine spark of genius, which I was by no means sure (in spite of my success) had been granted to me – that I felt as if I ought to go down on my knees before her, and entreat her to take her proper place of supremacy at once. But there! one does not go down on one's knees, combustively, as it were, before a woman over fifty, plain in feature, thin, dejected, and ill dressed. I contented myself with taking her hands (in their miserable old gloves) in mine, while I said cordially, 'Miss Crief, your drama seems to me full of original power. It has roused my enthusiasm: I sat up half the night reading it.'

The hands I held shook, but something (perhaps a shame for having evaded the knees business) made me tighten my hold and bestow upon her also a reassuring smile. She looked at me for a moment, and then, suddenly and noiselessly, tears rose and rolled down her cheeks. I dropped her hands and retreated. I had not thought her tearful: on the contrary, her voice and face had seemed rigidly controlled. But now here she was bending herself over the side of the chair with her head resting on her arms, not sobbing aloud, but her whole frame shaken by the strength of her emotion. I rushed for a glass of wine; I pressed her to take it. I did not quite know what to do, but, putting myself in her place, I decided to praise the drama; and praise it I did. I do not know when I have used so many adjectives. She raised her head and began to wipe her eyes.

'Do take the wine,' I said, interrupting myself in my cataract of language.

'I dare not,' she answered; then added humbly, 'that is, unless you have a biscuit here or a bit of bread.'

I found some biscuit; she ate two, and then slowly drank the wine, while I resumed my verbal Niagara. Under its influence – and that of the wine too, perhaps – she began to show new life. It was not that she looked radiant – she could not – but simply that she looked warm. I now perceived what had been the principal discomfort of her appearance heretofore: it was that she had looked all the time as if suffering from cold.

At last I could think of nothing more to say, and stopped. I really admired the drama, but I thought I had exerted myself sufficiently as an anti-hysteric, and that adjectives enough, for the present at least, had been administered. She had put down her empty wineglass, and was resting her hands on the broad cushioned arms of her chair with, for a thin person, a sort of expanded content.

'You must pardon my tears,' she said, smiling; 'it was the revulsion of feeling. My life was at a low ebb: if your sentence had been against me, it would have been my end.'

'Your end?'

'Yes, the end of my life; I should have destroyed myself.'

'Then you would have been a weak as well as wicked woman,' I said in a tone of disgust. I do hate sensationalism.

'Oh no, you know nothing about it. I should have destroyed only this poor worn tenement of clay. But I can well understand how *you* would look upon it. Regarding the desirableness of life, the prince and the beggar may have different opinions. We will say no more of it, but talk of the drama instead.' As she spoke the word 'drama' a triumphant brightness came into her eyes.

I took the manuscript from a drawer and sat down beside her. 'I suppose you know that there are faults,' I said, expecting ready acquiescence.

'I was not aware that there were any,' was her gentle reply.

Here was a beginning! After all my interest in her – and, I may say under the circumstances, my kindness – she received me in this way! However, my belief in her genius was too sincere to be altered by her whimsies; so I persevered. 'Let us go over it together,' I said. 'Shall I read it to you, or will you read it to me?'

'I will not read it, but recite it.'

'That will never do; you will recite it so well that we shall see only the good points, and what we have to concern ourselves with now is the bad ones.'

'I will recite it,' she repeated.

'Now, Miss Crief,' I said bluntly, 'for what purpose did you come to me? Certainly not merely to recite: I am no stage manager. In plain English, was it not your idea that I might help you in obtaining a publisher?'

'Yes, yes,' she answered, looking at me apprehensively, all her old manner returning.

I followed up my advantage, opened the little paper volume and began. I first took the drama line by line, and spoke of the faults of expression and structure; then I turned back and touched upon two or three glaring impossibilities in the plot. 'Your absorbed interest in the motive of the whole no doubt made you forget these blemishes,' I said apologetically.

But, to my surprise, I found that she did not see the blemishes – that she appreciated nothing I had said, comprehended nothing. Such unaccountable obtuseness puzzled me. I began again, going over the whole with even greater minuteness and care. I worked hard: the perspiration stood in beads upon my forehead as I struggled with her – what shall I call it – obstinacy? But it was not exactly obstinacy. She simply could not see the faults of her own work, any more than a blind man can see the smoke that dims a patch of blue sky. When I had finished my task the second time, she still remained as gently impassive as before. I leaned back in my chair exhausted, and looked at her.

Even then she did not seem to comprehend (whether she agreed with it or not) what I must be thinking. 'It is such a heaven to me that you like it!' she murmured dreamily, breaking the silence. Then, with more animation, 'And *now* you will let me recite it?'

I was too weary to oppose her; she threw aside her shawl and bonnet, and standing in the centre of the room, began.

And she carried me along with her: all the strong passages were doubly strong when spoken, and the faults, which seemed nothing to her, were made by her earnestness to seem nothing to me, at least for that moment. When it was ended, she stood looking at me with a triumphant smile.

'Yes,' I said, 'I like it, and you see that I do. But I like it because my taste is peculiar. To me originality and force are everything – perhaps because I have them not to any marked degree myself – but the world at large will not overlook as I do your absolutely barbarous shortcomings on account of them. Will you trust me to go over the drama and correct it at my pleasure?' This was a vast deal for me to offer; I was surprised at myself.

'No,' she answered softly, still smiling. 'There shall not be so much as a comma altered.' Then she sat down and fell into a reverie as though she were alone.

'Have you written anything else?' I said after a while, when I had become tired of the silence.

'Yes.'

'Can I see it? Or is it *them*?'

'It is *them*. Yes, you can see all.'

'I will call upon you for the purpose.'

'No, you must not,' she said, coming back to the present nervously. 'I prefer to come to you.'

At this moment Simpson entered to light the room, and busied himself rather longer than was necessary over the task. When he finally went out, I saw that my visitor's manner had sunk into its former depression: the presence of the servant seemed to have chilled her.

'When did you say I might come?' I repeated, ignoring her refusal.

'I did not say it. It would be impossible.'

'Well, then, when will you come here?' There was, I fear, a trace of fatigue in my tone.

'At your good pleasure, sir,' she answered humbly.

My chivalry was touched by this: after all, she was a woman. 'Come tomorrow,' I said. 'By the way, come and dine with me then; why not?' I was curious to see what she would reply.

'Why not, indeed? Yes, I will come. I am forty-three: I might have been your mother.'

This was not quite true, as I am over thirty: but I look young, while she – Well, I had thought her over fifty. 'I can hardly call you "mother", but we might compromise upon "aunt",' I said, laughing. 'Aunt what?'

'My name is Aaronna,' she gravely answered. 'My father was much disappointed that I was not a boy, and gave me as nearly as possible the name he had prepared – Aaron.'

'Then come and dine with me tomorrow, and bring with you the other manuscripts, Aaronna,' I said, amused at the quaint sound of the name. On the whole, I did not like 'aunt'.

'I will come,' she answered.

It was twilight and still raining, but she refused all offers of escort or carriage, departing with her maid, as she had come, under the brown umbrella. The next day we had the dinner. Simpson was astonished – and more than astonished, grieved – when I told him that he was to dine with the maid; but he could not complain in words, since my own guest, the mistress, was hardly more attractive. When our preparations were complete, I could not help laughing: the two prim little tables, one in the parlour and one in the anteroom, and Simpson disapprovingly going back and forth between them, were irresistible.

I greeted my guest hilariously when she arrived, and, fortunately, her manner was not quite so depressed as usual: I could never have accorded myself with a tearful mood. I had thought that perhaps she would make, for the occasion, some change in her attire; I have never known a woman who had not some scrap of finery, however small, in reserve for that unexpected occasion of which she is ever dreaming. But no: Miss Grief wore the same black gown, unadorned and unaltered. I was glad that there was no rain that day, so that the skirt did not at least look so damp and rheumatic.

She ate quietly, almost furtively, yet with a good appetite, and she did not refuse the wine. Then, when the meal was over and Simpson had removed the dishes, I asked for the new manuscripts. She gave me an old green copybook filled with short poems, and a prose sketch by itself; I lit a cigar and sat down at my desk to look them over.

'Perhaps you will try a cigarette?' I suggested, more for amusement than anything else, for there was not a shade of Bohemianism about her; her whole appearance was puritanical.

'I have not yet succeeded in learning to smoke.'

'You have tried?' I said, turning round.

'Yes: Serena and I tried, but we did not succeed.'

'Serena is your maid?'

'She lives with me.'

I was seized with inward laughter, and began hastily to look over her manuscripts with my back toward her, so that she might not see it. A vision had risen before me of those two forlorn women, alone in their room with locked doors, patiently trying to acquire the smoker's art.

But my attention was soon absorbed by the papers before

me. Such a fantastic collection of words, lines, and epithets I had never before seen, or even in dreams imagined. In truth, they were like the work of dreams: they were *Kubla Khan*, only more so. Here and there was radiance like the flash of a diamond, but each poem, almost each verse and line, was marred by some fault or lack which seemed wilful perversity, like the work of an evil sprite. It was like a case of jeweller's wares set before you, with each ring unfinished, each bracelet too large or too small for its purpose, each breastpin without its fastening, each necklace purposely broken. I turned the pages, marvelling. When about half an hour had passed, and I was leaning back for a moment to light another cigar, I glanced toward my visitor. She was behind me, in an easy-chair before my small fire, and she was – fast asleep! In the relaxation of her unconsciousness I was struck anew by the poverty her appearance expressed; her feet were visible, and I saw the miserable worn old shoes which hitherto she had kept concealed.

After looking at her for a moment, I returned to my task and took up the prose story; in prose she must be more reasonable. She was less fantastic perhaps, but hardly more reasonable. The story was that of a profligate and common-place man forced by two of his friends, in order not to break the heart of a dying girl who loves him, to live up to a high imaginary ideal of himself which her pure but mistaken mind has formed. He has a handsome face and sweet voice, and repeats what they tell them. Her long, slow decline and happy death, and his own inward ennui and profound weariness of the rôle he has to play, made the vivid points of the story. So far, well enough, but here was the trouble: through the whole narrative moved another character, a physician of tender heart and exquisite mercy, who practiced murder as a fine art, and was regarded (by the author) as a second Messiah! This was monstrous. I read it through twice, and threw it down; then, fatigued, I turned round and leaned back, waiting for her to wake. I could see her profile against the dark hue of the easy chair.

Presently she seemed to feel my gaze, for she stirred, then opened her eyes. 'I have been asleep,' she said, rising hurriedly.

'No harm in that, Aaronna.'

But she was deeply embarrassed and troubled, much more so than the occasion required; so much so, indeed, that I turned the conversation back upon the manuscripts as a diversion. 'I cannot stand that doctor of yours,' I said, indicating the prose story; 'no one would. You must cut him out.'

Her self-possession returned as if by magic. 'Certainly not,' she answered haughtily.

'Oh, if you do not care – I had laboured under the impression that you were anxious these things should find a purchaser.'

'I am, I am,' she said, her manner changing to deep humility with wonderful rapidity. With such alternations of feeling as this sweeping over her like great waves, no wonder she was old before her time.

'Then you must take out that doctor.'

'I am willing, but do not know how,' she answered, pressing her hands together helplessly. 'In my mind he belongs to the story so closely that he cannot be separated from it.'

Here Simpson entered, bringing a note for me: it was a line from Mrs. Abercrombie inviting me for that evening – an unexpected gathering, and therefore likely to be all the more agreeable. My heart bounded in spite of me; I forgot Miss Grief and her manuscripts for the moment as completely as though they had never existed. But, bodily, being still in the same room with her, her speech brought me back to the present.

'You have had good news?' she said.

'Oh no, nothing especial – merely an invitation.'

'But good news also,' she repeated. 'And now, as for me, I must go.'

Not supposing that she would stay much later in any case, I had that morning ordered a carriage to come for her at about that hour. I told her this. She made no reply beyond putting on her bonnet and shawl.

'You will hear from me soon,' I said; 'I shall do all I can for you.'

She had reached the door, but before opening it she stopped, turned and extended her hand. 'You are good,' she said: 'I give you thanks. Do not think me ungrateful or envious. It is only that you are young, and I am so – so old.' Then she opened the door and passed through the anteroom without pause, her maid accompanying her and Simpson with gladness lighting the way. They were gone. I dressed hastily and went out – to continue my studies in psychology.

Time passed; I was busy, amused and perhaps a little excited (sometimes psychology is exciting). But, though much occupied with my own affairs, I did not altogether neglect my self-imposed task regarding Miss Grief. I began by sending her prose story to a friend, the editor of a monthly magazine, with a letter making a strong plea for its admittance. It should have a chance first on its own merits. Then I forwarded the drama to a publisher, also an acquaintance, a man with a taste for phantasms and a soul above mere common popularity, as his own coffers knew to their cost. This done, I waited with conscience clear.

Four weeks passed. During this waiting period I heard nothing from Miss Grief. At last one morning came a letter from my editor. 'The story has force, but I cannot stand that doctor,' he wrote. 'Let her cut him out, and I might print it.' Just what I myself had said. The package lay there on my table, travel worn and grimed; a returned manuscript is, I think, the most melancholy object on earth. I decided to wait, before writing to Aaronna, until the second letter was received. A week later it came. 'Armor' was declined. The publisher had been 'impressed' by the power displayed in certain passages, but the 'impossibilities of the plot' rendered it 'unavailable for publication' – in fact, would 'bury it in ridicule' if brought before the public, a public 'lamentably' fond of amusement, 'seeking it, undaunted, even in the cannon's mouth.' I doubt if he knew himself what he meant. But one thing, at any rate, was clear: 'Armor' was declined.

Now, I am, as I have remarked before, a little obstinate. I was determined that Miss Grief's work should be received. I would alter and improve it myself, without letting her know: the end justified the means. Surely the sieve of my own good taste, whose mesh had been pronounced so fine and delicate, would serve for two. I began; and utterly failed.

I set to work first upon 'Armor'. I amended, altered, left out, put in, pieced, condensed, lengthened; I did my best, and all to no avail. I could not succeed in completing anything that satisfied me, or that approached, in truth, Miss Grief's own work just as it stood. I suppose I went over that manuscript twenty times: I covered sheets of paper with my copies. But the obstinate drama refused to be corrected; as it was it must stand or fall.

Wearied and annoyed, I threw it aside and took up the prose story: that would be easier. But, to my surprise, I found that that apparently gentle 'doctor' would not out: he was so closely interwoven with every part of the tale that to take him out was like taking out one especial figure in a carpet: that is, impossible, unless you unravel the whole. At last I did unravel the whole, and then the story was no longer good, or Aaronna's: it was weak, and mine. All this took time, for of course I had much to do in connection with my own life and tasks. But, though slowly and at my leisure, I really did try my best as regarded Miss Grief, and without success. I was forced at last to make up my mind that either my own powers were not equal to the task, or else that her perversities were as essential a part of her work as her inspirations, and not to be separated from it. Once during this period I showed two of the short poems to Isabel, withholding of course the writer's name. 'They were written by a woman,' I explained.

'Her mind must have been disordered, poor thing!' Isabel said in her gentle way when she returned them – 'at least, judging by these. They are hopelessly mixed and vague.'

Now, they were not vague so much as vast. But I knew that I could not make Isabel comprehend it, and (so complex a creature is man) I do not know that I wanted her to comprehend it. These were the only ones in the whole collection that I would have shown her, and I was rather glad that she did not like even these. Not that poor Aaronna's poems were evil: they were simply unrestrained, large, vast, like the skies or the wind. Isabel was bounded on all sides, like a violet in a garden bed. And I liked her so.

One afternoon, about the time when I was beginning to see that I could not 'improve' Miss Grief, I came upon the maid. I was driving, and she had stopped on the crossing to let the carriage pass. I recognised her at a glance (by her general forlornness), and called to the driver to stop. 'How is Miss Grief?' I said. 'I have been intending to write to her for some time.'

'And your note, when it comes,' answered the old woman on the crosswalk fiercely, 'she shall not see.'

'What?'

'I say she shall not see it. Your patronising face shows that you have no good news, and you shall not rack and stab her any more on *this* earth, please God, while I have authority.'

'Who has racked or stabbed her, Serena?'

'Serena, indeed! Rubbish! I'm no Serena: I'm her aunt. And as to who has racked and stabbed her, I say you, *you* – YOU literary men!' She had put her old head inside my carriage, and flung out these words at me in a shrill, menacing tone. 'But she shall die in peace in spite of you,' she continued. 'Vampires! you take her ideas and fatten on them, and leave her to starve. You know you do – *you* who have had her poor manuscripts these months and months!'

'Is she ill?' I asked in real concern, gathering that much at least from the incoherent tirade.

'She is dying,' answered the desolate old creature, her voice softening and her dim eyes filling with tears.

'Oh, I trust not. Perhaps something can be done. Can I help you in any way?'

'In all ways if you would,' she said, breaking down and beginning to sob weakly, with her head resting on the sill of the carriage window. 'Oh, what have we not been through together, we two! Piece by piece I have sold all.'

I am goodhearted enough, but I do not like to have old women weeping across my carriage door. I suggested, therefore, that she should come inside and let me take her home. Her shabby old skirt was soon beside me, and, following her directions, the driver turned toward one of the most wretched quarters of the city, the abode of poverty, crowded and unclean. Here, in a large bare chamber up many flights of stairs, I found Miss Grief.

As I entered I was startled: I thought she was dead. There seemed no life present until she opened her eyes, and even then they rested upon us vaguely, as though she did not know who we were. But as I approached a light came into them: she recognised me, and this sudden revivification, this return of the soul to the almost deserted body, was the most wonderful thing I ever saw. 'You have good news of the drama?' she whispered as I bent over her: 'tell me. I *know* you have good news.'

What was I to answer? Pray, what would you have answered, puritan?

'Yes, I have good news, Aaronna,' I said. 'The drama will appear.' (And who knows? Perhaps it will in some other world.)

She smiled, and her now brilliant eyes did not leave my face.

'He knows I'm your aunt: I told him,' said the old woman, coming to the bedside.

'Did you?' whispered Miss Grief, still gazing at me with a smile. 'Then please, dear Aunt Martha, give me something to eat.'

Aunt Martha hurried across the room, and I followed her. 'It's the first time she's asked for food in weeks,' she said in a husky tone.

She opened a cupboard door vaguely, but I could see nothing within. 'What have you for her?' I asked with some impatience, though in a low voice.

'Please God, nothing!' answered the poor old woman, hiding her reply and her tears behind the broad cupboard door. 'I was going out to get a little something when I met you.'

'Good Heavens! is it money you need? Here, take this and send; or go yourself in the carriage waiting below.'

She hurried out breathless, and I went back to the bedside, much disturbed by what I had seen and heard. But Miss Grief's eyes were full of life, and as I sat down beside her she whispered earnestly, 'Tell me.'

And I did tell her – a romance invented for the occasion. I venture to say that none of my published sketches could compare with it. As for the lie involved, it will stand among my few good deeds, I know, at the judgment bar.

And she was satisfied. 'I have never known what it was,' she whispered, 'to be fully happy until now.' She closed her eyes, and when the lids fell I again thought that she had passed away. But no, there was still pulsation in her small, thin wrist. As she perceived my touch she smiled. 'Yes, I am happy,' she said again, though without audible sound.

The old aunt returned; food was prepared, and she took some. I myself went out after wine that should be rich and pure. She rallied a little, but I did not leave her: her eyes dwelt upon me and compelled me to stay, or rather my conscience compelled me. It was a damp night, and I had a little fire made. The wine, fruit, flowers, and candles I had ordered made the bare place for the time being bright and fragrant. Aunt Martha dozed in her chair from sheer fatigue – she had watched many nights – but Miss Grief was awake, and I sat beside her.

'I make you my executor,' she murmured, 'as to the drama. But my other manuscripts place, when I am gone, under my head, and let them be buried with me. They are not many – those you have and these. See!'

I followed her gesture, and saw under her pillows the edges of two more copybooks like the one I had. 'Do not look at them – my poor dead children!' she said tenderly. 'Let them depart with me – unread, as I have been.'

Later she whispered, 'Did you wonder why I came to you? It was the contrast. You were young – strong – rich – praised – loved – successful: all that I was not. I wanted to look at you – and imagine how it would feel. You had success – but I had the greater power. Tell me, did I not have it?'

'Yes, Aaronna.'

'It is all in the past now. But I am satisfied.'

After another pause she said with a faint smile, 'Do you remember when I fell asleep in your parlour? It was the good and rich food. It was so long since I had had food like that!'

I took her hand and held it, conscience stricken, but now she hardly seemed to perceive my touch. 'And the smoking?' she whispered. 'Do you remember how you laughed? I saw it. But I had heard that smoking soothed – that one was no longer tired and hungry – with a cigar.'

In little whispers of this sort, separated by long rests and pauses, the night passed. Once she asked if her aunt was asleep, and when I answered in the affirmative she said, 'Help her to return home – to America: the drama will pay for it. I ought never to have brought her away.'

I promised, and she resumed her bright-eyed silence.

I think she did not speak again. Toward morning the change came, and soon after sunrise, with her old aunt kneeling by her side, she passed away.

All was arranged as she had wished. Her manuscripts, covered with violets, formed her pillow. No one followed her to the grave save her aunt and myself; I thought she would prefer it so. Her name was not 'Crief', after all, but 'Moncrief'; I saw it written out by Aunt Martha for the coffin plate, as follows: 'Aaronna Moncrief, aged forty-three years, two months, and eight days.'

I never knew more of her history than is written here. If there was more that I might have learned, it remained unlearned, for I did not ask.

And the drama? I keep it here in this locked case. I could have had it published at my own expense; but I think that now she knows its faults herself, perhaps, and would not like it.

I keep it; and, once in a while, I read it over – not as a *memento mori* exactly, but rather as a memento of my own good fortune, for which I should continually give thanks. The want of one grain made all her work void, and that one grain was given to me. She, with the greater power, failed – I, with the less, succeeded. But no praise is due to me for that. When

I die 'Armor' is to be destroyed unread: not even Isabel is to see it. For women will misunderstand each other; and, dear and precious to me as my sweet wife is, I could not bear that she or anyone should cast so much as a thought of scorn upon the memory of the writer, upon my poor dead, 'unavailable', unaccepted 'Miss Grief'.

VERNON LEE

LADY TAL

THE church of the Salute, with its cupolas and volutes, stared in at the long windows, white, luminous, spectral. A white carpet of moonlight stretched to where they were sitting, with only one lamp lit, for fear of mosquitoes. All the remoter parts of the vast drawing-room were deep in gloom; you were somehow conscious of the paintings and stuccos of the walls and vaulted ceilings without seeing them. From the canal rose plash of oar, gondolier's cry, and distant guitar twang and quaver of song; and from the balconies came a murmur of voices and women's laughter. The heavy scent of some flower, vague, white, southern, mingled with the cigarette smoke in that hot evening air, which seemed, by contrast to the Venetian day, almost cool.

As Jervase Marion lolled back (that lolling of his always struck one as out of keeping with his well-adjusted speech, his precise mind, the something conventional about him) on the ottoman in the shadow, he was conscious of a queer feeling, as if, instead of having arrived from London only two hours ago, he had never ceased to be here at Venice, and under Miss Vanderwerf's hospitable stuccoed roof. All those years of work, of success, of experience (or was it not rather of study?) of others, bringing with them a certain heaviness, baldness, and scepticism, had become almost a dream, and this present moment and the similar moment twelve years ago remaining as the only reality. Except his hostess, whose round, unchangeable face, the face of a world-wise, kind but somewhat frivolous baby, was lit up faintly by the regular puffs of her cigarette, all the people in the room were strangers to Marion: yet he knew them so well, he had known them so long.

There was the old peeress, her head tied up in a white pocket-handkerchief, and lolling from side to side with narcoticised benevolence, who, as it was getting on towards other people's bedtime, was gradually beginning to wake up from the day's slumber, and to murmur eighteenth-century witticisms and Blessingtonian anecdotes. There was the American Senator, seated with postage-stamp profile and the attitude of a bronze statesman, against the moonlight, one hand in his waistcoat, the other incessantly raised to his ear as in a stately 'Beg pardon?' There was the depressed Venetian naval officer who always made the little joke about not being ill when offered tea; the Roumanian Princess who cultivated the reputation of saying spiteful things cleverly, and wore all her pearls for fear of their tarnishing; the English cosmopolitan who was one day on the Bosphorus and the next in Bond Street, and was wise about singing and acting; the well turned out, subdued, Parisian-American aesthete talking with an English accent about modern pictures and ladies' dresses; and the awkward, enthusiastic English aesthete, who considered Ruskin a ranter and creaked over the marble floors with dusty, seven-mile boots. There was a solitary spinster fresh from higher efforts of some sort, unconscious that no one in Venice appreciated her classic profile, and that everyone in Venice stared at her mediaeval dress and collar of coins from the British Museum. There was the usual bevy of tight-waisted Anglo-Italian girls ready to play the guitar and sing, and the usual supply of shy, young artists from the three-franc pensions, wandering round the room, candle in hand, with the niece of the house, looking with shy intentness at every picture and sketch and bronze statuette and china bowl and lacquer box.

The smoke of the cigarettes mingled with the heavy scent of the flowers; the plash of oar and snatch of song rose from the canal; the murmur and laughter entered from the balcony. The old peeress lolled out her Blessingtonian anecdotes; the Senator raised his hand to his ear and said 'Beg pardon?' the Roumanian Princess laughed shrilly at her own malignant sayings; the hostess's face was periodically illumined by her cigarette and the hostess's voice periodically burst into a childlike: 'Why, you don't mean it!' The young men and women flirted in undertones about Symonds, Whistler, Tolstoy, and the way of rowing gondolas, with an occasional chord struck on the piano, an occasional string twanged on the guitar. The Salute, with its cupolas and volutes, loomed spectral in at the windows; the moonlight spread in a soft, shining carpet to their feet.

Jervase Marion knew it all so well, so well, this half-fashionable, half-artistic Anglo-American idleness of Venice, with its poetic setting and its prosaic reality. He would have known it, he felt, intimately, even if he had never seen it before; known it so as to be able to make each of these people say in print what they did really say. There is something in being a psychological novelist, and something in being a cosmopolitan American, something in being an inmate of the world of Henry James and a kind of Henry James, of a lesser magnitude, yourself: one has the pleasure of understanding so much, one loses the pleasure of misunderstanding so much more.

A singing boat came under the windows of Palazzo Bragadin, and as much of the company as could, squeezed on to the cushioned gothic balconies, much to the annoyance of such as were flirting outside, and to the satisfaction of such as were flirting within. Marion – who, much to poor Miss Vanderwerf's disgust, had asked to be introduced to no one as yet, but to be allowed to realise that evening, as he daintily put it, that Venice was the same and he a good bit changed – Marion leaned upon the parapet of a comparatively empty balcony and looked down at the canal. The moonbeams were weaving a strange, intricate pattern, like some old Persian tissue, in the dark water; further off the yellow and red lanterns of the singing boat were surrounded by black gondolas, each with its crimson, unsteady prow-light; and beyond, mysterious in the moonlight, rose the tower and cupola of St. George, the rigging of ships, and stretched a shimmering band of lagoon.

He had come to give himself a complete holiday here, after the grind of furnishing a three-volume novel for Blackwood (Why did he write so much? he asked himself; he had enough of his own, and to spare, for a dainty but frugal bachelor); and already vague notions of new stories began to arrive in his mind. He determined to make a note of them and dismiss them for the time. He had determined to be idle; and he was a very methodical man, valuing above everything (even above his consciousness of being a man of the world) his steady health, steady, slightly depressed spirits, and steady, monotonous, but not unmanly nor unenjoyable routine of existence.

Jervase Marion was thinking of this, and the necessity of giving himself a complete rest, not letting himself be dragged off into new studies of mankind and womankind; and listening, at the same time, half-unconsciously, to the scraps of conversation which came from the other little balconies, where a lot of heads were grouped, dark in the moonlight.

'I do hope it will turn out well – at least not too utterly

awful,' said the languid voice of a young English manufacturer's heir, reported to live exclusively off bread and butter and sardines, and to have no further desires in the world save those of the amiable people who condescended to shoot on his moors, yacht in his yachts, and generally devour his millions, 'it's ever so long since I've been wanting a sideboard. It's rather hard lines for a poor fellow to be unable to find a sideboard ready made, isn't it? And I have my doubts about it even now.'

There was a faint sarcastic tinge in the languid voice; the eater of bread and butter occasionally felt vague amusement at his own ineptness.

'Nonsense, my dear boy,' answered the cosmopolitan, who knew all about acting and singing; 'it's sure to be beautiful. Only you must *not* let them put on that rococo cornice, quite out of character, my dear boy.'

'A real rococo cornice is a precious lot better, I guess, than a beastly imitation Renaissance frieze cut with an oyster knife,' put in a gruff New York voice. 'That's my view, leastways.'

'I think Mr. Clarence had best have it made in slices, and each of you gentlemen design him a slice – that's what's called original nowadays – *c'est notre facon d'entendre l'art aujourd'hui*,' said the Roumanian Princess.

A little feeble laugh proceeded from Mr. Clarence. 'Oh,' he said, 'I shouldn't mind that at all. I'm not afraid of my friends. I'm afraid of myself, of my fickleness and weak-mindedness. At this rate I shall never have a sideboard at all, I fear.'

'There's a very good one, with three drawers and knobs, and a ticket "garantito vero noce a lire 45", in a joiner's shop at San Vio, which I pass every morning. You'd much better have that, Mr. Clarence. And it would be a new departure in art and taste, you know.'

The voice was a woman's; a little masculine, and the more so for a certain falsetto pitch. It struck Marion by its resolution, a sort of highbred bullying and a little hardness about it.

'Come, don't be cruel to poor Clarence, Tal darling,' cried Miss Vanderwerf, with her kind, infantine laugh.

'Why, what have I been saying, my dear thing?' asked the voice, with mock humility; 'I only want to help the poor man in his difficulties.'

'By the way, Lady Tal, will you allow me to take you to Rietti's one day?' added an aesthetic young American, with a shadowy Boston accent; 'he has some things you ought really to see, some quite good tapestries, a capital Gubbio vase. And he has a carved nigger really by Brustolon, which you ought to get for your red room at Rome. He'd look superb. The head's restored and one of the legs, so Rietti'd let him go for very little. He really is an awfully jolly bit of carving – and in that red room of yours –'

'Thanks, Julian. I don't think I seem to care much about him. The fact is, I have to see such a lot of ugly white men in my drawing-room, I feel I really couldn't stand an ugly black one into the bargain.'

Here Miss Vanderwerf, despite her solemn promise, insisted on introducing Jervase Marion to a lady of high literary tastes, who proceeded forthwith to congratulate him as the author of a novel by Randolph Tomkins, whom he abominated most of all living writers.

Presently there was a stir in the company, those of the balcony came trooping into the drawing-room, four or five young men and girls, surrounding a tall woman in a black walking-dress; people dropped in to these open evenings of Miss Vanderwerf's from their row on the lagoon or stroll at St. Mark's. Miss Vanderwerf jumped up.

'You aren't surely going yet, dearest?' she cried effusively. 'My darling child, it isn't half-past ten yet.'

'I must go; poor Gerty's in bed with a cold, and I must go and look after her.'

'Bother Gerty!' ejaculated one of the well turned out aesthetic young men.

The tall young woman gave him what Marion noted as a shutting-up look.

'Learn to respect my belongings,' she answered, 'I must really go back to my cousin.'

Jervase Marion had immediately identified her as the owner of that rather masculine voice with the falsetto tone; and apart from the voice, he would have identified her as the lady who had bullied the poor young man in distress about his sideboard. She was very tall, straight, and strongly built, the sort of woman whom you instinctively think of as dazzlingly fine in a ball frock; but at the same time active and stalwart, suggestive of long rides and drives and walks. She had handsome aquiline features, just a trifle wooden in their statuesque fineness, abundant fair hair, and a complexion, pure pink and white, which told of superb health. Marion knew the type well. It was one which, despite all the years he had lived in England, made him feel American, impressing him as something almost exotic. This great strength, size, cleanness of outline and complexion, this look of carefully selected breed, of carefully fostered health, was to him the perfect flower of the aristocratic civilisation of England. There were more beautiful types, certainly, and, intellectually, higher ones (his experience was that such women were shrewd, practical, and quite deficient in soul), but there was no type more well-defined and striking, in his eyes. This woman did not seem an individual at all.

'I must go,' insisted the tall lady, despite the prayers of her hostess and the assembled guests. 'I really can't leave that poor creature alone a minute longer.'

'Order the gondola, Kennedy; call Titta, please,' cried Miss Vanderwerf to one of the many youths whom the kindly old maid ordered about with motherly familiarity.

Mayn't I have the honour of offering mine?' piped the young man.

'Thanks, it isn't worth while. I shall walk.' Here came a chorus of protestations, following the tall young woman into the outer drawing-room, through the hall, to the head of the great flight of open-air stairs.

Marion had mechanically followed the noisy, squabbling, laughing crew. The departure of this lady suggested to him that he would slip away to his inn.

'Do let me have the pleasure of accompanying you,' cried one young man after another.

'*Do* take Clarence or Kennedy or Piccinillo, darling,' implored Miss Vanderwerf. 'You can't really walk home alone.'

'It's not three steps from here,' answered the tall one. 'And I'm sure it's much more proper for a matron of ever so many years standing to go home alone than accompanied by a lot of fascinating young creatures.'

'But, dear, you really don't know Venice; suppose you were spoken to! Just think.'

'Well, beloved friend, I know enough Italian to be able to answer.'

The tall lady raised one beautifully pencilled eyebrow, slightly, with a contemptuous little look. 'Besides, I'm big enough to defend myself, and see, here's an umbrella with a silver knob, or what passes for such in these degenerate days. Nobody will come near that.'

And she took the weapon from a rack in the hall, where

the big seventeenth-century lamp flickered on the portraits of doges in crimson and senators in ermine.

'As you like, dearest. I know that wilful must have her own way,' sighed Miss Vanderwerf, rising on tiptoe and kissing her on both cheeks.

'Mayn't I really accompany you?' repeated the various young men.

She shook her head, with the tall, pointed hat on it.

'No, you mayn't; good-night, dear friends,' and she brandished her umbrella over her head and descended the stairs, which went sheer down into the moonlit yard. The young men bowed. One, with the air of a devotee in St. Mark's, kissed her hand at the bottom of the flight of steps, while the gondolier unlocked the gate. They could see him standing in the moonlight and hear him say earnestly:

'I leave for Paris to-morrow; good-night.'

She did not answer him, but making a gesture with her umbrella to those above, she cried: 'Good-night.'

'Good-night,' answered the chorus above the stairs watching the tall figure pass beneath the gate and into the moonlit square.

'Well now,' said Miss Vanderwerf, settling herself on her ottoman again, and fanning herself after her exertions in the drawing-room, 'there is no denying that she's a strange creature, dear thing.'

'A fine figure-head cut out of oak, with a good, solid, wooden heart,' said the Roumanian Princess.

'No, no,' exclaimed the lady of the house. 'She's just as good as gold, – poor Lady Tal!'

II

'Tal?' asked Marion.

'Tal. Her name's Atalanta, Lady Atalanta Walkenshaw –

but everyone calls her Tal – Lady Tal. She's the daughter of Lord Ossian, you know.'

'And who is or was Walkenshaw? – is, I presume, otherwise she'd have married somebody else by this time.'

'Poor Tal!' mused Miss Vanderwerf. 'I'm sure she would have no difficulty in finding another husband to make up for that fearful old Walkenshaw creature. But she's in a very sad position for so young a creature, poor girl.'

'Ah!' ejaculated Marion, familiar with ladies thus to be commiserated, and remembering his friend's passion for romance, unquenchable by many serio-comic disenchantments, 'separated from her husband – that sort of thing! I thought so.'

'Now, why did you think that, you horrid creature?' asked his hostess eagerly. 'Well, now, there's no saying that you're not *real* psychological, Jervase. Now *do* tell what made you think of such a thing.'

'I don't know, I'm sure,' answered Marion, suppressing a yawn. He hated people who pried into his novelist consciousness, all the more so that he couldn't in the least explain its contents. 'Something about her – or nothing about her – a mere guess, a stupid random shot that happens to have hit right.'

'Why, that's just the thing, that you haven't hit quite right. That is, it's right in one way, and wrong in another. Oh, my! how difficult it is just to explain, when one isn't a clever creature like you? Well, Lady Tal isn't separated from her husband, but it's just the same as if she were –'

'I see. Mad? Poor thing!' exclaimed Marion with that air of concern which always left you in doubt whether it was utterly conventional, or might not contain a grain of sympathy after all.

'No, he's not mad. He's dead – been dead ever so long. She's one and thirty, you know – doesn't look it, does she?

– and was married at eighteen. But she can't marry again, for all that, because if she marries all his money goes elsewhere, and she's not a penny to bless herself with.'

'Ah – and why didn't she have proper settlements made?' asked Marion.

'That's just it. Because old Walkenshaw, who was a beast – just a beast – had a prejudice against settlements, and said he'd do much better for his wife than that – leave her everything, if only they didn't plague him. And then, when the old wretch died, after they'd been married a year or so, it turned out that he had left her everything, but only on condition of her not marrying again. If she did, it would all go to the next of kin. He hated the next of kin, too, they say, and wanted to keep the money away from him as long as possible, horrid old wretch! So there poor Tal is a widow, but unable to marry again.'

'Dear me!' ejaculated Marion, looking at the patterns which the moonlight, falling between the gothic balcony balustrade, was making on the shining marble floor; and reflecting upon the neat way in which the late Walkenshaw had repaid his wife for marrying him for his money; for of course she had married him for his money. Marion was not a stoic, or a cynic, or a philosopher of any kind. He fully accepted the fact that the daughters of Scotch lords should marry for money, he even hated all sorts of sentimental twaddle about human dignity. But he rather sympathised with this old Walkenshaw, whoever Walkenshaw might have been, who had just served a mercenary young lady as was right.

'I don't see that it's so hard, aunt,' said Miss Vanderwerf's niece, who was deeply in love with Bill Nettle, a penniless etcher. 'Lady Tal might marry again if she'd learn to do without all that money.'

'If she would be satisfied with only a little less,' interrupted the sharp-featured Parisian-American whom Miss

Vanderwerf wanted for a nephew-in-law. 'Why, there are dozens of men with plenty of money who have been wanting to marry her. There was Sir Titus Farrinder, only last year. He mayn't have had as much as old Walkenshaw, but he had a jolly bit of money, certainly.'

'Besides, after all,' put in the millionaire in distraction about the sideboard, 'why should Lady Tal want to marry again? She's got a lovely house at Rome.'

'Oh, come, come, Clarence!' interrupted Kennedy horrified; 'why, it's nothing but Japanese leather paper and Chinese fans.'

'I don't know,' said Clarence, crestfallen. 'Perhaps it isn't lovely. I thought it *rather* pretty – don't you really think it *rather* nice, Miss Vanderwerf?'

'Any house would be nice enough with such a splendid creature inside it,' put in Marion. These sort of conversations always interested him; it was the best way of studying human nature.

'Besides,' remarked the Roumanian Princess, 'Lady Tal may have had enough of the married state. And why indeed should a beautiful creature like that get married? She's got every one at her feet. It's much more amusing like that –'

'Well, all the same, I *do* think it's just terribly sad, to see a creature like that condemned to lead such a life, without anyone to care for or protect her, now poor Gerald Burne's dead.'

'Oh, her brother – her brother – do you suppose she cared for *him*?' asked the niece, pouring out the iced lemonade and Cyprus wine. She always rebelled against her aunt's romanticalness.

'Gerald Burne!' said Marion, collecting his thoughts, and suddenly seeing in his mind a certain keen-featured face, a certain wide curl of blond hair, not seen for many a long year. 'Gerald Burne! Do you mean an awfully handsome young Scotchman, who did something very distinguished in Afghanistan? You don't mean to say he was any relation of Lady Atalanta's? I never heard of his being dead, either. I thought he must be somewhere in India.'

'Gerald Burne was Lady Tal's half-brother – her mother had married a Colonel Burne before her marriage with Lord Ossian. He got a spear-wound or something out in Afghanistan,' explained one of the company.

'I thought it was his horse,' interrupted another.

'Anyhow,' resumed Miss Vanderwerf, 'poor Gerald was crippled for life – a sort of spinal disease, you know. That was just after old Sir Thomas Walkenshaw departed, so Tal and he lived together and went travelling from one place to another, consulting doctors, and that sort of thing, until they settled in Rome. And now poor Gerald is dead – he died two years ago – Tal's all alone in the world, for Lord Ossian's a wretched, tipsy, bankrupt old creature, and the other sisters are married. Gerald was just an angel, and you've no idea how devoted poor Tal was to him – he was just her life, I do believe.'

The young man called Ted looked contemptuously at his optimistic hostess.

'Well,' he said, 'I don't know whether Lady Tal cared much for her brother while he was alive. My belief is she never cared a jackstraw for anyone. Anyway, if she *did* care for him you must admit she didn't show it after his death. I never saw a woman look so utterly indifferent and heartless as when I saw her a month later. She made jokes, I remember, and asked me to take her to a curiosity shop. And she went to balls in London not a year afterwards.'

The niece nodded. 'Exactly. I always thought it perfectly

indecent. Of course Aunt says it's Tal's way of showing her grief, but it's a very funny one, anyhow.'

'I'm sure Lady Tal must regret her brother,' said the Roumanian Princess. 'Just think how convenient for a young widow to be able to say to all the men she likes: "Oh, do come and see poor Gerald."'

'Well, well!' remarked Miss Vanderwerf. 'Of course she did take her brother's death in a very unusual way. But still I maintain she's not heartless for all that.'

'Hasn't a pretty woman a right to be heartless, after all?' put in Marion.

'Oh, I don't care a fig whether Lady Tal is heartless or not,' answered Ted brusquely. 'Heartlessness isn't a social offence. What I object to most in Lady Tal is her being so frightfully mean.'

'Mean?'

'Why, yes; avaricious. With all those thousands, that woman manages to spend barely more than a few hundreds.'

'Well, but if she's got simple tastes?' suggested Marion.

'She hasn't. No woman was ever further from it. And of course it's so evident what her game is! She just wants to feather her nest against a rainy day. She's putting by five-sixths of old Walkenshaw's money, so as to make herself a nice little *dot*, to marry someone else upon one of these days.'

'A judicious young lady!' observed Marion.

'Well, really, Mr. Kennedy,' exclaimed the Roumanian Princess, 'you are ingenious and ingenuous! Do you suppose that our dear Tal is putting by money in order to marry some starving genius, to do love in a cottage with? Why, if she's not married yet, it's merely because she's not met a sufficient *parti*. She wants something very grand – a *Pezzo Grosso*, as they say here.'

'She couldn't marry as long as she had Gerald to look after,' said Miss Vanderwerf, fanning herself in the moonlight. 'She was too fond of Gerald.'

'She was afraid of Gerald, that's my belief, too,' corrected the niece. 'Those big creatures are always cowards. And Gerald hated the notion of her making another money marriage, though he seems to have arranged pretty well to live on old Walkenshaw's thousands.'

'Of course Gerald wanted to keep her all for himself; that was quite natural,' said Miss Vanderwerf; 'but I think that as long as he was alive she did not want anyone else. She thought only of him, poor creature –'

'And of a score of ball and dinner-parties and a few hundred acquaintances,' put in Ted, making rings with the smoke of his cigarette.

'And now,' said the Princess, 'she's waiting to find her *Pezzo Grosso.* And she wants money because she knows that a *Pezzo Grosso* will marry a penniless girl of eighteen, but won't marry a penniless woman of thirty; she must make up for being a little *passée* by loving him for his own sake, and for that, she must have money.'

'For all that, poor Tal's very simple,' wheezed the old peeress, apparently awakening from a narcotic slumber. 'She always reminds me of an anecdote poor dear Palmerston used to tell –'

'Anyhow,' said Kennedy, 'Lady Tal's a riddle, and I pity the man who tries to guess it. Good-night, dear Miss Vanderwerf – good-night, Miss Bessy. It's all settled about dining at the Lido, I hope. And you'll come, too, I hope, Mr. Marion.'

'I'll come with pleasure, particularly if you ask the enigmatic Lady Tal.'

'Much good it is to live in Venice,' thought Jervase Marion, looking out of his window on to the canal, 'if one spends two hours discussing a young woman six foot high looking out for a duke.'

III

Jervase Marion had registered three separate, well-defined, and solemn vows, which I recapitulate in the inverse order to their importance. The first was: Not to be enticed into paying calls during that month at Venice; the second, Not to drift into studying any individual character while on a holiday; and the third, a vow dating from more years back than he cared to think of, and resulting from infinite bitterness of spirit, Never to be entrapped, beguiled, or bullied into looking at the manuscript of an amateur novelist. And now he had not been in Venice ten days before he had broken each of these vows in succession; and broken them on behalf, too, of one and the same individual.

The individual in question was Lady Atalanta Walkenshaw, or, as he had already got accustomed to call her, Lady Tal. He had called upon Lady Tal; he had begun studying Lady Tal; and now he was actually untying the string which fastened Lady Tal's first attempt at a novel.

Why on earth had he done any of these things, much less all? Jervase Marion asked himself, leaving the folded parcel unopened on the large round table, covered with a black and red table-cloth, on which were neatly spread out his writing-case, blotter, inkstand, paper-cutter, sundry packets of envelopes, and boxes of cigarettes, two uncut *Athenaeums*, three dog-eared French novels (Marion secretly despised all English ones, and was for ever coveting that exquisite artistic sense, that admirable insincerity of the younger Frenchmen), a Baedeker, a Bradshaw, the photograph, done just before her death, of his mother in her picturesque, Puritan-looking widow's cap, and a little portfolio for unanswered letters, with flowers painted on it by his old friend, Biddy Lothrop.

Marion gave the parcel, addressed in a large, quill-pen

hand, a look of utter despair, and thrusting his hands ungracefully but desperately into the armhole of his alpaca writing-jacket, paced slowly up and down his darkened room on a side canal. He had chosen that room, rather than one on the Riva, thinking it would be less noisy. But it seemed to him now, in one of his nervous fits, as if all the noises of the world had concentrated on to that side canal to distract his brain, weaken his will, and generally render him incapable of coping with his own detestable weakness and Lady Tal's terrible determination. There was a plash of oar, a grind of keel, in that side canal, a cry of *Stali* or *Premè* from the gondoliers, only the more worrying for its comparative rareness. There was an exasperating blackbird who sang Garibaldi's hymn, in separate fragments, a few doors off, and an even more exasperating kitchen-maid, who sang the first bars of the umbrella trio of *Boccaccio*, without getting any further, while scouring her brasses at the window opposite, and rinsing out her saucepans, with a furtive splash into the canal. There was the bugle of the barracks, the bell of the parish church, the dog yelping on the boats of the Riva; everything in short which could madden a poor nervous novelist who has the crowning misfortune of looking delightfully placid.

Why on earth, or rather how on earth, had he let himself in for all this? 'All this' being the horrible business of Lady Atalanta, the visits to pay her, the manuscript to read, the judgment to pass, the advice to give, the lies to tell, all vaguely complicated with the song of that blackbird, the jar of that gondola keel, the jangle of those church bells. How on earth could he have been such a miserable worm? Marion asked himself, pacing up and down his large, bare room, mopping his head, and casting despairing glances at the mosquito curtains, the bulging yellow chest of drawers painted over with nosegays, the iron clothes-horse, the towel-stand, the large printed card setting forth in various tongues the necessity of travellers consigning all jewels and valuables to the secretary of the hotel at the Bureau.

He could not, at present, understand in the very least why he had given that young woman any encouragement; for he must evidently have given her some encouragement before she could have gone to the length of asking so great a favour of a comparative stranger. And the odd part of it was, that when he looked into the past, that past of a few days only, it seemed as if, so far from his having encouraged Lady Tal, it had been Lady Tal who had encouraged him. He saw her, the more he looked, in the attitude of a woman granting a favour, not asking one. He couldn't even explain to himself how the matter of the novel had ever come up. He certainly couldn't remember having said: 'I wish you would let me see your novel, Lady Tal,' or 'I should be curious to have a look at that novel of yours'; such a thing would have been too absurd on the part of a man who had always fled from manuscripts as from the plague. At the same time he seemed to have no recollection either of her having said the other thing, the more or less humble request for a reading. He recollected her saying: 'Mind you tell me the exact truth – and don't be afraid of telling me if it's all disgusting rubbish.' Indeed he could see something vaguely amused, mischievous, and a little contemptuous in the handsome, regular Scotch face; but that had been afterwards, after he had already settled the matter with her.

It was the sense of having been got the better of, and in a wholly unintelligible way, which greatly aggravated the matter. For Marion did not feel the very faintest desire to do Lady Atalanta a service. He would not have minded so much if she had wheedled him into it, – no man thinks the worse of himself for having been wheedled by a handsome young woman of fashion, – or if she had been an appealing or pathetic creature, one of those who seem to suggest that this is just all that can be done for them, and that perhaps one may regret not having done it over their early grave.

Lady Tal was not at all an appealing woman; she looked three times as strong, both in body and in mind, with her huge, strongly-knit frame, and clear, pink complexion, and eyes which evaded you, as himself and most of his acquaintances. And as to wheedling, how could she wheedle, this woman with her rather angular movements, brusque, sarcastic, bantering speech, and look of counting all the world as dust for an Ossian to trample underfoot? Moreover, Marion was distinctly aware of the fact that he rather disliked Lady Tal. It was not anything people said about her (although they seemed to say plenty), nor anything she said herself; it was a vague repulsion due to her dreadful strength, her appearance of never having felt anything, the hardness of those blue, bold eyes, the resolution of that well-cut, firmly closing mouth, the bantering tone of that voice, and the consequent impression which she left on him of being able to take care of herself to an extent almost dangerous to her fellow-creatures. Marion was not a sentimental novelist; his books turned mainly upon the little intrigues and struggles of the highly civilised portion of society, in which only the fittest have survived, by virtue of talon and beak. Yet he owned to himself, in the presence of Lady Atalanta Walkenshaw, or rather behind her back, that he did like human beings, and especially women, to have a soul; implying thereby that the lady in question affected him as being hampered by no such impediment to digestion, sleep, and worldly distinction.

It was this want of soul which constituted the strength of Lady Tal. This negative quality had much more than the value of a positive one. And it was Lady Tal's want of soul which had, somehow, got the better of him, pushed him, bullied him, without any external manifestation, and by a mere hidden force, into accepting, or offering to read that manuscript.

Jervase Marion was a methodical man, full of unformulated principles of existence. One of these consisted in always doing unpleasant duties at once, unless they were so unpleasant that he never did them at all. Accordingly, after a turn or two more up and down the room, and a minute or two lolling out of the window, and looking into that kitchen on the other side of the canal, with the bright saucepans in the background, and the pipkins with carnations and sweet basil on the sill, Marion cut the strings of the manuscript, rolled it backwards to make it lie flat, and with a melancholy little moan, began reading Lady Tal's novel.

'Violet –' it began.

'Violet! and her name's Violet too!' ejaculated Marion to himself.

'Violet is seated in a low chair in the gloom in the big bow window at Kieldar – the big bow window encircled by ivy and constructed it is said by Earl Rufus before he went to the crusades and from which you command a magnificent prospect of the broad champaign country extending for many miles, all dotted with oaks and farmhouses and bounded on the horizon by the blue line of the hills of B—shire – the window in which she had sat so often and cried as a child when her father Lord Rufus had married again and brought home that handsome Jewish wife with the *fardée* face and the exquisite dresses from Worth – Violet had taken refuge in that window in order to think over the events of the previous evening and that offer of marriage which her cousin Marmaduke had just made to her –'

'Bless the woman!' exclaimed Marion, 'what on earth is it all about?' And he registered the remark, to be used upon the earliest occasion in one of his own novels, that highly-connected and well-dressed young women of the present generation, appear to leave commas and semicolons, all in fact except full stops and dashes, to their social inferiors.

The remark consoled him, also, by its practical bearing on the present situation, for it would enable him to throw the weight of his criticisms on this part of Lady Tal's performance.

'You must try, my dear Lady Atalanta,' he would say very gravely, 'to cultivate a – a – somewhat more lucid style – to cut down your sentences a little – in fact to do what we pedantic folk call break up the members of a period. In order to do so, you must turn your attention very seriously to the subject of punctuation, which you seem to have – a – well – rather neglected hitherto. I will send for an invaluable little work on the subject – "Stops: and how to manage them", which will give you all necessary information. Also, if you can find it in the library of any of our friends here, I should recommend your studying a book which I used in my boyhood, – a great many years ago, alas! – called "Blair's Rhetoric".'

If that didn't quench Lady Tal's literary ardour, nothing ever would. But all the same he felt bound to read on a little, in order to be able to say he had done so.

IV

Jervase Marion fixed his eyes, the eyes of the spirit particularly, upon Lady Tal, as he sat opposite her, the next day, at the round dinner table, in Palazzo Bragadin.

He was trying to make out how on earth this woman had come to write the novel he had been reading. That Lady Tal should possess considerable knowledge of the world, and of men and women, did not surprise him in the least. He had recognised, in the course of various conversations, that this young lady formed an exception to the rule that splendid big creatures with regular features and superb complexions are invariably idiots.

That Lady Tal should even have a certain talent – about as cultivated as that of the little boys who draw horses on their copybooks – for plot and dialogue, was not astonishing at all, any more than that her sentences invariably consisted either of three words, or of twenty-seven lines, and that her grammar and spelling were nowhere. All this was quite consonant with Lady Tal's history, manner, talk, and with that particular beauty of hers – the handsome aquiline features, too clean-cut for anything save wood or stone, the bright, cold, blue eyes, which looked you in the face when you expected it least, and which looked away from you when you expected it least, also; the absence of any of those little subtle lines which tell of feeling and thought, and which complete visible beauty, while suggesting a beauty transcending mere visible things. There was nothing at all surprising in this. But Jervase Marion had found in this manuscript something quite distinct and unconnected with such matters: he had found the indications of a soul, a very decided and unmistakable soul.

And now, looking across the fruit and flowers, and the set out of old Venetian glass on Miss Vanderwerf's hospitable table, he asked himself in what portion of the magnificent person of Lady Atalanta Walkenshaw that soul could possibly be located.

Lady Tal was seated, as I have remarked, immediately opposite Marion, and between a rather battered cosmopolitan diplomatist and the young millionaire who had been in distress about a sideboard. Further along was the Roumanian Princess, and opposite, on the other side of Marion, an elderly American siren, in an extremely simple white muslin frock, at the first glance the work of the nursery maid, at the second of Worth, and symbolising the strange, dangerous fascination of a lady whom you took at first for a Puritan and a frump. On the other sat Miss Gertrude Ossian, Lady Tal's cousin, a huge young woman with splendid arms and shoulders and atrocious manners, who thought Venice such a bore because it was too hot to play at tennis and you couldn't ride on canals, and consoled herself by attempting to learn the guitar from various effete Italian youths, whom she alarmed and delighted in turn.

Among this interesting company Lady Tal was seated with that indefinable look of being a great deal too large, too strong, too highly connected, and too satisfied with herself and all things, for this miserable, effete, plebeian, and self-conscious universe.

She wore a beautifully-made dress of beautifully-shining silk, and her shoulders and throat and arms were as beautifully made and as shining as her dress; and her blond hair was as elaborately and perfectly arranged as it was possible to conceive. That blond hair, verging upon golden, piled up in smooth and regular plaits and rolls till it formed a kind of hard and fantastic helmet about her very oval face, and arranged in a close row of symmetrical little curls upon the high, white, unmarked forehead, and about the thin, black, perfectly-arched eyebrows – that hair of Lady Tal's symbolised, in the thought of Marion, all that was magnificent, conventional, and impassive in this creature. Those blue eyes also, which looked at you and away from you, when you expected each least, were too large, under the immense arch of eyebrow, to do more than look out indifferently upon the world. The mouth was too small in its beautiful shape for any contraction or expression of feeling, and when she smiled, those tiny white teeth seemed still to shut it. And altogether, with its finely-moulded nostrils, which were never dilated, and its very oval outline, the whole face affected Marion as a huge and handsome mask, as something clapped on and intended to conceal. To conceal what? It seemed to the novelist, as he listened to the stream of animated conventionalities, of jokes unconnected with any high spirits, that the mask of Lady Atalanta's face, like those great stone masks in Roman galleries and gardens, concealed the mere absence of everything. As Marion contemplated Lady Tal, he reviewed mentally that manuscript novel written in a hand as worn down as that of a journalist, and with rather less grammar and spelling than might be expected from a nursery maid; and he tried to connect the impression it had left on his mind with the impression which its author was making at the present moment.

The novel had taken him by surprise by its subject, and even more by its particular moral attitude. The story was no story at all, merely the unnoticed martyrdom of a delicate and scrupulous woman tied to a vain, mean, and frivolous man; the long starvation of a little soul which required affections and duties among the unrealities of the world. Not at all an uncommon subject nowadays; in fact, Marion could have counted you off a score of well-known novels on similar or nearly similar themes.

There was nothing at all surprising in the novel, the surprising point lay in its having this particular author.

Little by little, as the impression of the book became fainter, and the impression of the writer more vivid, Marion began to settle his psychological problem. Or rather he began to settle that there was no psychological problem at all. This particular theme was in vogue nowadays, this particular moral view was rife in the world; Lady Tal had read other people's books, and had herself written a book which was extremely like theirs. It was a case of unconscious, complete imitation. The explanation of Lady Tal's having produced a novel so very different from herself, was simply that, as a matter of fact, she had not produced that novel at all.

It was unlike herself because it belonged to other people, that was all.

'Tell me about my novel,' she said after dinner, beckoning Marion into one of the little gothic balconies overhanging the grand canal; the little balconies upon whose cushions and beneath whose drawn-up awning there is room for two, just out of earshot of any two others on the other balconies beyond.

Places for flirtation. But Lady Tal, Marion had instinctively understood, was not a woman who flirted. Her power over men, if she had any, or chose to exert it, must be of the sledge-hammer sort. And how she could possibly have any power over anything save a mere gaping masher, over anything that had, below its starched shirt front, sensitiveness, curiosity, and imagination, Marion at this moment utterly failed to understand.

The tone of this woman's voice, the very rustle of her dress, as she leaned upon the balcony and shook the sparks from her cigarette into the dark sky and the dark water, seemed to mean business and nothing but business.

She said:

'Tell me all about my novel. I don't intend to be put off with mere remarks about grammar and stops. One may learn all about that; or can't all that, and style, and so forth, be put in for one, by the printer's devil? I haven't a very clear notion what a printer's devil is, except that he's a person with a thumb. But he might see to such details, or somebody else of the same sort.'

'Quite so. A novelist of some slight established reputation would do as well, Lady Tal.'

Marion wondered why he had made that answer; Lady Tal's remark was impertinent only inasmuch as he chose to admit that she could be impertinent to him.

Lady Tal, he felt, but could not see, slightly raised

one of those immensely curved eyebrows of hers in the darkness.

'I thought that you, for instance, might get me through all that,' she answered; 'or some other novelist, as you say, of established reputation, who *was* benevolently inclined towards a poor, helpless ignoramus with literary aspirations.'

'Quite apart from such matters – and you are perfectly correct in supposing that there must be lots of professed novelists who would most gladly assist you with them – quite apart from such matters, your novel, if you will allow me to say a rude thing, is utterly impossible. You are perpetually taking all sorts of knowledge for granted in your reader. Your characters don't sufficiently explain themselves; you write as if your reader had witnessed the whole thing and merely required reminding. I almost doubt whether you have fully realised for yourself a great part of the situation; one would think you were repeating things from hearsay, without quite understanding them.'

Marion felt a twinge of conscience: that wasn't the impression left by the novel, but the impression due to the discrepancy between the novel and its author. That hateful habit of studying people, of turning them round, prodding and cutting them to see what was inside, why couldn't he leave it behind for awhile? Had he not come to Venice with the avowed intention of suspending all such studies?

Lady Tal laughed. The laugh was a little harsh. 'You say that because of the modelling of my face – I know all about modelling of faces, and facial angles, and cheek-bones, and eye cavities: I once learned to draw – people always judge of me by the modelling of my face. Perhaps they are right, perhaps they are wrong. I daresay I *have* taken too much for granted. One ought never to take anything for granted, in the way of human insight, ought one? Anyhow, perhaps you will show me when I have gone wrong, will you?'

'It will require a good deal of patience –' began Marion.

'On your part, of course. But then it all turns to profit with you novelists; and it's men's business to be patient, just because they never are.'

'I meant on your part, Lady Tal. I question whether you have any notion of what it means to recast a novel – to alter it throughout, perhaps not only once, but twice, or three times.'

'Make me a note of the main wrongness, and send me the MS., will you? I'll set about altering it at once, you'll see. I'm a great deal more patient than you imagine, Mr. Marion, when I want a thing – and I do want this – I want to write novels. I want the occupation, the interest, the excitement. Perhaps some day I shall want the money too. One makes pots of money in your business, doesn't one?'

Lady Atalanta laughed. She threw her cigarette into the canal, and with a crackle and a rustle of her light dress, straightened her huge person, and after looking for a moment into the blue darkness full of dim houses and irregularly scattered lights, she swept back into the hum of voices and shimmer of white dresses of Miss Vanderwerf's big drawing-room.

Jervase Marion remained leaning on the balcony, listening to the plash of oar and the bursts of hoarse voices and shrill fiddles from the distant music boats.

V

The temptations of that demon of psychological study proved too great for Marion; particularly when that tempter allied himself to an equally stubborn though less insidious demon apparently residing in Lady Atalanta: the demon of amateur authorship. So that, by the end of ten days, there was established, between Lady Tal's lodgings and Marion's hotel, a lively interchange of communication, porters and gondoliers for ever running to and fro between 'that usual tall young lady at San Vio,' and 'that usual short, bald gentleman on the Riva.' The number of parcels must have been particularly mysterious to these messengers, unless the proverbially rapid intuition (inherited during centuries of intrigue and spying) of Venetian underlings arrived at the fact that the seemingly numberless packets were in reality always one and the same, or portions of one and the same: the celebrated novel travelling to and fro, with perpetual criticisms from Marion and corrections from Lady Atalanta. This method of intercourse was, however, daily supplemented by sundry notes, in the delicate, neat little hand of the novelist, or the splashing writing of the lady, saying with little variation – 'Dear Lady Atalanta, I fear I may not have made my meaning very clear with respect to Chapter I, II, III, IV – or whatever it might be – will you allow me to give you some verbal explanations on the subject?' and 'Dear Mr. Marion, – *Do* come *at once*. I've got stuck over that beastly chapter V, VI, or VII, and positively *must* see you about it.'

'Well, I never!' politely ejaculated Miss Vanderwerf regularly every evening – 'if that Marion isn't the most *really* kind and patient creature on this earth!'

To which her friend the Princess, the other arbitress of Venetian society in virtue of her palace, her bric-à-brac, and that knowledge of Marie Corelli and Mrs. Campbell-Praed which balanced Miss Vanderwerf's capacity for grasping the meaning of Gyp – invariably answered in her best English colloquial:

'Well, my word! If that Lady Tal's not the most impudent amateur scribble-scrabble of all the amateur scribble-scrabbles that England produces.'

Remarks which immediately produced a lively discussion of Lady Tal and of Marion, including the toilettes of the one and the books of the other, with the result that neither retained a single moral, intellectual, or physical advantage; and the obvious corollary, in the mind of the impartial listener, that Jervase Marion evidently gave up much more of his time to Lady Tal and her novel than to Miss Vanderwerf and the Princess and their respective salons.

As a matter of fact, however, although a degree of impudence more politely described as energy and determination, on the part of Lady Tal; and of kindness, more correctly designated as feebleness of spirit, on the part of Marion, had undoubtedly been necessary in the first stages of this intercourse, yet nothing of either of these valuable social qualities had been necessary for its continuation. Although maintaining that manner of hers expressive of the complete rights which her name of Ossian and her additional inches constituted over all things and people, Lady Tal had become so genuinely enthusiastic for the novelist's art as revealed by Marion, that her perpetual intrusion upon his leisure was that merely of an ardent if somewhat inconsiderate disciple. In the eyes of this young lady, development of character, foreshortening of narrative, construction, syntax, nay, even grammar and punctuation, had become inexhaustible subjects of meditation and discussion, upon which every experience of life could be brought to bear.

So much for Lady Tal. As regards Marion, he had, not without considerable self-contempt, surrendered himself to the demon of character study. This passion for investigating into the feelings and motives of his neighbours was at once the joy, the pride, and the bane and humiliation of Marion's placid life. He was aware that he had, for years and years, cultivated this tendency to the utmost; and he was fully convinced that to study other folks and embody his studies in the most lucid form was the one mission of his life, and a mission in nowise inferior to that of any other highly gifted class of creatures. Indeed, if Jervase Marion, ever since his earliest manhood, had given way to a tendency to withdraw from all personal concerns, from all emotion or action, it was mainly because he conceived that this shrinkingness of nature (which foolish persons called egoism) was the necessary complement to his power of intellectual analysis; and that any departure from the position of dispassioned spectator of the world's follies and miseries would mean also a departure from his real duty as a novelist. To be brought into contact with people more closely than was necessary or advantageous for their intellectual comprehension; to think about them, feel about them, mistress, wife, son, or daughter, the bare thought of such a thing jarred upon Marion's nerves. So, the better to study, the better to be solitary, he had expatriated himself, leaving brothers, sisters (now his mother was dead) friends of childhood, all those things which invade a man's consciousness without any psychological profit; he had condemned himself to live in a world of acquaintances, of indifference; and, for sole diversion, he permitted himself, every now and then, to come abroad to places where he had not even acquaintances, where he could look at faces which had no associations for him, and speculate upon the character of total strangers. Only, being a methodical man, and much concerned for his bodily and intellectual health, he occasionally thought fit to suspend even this contact with mankind, and to spend six weeks, as he had intended spending those six weeks at Venice, in the contemplation of only bricks and mortar.

And now, that demon of psychological study had got the better of his determination. Marion understood it all now from the beginning: that astonishing feebleness of his towards Lady Atalanta, that extraordinary submission to this imperious and audacious young aristocrat's orders. The explanation was simple, though curious. He had divined in Lady Atalanta a very interesting psychological problem, considerably before he had been able to formulate the fact to himself: his novelist's intuition, like the scent of a dog, had set him on the track even before he knew the nature of the game, or the desire to pursue. Before even beginning to think about Lady Atalanta, he had begun to watch her; he was watching her now consciously; indeed all his existence was engrossed in such watching, so that the hours he spent away from her company, or the company of her novel, were so many gaps in his life.

Jervase Marion, as a result both of that shrinkingness of nature, and of a very delicate artistic instinct, had an aversion of such coarse methods of study as consist in sitting down in front of a human being and staring, in a metaphorical sense, at him or her. He was not a man of theories (their cut-and-driedness offending his subtlety); but had he been forced to formulate his ideas, he would have said that in order to perceive the real values (in pictorial language) of any individual, you must beware of isolating him or her; you must merely look attentively at the moving ocean of human faces, watching for the one face more particularly interesting than the rest, and catching glimpses of its fleeting expression, and of the expression of its neighbours as it appears and reappears. Perhaps, however, Marion's other reason against the sit-down-and-stare or walk-round-and-pray system of psychological study was really the stronger one in his nature, the more so that he would probably not have admitted its superior validity. This other reason was a kind of moral scruple against getting to know the secret mechanism of a soul, especially if such knowledge involved an appearance of intimacy with a person in whom he could never take more than a merely abstract, artistic interest. It was a mean taking advantage of superior strength, or the raising of expectations which could not be fulfilled; for Marion, although the most benevolent and serviceable of mortals, did not give his heart, perhaps because he had none to give, to anybody.

This scruple had occurred to Marion almost as soon as he discovered himself to be studying Lady Tal; and it occurred to him once or twice afterwards. But he despatched it satisfactorily. Lady Tal, in the first place, was making use of him in the most outrageous way, without scruple or excuse; it was only just that he, in his turn, should turn her to profit with equal freedom. This reason, however, savoured slightly of intellectual caddishness, and Marion rejected it with scorn. The real one, he came to perceive, was that Lady Tal gratuitously offered herself for study by her quiet, aggressive assumption of inscrutability. She really thrust her inscrutability down one's throat; her face, her manner, her every remark, her very novel, were all so many audacious challenges to the more psychological members of the community. She seemed to be playing on a gong and crying: 'Does anyone feel inclined to solve a riddle? Is there any person who thinks himself sufficiently clever to understand me?' And when a woman takes up such an attitude, it is only natural, human and proper that the first novelist who comes along that way should stop and say: 'I intend to get to the bottom of you; one, two, three, I am going to begin.'

So Jervase Marion assiduously cultivated the society of Lady Atalanta, and spent most of his time instructing her in the art of the novelist.

VI

One morning Marion, by way of exception, saw and studied Lady Tal without the usual medium of the famous novel. It was early, with the very first autumn crispness in the blue morning, in the bright sun which would soon burn, but as yet barely warmed. Marion was taking his usual ramble through the tortuous Venetian alleys, and as usual he had found himself in one of his favourite haunts, the market on the further slope of the Rialto.

That market – the yellow and white awning and the white houses against the delicate blue sky; the bales and festoons of red and green and blue and purple cotton stuffs outside the little shops, and below that the shawled women pattering down the bridge steps towards it; the monumental display of piled up peaches and pears, and heaped up pumpkins and mysterious unknown cognate vegetables, round and long, purple, yellow, red, grey, among the bay leaves, the great, huge, smooth, green-striped things, cut open to show their red pulp, the huger things looking as if nature had tried to gild and silver them unsuccessfully, tumbled on to the pavement; the butchers' shops with the gorgeous bullocks' hearts and sacrificial fleeced lambs; the endless hams and sausages – all this market, under the blue sky, with this lazy, active, noisy, brawling, friendly population jerking and lolling about it, always seemed to Marion one of the delightful spots of Venice, pleasing him with a sense (although he knew it to be all false) that here *was* a place where people could eat and drink and laugh and live without any psychological troubles.

On this particular morning, as this impression with the knowledge of its falseness was as usual invading Marion's consciousness, he experienced a little shock of surprise, incongruity, and the sudden extinction of a pleasingly unreal mood, on perceiving, coming towards him, with hand cavalierly on hip and umbrella firmly hitting the ground, the stately and faultlessly coated and shirted and necktied figure of Lady Atalanta.

'I have had a go already at *Christina*,' she said, after extending to Marion an angular though friendly handshake, and a cheerful frank inscrutable smile of her big blue eyes and her little red mouth. 'That novel is turning me into another woman: the power of sinning, as the Salvationists say, has been extracted out of my nature even by the rootlets; I sat up till two last night after returning from the Lido, and got up this morning at six, all for the love of *Christina* and literature. I expect Dawson will give me warning; she told me yesterday that she "had never *know* any other lady that writes so much or used them big sheets of paper, quite *henormous*, my lady." Dear old place, isn't it? Ever tasted any of that fried pumpkin? It's rather nasty but quite good; have some? I wonder we've not met here before; I come here twice a week to shop. You don't mind carrying parcels, do you?' Lady Tal had stopped at one of the front stalls, and having had three vast yellow paper bags filled with oranges and lemons, she handed the two largest to Marion.

'You'll carry them for me, won't you, there's a good creature: like that I shall be able to get rather more rolls than I usually can. It's astonishing how much sick folk care for rolls. I ought to explain I'm going to see some creatures at the hospital. It takes too long going there in the gondola from my place, so I walk. If you were to put those bags well on your chest like that, under your chin, they'd be easier to hold, and there'd be less chance of the oranges bobbing out.'

At a baker's in one of the little narrow streets near the church of the Miracoli, Lady Atalanta provided herself with a bag of rolls, which she swung by the string to her wrist. Marion then perceived that she was carrying under her arm a parcel of paper-covered books, fastened with an elastic band.

'Now we shall have got everything except some flowers, which I daresay we can get somewhere on the way,' remarked Lady Tal. 'Do you mind coming in here?' and she entered one of those little grocer's shops, dignified with the arms of Savoy in virtue of the sale of salt and tobacco, and where a little knot of vague, wide-collared individuals usually hang about among the various-shaped liqueur bottles in an atmosphere of stale cigar, brandy and water, and kitchen soap.

'May – I – a – a – ask for anything for you, Lady Tal?' requested Marion, taken completely by surprise by the rapidity of his companion's movements. 'You want stamps, I presume; may I have the honour of assisting you in your purchase?'

'Thanks, it isn't stamps; it's snuff, and you wouldn't know what sort to get.' And Lady Tal, making her stately way through the crowd of surprised loafers, put a franc on the counter and requested the presiding female to give her four ounces of *Semolino*, but of the good sort – 'It's astonishing how faddy those old creatures are about their snuff!' remarked Lady Tal, pocketing her change. 'Would you put this snuff in your pocket for me? Thanks. The other sort's called *Bacubino*, it's dark and clammy, and it looks nasty. Have you ever taken snuff? I do sometimes to please my old creatures; it makes me sneeze, you know, and they think that awful fun.'

As they went along lady Atalanta suddenly perceived, in a little green den, something which attracted her attention.

'I wonder whether they're fresh?' she mused. 'I suppose you can't tell a fresh egg when you see it, can you, Mr. Marion? Never mind, I'll risk it. If you'll take this third bag of oranges, I'll carry the eggs – they might come to grief in your hands, you know.'

'What an odious, odious creature a woman is,' thought Marion. He wondered, considerably out of temper, why he should feel so miserable at having to carry all those oranges. Of course with three gaping bags piled on his chest there was the explanation of acute physical discomfort; but that wasn't sufficient. It seemed as if this terrible, aristocratic giantess were doing it all on purpose to make him miserable. He saw that he was intensely ridiculous in her eyes, with those yellow bags against his white waistcoat and the parcel of snuff in his coat pocket; his face was also, he thought, streaming with perspiration, and he couldn't get at his handkerchief. It was childish, absurd of him to mind; for, after all, wasn't Lady Atalanta equally burdened? But she, with her packets of rolls, and packet of books, and basket of eggs, and her umbrella tucked under her arm, looked serene and even triumphant in her striped flannel.

'I beg your pardon – would you allow me to stop a minute and shift the bags to the other arm?' Marion could no longer resist that fearful agony. 'If you go on I'll catch you up in a second.'

But just as Marion was about to rest the bags upon the marble balustrade of a bridge, his paralysed arm gave an unaccountable jerk, and out flew one of the oranges, and rolled slowly down the stone steps of the bridge.

'I say, don't do that! You'll have them all in the canal!' cried Lady Atalanta, as Marion quickly stooped in vain pursuit of the escaped orange, the movement naturally, and as if it were being done on purpose, causing another orange to fly out in its turn; a small number of spectators, gondoliers and workmen from under the bridge, women nursing babies at neighbouring windows, and barefooted urchins from nowhere in particular, starting up to enjoy the extraordinary complicated conjuring tricks which the stout gentleman in the linen coat and Panama hat had suddenly fallen to execute.

'Damn the beastly things!' ejaculated Marion, forgetful of Lady Atalanta and good breeding, and perceiving only the oranges jumping and rolling about, and feeling his face grow redder and hotter in the glare on that white stone bridge. At that moment, as he raised his eyes, he saw, passing along, a large party of Americans from his hotel; Americans whom he had avoided like the plague, who, he felt sure, would go home and represent him as a poor creature and a snob disavowing his 'people'. He could hear them, in fancy, describing how at Venice he had turned flunky to one of your English aristocrats, who stood looking and making game of him while he ran after her oranges, 'and merely because she's the daughter of an Earl or Marquis or such like.'

'Bless my heart, how helpless is genius when it comes to practical matters!' exclaimed lady Atalanta. And putting her various packages down carefully on the parapet, she calmly collected the bounding oranges, wiped them with her handkerchief, and restored them to Marion, recommending him to 'stick them loose in his pockets.'

Marion had never been in a hospital (he had been only a boy, and in Europe with his mother, a Southern refugee, at the time of the War), the fact striking him as an omission in his novelist's education. But he felt as if he would never wish to describe the one into which he mechanically followed Lady Tal. With its immense, immensely lofty wards, filled with greyish light, and radiating like the nave and transepts of a vast church from an altar with flickering lights and kneeling figures, it struck Marion, while he breathed that hot, thick air, sickly with carbolic and chloride of lime, as a most gruesome and quite objectionably picturesque place. He had a vague notion that the creatures in the rows and rows of greyish white beds ought to have St. Vitus's dance or leprosy or some similar mediaeval disease. They were nasty enough objects, he thought, as he timidly followed Lady Tal's rapid and resounding footsteps, for anything. He had, for all the prosaic quality of his writings, the easily foused imagination of a nervous man: and it seemed to him as if they were all of them either skeletons gibbering and screeching in bed, or frightful yellow and red tumid creatures, covered with plasters and ligatures, or old ladies recently liberated from the cellar in which, as you may periodically read in certain public prints, they had been kept by barbarous nephews or grandchildren –

'Dear me, dear me, what a dreadful place!' he kept ejaculating, as he followed Lady Atalanta, carrying her bags of oranges and rolls, among the vociferating, grabbing beldames in bed, and the indifferent nuns and serving wenches toiling about noisily: Lady Tal going methodically her way, business-like, cheerful, giving to one some snuff, to another an orange or a book, laughing, joking in her bad Italian, settling the creatures' disagreeable bed-clothes and pillows for them, as if instead of cosseting dying folk, she was going round to the counters of some huge shop. A most painful exhibition, thought Marion.

'I say, suppose you talk to her, she's a nice little commonplace creature who wanted to be a school-mistress and is awfully fond of reading novels – tell her – I don't know how to explain it – that you write novels. See, Teresina, this gentleman and I are writing a book together, all about a lady who married a silly husband – would you like to hear about it?'

Stroking the thin white face, with the wide forget-me-not eyes, of the pretty, thin little blonde, Lady Tal left Marion, to his extreme discomfort, seated on the edge of a straw chair by the side of the bed, a bag of oranges on his knees and absolutely no ideas in his head.

'She is so good,' remarked the little girl, opening and shutting a little fan which Lady Tal had just given her, 'and so beautiful. Is she your sister? She told me she had a brother whom she was very fond of, but I thought he was dead. She's like an angel in Paradise.'

'Precisely, precisely,' answered Marion, thinking at the same time what an uncommonly uncomfortable place Paradise must, in that case, be. All this was not at all what he had imagined when he had occasionally written about young ladies consoling the sick; this businesslike, bouncing, cheerful shake-up-your-pillows and shake-up-your-soul mode of proceeding.

Lady Tal, he decided within himself, had emphatically no soul; all he had just witnessed, proved it.

'Why do you do it?' he suddenly asked, as they emerged from the hospital cloisters. He knew quite well: merely because she was so abominably active.

'I don't know. I like ill folk. I'm always so disgustingly well myself; and you see with my poor brother, I'd got accustomed to ill folk, so I suppose I can't do without. I should like to settle in England – if it weren't for all those hateful relations of mine and of my husband's – and go and live in the East End and look after sick creatures. At least I think I should; but I know I shouldn't.'

'Why not?' asked Marion.

'Why? Oh, well, it's making oneself conspicuous, you know, and all that. One hates to be thought eccentric, of course. And then, if I went to England, of course I should have to go into society, otherwise people would go and say that I was out of it and had been up to something or other. And if I went into society, that would mean doing simply nothing else, not even the little I do here. You see I'm not an independent woman; all my husband's relations are perpetually ready to pull me to pieces on account of his money! There's nothing they're not prepared to invent about me. I'm too poor and too expensive to do without it, and as long as I take his money, I must see to no one being able to say anything that would have annoyed him – see?'

'I see,' answered Marion.

At that moment Lady Atalanta perceived a gondola turning a corner, and in it the young millionaire whom she had chaffed about his sideboard.

'Hi, hi! Mr. Clarence!' she cried, waving her umbrella.

'Will you take me to that curiosity-dealer's this afternoon?'

Marion looked at her, standing there on the little wharf, waving her red umbrella and shouting to the gondola; her magnificent rather wooden figure more impeccably magnificent, uninteresting in her mannish flannel garments, her handsome pink and white face, as she smiled that inexpressive smile with all the pearl-like little teeth, more than ever like a big mask –

'No soul, decidedly no soul,' said the novelist to himself. And he reflected that women without souls were vaguely odious.

VII

'I have been wondering of late why I liked you?' said Lady Tal one morning at lunch, addressing the remark to Marion, and cut short in her speech by a burst of laughter from that odious tomboy of a cousin of hers (how could she endure that girl? Marion reflected) who exclaimed, with an affectation of milkmaid archness:

'Oh, Tal! how *can* you be so rude to the *gentleman*? You oughtn't to say to people you wonder why you like them. Ought she, Mr. Marion?'

Marion was silent. He felt a weak worm for disliking this big blond girl with the atrocious manners, who insisted on pronouncing his name *Mary Anne*, with unfailing relish of the joke. Lady Tal did not heed the interruption, but repeated pensively, leaning her handsome cleft chin on her hand, and hacking at a peach with her knife: 'I have been wondering why I like you, Mr. Marion (I usedn't to, but made up to you for *Christina's* benefit), because you are not a bit like poor Gerald. But I've found out now and I'm pleased. There's nothing so pleasant in this world as finding out *why* one thinks or does things, is there? Indeed it's the only pleasant thing, besides riding in the Campagna and drinking iced water on a hot day. The reason I like you is because you have seen a lot of the world and of people, and still take nice views of them. The people one meets always think to show their cleverness by explaining everything by nasty little motives; and you don't. It's nice of you, and it's clever. It's cleverer than your books even, you know.'

In making this remark (and she made it with an aristocratic indifference to being personal) Lady Atalanta had most certainly hit the right nail on the head. That gift, a rare one, of seeing the simple, wholesome, and even comparatively noble, side of things; of being, although a pessimist, no misanthrope, was the most remarkable characteristic of Jervase Marion; it was the one which made him, for all his old bachelor ways and his shrinking from close personal contact, a man and a manly man, giving this analytical and nervous person a certain calmness and gentleness and strength.

But Lady Tal's remark, although in the main singularly correct, smote him like a rod. For it so happened that for once in his life Marion had not been looking with impartial, serene, and unsuspecting eyes upon one of his fellow-sufferers in this melancholy world; and that one creature to whom he was not so good as he might be, was just Lady Tal.

He could not really have explained how it was. But there was the certainty, that while recognising in Lady Tal's conversation, in her novel, in the little she told him of her life, a great deal which was delicate, and even noble, wherewithal to make up a somewhat unusual and perhaps not very superficially attractive, but certainly an original and desirable personality, he had got into the habit of explaining whatever in her was obscure and contradictory by unworthy reasons; and even of making allowance for the possibility of all the seeming good points proving, some day, to be a delusion and a snare. Perhaps it depended upon the constant criticisms he was hearing on all sides of Lady Atalanta's character and conduct: the story of her mercenary marriage, the recital of the astounding want of feeling displayed upon the occasion of her brother's death, and that perpetual, and apparently too well founded suggestion that this young lady, who possessed fifteen thousand a year and apparently spent about two, must be feathering her nest and neatly evading the intentions of her late lamented. Moreover there was something vaguely disagreeable in the extraordinary absence of human emotion displayed in such portion of her biography as might be considered public property.

Marion, heaven knows, didn't like women who went in for *grande passion*; in fact passion, which he had neither experienced nor described, was distinctly repulsive to him. But, after all, Lady Tal was young, Lady Tal was beautiful, and Lady Tal had for years and years been a real and undoubted widow; and it was therefore distinctly inhuman on the part of Lady Tal to have met no temptations to part with her heart, and with her jointure. It was ugly; there was no doubt it was ugly. The world, after all, *has* a right to demand that a young lady of good birth and average education should have a heart. It was doubtless also, he said to himself, the fault of Lady Atalanta's physique, this suspicious attitude of his; nature had bestowed upon her a face like a mask, muscles which never flinched, nerves apparently hidden many inches deeper than most folk's: she was enigmatic, and a man has a right to pause before an enigma. Furthermore – But Marion could not quite understand that furthermore.

He understood it a few days later. They had had the usual *séance* over *Christina* that morning; and now it was evening, and three or four people had dropped in at Lady Tal's after the usual stroll at St. Mark's. Lady Tal had hired a small house, dignified with the title of Palazzina, on the Zattere. It was modern, and the aesthetic colony at Venice sneered at a woman with that amount of money inhabiting anything short of a palace. They themselves being mainly Americans, declared they couldn't feel like home in a dwelling which was not possessed of historical reminiscences. The point of Lady Tal's little place, as she called it, was that it possessed a garden; small indeed, but round which, as she remarked, one solitary female could walk. In this garden she and Marion were at this moment walking. The ground floor windows were open, and there issued from the drawing-room a sound of cups and saucers, of guitar strumming and laughter, above which rose the loud voice, the aristocratic kitchen-maid pronunciation of Lady Atalanta's tomboy cousin.

'Where's Tal? I declare if Tal hasn't gone off with Mary Anne! Poor Mary Anne! She's tellin' him all about *Christina*, you know; how she can't manage that row between Christina and Christina's mother-in-law, and the semicolons and all that. *Christina's* the novel, you know. You'll be expected to ask for *Christina* at your club, you know, when it comes out, Mr. Clarence. I've already written to all my cousins to get it from Mudie's –'

Marion gave a little frown, as if his boot pinched him, as he walked on the gravel down there, among the dark bushes, the spectral little terra-cotta statues, with the rigging of the ships on the Giudecca canal black against the blue evening sky, with a vague, sweet, heady smell of *Olca fragrans* all round. Confound that girl! Why couldn't he take a stroll in a garden with a handsome woman of thirty without the company being informed that it was only on account of Lady Tal's novel. That novel, that position of literary adviser, of a kind of male daily governess, would make him ridiculous. Of course Lady Tal was continually making use of him, merely making use of him in her barefaced and brutal manner: of course she didn't care a hang about him except to help her with that novel: of course as soon as that novel was done with she would drop him. He knew all that, and it was natural. But he really didn't see the joke of being made conspicuous and grotesque before all Venice –

'Shan't we go in, Lady Tal?' he said sharply, throwing away his cigarette. 'Your other guests are doubtless sighing for your presence.'

'And this guest here is not. Oh dear, no; there's Gertrude to look after them and see to their being happy; besides, I don't care whether they are. I want to speak to you. I can't understand your thinking that situation strained. I should have thought it the commonest thing in the world, I mean, gracious – I can't understand your not understanding!'

Jervase Marion was in the humour when he considered Lady Tal a legitimate subject of study, and intellectual vivisection a praiseworthy employment. Such study implies, as a rule, a good deal of duplicity on the part of the observer; duplicity doubtless sanctified, like all the rest, by the high mission of prying into one's neighbour's soul.

'Well,' answered Marion – he positively hated that good French Alabama name of his, since hearing it turned into Mary Anne – 'of course one understands a woman avoiding, for many reasons, the temptation of one individual passion; but a woman who makes up her mind to avoid the temptation of all passion in the abstract, and what is more, acts consistently and persistently with this object in view, particularly when she has never experienced passion at all, when she has not even burnt the tips of her fingers once in her life –; that does seem rather far fetched, you must admit.'

Lady Tal was not silent for a moment, as he expected she would be. She did not seem to see the danger of having the secret of her life extracted out of her.

'I don't see why you should say so, merely because the

person's a woman. I'm sure you must have met examples enough of men who, without ever having been in love, or in danger of being in love – poor little things – have gone through life with a resolute policy of never placing themselves in danger, of never so much as taking their heart out of their waistcoat pockets to look at it, lest it might suddenly be jerked out of their possession.'

It was Marion who was silent. Had it not been dark, Lady Tal might have seen him wince and redden; and he might have seen Lady Tal smile a very odd but not disagreeable smile. And they fell to discussing the technicalities of that famous novel.

Marion outstayed for a moment or two the other guests. The facetious cousin was strumming in the next room, trying over a Venetian song which the naval captain had taught her. Marion was slowly taking a third cup of tea – he wondered why he should be taking so much tea, it was very bad for his nerves, – seated among the flowering shrubs, the bits of old brocade and embroidery, the various pieces of bric-à-brac which made the drawing-room of Lady Tal look, as all distinguished modern drawing-rooms should, like a cross between a flower show and a pawnbroker's, and as if the height of modern upholstery consisted in avoiding the use of needles and nails, and enabling the visitors to sit in a little heap of variegated rags. Lady Tal was arranging a lamp, which burned, or rather smoked, at this moment, surrounded by lace petticoats on a carved column.

'Ah,' she suddenly said, 'it's extraordinary how difficult it is to get oneself understood in this world. I'm thinking about *Christina*, you know. I never *do* expect any one to understand anything, as a matter of fact. But I thought that was probably because all my friends hitherto have been all frivolous poops who read only the Peerage and the sporting papers. I should have thought, now, that writing novels would have made you different. I suppose, after all, it's all a question of physical constitution and blood relationship – being able to understand other folk, I mean. If one's molecules aren't precisely the same and in the same place (don't be surprised, I've been reading Carpenter's "Mental Physiology"), it's no good. It's certain that the only person in the world who has ever understood me one bit was Gerald.'

Lady Tal's back was turned to Marion, her tall figure a mere dark mass against the light of the lamp, and the lit-up white wall behind.

'And still,' suddenly remarked Marion, 'you were not – not – *very* much attached to your brother, were you?'

The words were not out of Marion's mouth before he positively trembled at them. Good God! what had he allowed himself to say? But he had no time to think of his own words. Lady Tal had turned round, her eyes fell upon him. Her face was pale, very quiet; not angry, but disdainful. With one hand she continued to adjust the lamp.

'I see,' she said coldly, 'you have heard all about my extraordinary behaviour, or want of extraordinary behaviour. It appears I did surprise and shock my acquaintances very much by my proceedings after Gerald's death. I suppose it really is the right thing for a woman to go into hysterics and take to her bed and shut herself up for three months at least, when her only brother dies. I didn't think of that at the time; otherwise I should have conformed, of course. It's my policy always to conform, you know. I see now that I made a mistake, showed a want of *savoir-vivre*, and all that – I stupidly consulted my own preferences, and I happened to prefer keeping myself well in hand. I didn't seem to like people's sympathy; now the world, you know, has a right to give one its sympathies under certain circumstances, just as a foreign man has a right to leave his card when he's been introduced. Also, I knew that Gerald would have just hated my making myself a *motley to the view* – you mightn't think it, but we used to read Shakespeare's sonnets, he and I – and, you see, I cared for only one mortal thing in the world, to do what Gerald wanted. I never have cared for any other thing, really; after all, if I don't want to be conspicuous, it's because Gerald would have hated it – I never shall care for anything in the world besides that. All the rest's mere unreality. One thinks one's alive, but one isn't.'

Lady Atalanta had left off fidgeting with the lamp. Her big blue eyes had all at once brightened with tears which did not fall; but as she spoke the last words, in a voice suddenly husky, she looked down at Marion with an odd smile, tearing a paper spill with her large, well-shaped fingers as she did so.

'Do you see?' she added, with that half-contemptuous smile, calmly mopping her eyes. 'That's how it is, Mr. Marion.'

A sudden light illuminated Marion's mind; a light, and with it something else, he knew not what, something akin to music, to perfume, beautiful, delightful, but solemn. He was aware of being moved, horribly grieved, but at the same moment intensely glad; he was on the point of saying he didn't know beforehand what, something which, however, would be all right, natural, like the things, suddenly improvised, which one says occasionally to children.

'My dear young lady –'

But the words did not pass Marion's lips. He remembered suddenly by what means and in what spirit he had elicited this unexpected burst of feeling on the part of Lady Tal. He could not let her go on, he could not take advantage of her; he had not the courage to say: 'Lady Tal, I am a miserable cad who was prying into your feelings; I'm not fit to be spoken to!' And with the intolerable shame at his own caddishness came that old shrinking from any sort of spiritual contact with others.

'Quite so, quite so,' he merely answered, looking at his boots and moving that ring of his mother's up and down his watch chain. 'I quite understand. And as a matter of fact you are quite correct in your remark about our not being always alive. Or rather we *are* usually alive, when we are living our humdrum little natural existence, full of nothing at all; and during the moments when we do really seem to be alive, to be feeling, living, we are not ourselves, but somebody else.'

Marion had had no intention of making a cynical speech. He had been aware of having behaved like a cad to Lady Tal, and in consequence, had somehow informed Lady Tal he considered her as an impostor. He had reacted against that first overwhelming sense of pleasure at the discovery of the lady's much-questioned soul. Now he was prepared to tell her that she had none.

'Yes,' answered Lady Tal, lighting a cigarette over the high lamp, 'that's just it. I shall borrow that remark and put it into *Christina*. You may use up any remark of mine, in return, you know.'

She stuck out her under lip with that ugly little cynical movement which was not even her own property, but borrowed from women more trivial than herself like the way of carrying the elbows, and the pronunciation of certain words: a mark of caste, as a blue triangle on one's chin or a yellow butterfly on one's forehead might be, and not more graceful or engaging.

'One thinks one has a soul sometimes,' she mused. 'It isn't true. It would prevent one's clothes fitting, wouldn't it? One really acts in this way or that because *it's better form*. You see here on the Continent it's good form to tear one's hair and roll on the floor, and to pretend to have a soul; we've got beyond that, as we've got beyond women trying to seem to know about art and literature. Here they do, and make idiots of themselves. Just now you thought I'd got a soul, didn't you,

Mr. Marion? You've been wondering all along whether I had one. For a minute I managed to make you believe it – it was rather mean of me, wasn't it? I haven't got one. I'm a great deal too well-bred.'

There was a little soreness under all this banter; but how could she banter? Marion felt he detested the woman, as she put out her elbow and extended a stiff handsome hand, and said:

'Remember poor old *Christina* to-morrow morning, there's a kind man,' with that little smile of close eyes and close lips. He detested her just in proportion as he had liked her half an hour ago. Remembering that little gush of feeling of his own, he thought her a base creature, as he walked across the little moonlit square with the well in the middle and the tall white houses all round.

Jervase Marion, the next morning, woke up with the consciousness of having been very unfair to Lady Tal, and, what was worse, very unfair to himself. It was one of the drawbacks of friendship (for, after all, this was a kind of friendship) that he occasionally caught himself saying things quite different from his thoughts and feelings, masquerading towards people in a manner distinctly humiliating to his self-respect. Marion had a desire to be simple and truthful; but somehow it was difficult to be simple and truthful as soon as other folk came into play; it was difficult and disagreeable to show one's real self; that was another reason for living solitary on a top flat at Westminster, and descending therefrom in the body, but not in the spirit, to move about among mere acquaintances, disembodied things, with whom there was no fear of real contact. On this occasion he had let himself come in contact with a fellow-creature; and behold, as a result, he had not only behaved more or less like a cad, but he had done that odious thing of pretending to feel differently from how he really did.

From how he had really felt at the moment, be it well understood. Of course Marion, in his capacity of modern analytical novelist, was perfectly well aware that feelings are mere momentary matters; and that the feeling which had possessed him the previous evening, and still possessed him at the present moment, would not last. The feeling, he admitted to himself (it is much easier to admit such things to one's self, when one makes the proviso that it's all a mere passing phase, one's eternal immutable self, looking on placidly at one's momentary changing self), the feeling in question was vaguely admiring and pathetic, as regarded Lady Tal. He even confessed to himself that there entered into it a slight dose of poetry. This big, correct young woman, with the beautiful inexpressive face and the ugly inexpressive manners, carrying through life a rather exotic little romance which no one must suspect, possessed a charm for the imagination, a decided value. Excluded for some reason (Marion blurred out his knowledge that the reasons were the late Walkenshaw's thousands) from the field for emotions and interests which handsome, big young women have a right to, and transferring them all to a nice crippled brother, who had of course not been half as nice as she imagined, living a conventional life, with a religion of love and fidelity secreted within it, this well-born and well-dressed Countess Olivia of modern days, had appealed very strongly to a certain carefully guarded tenderness and chivalry in Marion's nature; he saw her, as she had stood arranging that lamp, with those unexpected tears brimming in her eyes.

Decidedly. Only that, of course, wasn't the way to treat it. There was nothing at all artistic in that, nothing modern. And Marion was essentially modern in his novels. Lady Tal, doing the Lady Olivia, with a dead brother in the background, sundry dukes in the middle distance, and no enchanting page (people seemed unanimous in agreeing that

Lady Tal had never been in love) perceptible anywhere; all that was pretty, but it wasn't the right thing. Jervase Marion thought Lady Tal painfully conventional (although of course her conventionality gave all the value to her romantic quality) because she slightly dropped her final g's, and visibly stuck out her elbows, and resolutely refused to display emotion of any kind. Marion himself was firmly wedded to various modes of looking at human concerns, which corresponded, in the realm of novel-writing, to these same modern conventionalities of Lady Atalanta's. The point of it, evidently, must be that the Lady of his novel would have lived for years under the influence of an invalid friend (the brother should be turned into a woman with a mortal malady, and a bad husband, something in the way of Emma and Tony in 'Diana of the Crossways', of intellectual and moral quality immensely superior to her own); then, of course, after the death of the Princess of Trasimeno (she being the late Gerald Burne), Lady Tal (Marion couldn't fix on a name for her) would gradually be sucked back into frivolous and futile and heartless society; the *hic* of the whole story being the slow ebbing of that noble influence, the daily encroachments of the baser sides of Lady Tal's own nature, and of the base side of the world. She would have a chance, say by marrying a comparatively poor man, of securing herself from that rising tide of worldly futility and meanness; the reader must think that she really was going to love the man, to choose him. Or rather, it would be more modern and artistic, less romantic, if the intelligent reader were made to foresee the dismal necessity of Lady Tal's final absorption into moral and intellectual nothingness. Yes – the sort of thing she would live for, a round of monotonous dissipation, which couldn't amuse her; of expenditure merely for the sake of expenditure, of conventionality merely for the sake of conventionality; – and the sham, clever, demoralised women, with their various semi-imaginary grievances against the world, their husbands and children, their feeble self-conscious hankerings after mesmerism, spiritualism, Buddhism, and the other forms of intellectual adulteration – he saw it all. Marion threw his cigar into the canal, and nursed his leg tighter, as he sat all alone in his gondola, and looked up at the bay trees and oleanders, the yellow straw blinds of Lady Tal's little house on the Zattere.

It would make a capital novel. Marion's mind began to be inundated with details: all those conversations about Lady Tal rushed back into it, her conventionality, perceptible even to others, her disagreeable parsimoniousness, visibly feathering her nest with the late Walkenshaw's money, while quite unable to screw up her courage to deliberately forego it, that odd double-graspingness of nature.

That was evidently the final degradation. It would be awfully plucky to put it in, after showing what the woman had been and might have been; after showing her coquettings with better things (the writing of that novel, for instance, for which he must find an equivalent). It would be plucky, modern, artistic, to face the excessive sordidness of this ending. And still – and still – Marion felt a feeble repugnance to putting it in; it seemed too horrid. And at the same moment, there arose in him that vague, disquieting sense of being a cad, which had distressed him that evening. To suspect a woman of all that – and yet, Marion answered himself with a certain savageness, he knew it to be the case.

VIII

They had separated from the rest of the picnickers, and were walking up and down that little orchard or field – rows of brown maize distaffs and tangles of reddening half trodden-down maize leaves, and patches of tall grass powdered with hemlock under the now rather battered vine garlands, the pomegranate branches weighed down by their vermilion fruit, the peach branches making a Japanese pattern of narrow crimson leaves against the blue sky – that odd cultivated corner in the God-forsaken little marsh island, given up to sea-gulls and picnickers, of Torcello.

'Poor little Clarence,' mused Lady Tal, alluding to the rather feeble-minded young millionaire, who had brought them there, five gondolas full of women in lilac and pink and straw-coloured frocks, and men in white coats, three guitars, a banjo, and two mandolins, and the corresponding proportion of table linen, knives and forks, pies, bottles, and sweetmeats with crinkled papers round them. 'Poor little Clarence, he isn't a bad little thing, is he? He wouldn't be bad to a woman who married him, would he?'

'He would adore her,' answered Jervase Marion, walking up and down that orchard by Lady Tal's side. 'He would give her everything the heart of woman could desire; carriages, horses, and diamonds, and frocks from Worth, and portraits by Lenbach and Sargent, and bric-à-brac, and – ever so much money for charities, hospitals, that sort of thing – and – and complete leisure and freedom and opportunities for enjoying the company of men not quite so well off as himself.'

Marion stopped short, his hands thrust in his pockets, and with that frown which made people think that his boots pinched. He was looking down at his boots at this moment, though he was really thinking of that famous novel, his, not Lady Tal's; so Lady Tal may have perhaps thought it was the boots that made him frown, and speak in a short, cross little way. Apparently she thought so, for she took no notice of his looks, his intonation, or his speech.

'Yes,' she continued musing, striking the ground with her umbrella, 'he's a good little thing. It's good to bring us all to Torcello, with all that food and those guitars, and banjos and things, particularly as we none of us throw a word at him in return. And he seems so pleased. It shows a very amiable, self-effacing disposition, and that's after all, the chief thing in marriage. But, Lord! how dreary it would be to see that man at breakfast, and lunch, and dinner! or if one didn't, merely to know that there he must be, having breakfast, lunch and dinner somewhere – for I suppose he would have to have them – that man existing somewhere on the face of the globe, and speaking of one as "my wife". Fancy knowing the creature was always smiling, whatever one did, and never more jealous than my umbrella. Wouldn't it feel like being one of the fish in that tank we saw? Wouldn't living with the Bishop – is he a bishop? – of Torcello, in that musty little house with all the lichen stains and mosquito nests, and nothing but Attila's throne to call upon – be fun compared with that? Yes, I suppose it's wise to marry Clarence. I suppose I shall do right in making him marry my cousin. You know' – she added, speaking all these words slowly – 'I could make him marry anybody, because he wants to marry me.'

Marion gave a little start as Lady Tal had slowly pronounced those two words, 'my cousin'. Lady, Tal noticed it.

'You thought I had contemplated having Clarence myself?' she said, looking at the novelist with a whimsical, amused look. 'Well, so I have. I have contemplated a great many things, and not had the courage to do them. I've contemplated going off to Germany, and studying nursing; and going off to France, and studying painting; I've contemplated turning Catholic, and going into a convent. I've contemplated – well – I'm contemplating at present – becoming a *great* novelist, as you know. I've contemplated marrying poor men, and becoming their amateur charwoman; and I've contemplated marrying rich men, and becoming – well, whatever a penniless woman does become when she marries a rich man;

but I've done that once before, and once is enough of any experience in life, at least for a person of philosophic cast of mind, don't you think? I confess I have been contemplating the possibility of marrying Clarence, though I don't see my way to it. You see, it's not exactly a pleasant position to be a widow and not to be one, as I am, in a certain sense. Also, I'm bored with living on my poor husband's money, particularly as I know he wished me to find it as inconvenient as possible to do so. I'm bored with keeping the capital from that wretched boy and his mother, who would get it all as soon as I was safely married again. That's it. As a matter of fact I'm bored with all life, as I daresay most people are; but to marry this particular Clarence, or any other Clarence that may be disporting himself about, wouldn't somehow diminish the boringness of things. Do you see?'

'I see,' answered Marion. Good Heavens, what a thing it is to be a psychological novelist! and how exactly he had guessed at the reality of Lady Atalanta's character and situation. He would scarcely venture to write that novel of his; he might as well call it *Lady Tal* at once. It was doubtless this discovery which made him grow suddenly very red and feel an intolerable desire to say he knew not what.

They continued walking up and down that little orchard, the brown maize leaves all around, the bright green and vermilion enamel of the pomegranate trees, the Japanese pattern, red and yellow, of the peach branches, against the blue sky above.

'My dear Lady Tal,' began Marion, 'my dear young lady, will you allow – an elderly student of human nature to say – how – I fear it must seem very impertinent – how thoroughly – taking your whole situation as if it were that of a third person – he understanding its difficulties – and, taking the situation no longer quite as that of a third person, how earnestly he hopes that –'

Marion was going to say 'you will not derogate from the real nobility of your nature.' But only a fool could say such a thing; besides, of course, Lady Tal *must* derogate. So he finished off:

'That events will bring some day a perfectly satisfactory, though perhaps unforeseen, conclusion for you.'

Lady Tal was paying no attention. She plucked one of the long withered peach leaves, delicate, and red, and transparent, like a Chinese visiting card, and began to pull it through her fingers.

'You see,' she said, 'of the income my husband left me, I've been taking only as much as seemed necessary – about two thousand a year. I mean necessary that people shouldn't see that I'm doing this sort of thing; because, after all, I suppose a woman could live on less, though I am an expensive woman. – The rest, of course, I've been letting accumulate for the heir; I couldn't give it him, for that would have been going against my husband's will. But it's rather boring to feel one's keeping that boy, – such a nasty young brute as he is – and his horrid mother out of all that money, merely by being there. It's rather humiliating, but it would be more humiliating to marry another man for his money. And I don't suppose a poor man would have me; and perhaps I wouldn't have a poor man. Now, suppose I were the heroine of your novel – you know you *are* writing a novel about me, that's what makes you so patient with me and *Christina*, you're just walking round, and looking at me –'

'Oh, my dear Lady Tal – how – how can you think such a thing!' gobbled out Marion indignantly. And really, at the moment of speaking, he did feel a perfectly unprofessional interest in this young lady, and was considerably aggrieved at this accusation.

'Aren't you? Well, I thought you were. You see I have novel on the brain. Well, just suppose you *were* writing that novel, with me for a heroine, what would you advise me? One has got accustomed to having certain things – a certain amount of clothes, and bric-à-brac and horses, and so forth, and to consider then necessary. And yet, I think if one were to lose them all to-morrow, it wouldn't make much difference. One would merely say: "Dear me, what's become of it all?" And yet I suppose one does require them – other people have them, so I suppose it's right one should have them also. Other people like to come to Torcello in five gondolas with three guitars, a banjo, and lunch, and to spend two hours feeding and littering the grass with paper bags; so I suppose one ought to like it too. If it's right, I like it. I always conform, you know; only it's rather dull work, don't you think, considered as an interest in life? Everything is dull work, for the matter of that, except dear old *Christina*. What do you think one might do to make things a little less dull? But perhaps everything is equally dull –'

Lady Tal raised one of those delicately-pencilled, immensely arched eyebrows of hers, with a sceptical little sigh, and looked in front of her, where they were standing.

Before them rose the feathery brown and lilac of the little marsh at the end of the orchard, long seeding reeds, sere grasses, sea lavender, and Michaelmas daisy; and above that delicate bloom, on an unseen strip of lagoon, moved a big yellow and brown sail, slowly flapping against the blue sky. From the orchard behind, rose at intervals the whirr of a belated cicala; they heard the dry maize leaves crack beneath their feet.

'It's all very lovely,' remarked Lady Tal pensively; 'but it doesn't somehow fit in properly. It's silly for people like me to come to such a place. As a rule, since Gerald's death, I only go for walks in civilised places: they're more in harmony with my frocks.'

Jervase Marion did not answer. He leaned against the

bole of a peach tree, looking out at the lilac and brown sea marsh and the yellow sail, seeing them with that merely physical intentness which accompanies great mental preoccupation. He was greatly moved. He was aware of a fearful responsibility. Yet neither the emotion nor the responsibility made him wretched, as he always fancied that all emotion or responsibility must.

He seemed suddenly to be in this young woman's place, to feel the already begun, and rapid increasing withering-up of this woman's soul, the dropping away from it of all real, honest, vital interests. She seemed to him in horrible danger, the danger of something like death. And there was but one salvation: to give up that money, to make herself free – Yes, yes, there was nothing for it but that. Lady Tal, who usually struck him as so oppressively grown up, powerful, able to cope with everything, affected him at this moment as a something very young, helpless, almost childish; he understood so well that during all those years this big woman in her stiff clothes, with her inexpressive face, had been a mere child in the hands of her brother, that she had never thought, or acted, or felt for herself; that she had not lived.

Give up that money; give up that money; marry some nice young fellow who will care for you; become the mother of a lot of nice little children – The words went on and on in Marion's mind, close to his lips; but they could not cross them. He almost saw those children of hers, the cut of their pinafores and sailor clothes, the bend of their blond and pink necks; and that nice young husband, blond of course, tall of course, with vague, regular features, a little dull perhaps, but awfully good. It was so obvious, so right. At the same time it seemed rather tame; and Marion, he didn't know why, while perceiving its extreme rightness and delightfulness, couldn't help wincing a little bit at the prospect –

Lady Tal must have been engaged simultaneously in some

similar contemplation, for she suddenly turned round, and said:

'But after all, anything else might perhaps be just as boring as all this. And fancy having given up that money all for nothing; one would feel such a fool. On the whole, my one interest in life is evidently destined to be *Christina*, and the solution of all my doubts will be the appearance of the "New George Eliot of fashionable life"; don't you think that sounds like the heading in one of your American papers, the Buffalo *Independent*, or Milwaukee *Republican?*'

Marion gave a little mental start.

'Just so, just so,' he answered hurriedly: 'I think it would be a fatal thing – a very fatal thing for you to – well – to do anything rash, my dear Lady Tal. After all, we must remember that there is such a thing as habit; a woman accustomed to the life you lead, although I don't deny it may sometimes seem dull, would be committing a mistake, in my opinion a great mistake, in depriving herself, for however excellent reasons, of her fortune. Life is dull, but, on the whole, the life we happen to live is usually the one which suits us best. My own life, for instance, strikes me at moments, I must confess, as a trifle dull. Yet I should be most unwise to change it, most unwise. I think you are quite right in supposing that novel-writing, if you persevere in it, will afford you a – very – well – a – considerable interest in life.'

Lady Tal yawned under her parasol.

'Don't you think it's time for us to go back to the rest of our rabble?' she asked. 'It must be quite three-quarters of an hour since we finished lunch, so I suppose it's time for tea, or food of some sort. Have you ever reflected, Mr. Marion, how little there would be in picnics, and in life in general, if one couldn't eat a fresh meal every three-quarters of an hour?'

IX

Few things, of the many contradictory things of this world, are more mysterious than the occasional certainty of sceptical men. Marion was one of the most sceptical of sceptical novelists; the instinct that nothing really depended upon its supposed or official cause, that nothing ever produced its supposed or official effect, that all things were always infinitely more important or unimportant than represented, that nothing is much use to anything, and the world a mystery and a muddle; this instinct, so natural to the psychologist, regularly honeycombed his existence, making it into a mere shifting sand, quite unfit to carry the human weight. Yet at this particular moment, Marion firmly believed that if only Lady Atalanta could be turned into a tolerable novelist, the whole problem of Lady Atalanta's existence would be satisfactorily solved, if only she could be taught construction, style, punctuation, and a few other items; if only one could get into her head the difference between a well-written thing, and an ill-written thing, then, considering her undoubted talent – for Marion's opinion of Lady Tal's talent had somehow increased with a bound. Why he should think *Christina* a more remarkable performance now that he had been tinkering at it for six weeks, it is difficult to perceive. He seemed certainly to see much more in it. Through that extraordinary difficulty of expression, he now felt the shape of a personality, a personality contradictory, enigmatical, not sure of itself, groping, as it were, to the light. *Christina* was evidently the real Lady Tal, struggling through that overlaying of habits and prejudices which constituted the false one.

So, *Christina* could not be given too much care; and certainly no novel was ever given more, both by its author and by its critic. There was not a chapter, and scarcely a paragraph, which had not been dissected by Marion and re-written by Lady Tal; the critical insight of the one being outdone only by the scribbling energy of the other. And now, it would soon be finished. There was only that piece about Christina's reconciliation with her sister-in-law to get into shape. Somehow or other the particular piece seemed intolerably difficult to do; the more Lady Tal worked at it, the worse it grew; the more Marion expounded his views on the subject, the less did she seem able to grasp them.

They were seated on each side of the big deal table, which, for the better development of *Christina*, Lady Tal had installed in her drawing-room, and which at this moment presented a lamentable confusion of foolscap, of mutilated pages, of slips for gumming on, of gum-pots, and scissors. The scissors, however, were at present hidden from view, and Lady Tal, stooping over the litter, was busily engaged looking for them.

'Confound those beastly old scissors!' she exclaimed, shaking a heap of MS. with considerable violence.

Marion, on his side, gave a feeble stir to the mass of paper, and said, rather sadly: 'Are you sure you left them on this table?'

He felt that something was going wrong. Lady Tal had been unusually restive about the alterations he wanted her to make.

'You are slanging those poor scissors because you are out of patience with things in general, Lady Tal.'

She raised her head, and leaning both her long, well-shaped hands on the table, looked full at Marion:

'Not with things in general, but with things in particular. With *Christina*, in the first place; and then with myself; and then with you, Mr. Marion.'

'With me?' answered Marion, forcing out a smile of pseudo-surprise. He had felt all along that she was irritated with him this morning.

'With you' – went on the lady, continuing to rummage for the scissors – 'with you, because I don't think you've been quite fair. It isn't fair to put it into an unfortunate creature's head that she is an incipient George Eliot, when you know that if she were to slave till doomsday, she couldn't produce a novel fit for the *Family Herald*. It's very ungrateful of me to complain, but you see it is rather hard lines upon me. You can do all this sort of thing as easy as winking, and you imagine that everyone else must. You put all your own ideas into poor *Christina*, and you just expect me to be able to carry them out, and when I make a hideous hash, you're not satisfied. You think of that novel just as if it were you writing it – you know you do. Well, then, when a woman discovers at last that she can't make the beastly thing any better; that she's been made to hope too much, and that too much is asked of her, you understand it's rather irritating. I am sick of re-writing that thing, sick of every creature in it.'

And Lady Tal gave an angry toss to the sheets of manuscript with the long pair of dressmaker's scissors, which she had finally unburied. Marion felt a little pang. The pang of a clever man who discovers himself to be perpetrating a stupidity. He frowned that little frown of the tight boots.

Quite true. He saw, all of a sudden, that he really had been over-estimating Lady Tal's literary powers. It appeared to him monstrous. The thought made him redden. To what unjustifiable lengths had his interest in the novel – the novel in the abstract, anybody's novel; and (he confessed to himself) the interest in one novel in particular, his own, the one in which Lady Tal should figure – led him away! Perceiving himself violently to be in the wrong, he proceeded to assume the manner, as is the case with most of us under similar circumstances (perhaps from a natural instinct of balancing matters) of a person conscious of being in the right.

'I think,' he said, dryly, 'that you have rather overdone

this novel, Lady Tal – worked at it too much, talked of it too much too, sickened yourself with it.'

'– And sickened others,' put in Lady Atalanta gloomily.

'No, no, no – not others – only yourself, my dear young lady,' said Marion paternally, in a way which clearly meant that she had expressed the complete truth, being a rude woman, but that he, being a polite man, could never admit it. As a matter of fact, Marion was not in the least sick of *Christina*, quite the reverse.

'You see,' he went on, playing with the elastic band of one of the packets of MS., 'you can't be expected to know these things. But no professed novelist – no one of any experience – no one, allow me to say so, except a young lady, could possibly have taken such an overdose of novel-writing as you have. Why, you have done in six weeks what ought to have taken six months! The result, naturally, is that you have lost all sense of proportion and quality; you really can't see your novel any longer, that's why you feel depressed about it.'

Lady Tal was not at all mollified.

'That wasn't a reason for making me believe I was going to be George Eliot and Ouida rolled into one, with the best qualities of Goethe and Dean Swift into the bargain,' she exclaimed.

Marion frowned, but this time internally. He really had encouraged Lady Tal quite unjustifiably. He doubted, suddenly, whether she would ever get a publisher; therefore he smiled, and remarked gently:

'Well, but – in matters of belief, there are two parties, Lady Tal. Don't you think you may be partly responsible for this – this little misapprehension?'

Lady Tal did not answer. The insolence of the Ossian was roused. She merely looked at Marion from head to foot; and the look was ineffably scornful. It seemed to say: 'This is what comes of a woman like me associating with Americans and novelists.'

'I've not lost patience,' she said after a moment; 'don't think that. When I make up my mind to a thing I just do it. So I shall finish *Christina*, and print her, and publish her, and dedicate her to you. Only, catch me ever writing another novel again! – and' – she added, smiling with her closed teeth as she extended a somewhat stiff hand to Marion – 'catch you reading another novel of mine again either, now that you've made all the necessary studies of me for *your* novel!'

Marion smiled politely. But he ran downstairs, and through the narrow little paved lane to the ferry at San Vio with a bent head.

He had been a fool, a fool, he repeated to himself. Not, as he had thought before, by exposing Lady Tal to disappointment and humiliation, but by exposing himself.

Yes, he understood it all. He understood it when, scarcely out of Lady Tal's presence, he caught himself, in the garden, looking up at her windows, half expecting to see her, to hear some rather rough joke thrown at him as a greeting, just to show she was sorry – He understood it still better, when, every time the waiter knocked in the course of the day, he experienced a faint expectation that it might be a note from Lady Tal, a line to say: 'I was as cross as two sticks, this morning, wasn't I?' or merely: 'don't forget to come to-morrow.'

He understood. He and the novel, both chucked aside impatiently by this selfish, capricious, imperious young aristocrat: the two things identified, and both now rejected as unworthy of taking up more of her august attention! Marion felt the insult to the novel – her novel – almost more than to himself. After all, how could Lady Tal see the difference between him and the various mashers of her acquaintance, perceive that he was the salt of the earth?

She had not wherewithal to perceive it. But that she should not perceive the dignity of her own work, how infinitely finer that novel was than herself, how it represented all her own best possibilities; that she should be ungrateful for the sensitiveness with which he had discovered its merit, *her* merits, in the midst of that confusion of illiterate fashionable rubbish –

And when that evening, having his coffee at St. Mark's, he saw Lady Tal's stately figure, her white dress, amongst the promenaders in the moonlight, a rabble of young men and women at her heels, it struck him suddenly that something was over. He thought that, if Lady Tal came to London next spring; he would not call upon her unless sent for; and he was sure she would not send for him, for as to *Christina*, *Christina* would never get as far as the proof-sheets; and unless *Christina* re-appeared on the surface, he also would remain at the bottom.

Marion got up from his table, and leaving the brightly illuminated square and the crowd of summer-like promenaders, he went out on to the Riva, and walked slowly towards the arsenal. The contrast was striking. Out here it looked already like winter. There were no chairs in front of the cafés, there were scarcely any gondola-lights at the mooring places. The passers-by went along quickly, the end of their cloak over their shoulder. And from the water, which swished against the marble landings, came a rough, rainy wind. It was dark, and there were unseen puddles along the pavement.

This was the result of abandoning, for however little, one's principles. He had broken through his convictions by accepting to read a young lady's MS. novel. It did not seem a very serious mistake. But through that chink, what disorderly powers had now entered his well-arranged existence!

What the deuce did he want with the friendship of a Lady Tal? He had long made up his mind to permit himself only such friendship as could not possibly involve any feeling, as could not distress or ruffle him by such incidents as illness, death, fickleness, ingratitude. The philosophy of happiness, of that right balance of activities necessary for the dispassionate student of mankind, consisted in never having anything that one could miss, in never wanting anything. Had he not long ago made up his mind to live contemplative only of external types, if not on a column like Simon Stylites, at least in its meaner modern equivalent, a top flat at Westminster?

Marion felt depressed, ashamed of his depression, enraged at his shame; and generally intolerably mortified at feeling anything at all, and still more, in consequence, at feeling all this much.

As he wandered up and down one of the stretches of the Riva, the boisterous wind making masts and sails creak, and his cigar-smoke fly wildly about, he began, however, to take a little comfort. All this, after all, was so much experience; and experience was necessary for the comprehension of mankind. It was preferable, as a rule, to use up other people's experience; to look down, from that top flat at Westminster, upon grief and worry and rage *in corpore vili*, at a good five storeys below one. But, on reflection, it was doubtless necessary occasionally to get impressions a little nearer; the very recognition of feeling in others presupposed a certain minimum of emotional experience in oneself.

Marion had a sense of humour, a sense of dignity, and a corresponding aversion to being ridiculous. He disliked extremely having played the part of the middle-aged fool. But if ever he should require, for a future novel, a middle-aged fool, why, there he would be, ready to hand. And really, unless he had thus miserably broken through his rules of life, thus contemptibly taken an interest in a young lady six-foot high, the daughter of a bankrupt earl, with an inexpressive face and a sentimental novel, he would never, never have got to fathom, as he now fathomed, the character of the intelligent woman of the world, with aspirations ending in frivolity, and a heart entirely rusted over by insolence.

Ah, he *did* understand Lady Tal. He had gone up to his hotel; and shut his window with a bang, receiving a spout of rain in his face, as he made that reflection. Really, Lady Tal might be made into something first-rate.

He threw himself into an arm-chair and opened a volume of the correspondence of Flaubert.

X

'I am glad to have made an end of *Christina*,' remarked Lady Tal, when they were on Miss Vanderwerf's balcony together. *Christina* had been finished, cleaned up, folded, wrapped in brown paper, stringed, sealing-waxed and addressed to a publisher, a week almost ago. During the days separating this great event from this evening, the last of Lady Atalanta's stay in Venice, the two novelists had met but little. Lady Tal had had farewell visits to pay, farewell dinners and lunches to eat. So had Jervase Marion; for, two days after Lady Tal's return to her apartment near the Holy Apostles at Rome, he would be setting out for that dear, tidy, solitary flat at Westminster.

'I am glad to have made an end of *Christina*,' remarked Lady Tal, 'it had got to bore me fearfully.'

Marion winced. He disliked this young woman's ingratitude and brutality. It was ill-bred and stupid; and of all things in the world, the novelist from Alabama detested ill-breeding and stupidity most. He was angry with himself for minding these qualities in Lady Tal. Had he not long made up his mind that she possessed them, *must* possess them?

There was a pause. The canal beneath them was quite

dark, and the room behind quite light; it was November, and people no longer feared lamps on account of mosquitoes, any more than they went posting about in gondolas after illuminated singing boats. The company, also, was entirely collected within doors; the damp sea-wind, the necessity for shawls and overcoats, took away the Romeo and Juliet character from those little gothic balconies, formerly crowded with light frocks and white waistcoats.

The temperature precluded all notions of flirtation; one must intend business, or be bent upon catching cold, to venture outside.

'How changed it all is!' exclaimed Lady Tal, 'and what a beastly place Venice does become in autumn. If I were a benevolent despot, I should forbid any rooms being let or hotels being opened beyond the 15th of October. I wonder why I didn't get my bags together and go earlier! I might have gone to Florence or Perugia for a fortnight, instead of banging straight back to Rome. Oh, of course, it was all along of *Christina!* What were we talking about? Ah, yes, about how changed it all was. Do you remember the first evening we met here, a splendid moonlight, and ever so hot? When was it? Two months ago? Surely more. It seems years ago. I don't mean merely on account of the change of temperature, and leaving off cotton frocks and that: I mean we seem to have been friends so long. You will write to me sometimes, won't you, and send any of your friends to me? Palazzo Malaspini, Santi Apostoli (just opposite the French Embassy, you know), after five nearly always, in winter. I wonder,' continued Lady Tal, musingly, leaning her tweed elbow on the damp balustrade, 'whether we shall ever write another novel together; what do you think, Mr. Marion?'

Something seemed suddenly to give away inside Marion's soul. He saw, all at once, those big rooms, which he had often heard described (a woman of her means ought to be ashamed of such furniture, the Roumanian Princess had remarked), near the Holy Apostles at Rome: the red damask walls, the big palms and azaleas, with pieces of embroidery wrapped round the pots, the pastel of Lady Tal by Lenbach, the five hundred photographs dotted about, and fifteen hundred silver objects of indeterminable shape and art, and five dozen little screens all covered with odd bits of brocade – of course there was all that: and the door curtain raised, and the butler bowing in, and behind him the whitish yellowish curl, and pinky grey face of Clarence. And then he saw, but not more distinctly, his writing-table at Westminster, the etchings round his walls, the collection of empty easy-chairs, each easier and emptier, with its book-holding or leg-stretching apparatus, than its neighbour. He became aware of being old, remarkably old, of a paternal position towards this woman of thirty. He spoke in a paternal tone –

'No!' he answered, 'I think not. I shall be too busy. I must write another novel myself.'

'What will your novel be about?' asked Lady Tal, slowly, watching her cigarette cut down through the darkness into the waters below. 'Tell me.'

'My novel? What will my novel be about?' repeated Marion, absently. His mind was full of those red rooms at Rome, with the screens, and the palms, and odious tow-coloured head of Clarence. 'Why, my novel will be the story of an old artist, a sculptor – I don't mean a man of the Renaissance, I mean old in years, elderly, going on fifty – who was silly enough to imagine it was all love of art which made him take a great deal of interest in a certain young lady and her paintings –'

'You said he was a sculptor just now,' remarked Lady Tal calmly.

'Of course I meant in her statues – modelling – what d'you call it –'

'And then?' asked Lady Tal after a pause, looking down into the canal. 'What happened?'

'What happened?' repeated Marion, and he heard his own voice with surprise, wondering how it could be his own, or how he could know it for his, so suddenly had it grown quick and husky and unsteady – 'What happened? Why – that he made an awful old fool of himself. That's all.'

'That's all!' mused Lady Tal. 'Doesn't it seem rather lame? You don't seem to have got sufficient *dénouement*, do you? Why shouldn't we write that novel together? I'm sure I could help you to something more conclusive than that. Let me see. Well, suppose the lady were to answer: 'I am as poor as a rat, and I fear I'm rather expensive. But I *can* make my dresses myself if only I get one of those wicker dolls, I call them Theresa, you know; and I *might* learn to do my hair myself; and then I'm going to be a great painter – no, sculptor, I mean – and make pots of money; so suppose we get married.' Don't you think Mr. Marion, that would be more *modern* than your *dénouement*? You would have to find out what that painter – no, sculptor, I beg your pardon – would answer. Consider that both he and the lady are rather lonely, bored, and getting into the sere and yellow – We ought to write that novel together, because I've given you the ending – and also because I really can't manage another all by myself, now that I've got accustomed to having my semicolons put in for me –'

As Lady Atalanta spoke these words, a sudden downpour of rain drove her and Marion back into the drawing-room.

SARAH GRAND

THE UNDEFINABLE: A FANTASIA

That certain Something.
RUSKIN

IT was a hot summer evening, and I had gone into the studio after dinner to sit opposite my last-accomplished work, and smoke a cigarette to add to my joy in the contemplation thereof. It is a great moment even for a great artist when he can sit and sigh in solitary satisfaction before a finished picture. I had looked at it while I was waiting for dinner, and even in that empty hour it had seemed most masterly; so that now, when I may perhaps – if I apologise in advance for the unacademical vulgarism of the idea – be allowed to say that I was comfortably replete, I expected to feel in it that which surpasses the merely masterly of talent (to which degree of excellence ordinary painters, undowered by the divine afflatus, may attain by eminent industry) and approaches the superb – ecstatic. Well, in a word, if I may venture – with all becoming diffidence, and only, it will be understood, for the good-natured purpose of making myself intelligible to the general reader – if I may venture to quote a remarkable critic of mine, a most far-seeing fellow, who, in recognising the early promise of my work, in the early days when I was still struggling to scale those heights to which I afterwards so successfully attained, aptly described whatever of merit I had then displayed as 'the undefinable of genius' – this was what I had come to recognise on the great canvas before me, to feel, to revel in, to *know* in the utmost significance of the term as something all-comprehensive enough to be evident to the meanest man's capacity in its power to make him feel, while yet remaining beyond the range of language to convey. I had sat some time, however; my cigarette was half finished; the enjoyable sensation of having dined was uninterrupted by any feeling of regret on the subject of what I had eaten. I had, in fact, forgotten what I had eaten, which, when the doctor has put us under stoppages, as the military phrase is, and we have, nevertheless, ventured upon forbidden fruit, I take to be a proof that we have done so with impunity. The balmy summer air blew in upon me freshly from the garden through the south lattice of the studio; blackbird and thrush no longer lilted their love-songs – it was late; but a nightingale from the top of a tall tree, unseen, filled the innermost recesses of audition with inimitable sound. The hour, the scene – and the man, I may say – were all that is best calculated to induce the proper appreciation of a noble work of art; and the pale grey shades of evening had been dispelled by the radiant intensity of the electric light; but, although I had reclined in a deep easy-chair long enough to finish a cigarette, not a single fibre of feeling had responded to the call of the canvas upon it. I felt the freshness, the nightingale's note in the stillness; that luxurious something of kinship which comes from the near neighbourhood of a great city with companionable effect when one is well disposed. But the work of art before me moved me no more than a fresh canvas standing ready stretched upon the easel, with paints and palette lying ready for use beside it would have done – not so much, in fact, for such preparations were only made when a new idea was burning in my being to be expressed;

I should have been feeling it then; but now I was conscious of nothing more entrancing than the cold ashes of an old one. Yes! cold ashes, quite extinct, they were, and I found myself forced to acknowledge it, although, of course, I assured myself at the same time that the fault was in my mood of the moment, not in the picture. If I went out into the streets and brought in a varied multitude to gaze, I never doubted but that I should hear them shout again those paeans of praise to which I had long become accustomed – accustomed, too, as we are to the daily bread which we eat without much thought or appetite, but cannot do without. But certainly on this particular evening, while I gazed, persistent thoughts obtruded themselves instead of refined sensations. As I rounded that exquisite arm I remembered now that I had had in my mind the pleasurable certainty that the smiles of the Lady Catherine Claridge, her little invitations to 'come when you have nothing better to do – but not on my regular day, you know. *You* will always find me at home,' and her careless-seeming hint of a convenient hour, meant as much as I cared to claim. There had been in her blush, I knew, the material for my little romance of that season. And then, as I flecked in those floating clouds, I had been calculating the cost of these little romances, and deciding the sum it would be necessary to set upon this picture, in order to cover the more than usually extravagant outlay which would be entailed by her gentle ladyship's idea of my princely habits. When I was engaged upon those love-limpid eyes, it had occurred to me to calculate how much a year I should lose by spending the price of this picture, instead of reserving it as capital to be invested; and here I had asked myself, was it wise to lavish so much on one caprice? Then suddenly my mind had glanced off to the last Levée. I had certainly been slighted on that occasion – obviously neglected – allowed to pass with the kind of nod of recognition which does for a faithful lackey.

At the recollection of it my forehead contracted with anger, the pride of performance forsook me, my effect had not come to those eyes, and I threw down my brush in disgust. I had gone over all that ground afterwards, for it is well known that I am nothing if not painstaking, and, indeed, my work is everywhere quoted in proof of the assertion that genius obviously *is* an infinite capacity for taking pains. But now again, as I gazed, the effect that I had tried for was absent; the whole work answered no more to my expectation than if it had been altogether stale, flat, and unprofitable; and there gradually took possession of me a great amazement, not to say alarm, as I forced myself to acknowledge that there must be some blunting of my faculties to account for the powerlessness of the picture to move me as it ought. What could be the matter with me? Loss of nerve-power? Visions of delicate artistic susceptibilities injured when not actually wiped out by the coarse influences of indigestion, horrid possibilities, had begun to assail me rudely, when the ringing of the studio bell suddenly startled me back to my normal state of mind. It rang once sharply, and, although it is not my habit to answer bells for myself, I arose on some unaccountable impulse, and, going to the outer door of the studio, which opened on to a flight of steps leading down into the road, did so on this occasion.

A young woman was waiting without. The electric light from behind me fell full upon her face. I did not think her particularly attractive in appearance, and the direct look of her eyes into mine was positively distasteful. It was the kind of glance which either fascinates or creates a feeling of repulsion. Coming from a creature whose exterior does not please, such a glance inevitably repels, especially if there is anything commanding in it, and more particularly the command of a strong nature in an inferior position, when it is likely to cause a degree of irritation which would, amongst unrefined people, result in an outburst of rough hostility; but with us, of course, only expresses itself in a courtly coldness.

'Do you want a model?' the young woman asked, speaking without a particle of respect or apology, as if to an equal.

I would have answered in the negative shortly, and shut the door, but for – I had it just now, but for the moment it has escaped me. However, I shall remember it by and by, and for the present it is only necessary to state that I did not say 'No', and shut the door. I hesitated.

'You can't tell, of course, until you see me,' the applicant pursued in a confident tone. 'I had better come in and show myself.'

And involuntarily I stood aside to let her pass, conscious at the same time that I was bending my body from the waist, although I certainly never meant to bow to a model. My position necessitates so many bows, however, that it has really become more natural for me to acknowledge the approach of a fellow-creature so, than in any other posture.

Ah! now I recall what it was that had made me hesitate – her voice. It was not the voice of a common model. And as she passed into the studio before me now, she struck me as not being a common person of any kind. Someone in distress, I thought, driven to earn an honest penny. All sorts of people come in this way to us artists, and we do what we can for them without asking questions. Sometimes we get an invaluable model with distinct marks of superior breeding, in this way; a king's daughter, displaying in every lineament the glory of race, which inspires. Oftener it is a pretty 'young lady' out of a situation. The latter appears in every academy by the name of some classical celebrity. But then, again, we have applicants like the present, not attractive, whom it would be folly to engage to sit, however willing we may be to oblige them by employing them. In such cases a sovereign or so is gratefully accepted, as a rule, and there the matter ends; and I had put my hand in my pocket now as I followed my visitor in, thinking for a moment that I could satisfy her with such substantial proof of sympathy, and get rid of her; but directly she stopped and turned to me, I felt an unaccountable delicacy about doing so. 'This is no beggar, no ordinary object of charity,' I thought; 'it would be an insult to offer her anything that she has not earned.'

She had placed herself full in the light for my inspection, with her back to my picture, and I looked at her attentively, gauging the possibility of making anything out of such a face, and the rather tall bundle of loose, light wraps which was the figure she presented. 'Hopeless!' was my first impression; 'I'm not sure,' the second; and the third, 'Skin delicate, features regular, eyes' – but there the fault was, I discovered, not in the shape or colour, but in the expression of them. They were the mocking eyes of that creature most abhorrent to the soul of man, a woman who claims to rule and does not care to please; eyes out of which an imperious spirit shone independently, not looking up, but meeting mine on the same level. Now, a really attractive, womanly woman looks up, clings, depends, so that a man can never forget his own superiority in her presence.

'Well?' she broke in upon my reflections, prolonging the word melodiously.

And instantly it occurred to me that as I had not yet begun another serious work, I might as well do a good deed, and keep my hand in at the same time, by making a study of her. Certainly, the type was uncommon.

'Yes,' I replied, speaking, to my own surprise, in a satisfied tone, as if I were receiving instead of conferring a favour, although I cannot understand why I should have done so 'You may come tomorrow and give me some sittings. Be here at ten.'

She was turning away without a word, and she had not ventured to look at the picture; but this I thought was natural diffidence, so I called her back, feeling that a man in my position might, without loss of dignity, give the poor creature a treat.

'You may look at the picture if you like,' I said, speaking involuntarily very much as I should have done to – well, to the Lady Catherine Claridge herself!

She glanced at the picture over her shoulder. 'Pooh!' she said. 'Do you call that a picture?' And then she looked up in my face and laughed.

When next I found myself thinking coherently, it was about her teeth. 'What wonderful white ones she has!' I was saying to myself. But the studio door was shut, and all echo of her departing footsteps had died away long before I arrived at that reflection.

The next morning I was in the studio before ten o'clock, and the first thing I did was to cover my new work with a curtain, and then I set my palette. But a quarter past ten arrived and no model. Half-past – this was hardly respectful. Eleven, twelve, luncheon, light literature, a drive, the whole day – what could the woman mean? I had intended to take tea with Lady Catherine, but just as I approached the house, I was suddenly seized with a curious dislike of the visit, an unaccountable distaste for herself and everything about her, which impelled me to drive on past the place without casting a glance in that direction. I wondered afterwards if she had seen me, but I did not care in the least whether she had or not.

After dinner, as on the previous evening, I retired to the studio to enjoy a cigarette; but this time I sat with my back to the picture, before which the curtain still remained drawn, and looked out of the lattice at the lights which leaves take when fluttering in the moonlight; and listened to the nightingale – until there stole upon my senses something – that something which did not come to me out of my picture the night before. I found myself in a moment drinking in the beauty of the night with long, deep sighs, and thinking thoughts – thoughts like the thoughts of youth, which are 'long, long thoughts'. I had even felt the first thrill of a great aspiration, when I was disturbed again by the ringing of the studio bell. Again, involuntarily, I hastened to open the door, and there she stood in exactly the same position at the foot of the steps, looking up at me with her eyes that repelled – but no! I was mistaken. How could I have thought her eyes repellent? They were merrily-dancing, mischievous eyes, that made you smile in spite of yourself.

'Well, I didn't come, you see,' she said in a casual way. 'I knew you wouldn't be ready for me.'

'Not ready for you?' I exclaimed, without thinking whether I ought to condescend to parley with a model. 'Why, I waited for you the whole morning.'

'Oh, that is nothing,' she answered cheerfully – 'nothing, at least, if nothing comes of it. You must wait, you know, to recover yourself. You've lost such a lot. What is the use of having paint on your palette if the rage to apply it is not *here?*' She looked up at me with big, bright, earnest eyes as she spoke, and clasped her hands over her chest. Then she stooped and peeped unceremoniously under my arm into the studio. 'Ah!' she said, 'you have covered that thing up' – meaning my picture! 'That's right. And you've been sitting by the lattice – there's your chair. Last night it was in front of the easel. Well! I will look in to-morrow, just to see how you are getting on. No trouble, I assure you. There! you can shut the door. If you stand there when I am gone, staring at the spot where I stood as you did last night, you'll be in a draught and catch cold, which is risky for a middle-aged man, just now especially, with so much influenza about. Good-night!'

She turned to walk away as she spoke, and her gait was like music in motion, she moved so rhythmically.

'What an extraordinary person!' I exclaimed, when she was out of sight. While she was with me, however, she did not seem extraordinary, and it was only after she had gone that I even recognised the utter incongruity of my own attitude towards her when under the immediate influence of her singular personality.

But what was it that set me thinking of Martha troubled about many things when she mentioned the draught and the influenza? And also reminded me that to be a great artist one must be a great man in the sense of being a good one?

Now, somehow, next morning I knew better than to expect her at ten o'clock. I noticed that the paint had dried on my palette, and ordered my man to clean it, but I did not set it afresh, for what, I asked myself, is the use of paint on a palette if one has nothing to express?

The day was devoted to social duties. I went in and out several times, asking always on my return if anyone had been, to which my man, an old and faithful servant, invariably replied as if he understood me, 'Not even a model, sir.'

I had had to attend a Levée in the afternoon, and when it was over, one of the dukes, a noted connoisseur, asked me if I would 'be so good' as to show him my new picture – the exact expression was: 'Your last great work.' Other gentlemen came up while he was speaking to me, and it ended in several of them returning with me forthwith to view the picture.

I had not looked at it myself since I had covered it up, and now that I was forced to draw the curtain from before it, I felt it to be a distasteful duty.

'Well, that *is* a picture!' the duke exclaimed, and all the other gentlemen praised the work in a choice variety of elegantly-selected phrases. They even looked as if they liked it, a fact which clearly proved to me they had not one of them got further than I had myself before dinner on the eventful evening when *she* first appeared.

I was to have dined out that day, but just as I was about to step into my carriage, I saw a figure in loose, light draperies, charmingly disposed, approaching. (What was it made me think of Lot's wife?) I turned back into the house on the instant, and retired to the studio, the outer door of which I opened at once for her convenience.

She walked straight in without ceremony.

'You were going to some feeding function to-night, I suppose,' she observed. Then she looked round, chose a chair, and sat herself down deliberately.

I remained standing myself with my hands folded, regarding her with an expression in which I hoped she would see good-natured tolerance of one of the whimsical sex struggling with a certain amount of impatience carefully controlled. And she did study my face and attitude critically for some seconds; then she shook her head.

'Don't like it!' she exclaimed. 'No native dignity in it, because anybody could see that you are posing.'

Involuntarily I altered my position, planting myself more firmly on my feet.

'That's better,' she said, and then she looked at me again, frowning intently, and once more shook her head. 'You live too well, you know,' she admonished me. 'There is a certain largeness in your very utterance which bespeaks high feeding, and an oleo-saccharine quality in the courtly urbanity even of your every-day manner which comes of constant repletion. One is obliged to fall into it oneself to express it properly,' she added apologetically. 'But you are a prince now, you know; you're not an artist. You've eaten all that out of yourself.'

'I am not a great eater,' I protested, in a tone which should have shown her that I was gravely offended by the liberty of language she allowed herself.

'Well, don't be huffy,' she said. 'It is not so much in the matter of meat and drink that your appetite is gross, I allow; it was the Tree of Life to which I alluded. You cannot pretend that you only nibble at that! You know you deny yourself none of it, so long as what you can reach is sufficiently refined to please you. You have fed your senses to such a monstrous girth that they have crowded the soul out of you. What you put into your pictures now is knowledge, not inspiration. But that is the way with all of you artist-princes at present. Inspiration is extinct at Hampstead and in St. John's Wood, and even here, on Melbury Hill, there is scarcely a flicker.' She slowly removed her outer wrap, and as she put the long pin with a black glass head which had held it together carefully back in it, she added emphatically: 'People may look at your pictures to their heads' content, but their hearts you never touch.'

She sat still, looking gravely at the ground, for a few seconds after this last utterance; then she rose in her deliberate, languid way, and went, with her long wrap depending from her left arm and gracefully trailing after her, up to the picture, and drew aside the curtain that concealed it.

'Now, look at that!' she exclaimed. 'Your flesh is flesh, and your form is form; likewise your colour is colour, and your draperies are drapery – although too luxuriant, as a rule; you riot in fullness and folds with an effect that is wormy – but there isn't a scrap of human interest in the whole composition, and the consequence is a notable flatness and insipidity, as of soup without salt.' She looked close into the picture, then drew back and contemplated it from a little distance, with her head on one side, and then she carefully covered it up with the curtain, remarking as she did so contemptuously, 'There is not a scrap of "that certain something" in it, you know; it is merely a clever contrivance of paint upon canvas.'

'But there is pleasure in the contemplation of a coat of colour laid on with a master's hand,' I modestly observed, changing my balance from one leg to the other, and crisping the fingers of my left hand as they lay upon the right.

'For some people,' she replied; 'there is an order of mind, mind in its infancy, which can be so diverted. We have a pet frame-maker at home (*Who can she be?*), and one day when he brought back a new picture we thought we would give him a treat, so we took him into the picture gallery (*A picture gallery argues a mansion*), and invited him to look at the pictures, and then we watched him walking down the long length of it slowly, passing in review a whole sequence of art, ancient and modern. (*She must belong to considerable people, there are not many such private collections.*) But not a muscle of his face moved until he came to an exquisite little modern gem – it was not one of yours,' she hastened to assure me. I made a deprecating gesture to show her I had not the egotism to suppose it might be. 'Gems by you are exceedingly difficult to procure,' she proceeded, in a tone which suggested something sarcastical, but I failed to comprehend. 'Well,' she pursued, 'our good frame-maker stopped opposite to that gem. His countenance, which had been sombre as that of one who patiently accomplishes a task, now cleared, his eyes brightened intelligently, his cheeks flushed, his lips parted to exclaim, and I thought to myself, 'Now for a genuine glimpse of the soul of a working man!' He looked again, as if to make sure before he committed himself, then, turning to me, he exclaimed triumphantly, '*I* made that frame!'

'Ah – yes,' I was conscious of murmuring politely. 'Extremely good! But we were talking about paint.'

'Oh, well, of course, if you can't see the point –' She shrugged her shoulders and turned the palms of her hands outwards. Then she sat down again and looked at my feet. I shifted them uneasily.

'I was going out to dinner,' I ventured at last, breaking in upon her meditations tentatively.

'I know,' she responded, with a sigh, as if she were wearied in mind. 'It would be just as well to send the carriage back. There is no use keeping the coachman and horses at the door. I daresay the cook has some cutlets that will do for us.'

'I am sure I shall be delighted if you will do me the honour –' I was beginning, when again she laughed in my face, showing much of her magnificent set of strong white teeth. Why did I never dream of opposing her?

'Oh, come now!' she exclaimed, apparently much amused; 'you are not at Court, you know. Here in the studio you should be artistic, not artificial; and what you don't feel you shouldn't pretend to feel. Shall we dine here? Put that thing back,' – pointing to the picture – 'pull out the throne – it will make a capital low table – and order in two easy-chairs for us to recline upon opposite to each other. You are nothing if not classical in appearance. Fancy you in a frock-coat, with spats upon your boots! and you in modern evening dress! It is absurd! You should wear a toga.'

I was going to say something about the incongruity of such a costume, but she would not let me speak. 'Just wait a moment,' she said; 'it is my innings. And nobody knows better than I do that High Street, Kensington, would be more amazed than edified by the apparition of yourself in a toga, or, better still – for I take you to be more Greek than Roman – clad in the majestic folds of the *himation* and without a cravat – admirably as either would set off your attractive personal appearance. Here on the hill, however, it is different. I tell you, you are nothing if not classical, both in your person and your work; but a modern man must add of the enlightenment of to-day that which was wanting to the glory of the Greeks. Your work at present is purely Greek – form without character, passionless perfection, imperfectly perfect, wanting the spirit part, which was not in Greece, but is, or ought to be, in you; without which the choicest masterpiece of old was merely "icily regular, splendidly null", with which the veriest street arab put upon canvas is "equal to the god!" I tell you, you are a true Greek, but you must be something more, for this is not Athens in Greece, but Melbury Hill, Kensington, London, W. – coming whence we will accept nothing but positive perfection, which is form *and* character, flesh and blood, body and soul, the divine in the human – But there!' she broke off. 'That is as much as you must have at present. And I am fatigued. Do get the room arranged and order in dinner, while I retire to refresh myself by indulging in the comfort of a bath. I suppose I shall find one somewhere, with hot and cold water laid on.'

She walked with easy grace out of the studio into the house when she had spoken, leaving me gravely perplexed. And again I wonder why, at the time, it never occurred to me to oppose her; but certainly it never did.

My difficulty now was how to make the arrangements she required without taking the whole establishment into my confidence; but while I still stood in the attitude in which she had left me – an attitude, I believe, of considerable dignity, the right foot being a little in advance, at right angles to the left, and the left elbow supported on the back of the right hand, so that the fingers caressed the left cheek – my faithful old confidential servant entered.

'Beg pardon, sir,' he began – and I could see that he was perturbed and anxious, like one in dread lest he shall not perform the duty exacted of him satisfactorily – 'but the lady said you wanted me to arrange the scene for the new picture.'

Instantly I understood her delicate manner of getting me

out of my difficulty, and having given my man full directions, I stood looking on while the necessary arrangements were being completed, making a suggestion now and then as to the disposition of table decorations, and myself choosing the draperies that were to decorate the lounges upon which we were to recline. While so engaged, I, as it were – if I may venture to use such an expression – warmed to the work. At first I had looked on as a grown-up person might do when viewing with pleased toleration the preparations for some childish frolic; but as the arrangements neared completion, and I gradually beheld one end of my studio transformed with the help of rare ancient vessels, statues, and furniture of the most antique design, which I had collected for the purposes of my art, into such a scene as Apelles himself might have countenanced, I felt an unwonted glow of enthusiasm, and fell to adjusting hangings and dragging lounges about myself. It was a close evening, and the extraordinary exertion made me so hot, that, without a thought of my dignity, I dashed my coat and vest on the floor, and worked in my shirt-sleeves.

'That's right!' said a tuneful voice at last, and upon looking round, I saw my model – or guest of the evening, shall I say? She was standing between two heavy curtains which screened off one side of the studio from an outer apartment. Her right hand was raised high in the act of holding one of the curtains back, and her bare, round arm shone ivory-white against the dark folds of the curtains. It was a striking attitude, instinct with a singular grace and charm, both of which, on looking back, I now recognise as having been eminently characteristic; and their immediate effect upon me was to make me entreat her not to move for a moment until I had caught the pose in a rapid sketch. She signified her consent by standing quiescent as a statue, while I hastily got out my materials, choosing charcoal for my medium, and set to work. And so great was my eagerness that I actually remained in my shirt-sleeves without being aware of the fact – a statement which will, I know, astonish my friends, and appear to them to be incredible, even upon my own authority. But there must have been something powerfully – what shall I say? – demoralising? – about this extraordinary woman. And yet it was not at all that, but elevating rather; even my model manservant, to judge by his countenance, felt her effect. Her mere presence seemed to be making him, 'the reptile equal' – for the moment in his own estimation – 'to the god', that is to say, to me. Under the strange, benign influence of her appearance as she stood there, I could see that he had suddenly ceased to be an impassive serving-machine, and had become an emotional human being. There was interest in his eyes, and admiration, besides an all-devouring anxiety to be equal to the occasion – a disinterested trepidation on my account, as well as on his own. He was fearful that I should not answer to expectation, as was evident from the way that he, hitherto the most respectful of fellows, forgot himself, and ventured upon the liberty of looking on, first at the model and then at my sketch as it progressed. He came and peeped over my shoulder, went up to the model for a nearer view, then stepped off again to see her from another point, as we do when studying a fascinating object; and so inevitable did it seem even for a manservant to think and feel in her presence, that I allowed his demonstrations to pass unreproved, as though it were part of the natural order of things for a lackey so to comport himself.

But in the meantime the attention to my subject which the making of the sketch necessitated brought about a revelation. As I rapidly read each lineament for the purpose of fixing it on my paper, I asked myself involuntarily how I could possibly have supposed for a moment that this magnificent creature was unattractive? Why, from the crown of her head to the sole of her foot – what expression! There was a volume of verse in her glance – Oh, Sappho! – a bounteous vitality in her whole person – Oh, Ceres! – an atmosphere of life, of love, surrounded her – Oh, Venus! – a modest reserve of womanhood – Diana! – a –

'Get on, do!' she broke in upon my fervid analysis.

An *aplomb*, I concluded, a confidence of intellect; decision, intelligence, and force of fine feeling combined in her which brought her up to date.

'Yes,' she observed, dropping the curtain, and coming forward when I had finished my sketch – in which, by the way, she took not the slightest interest, for she did not cast so much as a glance upon it. 'Yes,' she repeated, as if in answer to my thoughts – I wonder if perchance I had uttered them aloud? 'Yes, you are right. I commend you. I *am* a woman with all the latest improvements. The creature the world wants. Nothing can now be done without me.' She silently surveyed me after this with critical eyes. 'But hop out of that ridiculous dress, *do*,' she said at last, 'and get into something suitable for summer, for a man of your type, and for the occasion.'

I instantly unbuttoned a brace.

'Hold on a moment,' she said rather hastily. 'Where is your classical wardrobe?'

My man, who had been waiting on her words, as it were, ran to a large carved chest at the further end of the studio, and threw up the lid for answer.

'Johnson, as he appears in St. Paul's Cathedral, may be all very well for people at church to contemplate; but that isn't my idea of a dinner dress,' she proceeded.

She was walking towards the chest as she spoke, and I noticed that her own dress, which had struck me at first as purely classical, was not really of any form with which I was acquainted, ancient or modern; but was of a design which I believe to be perfectly new, or, at all events, a most original variation upon already-known designs. It was made of several exquisitely harmonized tints of soft silk.

When she reached the great chest, she stood a moment looking into it, and then began to pull the things out and throw them on the floor behind her, diving down deeper and deeper into the chest, till she had to stand on tip-toe to reach in at all, and the upper part of her body disappeared at every plunge. Near the bottom she found what she wanted. This proved to be a short-sleeved tunic, reaching to the knees, with a handsome Greek border embroidered upon it; some massive gold bracelets; a pair of sandals; and a small harp, such as we associate with Homer.

She gathered all these things up in her arms, brought them to me, and threw them down at my feet. 'There!' she exclaimed; 'be quick! I want my dinner.'

With which she delicately withdrew until my toilette was complete.

When she returned, she held in her hand a laurel wreath, tied at the back with a bow of ribbon, and with the leaves lying symmetrically towards the front, where they met in a point. It was the form which appears in ancient portraits crowning the heads of distinguished men.

I had placed myself near a pedestal, with the harp in my hand, and, as she approached, felt conscious of nothing but my bare legs. My man, who had helped to attire me, also stood by, with deprecating glances entreatingly bespeaking her approval.

Having crowned me, she stepped back to consider the effect, and instantly she became convulsed with laughter. My servant assumed a dejected attitude upon this, and silently slunk away.

'Oh, dear! Oh, dear!' she exclaimed. 'If Society could only see you now! It isn't that you don't look well,' she hastened to reassure me – 'and I trust you will kindly excuse my inopportune mirth. It is a disease of the mind which I inherit from an ancestor of mine, who was a funny man. He worked for a comic paper, and was expected to make new jokes every week on the three same subjects: somebody drunk, somebody's mother-in-law, something unhappy – or low for preference – in married life; a consequence of which strain upon his mind was the setting up of the deplorable disease of inopportune mirth, which has unfortunately been transmitted to me. But I am altogether an outcome of the age, you will perceive, an impossible mixture of incongruous qualities, which are all in a ferment at present, but will eventually resolve themselves, as chemical combinations do, into an altogether unexpected, and, seeing that already the good is outweighing the bad and indifferent ingredients, admirable composition, we will hope. But, as I was going to say, those ambrosial locks and that classic jowl of yours, not to mention your manly arms embraceleted, and –' But here she hesitated, apparently not liking to mention my legs, although she looked at them. 'Well,' she hurriedly summed up, 'I always said you would look lovely in a toga, and the short tunic is also artistic in its own way. But now let us dine; I am mortal hungry.'

I was about to hasten, harp in hand, across the studio to ring for dinner, but the moment I moved she went off again into convulsions of laughter.

'Excuse me,' she implored, drying her eyes, 'but it *is* so classical! I can't help it, really! Just to see you go gives me little electric shocks all over! But don't be huffy. You never looked nicer, I declare. And you can put on a toga, you know, if the tunic isn't enough. It *is* somewhat skimpy, I confess, for a man of your girth.'

When she had spoken, she went to the chest and obligingly looked me out some yards of stuff, which she said, when properly draped, would do for a toga; and having arranged it upon my shoulders to please herself, she conducted me to one of the couches, remarking that dinner would be sure to come all in good time, and recommending me to employ the interval in cultivating a cheerful frame of mind, 1, 2, 3, 4, 5, 6, 7 – a copybook precept, good for the digestion when practised, she insisted, as she thoughtfully adjusted my harp; after which she begged me to assume a classical attitude, and then proceeded to dispose herself in like manner on the other couch opposite.

'This is delicious,' she said, sighing luxuriously as she sank upon it. 'I guess the Greeks and Romans never really knew what comfort was. Imagine an age without springs!'

Dinner was now served by my man, who was, I could see, still shaking in his shoes with anxiety lest everything should not be to her mind. He had donned a red gown, similar to that worn by attendants at the Royal Academy on state occasions, and was suffering a good deal from the heat in consequence. But the dinner was all that could be desired, as my guest herself observed. And she should have known, too, for she ate with a will. 'I must tell you,' she explained, 'Æsculapius prescribed a tonic for me on one occasion, and I have been taking it, off and on, ever since, so that I am almost all appetite.'

What was it that made me think at that moment of Venus's visit to Æsculapius?

We were now at dessert, nibbling fruit and sipping wine, and my face was suffused with smiles, but my companion looked grave, and I thought that her mood was resolving itself into something serious by the sober way she studied my face.

'Excuse me, but your wreath is all on one side,' she remarked at last – quite by the way, however.

I rose hastily to readjust the wreath at a mirror, and then returned and leisurely resumed my seat. I had been about to speak, but something new in the demeanour of the lady opposite caused me to forget my intention. There was an indescribable grace in her attitude, a perfect *abandon* to the repose of the moment which was in itself an evidence of strength in reserve, and fascinating to a degree. But the curious thing about the impression that she was now making upon me is that she had not moved. She had been reclining in an easy manner since the servant left the room, with her arm resting on the back of her couch, twirling a flower in her fingers, and hadn't swerved from the pose a fraction; only a certain quietude had settled upon her, and was emanating from her forcibly, as I felt. And with this quietude there came to me quite suddenly a new and solemn sense of responsibility, something grave and glad which I cannot explain, something which caused me an exquisite sense of pleasurable emotion, and made me feel the richer for the experience. My first thought was of England and America, of the glorious womanhood of this age of enlightenment, compared with the creature as she existed merely for man's use and pleasure of old; the toy-woman, drudge, degraded domestic animal, beast of intolerable burdens. How could the sons of slaves ever be anything but slaves themselves? slaves of various vices, the most execrable form of bondage. To paint – to paint this woman as she is! – in her youth, in her strength, in her beauty – in her insolence, even! in the fearless candour of her perfect virtue; the trifler of an idle hour, the strong, true spirit of an arduous day – to paint her so that man may feel her divinity and worship that!

I had covered my eyes with my hands, so as the better to control my emotions and collect my thoughts; but now a current of cold air playing upon my limbs, and the faint sith of silk, aroused me. I looked up. The couch was empty.

The next morning she arrived by ten o'clock in a very ugly old grey cloak. I was engaged at the moment in reading the report in a morning paper of the dinner at which I ought to have appeared on the previous evening, and the letter of apology for my unavoidable absence which I forgot to mention that my guest had induced me to send. She came and read the report over my shoulder.

'That is graceful,' was her comment upon my letter. 'You are a charming phrase-maker. Such neatness of expression is not common. But,' she added severely, 'it is also disgraceful, because you didn't mean a word of it. And an artist should be an honest, earnest man, incapable of petty subterfuge; otherwise, however great he may be, he falls short of the glory, just as you do. But there!' she added plaintively, 'you know all that – or, at all events, you used to know it.'

'"He is the greatest artist who has the greatest number"' – I was beginning, when she interrupted me abruptly.

'Oh, I know! You have it all off by heart so pat!' she exclaimed. 'But what good do precepts do you? Why, if maxims could make an artist, I should be one myself, for I know them all; and I am no artist!'

'I don't know that,' slipped from me unawares.

'That is because you have become a mere appraiser of words,' she declared. 'You, as an artist, would have divined that if I could paint myself I should not be here. I should be doing what I want for myself, instead of using my peculiar power to raise you to the necessary altitude.'

'Oh, of course!' I hastened to agree, apologetically, feeling myself on familiar ground at last. 'The delicate, subtly-inspiring presence is the woman's part; the rough work is for man, the interpreter. No woman has ever truly distinguished herself except in her own sphere.'

'Now, no cant, *please*,' she exclaimed. 'You are not a pauper priest, afraid that the offertory will fall off if he doesn't keep the upper hand of all the women in the parish.'

'But,' I protested, 'few women have ever –'

'Now just reflect,' she interrupted, 'and you will remember that in the days of our slavery there were more great women than there have ever been great men who were also slaves; so that now that our full emancipation is imminent, why, you shall see what you shall see.'

'Then why don't you paint?' I asked her blandly.

'All in good time,' she answered suavely. 'But I have not come to bandy words with you, nor to be irritated by hearing nonsensical questions asked by a man of your age and standing. I am here to be painted. Just set your palette while I see to my attire. You seem to have forgotten lately that a woman is a creature of clothes in these days – and there never were more delightful days, by the way, since the world began.'

When she returned, she ascended the throne, but before falling into a set attitude, she addressed me: 'The great stories of the world are deathless and ageless, because of the human nature that is in them, and you know that in your head, but your heart does not feel it a bit. Your sentiments are irreproachable, but they have survived the vivifying flush of feeling, parent of sympathetic insight, upon which you formed them, and the mere dry knowledge that remains is no use for creative purposes. All through Nature strong emotion is the motive of creation, and in art, also, the power to create is invariably the outcome of an ardent impulse. But there you stand, in full conceit beside your canvas, with your palette and brushes in your hand, a mere cool, calculating workman, without an atom of love or reverence, not to mention inspiration, to warm your higher faculties into life and action; and in that mood you have the assurance to believe that you have only to choose to paint me as I am, and you will be able to do so – able to paint, not merely a creature of a certain shape, but a creature of boundless possibilities, instinct with soul – no, though, I wrong you,' she broke off scornfully. 'The soul of me, the part that an artist should specially crave to render through the medium of this outer shell, which of itself alone is hardly worth the trouble of copying on to the canvas, has never cost you a thought. Rounded form, healthy flesh, and lively glances are all that appeal to you now.'

I bent my head, considering if this were true; but even while I asked myself the question I was conscious of a curious shock – a shock of awakening, as it were, a thrill that traversed my body in warm, swift currents, making me tingle. I knew what it was in a moment – her enthusiasm. She had communicated it to me occultly, a mere spark of it at first, but even that was animating to a degree that was delicious.

'Don't put anything on canvas that you cannot glorify,' she resumed. 'The mere outer husk of me is nothing, I repeat; you must interpret – you must reveal the beyond of that – the grace, I mean, all resplendent within.' She clasped her hands upon her breast, and looked into my eyes. 'You remember your first impression when I offered myself as a model?' she pursued. I felt ashamed of my own lack of thought, and hung my head. 'Compare your present idea of my attractions with that, and see for yourself how far you have lapsed. You have descended from art to artificiality, I tell you. You have ceased to see and render like a sentient being; you are nothing now but a painting machine. *Now!*' she exclaimed, clapping her hands together, 'stand straight and look at me!'

Like one electrified, I obeyed.

'I am the woman who stood at the outer door of your studio and summoned you to judge me; the same whom, in your spiritual obscurity, you then found wanting. Rend now that veil of flesh, and look! Who was at fault?'

'I was,' burst from me involuntarily.

When I had spoken, I clasped my palette, and hastily

selected a brush. Her exaltation had rapidly gained upon me. I was consumed with the rage to paint her – or, rather, to paint that in her which I suddenly saw and could reproduce upon canvas, but could not otherwise express.

Slowly, without another word, she lapsed into an easy attitude, fixing her wonderful eyes upon mine. For a moment my vision was clouded; I saw nothing but mist. As that cleared, however, there penetrated to the inner recesses of my being – there was revealed to me – But the tone-poets must find the audible expression of it. My limit is to make it visible.

But never again, I said to myself as I painted, shall mortal stand before a work of mine unmoved; never again shall it be said: 'Well, it may be my ignorance, which it would be bad taste for me to display in the presence of a picture by so great a man; but, all the same, I must say I can't see anything in it.' No, never again! if I have to sacrifice every delight of the body to keep my spiritual vision unobscured; for there is no joy like this joy, nothing else which is human which so nearly approaches the divine as the exercise of this power.

'For heaven's sake don't move!' I implored.

She had not moved, but the whole expression of her face had changed with an even more disastrous effect. The glorious light which had illuminated such enthusiasm in me had passed out of her eyes, giving place to that cold, critical expression which repelled, and she smiled enigmatically.

'I can't stand here all day,' she said, stepping down from the throne. 'You know now what you want.'

She was at the outer door as she pronounced those words, and the instant after she had uttered them she was gone, absolutely gone, before I could remonstrate.

I had thrown myself on my knees to beg for another hour, and now, when I realised the cruelty of her callous desertion of me at such a juncture, I sank beside the easel utterly overcome, and remained for I cannot tell how long in a kind of stupor, from which, however, I was at length aroused by a deep-drawn sigh.

I looked up, and then I rose to my feet.

It was my faithful servant who had sighed. He was standing at gaze before the all-unfinished work. I looked at it myself.

'It is wonderful, sir,' he said, speaking in an undertone, as if in the presence of something sacred.

Yes, it was wonderful, even then, and what would it be when it was finished? Finished! How could I finish it without a model – without that model in particular? I recognised her now – a free woman, a new creature, a source of inspiration the like of which no man hitherto has even imagined in art or literature. Why had she deserted me? – for she had, and I knew it at once. I felt she would not return, and she never did; nor have I ever been able to find her, although I have been searching for her ever since. You may see me frequently in the corner of an open carriage, with my man seated on the box beside the coachman; and as we drive through the streets, we gaze up at the windows, and into the faces of the people we pass, in the hope that some day we shall see her; but never a glimpse, as yet, have we obtained.

My man says that such capricious conduct is just what you might expect of a woman, old-fashioned or new; but I cannot help thinking myself that both in her coming and her going, her insolence and her ideality, her gravity and her levity, there was a kind of allegory. 'With all my faults, nothing uncommonly great can be done without my countenance,' this was what she seemed to have said to me; 'but my countenance you shall not have to perfection until the conceit of you is conquered, and you acknowledge all you owe me. Give me my due; and when *you* help *me*, I will help *you!*'

EDITH WHARTON

THE MUSE'S TRAGEDY

DANYERS afterwards liked to fancy that he had recognised Mrs. Anerton at once; but that, of course, was absurd, since he had seen no portrait of her – she affected a strict anonymity, refusing even her photograph to the most privileged – and from Mrs. Memorall, whom he revered and cultivated as her friend, he had extracted but the one impressionist phrase: 'Oh, well, she's like one of those old prints where the lines have the value of colour.'

He was almost certain, at all events, that he had been thinking of Mrs. Anerton as he sat over his breakfast in the empty hotel restaurant, and that, looking up on the approach of the lady who seated herself at the table near the window, he had said to himself, '*That might be she.*'

Ever since his Harvard days – he was still young enough to think of them as immensely remote – Danyers had dreamed of Mrs. Anerton, the Silvia of Vincent Rendle's immortal sonnet cycle, the Mrs. A. of the *Life and Letters*. Her name was enshrined in some of the noblest English verse of the nineteenth century – and of all past or future centuries, as Danyers, from the standpoint of a maturer judgment, still believed. The first reading of certain poems – of the *Antinous*, the *Pia Tolomei*, the *Sonnets to Silvia* – had been epochs in Danyers' growth, and the verse seemed to gain in mellowness, in amplitude, in meaning as one brought to its interpretation more experience of life, a finer emotional sense. Where, in his boyhood, he had felt only the perfect, the almost austere beauty of form, the subtle interplay of vowel sounds, the rush and fullness of lyric emotion, he now thrilled to the close-packed significance of each line, the allusiveness of each word – his imagination lured hither and thither on fresh trails of thought, and perpetually spurred by the sense that, beyond what he had already discovered, more marvellous regions lay waiting to be explored. Danyers had written, at college, the prize essay on Rendle's poetry (it chanced to be the moment of the great man's death); he had fashioned the fugitive verse of his own Storm and Stress period on the forms which Rendle had first given to English meter, and when two years later the *Life and Letters* appeared, and the Silvia of the sonnets took substance as Mrs. A., he had included in his worship of Rendle the woman who had inspired not only such divine verse but such playful, tender, incomparable prose.

Danyers never forgot the day when Mrs. Memorall happened to mention that she knew Mrs. Anerton. He had known Mrs. Memorall for a year or more, and had somewhat contemptuously classified her as the kind of woman who runs cheap excursions to celebrities; when one afternoon she remarked, as she put a second lump of sugar in his tea:

'Is it right this time? You're almost as particular as Mary Anerton.'

'Mary Anerton?'

'Yes, I never *can* remember how she likes her tea. Either it's lemon *with* sugar, or lemon without sugar, or cream without either, and whichever it is must be put into the cup before the tea is poured in; and if one hasn't remembered, one must begin all over again. I suppose it was Vincent Rendle's way of taking his tea and has become a sacred rite.'

'Do you *know* Mrs. Anerton?' cried Danyers, disturbed by this careless familiarity with the habits of his divinity.

'"And did I once see Shelley plain?" Mercy, yes! She and I were at school together – she's an American, you know. We were at a *pension* near Tours for nearly a year; then she went back to New York, and I didn't see her again till after her marriage. She and Anerton spent a winter in Rome while my husband was attached to our Legation there, and she used to be with us a great deal.' Mrs. Memorall smiled reminiscently. 'It was *the* winter.'

'The winter they first met?'

'Precisely – but unluckily I left Rome just before the meeting took place. Wasn't it too bad? I might have been in the *Life and Letters*. You know he mentions that stupid Madame Vodki, at whose house he first saw her.'

'And did you see much of her after that?'

'Not during Rendle's life. You know she has lived in Europe almost entirely, and though I used to see her off and on when I went abroad, she was always so engrossed, so preoccupied, that one felt one wasn't wanted. The fact is, she cared only about his friends – she separated herself gradually from all her own people. Now, of course, it's different; she's desperately lonely; she's taken to writing to me now and then; and last year, when she heard I was going abroad, she asked me to meet her in Venice, and I spent a week with her there.'

'And Rendle?'

Mrs. Memorall smiled and shook her head. 'Oh, I never was allowed a peep at *him*; none of her old friends met him, except by accident. Ill-natured people say that was the reason she kept him so long. If one happened in while he was there, he was hustled into Anerton's study, and the husband mounted guard till the inopportune visitor had departed. Anerton, you know, was really much more ridiculous about it than his wife. Mary was too clever to lose her head, or at least to show she'd lost it – but Anerton couldn't conceal his pride in the conquest. I've seen Mary shiver when he spoke of Rendle as *our poet*. Rendle always had to have a certain seat at the dinner table, away from the draft and not too near the fire, and a box of cigars that no one else was allowed to touch, and a writing-table of his own in Mary's sitting-room – and Anerton was always telling one of the great man's idiosyncrasies: how he never would cut the ends of his cigars, though Anerton himself had given him a gold cutter set with a star sapphire, and how untidy his writing-table was, and how the housemaid had orders always to bring the wastepaper basket to her mistress before emptying it, lest some immortal verse should be thrown into the dustbin.'

'The Anertons never separated, did they?'

'Separated? Bless you, no. He never would have left Rendle! And besides, he was very fond of his wife.'

'And she?'

'Oh, she saw he was the kind of man who was fated to make himself ridiculous, and she never interfered with his natural tendencies.'

From Mrs. Memorall, Danyers further learned that Mrs. Anerton, whose husband had died some years before her poet, now divided her life between Rome, where she had a small apartment, and England, where she occasionally went to stay with those of her friends who had been Rendle's. She had been engaged, for some time after his death, in editing some juvenilia which he had bequeathed to her care; but that task being accomplished, she had been left without definite occupation, and Mrs. Memorall, on the occasion of their last meeting, had found her listless and out of spirits.

'She misses him too much – her life is too empty. I told her so – I told her she ought to marry.'

'Oh!'

'Why not, pray? She's a young woman still – what many

people would call young,' Mrs. Memorall interjected, with a parenthetic glance at the mirror. 'Why not accept the inevitable and begin over again? All the King's horses and all the King's men won't bring Rendle to life – and besides, she didn't marry *him* when she had the chance.'

Danyers winced slightly at this rude fingering of his idol. Was it possible that Mrs. Memorall did not see what an anticlimax such a marriage would have been? Fancy Rendle 'making an honest woman' of Silvia; for so society would have viewed it! How such a reparation would have vulgarised their past – it would have been like 'restoring' a masterpiece; and how exquisite must have been the perceptions of the woman who, in defiance of appearances, and perhaps of her own secret inclination, chose to go down to posterity as Silvia rather than as Mrs. Vincent Rendle!

Mrs. Memorall, from this day forth, acquired an interest in Danyers' eyes. She was like a volume of unindexed and discursive memoirs, through which he patiently plodded in the hope of finding embedded amid layers of dusty twaddle some precious allusion to the subject of his thought. When, some months later, he brought out his first slim volume, in which the remodelled college essay on Rendle figured among a dozen somewhat overstudied 'appreciations', he offered a copy to Mrs. Memorall; who surprised him, the next time they met, with the announcement that she had sent the book to Mrs. Anerton.

Mrs. Anerton in due time wrote to thank her friend. Danyers was privileged to read the few lines in which, in terms that suggested the habit of 'acknowledging' similar tributes, she spoke of the author's 'feeling and insight', and was 'so glad of the opportunity', etc. He went away disappointed, without clearly knowing what else he had expected.

The following spring, when he went abroad, Mrs. Memorall offered him letters to everybody, from the Archbishop of

Canterbury to Louise Michel. She did not include Mrs. Anerton, however, and Danyers knew, from a previous conversation, that Silvia objected to people who 'brought letters'. He knew also that she travelled during the summer, and was unlikely to return to Rome before the term of his holiday should be reached, and the hope of meeting her was not included among his anticipations.

The lady whose entrance broke upon his solitary repast in the restaurant of the Hotel Villa d'Este had seated herself in such a way that her profile was detached against the window, and thus viewed, her domed forehead, small arched nose, and fastidious lip suggested a silhouette of Marie Antoinette. In the lady's dress and movements – in the very turn of her wrist as she poured out her coffee – Danyers thought he detected the same fastidiousness, the same air of tacitly excluding the obvious and unexceptional. Here was a woman who had been much bored and keenly interested. The waiter brought her a *Secolo*, and as she bent above it Danyers noticed that the hair rolled back from her forehead was turning grey; but her figure was straight and slender, and she had the invaluable gift of a girlish back.

The rush of Anglo-Saxon travel had not set toward the lakes, and with the exception of an Italian family or two, and a hump-backed youth with an *abbé*, Danyers and the lady had the marble halls of the Villa d'Este to themselves.

When he returned from his morning ramble among the hills he saw her sitting at one of the little tables at the edge of the lake. She was writing, and a heap of books and newspapers lay on the table at her side. That evening they met again in the garden. He had strolled out to smoke a last cigarette before dinner, and under the black vaulting of ilexes, near the steps leading down to the boat landing, he found her leaning on the parapet above the lake. At the sound of his approach she turned and looked at him. She had thrown a black lace scarf over her head, and in this somber setting her face seemed thin and unhappy. He remembered afterwards that her eyes, as they met his, expressed not so much sorrow as profound discontent.

To his surprise she stepped toward him with a detaining gesture.

'Mr. Lewis Danyers, I believe?'

He bowed.

'I am Mrs. Anerton. I saw your name on the visitors' list and wished to thank you for an essay on Mr. Rendle's poetry – or rather to tell you how much I appreciated it. The book was sent to me last winter by Mrs. Memorall.'

She spoke in even melancholy tones, as though the habit of perfunctory utterance had robbed her voice of more spontaneous accents; but her smile was charming.

They sat down on a stone bench under the ilexes, and she told him how much pleasure his essay had given her. She thought it the best in the book – she was sure he had put more of himself into it than into any other; was she not right in conjecturing that he had been very deeply influenced by Mr. Rendle's poetry? *Pour comprendre il faut aimer*, and it seemed to her that, in some ways, he had penetrated the poet's inner meaning more completely than any other critic. There were certain problems, of course, that he had left untouched; certain aspects of that many-sided mind that he had perhaps failed to seize –

'But then you are young,' she concluded gently, 'and one could not wish you, as yet, the experience that a fuller understanding would imply.'

II

She stayed a month at Villa d'Este, and Danyers was with her daily. She showed an unaffected pleasure in his society;

a pleasure so obviously founded on their common veneration of Rendle, that the young man could enjoy it without fear of fatuity. At first he was merely one more grain of frankincense on the altar of her insatiable divinity; but gradually a more personal note crept into their intercourse. If she still liked him only because he appreciated Rendle, she at least perceptibly distinguished him from the herd of Rendle's appreciators.

Her attitude toward the great man's memory struck Danyers as perfect. She neither proclaimed nor disavowed her identity. She was frankly Silvia to those who knew and cared; but there was no trace of the Egeria in her pose. She spoke often of Rendle's books, but seldom of himself; there was no posthumous conjugality, no use of the possessive tense, in her abounding reminiscences. Of the master's intellectual life, of his habits of thought and work, she never wearied of talking. She knew the history of each poem; by what scene or episode each image had been evoked; how many times the words in a certain line had been transposed; how long a certain adjective had been sought, and what had at last suggested it; she could even explain that one impenetrable line, the torment of critics, the joy of detractors, the last line of *The Old Odysseus*.

Danyers felt that in talking of these things she was no mere echo of Rendle's thought. If her identity had appeared to be merged in his it was because they thought alike, not because he had thought for her. Posterity is apt to regard the women whom poets have sung as chance pegs on which they hung their garlands; but Mrs. Anerton's mind was like some fertile garden wherein, inevitably, Rendle's imagination had rooted itself and flowered. Danyers began to see how many threads of his complex mental tissue the poet had owed to the blending of her temperament with his; in a certain sense Silvia had herself created the *Sonnets to Silvia*.

To be the custodian of Rendle's inner self, the door, as it were, to the sanctuary, had at first seemed to Danyers so comprehensive a privilege that he had the sense, as his friendship with Mrs. Anerton advanced, of forcing his way into a life already crowded. What room was there, among such towering memories, for so small an actuality as his? Quite suddenly, after this, he discovered that Mrs. Memorall knew better: his fortunate friend was bored as well as lonely.

'You have had more than any other woman!' he had exclaimed to her one day: and her smile flashed a derisive light on his blunder. Fool that he was, not to have seen that she had not had enough! That she was young still – do years count? – tender, human, a woman; that the living have need of the living.

After that, when they climbed the alleys of the hanging park, resting in one of the little ruined temples, or watching, through a ripple of foliage, the remote blue flash of the lake, they did not always talk of Rendle or of literature. She encouraged Danyers to speak of himself; to confide his ambitions to her; she asked him the questions which are the wise woman's substitute for advice.

'You must write,' she said, administering the most exquisite flattery that human lips could give.

Of course he meant to write – why not do something great in his turn? His best, at least; with the resolve, at the outset, that his best should be *the* best. Nothing less seemed possible with that mandate in his ears. How she had divined him; lifted and disentangled his groping ambitions; laid the awakening touch on his spirit with her creative *Let there be light!*

It was his last day with her, and he was feeling very hopeless and happy.

'You ought to write a book about *him*,' she went on gently.

Danyers started; he was beginning to dislike Rendle's way of walking in unannounced.

'You ought to do it,' she insisted. 'A complete interpretation – a summing up of his style, his purpose, his theory of life and art. No one else could do it as well.'

He sat looking at her perplexedly. Suddenly – dared he guess?

'I couldn't do it without you,' he faltered.

'I could help you – I would help you, of course.'

They sat silent, both looking at the lake.

It was agreed, when they parted, that he should rejoin her six weeks later in Venice. There they were to talk about the book.

III

Lago d'Iseo, August 14th.

When I said good-bye to you yesterday I promised to come back to Venice in a week: I was to give you your answer then. I was not honest in saying that; I didn't mean to go back to Venice or to see you again. I was running away from you – and I mean to keep on running! If *you* won't, *I* must. Somebody must save you from marrying a disappointed woman of – well, you say years don't count, and why should they, after all, since you are not to marry me?

That is what I dare not go back to say. *You are not to marry me*. We have had our month together in Venice (such a good month, was it not?) and now you are to go home and write a book – any book but the one we – didn't talk of! – and I am to stay here, attitudinising among my memories like a sort of female Tithonus. The dreariness of this enforced immortality!

But you shall know the truth. I care for you, or at least for your love, enough to owe you that.

You thought it was because Vincent Rendle had loved me that there was so little hope for you. I had had what I wanted to the full; wasn't that what you said? It is just when a man begins to think he understands a woman that he may be sure he doesn't! It is because Vincent Rendle *didn't love me* that there is no hope for you. I never had what I wanted, and never, never, never will I stoop to wanting anything else.

Do you begin to understand? It was all a sham then, you say? No, it was all real as far as it went. You are young – you haven't learned, as you will later, the thousand imperceptible signs by which one gropes one's way through the labyrinth of human nature; but didn't it strike you, sometimes, that I never told you any foolish little anecdotes about him? His trick, for instance, of twirling a paper knife round and round between his thumb and forefinger while he talked; his mania for saving the backs of notes; his greediness for wild strawberries, the little pungent Alpine ones; his childish delight in acrobats and jugglers; his way of always calling me *you – dear you*, every letter began – I never told you a word of all that, did I? Do you suppose I could have helped telling you, if he had loved me? These little things would have been mine, then, a part of my life – of our life – they would have slipped out in spite of me (it's only your unhappy woman who is always reticent and dignified). But there never was any 'our life'; it was always 'our lives' to the end . . .

If you knew what a relief it is to tell someone at last, you would bear with me, you would let me hurt you! I shall never be quite so lonely again, now that someone knows.

Let me begin at the beginning. When I first met Vincent Rendle I was not twenty-five. That was twenty years ago. From that time until his death, five years ago, we were fast friends. He gave me fifteen years, perhaps the best fifteen years, of his life. The world, as you know, thinks that his greatest poems were written during those years; I am supposed to have 'inspired' them, and in a sense I did. From the first, the intellectual sympathy between us was almost complete; my mind must have been to him (I fancy) like some perfectly tuned instrument on which he was never tired of playing. Someone told me of his once saying of me that I 'always understood'; it is the only praise I ever heard of his giving me. I don't even know if he thought me pretty, though I hardly think my appearance could have been disagreeable to him, for he hated to be with ugly people. At all events he fell into the way of spending more and more of his time with me. He liked our house; our ways suited him. He was nervous, irritable; people bored him and yet he disliked solitude. He took sanctuary with us. When we travelled he went with us; in the winter he took rooms near us in Rome. In England or on the Continent he was always with us for a good part of the year. In small ways I was able to help him in his work; he grew dependent on me. When we were apart he wrote to me continually – he liked to have me share in all he was doing or thinking; he was impatient for my criticism of every new book that interested him; I was a part of his intellectual life. The pity of it was that I wanted to be something more. I was a young woman and I was in love with him – not because he was Vincent Rendle, but just because he was himself!

People began to talk, of course – I was Vincent Rendle's Mrs. Anerton; when the *Sonnets to Silvia* appeared, it was whispered that I was Silvia. Wherever he went, I was invited; people made up to me in the hope of getting to know him; when I was in London my doorbell never stopped ringing. Elderly peeresses, aspiring hostesses, lovesick girls and struggling authors overwhelmed me with their assiduities. I hugged my success, for I knew what it meant – they thought that Rendle was in love with me! Do you know, at times, they almost made me think so too? Oh, there was no phase of folly I didn't go through. You can't imagine the excuses a woman will invent for a man's not telling her that he loves her – pitiable arguments that she would see through at a glance if any other woman used them! But all the while, deep down, I knew he had never cared. I should have known it if he had made love to me every day of his life. I could never guess whether he knew what people said about us – he listened so little to what people said; and cared still less, when he heard. He was always quite honest and straightforward with me; he treated me as one man treats another; and yet at times I felt he *must* see that with me it was different. If he did see, he made no sign. Perhaps he never noticed – I am sure he never meant to be cruel. He had never made love to me; it was no fault of his if I wanted more than he could give me. The *Sonnets to Silvia*, you say? But what are they? A cosmic philosophy, not a love poem; addressed to Woman, not to a woman!

But then, the letters? Ah, the letters! Well, I'll make a clean breast of it. You have noticed the breaks in the letters here and there, just as they seem to be on the point of growing a little – warmer? The critics, you may remember, praised the editor for his commendable delicacy and good taste (so rare in these days!) in omitting from the correspondence all personal allusions, all those *détails intimes* which should be kept sacred from the public gaze. They referred, of course, to the asterisks in the letters to Mrs. A. Those letters I myself prepared for publication; that is to say, I copied them out for the editor, and every now and then I put in a line of asterisks to make it appear that something had been left out. You understand? The asterisks were a sham – *there was nothing to leave out.*

No one but a woman could understand what I went through during those years – the moments of revolt, when I felt I must break away from it all, fling the truth in his face and never see him again; the inevitable reaction, when not to see him seemed the one unendurable thing, and I trembled lest a look or word of mine should disturb the poise of our friendship; the silly days when I hugged the delusion that he *must* love me, since everybody thought he did; the long periods of numbness, when I didn't seem to care whether he loved me or not. Between these wretched days came others when our intellectual accord was so perfect that I forgot everything else in the joy of feeling myself lifted up on the wings of his thought. Sometimes, then, the heavens seemed to be opened.

All this time he was so dear a friend! He had the genius of friendship, and he spent it all on me. Yes, you were right when you said that I have had more than any other woman. *Il faut de l'adresse pour aimer*, Pascal says; and I was so quiet, so cheerful, so frankly affectionate with him, that in all those years I am almost sure I never bored him. Could I have hoped as much if he had loved me?

You mustn't think of him, though, as having been tied to my skirts. He came and went as he pleased, and so did his fancies. There was a girl once (I am telling you everything), a lovely being who called his poetry 'deep' and gave him *Lucile* on his birthday. He followed her to Switzerland one summer, and all the time that he was dangling after her (a little too conspicuously, I always thought, for a Great Man), he was writing to *me* about his theory of vowel combinations – or was it his experiments in English hexameter? The letters were dated from the very places where I knew they went and sat by waterfalls together and he thought out adjectives for her hair. He talked to me about it quite frankly afterwards. She was perfectly beautiful and it had been a pure delight to watch her; but she *would* talk, and her mind, he said, was 'all elbows'. And yet, the next year, when her marriage was announced, he went away alone, quite suddenly . . . and it was just afterwards that he published *Love's Viaticum*. Men are queer!

After my husband died – I am putting things crudely, you see – I had a return of hope. It was because he loved me, I argued, that he had never spoken; because he had always hoped some day to make me his wife; because he wanted to spare me the 'reproach'. Rubbish! I knew well enough, in my heart of hearts, that my one chance lay in the force of habit. He had grown used to me; he was no longer young; he dreaded new people and new ways; *il avait pris son pli*. Would it not be easier to marry me?

I don't believe he ever thought of it. He wrote me what people call 'a beautiful letter'; he was kind, considerate, decently commiserating; then, after a few weeks, he slipped into his old way of coming in every afternoon, and our interminable talks began again just where they had left off. I heard later that people thought I had shown 'such good taste' in not marrying him.

So we jogged on for five years longer. Perhaps they were the best years, for I had given up hoping. Then he died.

After his death – this is curious – there came to me a kind of mirage of love. All the books and articles written about him, all the reviews of the *Life*, were full of discreet allusions to Silvia. I became again the Mrs. Anerton of the glorious days. Sentimental girls and dear lads like you turned pink when somebody whispered, 'That was Silvia you were talking to.' Idiots begged for my autograph – publishers urged me to write my reminiscences of him – critics consulted me about the reading of doubtful lines. And I knew that, to all these people, I was the woman Vincent Rendle had loved.

After a while that fire went out too and I was left alone with my past. Alone – quite alone; for he had never really been with me. The intellectual union counted for nothing now. It had been soul to soul, but never hand in hand, and there were no little things to remember him by.

Then there set in a kind of Arctic winter. I crawled into myself as into a snow hut. I hated my solitude and yet dreaded anyone who disturbed it. That phase, of course, passed like the others. I took up life again, and began to read the papers and consider the cut of my gowns. But here was one question that I could not be rid of, that haunted me night and day. Why had he never loved me? Why had I been so much to him, and no more? Was I so ugly, so essentially unlovable, that though a man might cherish me as his mind's comrade, he could not care for me as a woman? I can't tell you how that question tortured me. It became an obsession.

My poor friend, do you begin to see? I had to find out what some other man thought of me. Don't be too hard on me! Listen first – consider. When I first met Vincent Rendle I was a young woman, who had married early and led the quietest kind of life; I had had no 'experiences'. From the hour of our first meeting to the day of his death I never looked at any other man, and never noticed whether any other man looked at me. When he died, five years ago, I knew the extent of my powers no more than a baby. Was it too late to find out? Should I never know *why*?

Forgive me – forgive me. You are so young; it will be an episode, a mere 'document', to you so soon! And, besides, it wasn't as deliberate, as cold-blooded as these disjointed lines have made it appear. I didn't plan it, like a woman in a book. Life is so much more complex than any rendering of it can be. I liked you from the first – I was drawn to you (you must have seen that) – I wanted you to like me; it was not a mere psychological experiment. And yet in a sense it was that, too – I must be honest. I had to have an answer to that question; it was a ghost that had to be laid.

At first I was afraid – oh, so much afraid – that you cared

for me only because I was Silvia, that you loved me because you thought Rendle had loved me. I began to think there was no escaping my destiny.

How happy I was when I discovered that you were growing jealous of my past; that you actually hated Rendle! My heart beat like a girl's when you told me you meant to follow me to Venice.

After our parting at Villa d'Este my old doubts reasserted themselves. What did I know of your feeling for me, after all? Were you capable of analysing it yourself? Was it not likely to be two-thirds vanity and curiosity, and one-third literary sentimentality? You might easily fancy that you cared for Mary Anerton when you were really in love with Silvia – the heart is such a hypocrite! Or you might be more calculating than I had supposed. Perhaps it was you who had been flattering *my* vanity in the hope (the pardonable hope!) of turning me, after a decent interval, into a pretty little essay with a margin.

When you arrived in Venice and we met again – do you remember the music on the lagoon, that evening, from my balcony? – I was so afraid you would begin to talk about the book – the book, you remember, was your ostensible reason for coming. You never spoke of it, and I soon saw your one fear was *I* might do so – might remind you of your object in being with me. Then I knew you cared for me! yes, at that moment really cared! We never mentioned the book once, did we, during that month in Venice?

I have read my letter over; and now I wish that I had said this to you instead of writing it. I could have felt my way then, watching your face and seeing if you understood. But, no, I could not go back to Venice; and I could not tell you (though I tried) while we were there together. I couldn't spoil that month – my one month. It was so good, for once in my life, to get away from literature.

You will be angry with me at first – but, alas! not for long. What I have done would have been cruel if I had been a younger woman; as it is, the experiment will hurt no one but myself. And it will hurt me horribly (as much as, in your first anger, you may perhaps wish), because it has shown me, for the first time, all that I have missed.

KATE CHOPIN

EMANCIPATION: A LIFE FABLE

THERE was once an animal born into this world, and opening his eyes upon Life, he saw above and about him confining walls, and before him were bars of iron through which came air and light from without; this animal was born in a cage.

Here he grew, and throve in strength and beauty under care of an invisible protecting hand. Hungering, food was ever at hand. When he thirsted water was brought, and when he felt the need of rest, there was provided a bed of straw upon which to lie: and here he found it good, licking his handsome flanks, to bask in the sunbeam that he thought existed but to lighten his home.

Awaking one day from his slothful rest, lo! the door of his cage stood open: accident had opened it. In the corner he crouched, wondering and fearingly. Then slowly did he approach the door, dreading the unaccustomed, and would have closed it, but for such a task his limbs were purposeless. So out the opening he thrust his head, to see the canopy of the sky grow broader, and the world waxing wider.

Back to his corner but not to rest, for the spell of the Unknown was over him, and again and again he goes to the open door, seeing each time more Light.

Then one time standing in the flood of it; a deep

in-drawn breath – a bracing of strong limbs, and with a bound he was gone.

On he rushes, in his mad flight, heedless that he is wounding and tearing his sleek sides – seeing, smelling, touching of all things; even stopping to put his lips to the noxious pool, thinking it may be sweet.

Hungering there is no food but such as he must seek and ofttimes fight for; and his limbs are weighted before he reaches the water that is good to his thirsting throat.

So does he live, seeking, finding, joying and suffering. The door which accident had opened is open still, but the cage remains forever empty!

OLIVE SCHREINER

THREE DREAMS IN A DESERT

Under a Mimosa-Tree

AS I travelled across an African plain the sun shone down hotly. Then I drew my horse up under a mimosa-tree, and I took the saddle from him and left him to feed among the parched bushes. And all to right and to left stretched the brown earth. And I sat down under the tree, because the heat beat fiercely, and all along the horizon the air throbbed. And after a while a heavy drowsiness came over me, and I laid my head down against my saddle, and I fell asleep there. And, in my sleep, I had a curious dream.

I thought I stood on the border of a great desert, and the sand blew about everywhere. And I thought I saw two great figures like beasts of burden of the desert, and one lay upon the sand with its neck stretched out, and one stood by it. And I looked curiously at the one that lay upon the ground, for it had a great burden on its back, and the sand was thick about it, so that it seemed to have piled over it for centuries.

And I looked very curiously at it. And there stood one beside me watching. And I said to him, 'What is this huge creature who lies here on the sand?'

And he said, 'This is woman; she that bears men in her body.'

And I said, 'Why does she lie here motionless with the sand piled round her?'

And he answered, 'Listen, I will tell you! Ages and ages long she has lain here, and the wind has blown over her. The oldest, oldest, oldest man living has never seen her move: the oldest, oldest book records that she lay here then, as she lies here now, with the sand about her. But listen! Older than the oldest book, older than the oldest recorded memory of man, on the Rocks of Language, on the hard-baked clay of Ancient Customs, now crumbling to decay, are found the marks of her footsteps! Side by side with his who stands beside her you may trace them; and you know that she who now lies there once wandered free over the rocks with him.'

And I said, 'Why does she lie there now?'

And he said, 'I take it, ages ago the Age-of-dominion-of-muscular-force found her, and when she stooped low to give suck to her young, and her back was broad, he put his burden of subjection on to it, and tied it on with the broad band of Inevitable Necessity. Then she looked at the earth and the sky, and knew there was no hope for her; and she lay down on the sand with the burden she could not loosen. Ever since she has lain here. And the ages have come, and the ages have gone, but the band of Inevitable Necessity has not been cut.'

And I looked and saw in her eyes the terrible patience of the centuries; the ground was wet with her tears, and her nostrils blew up the sand.

And I said, 'Has she ever tried to move?'

And he said, 'Sometimes a limb has quivered. But she is wise; she knows she cannot rise with the burden on her.'

And I said, 'Why does not he who stands by her leave her and go on?'

And he said. 'He cannot. Look –'

And I saw a broad band passing along the ground from one to the other, and it bound them together.

He said, 'While she lies there he must stand and look across the desert.'

And I said, 'Does he know why he cannot move?'

And he said, 'No.'

And I heard a sound of something cracking and I looked and I saw the band that bound the burden on to her back broken asunder; and the burden rolled on to the ground.

And I said, 'What is this?'

And he said, 'The Age-of-nervous-force has killed him with the knife he holds in his hand; and silently and invisibly he has crept up to the woman, and with that knife of Mechanical Invention he has cut the band that bound the burden to her back. The Inevitable Necessity is broken. She must rise now.'

And I saw that she still lay motionless on the sand, with her eyes open and her neck stretched out. And she seemed to look for something on the far-off border of the desert that never came. And I wondered if she were awake or asleep. And as I looked her body quivered, and a light came into her eyes, like when a sunbeam breaks into a dark room.

I said, 'What is it?'

He whispered 'Hush! the thought has come to her, "Might I not rise?"'

And I looked. And she raised her head from the sand, and I saw the dent where her neck had lain so long. And she looked at the earth, and she looked at the sky, and she looked at him who stood by her: but he looked out across the desert.

And I saw her body quiver; and she pressed her front knees to the earth, and veins stood out; and I cried, 'She is going to rise!'

But only her sides heaved, and she lay still where she was.

But her head she held up; she did not lay it down again. And he beside me said, 'She is very weak. See, her legs have been crushed under her so long.'

And I saw the creature struggle: and the drops stood out on her.

And I said, 'Surely he who stands beside her will help her?'

And he beside me answered, 'He cannot help her: *she must help herself*. Let her struggle till she is strong.'

And I cried, 'At least he will not hinder her! See, he moves farther from her, and tightens the cord between them, and he drags her down.'

And he answered, 'He does not understand. When she moves she draws the band that binds them, and hurts him, and he moves farther from her. The day will come when he will understand, and will know what she is doing. Let her once stagger on to her knees. In that day he will stand close to her, and look into her eyes with sympathy.'

And she stretched her neck, and the drops fell from her. And the creature rose an inch from the earth and sank back.

And I cried, 'Oh, she is too weak! she cannot walk! The long years have taken all her strength from her. Can she never move?'

And he answered me, 'See the light in her eyes!'

And slowly the creature staggered on to its knees.

And I awoke: and all to the east and to the west stretched the barren earth, with the dry bushes on it. The ants ran up and down in the red sand, and the heat beat fiercely. I looked up through the thin branches of the tree at the blue sky overhead. I stretched myself, and I mused over the dream I had had. And I fell asleep again, with my head on my saddle. And in the fierce heat I had another dream.

I saw a desert and I saw a woman coming out of it. And she came to the bank of a dark river; and the bank was steep and high. And on it an old man met her, who had a long white beard; and a stick that curled was in his hand, and on it was written Reason. And he asked her what she wanted; and she said, 'I am woman; and I am seeking for the land of Freedom.'

And he said, 'It is before you.'

And she said, 'I see nothing before me but a dark flowing river, and a bank steep and high, and cuttings here and there with heavy sand in them.'

And he said, 'And beyond that?'

She said, 'I see nothing, but sometimes, when I shade my eyes with my hand, I think I see on the further bank trees and hills, and the sun shining on them!'

He said, 'That is the Land of Freedom.'

She said, 'How am I to get there?'

He said, 'There is one way, and one only. Down the banks of Labour, through the water of Suffering. There is no other.'

She said, 'Is there no bridge?'

He answered, 'None.'

She said, 'Is the water deep?'

He said, 'Deep.'

She said, 'Is the floor worn?'

He said, 'It is. Your foot may slip at any time, and you may be lost.'

She said, 'Have any crossed already?'

He said, 'Some have *tried!*'

She said, 'Is there a track to show where the best fording is?'

He said, 'It has to be made.'

She shaded her eyes with her hand; and she said, 'I will go.'

And he said, 'You must take off the clothes you wore in the desert: they are dragged down by them who go into the water so clothed.'

And she threw from her gladly the mantle of Ancient-received-opinions she wore, for it was worn full of holes. And she took the girdle from her waist that she had treasured so long, and the moths flew out of it in a cloud. And he said, 'Take the shoes of dependence off your feet.'

And she stood there naked, but for one white garment that clung close to her.

And he said. 'That you may keep. So they wear clothes in the Land of Freedom. In the water it buoys; it always swims.'

And I saw on its breast was written Truth; and it was white; the sun had not often shone on it; the other clothes had covered it up. And he said, 'Take this stick; hold it fast. In that day when it slips from your hand you are lost. Put it down before you; feel your way: where it cannot find a bottom do not set your foot.'

And she said, 'I am ready; let me go.'

And he said, 'No – but stay; what is that – in your breast?'

She was silent.

He said, 'Open it, and let me see.'

And she opened it. And against her breast was a tiny thing, who drank from it, and the yellow curls above his forehead pressed against it; and his knees were drawn up to her, and he held her breast fast with his hands.

And Reason said, 'Who is he, and what is he doing here?'

And she said, 'See his little wings –'

And Reason said, 'Put him down.'

And she said, 'He is asleep, and he is drinking! I will carry him to the Land of Freedom. He has been a child so long, so long, I have carried him. In the Land of Freedom he will be a man. We will walk together there, and his great white wings will overshadow me. He has lisped one word only to me in the desert – "Passion!" I have dreamed he might learn to say "Friendship" in that land.'

And Reason said, 'Put him down!'

And she said, 'I will carry him so – with one arm, and with the other I will fight the water.'

He said, 'Lay him down on the ground. When you are in the water you will forget to fight, you will think only of him. Lay him down.' He said, 'He will not die. When he finds you have left him alone he will open his wings and fly. He will be in the Land of Freedom before you. Those who reach the Land of Freedom, the first hand they see stretching down the bank to help them shall be Love's. He will be a man then, not a child. In your breast he cannot thrive; put him down that he may grow.'

And she took her bosom from his mouth, and he bit her, so that the blood ran down on to the ground. And she laid him down on the earth; and she covered her wound. And she bent and stroked his wings. And I saw the hair on her forehead turned white as snow, and she had changed from youth to age.

And she stood far off on the bank of the river. And she said, 'For what do I go to this far land which no one has ever reached? *Oh, I am alone! I am utterly alone!*'

And Reason, that old man, said to her, 'Silence! what do you hear?'

And she listened intently, and she said, 'I hear a sound of feet, a thousand times ten thousand and thousands of thousands, and they beat this way!'

He said, 'They are the feet of those that shall follow you. Lead on! make a track to the water's edge! Where you stand now, the ground will be beaten flat by ten thousand times ten thousand feet.' And he said, 'Have you seen the locusts how they cross a stream? First one comes down to the water-edge, and it is swept away, and then another comes and then another, and then another, and at last with their bodies piled up a bridge is built and the rest pass over.'

She said, 'And, of those that come first, some are swept away, and are heard of no more; their bodies do not even build the bridge?'

'And are swept away, and are heard of no more – and what of that?' he said.

'And what of that –' she said.

'They make a track to the water's edge.'

'They make a track to the water's edge –' And she said, 'Over that bridge which shall be built with our bodies, who will pass?'

He said, '*The entire human race*.'

And the woman grasped her staff.

And I saw her turn down that dark path to the river.

And I awoke; and all about me was the yellow afternoon light: the sinking sun lit up the fingers of the milk bushes; and my horse stood by me quietly feeding. And I turned on my side, and I watched the ants run by thousands in the red sand. I thought I would go on my way now – the afternoon was cooler. Then a drowsiness crept over me again, and I laid back my head and fell asleep.

And I dreamed a dream.

I dreamed I saw a land. And on the hills walked brave women and brave men, hand in hand. And they looked into each other's eyes, and they were not afraid.

And I saw the women also hold each other's hands.

And I said to him beside me, 'What place is this?'

And he said, 'This is heaven.'

And I said, 'Where is it?'

And he answered, 'On earth.'
And I said, 'When shall these things be?'
And he answered, 'IN THE FUTURE.'

And I awoke, and all about me was the sunset light; and on the low hills the sun lay, and a delicious coolness had crept over everything; and the ants were going slowly home. And I walked towards my horse, who stood quietly feeding. Then the sun passed down behind the hills; but I knew that the next day he would arise again.

OLIVE SCHREINER

LIFE'S GIFTS

I saw a woman sleeping. In her sleep she dreamt Life stood before her, and held in each hand a gift – in the one Love, in the other Freedom. And she said to the woman. 'Choose!'

And the woman waited long: and she said, 'Freedom!'

And Life said, 'Thou hast well chosen. If thou hadst said, 'Love', I would have given thee that thou didst ask for; and I would have gone from thee, and returned to thee no more. Now, the day will come when I shall return. In that day I shall bear both gifts in one hand.'

I heard the woman laugh in her sleep.

EDITH WHARTON

THE VALLEY OF CHILDISH THINGS

ONCE upon a time a number of children lived together in the Valley of Childish Things, playing all manner of delightful games, and studying the same lesson-books. But one day a little girl, one of their number, decided that it was time to see something of the world about which the lesson-books had taught her; and as none of the other children cared to leave their games, she set out alone to climb the pass which led out of the valley.

It was a hard climb, but at length she reached a cold, bleak table-land beyond the mountains. Here she saw cities and men, and learned many useful arts, and in so doing grew to be a woman. But the table-land was bleak and cold, and when she had served her apprenticeship she decided to return to her old companions in the Valley of Childish Things, and work with them instead of with strangers.

It was a weary way back, and her feet were bruised by the stones, and her face was beaten by the weather; but half way down the pass she met a man, who kindly helped her over the roughest places. Like herself, he was lame and weather-beaten; but as soon as he spoke she recognised him as one of her old playmates. He too had been out in the world, and was going back to the valley; and on the way they talked together of the work they meant to do there. He had been a dull boy, and she had never taken much notice of him; but as she listened to his plans for building bridges and draining swamps and cutting roads through the jungle, she thought to herself, 'Since he has grown into such a fine fellow, what splendid men and women my other playmates must have become!'

But what was her surprise to find, on reaching the valley, that her former companions, instead of growing into men and women, had all remained little children. Most of them were playing the same old games, and the few who affected to be working were engaged in such strenuous occupations as building mudpies and sailing paper boats in basins. As for the lad who had been the favourite companion of her studies, he was playing marbles with all the youngest boys in the valley.

At first the children seemed glad to have her back, but soon she saw that her presence interfered with their games; and when she tried to tell them of the great things that were being done on the table-land beyond the mountains, they picked up their toys and went farther down the valley to play.

Then she turned to her fellow-traveller, who was the only grown man in the valley; but he was on his knees before a dear little girl with blue eyes and a coral necklace, for whom he was making a garden out of cockle-shells and bits of glass, and broken flowers stuck in sand.

The little girl was clapping her hands and crowing (she was too young to speak articulately); and when she who had grown to be a woman laid her hand on the man's shoulder, and asked him if he did not want to set to work with her building bridges, draining swamps, and cutting roads through the jungle, he replied that at that particular moment he was too busy.

And as she turned away, he added in the kindest possible way, 'Really, my dear, you ought to have taken better care of your complexion.'

BIOGRAPHICAL NOTES

Kate (O'Flaherty) Chopin (1850–1904) was born in St Louis. Her father was killed in a railroad accident when she was four, and she was raised by her mother's wealthy French Creole family. She attended the Academy of the Sacred Heart in St Louis from 1860 to 1868, and in 1870 married Oscar Chopin, a cotton factor from New Orleans. She had six children in the next nine years. Oscar's business failed in 1880, however, and he died two years later. She took her children back to live with her mother in St Louis, and began writing following her mother's death in 1885. Her first novel, *At Fault* (1891), was not very successful, although it dealt with the theme of women's sexual passion that she returned to regularly. She next wrote local colour stories about rural Louisiana, many of them collected as *Bayou Folk* (1984) and *A Night in Acadie* (1897.) Her frank treatment of sexuality created scandal, however; her greatest work, *The Awakening* (1899), provoked an uproar of hostile criticism. She wrote very little afterwards, and died only five years later, of a brain hemorrhage, in her home in St Louis.

Victoria Cross(e) (***Annie Sophie Cory***) (1868–1952) was the daughter of Fanny (Griffin) and Arthur Cory, a colonel in the Indian army; her sister 'Laurence Hope' (Adela Nicolson) became a poet and another sister, Isabell Tate, edited the *Sind Gazette*. Cross grew up in India and never married. She travelled throughout the world with her uncle, finally settling in Monte Carlo, where she wrote several popular novels. Among the best known were *The Woman Who Didn't* (1895), thus retitled by her publisher John Lane so as to allude to Grant

Allen's *The Woman Who Did*; *Anna Lombard* (1898), about a married woman who continues a pre-marital affair; *Life of My Heart*, about an interracial couple; and her last work, *Martha Brown, MP* (1935).

George Egerton (*Mary Chavelita Dunne*) (1859–1945) was born in Australia. During her childhood she lived in New Zealand, Chile, Wales, Ireland, and Germany; after her mother's death in 1875 she cared for her younger siblings, and held various jobs in Dublin, London, and New York. In 1887 she eloped to Norway with Henry Higginson, a friend of her father's and a bigamist; Higginson died there two years later. While in Norway she read the works of Ibsen and Strindberg, and on returning to London in 1890 she began a translation of Knut Hamsun's novel *Hunger*, which was published in 1899. In 1891 she married Goerge Egerton Clairmonte and moved to Ireland. She gave birth to a son in 1895, but her marriage ended soon afterwards. In 1901 she married Reginald Golding Bright, a drama critic fifteen years younger than herself. Her writing career began with a collection of short stories published as *Keynotes* in 1893 with great success. A second volume, *Discords*, appeared the following year; her other works include *Young Ofeg's Ditties* (1895), *Symphonies* (1897), *Fantasias* (1898), *The Wheel of God* (1898), *Rosa Amorosa* (1901), and *Flies in Amber* (1905). She also wrote a number of unsuccessful plays. She died at her home at Ifield Park, Crawley.

George Fleming (*Julia Constance Fletcher*) (1853–1938) was born in America, but spent her most productive years in Europe, where she finally settled in Rome. She met and impressed Oscar Wilde both as a writer and as a conversationalist; he dedicated his poem 'Ravenna' (1878) to her. She translated the Venetian poet Gaspara Stampa and Edmond Rostand. *A Nile Novel* (1876; republished as *Kismet* in 1877) was her first success; it is the story of an American woman in Egypt, who must break free from an engagement to be with the man she loves. Other titles included *The Truth about Clement Ker* (1889), about a woman in an unhappy marriage; *Mirage* (1877), a parody of Wilde set in the Middle East; *The Head of the Medusa* (1880), *Vestigia* (1884), *Andromeda* (1885), *For Plain Women Only* (1895), and *Little Stories about Women* (1897).

Charlotte (Perkins) Stetson Gilman (1860–1935) was born in Hartford, Connecticut. Her father, a nephew of Harriet Beecher Stowe, abandoned his family shortly after Charlotte's birth, leaving his wife and children in near poverty. Charlotte received limited formal education and began working very young as an artist and governess. She married Charles Walter Stetson, an artist, in 1884, and gave birth to a daughter the following year; but she then suffered an extended depression, for which she took the rest cure prescribed by Dr. S. Weir Mitchell. A trip to California without her husband in 1885 proved more restorative. She concluded that her sanity required a separation, and took her daughter to Pasadena in 1888, obtaining a divorce in 1894. In 1900 she married her first cousin, George Houghton Gilman, who supported her activities as writer, lecturer, and campaigner for women's rights. She began writing as a journalist in the 1890s, to earn a living; her short story, 'The Yellow Wallpaper,' appeared in 1892. On a trip to England she met Shaw and the Webbs and became an advocate of Fabian socialism. Most of her writings were essays on women's issues, including *Women and Economics* (1898), *Concerning Children* (1900), *The Home* (1903), *The Man-Made World* (1911), and *His Religion and Hers* (1923). From 1909 to 1916 she edited her own novels, *What Diantha Did* (1910) and *The Crux* (1911). In 1935 she published her autobiography, *The Living of Charlotte Perkins Gilman*. The same year, suffering from cancer and mourning her husband's sudden death a year before, she took her own life.

Sarah Grand (*Frances Elizabeth Bellenden (Clarke) McFall*) (1854–1943) was born in Ireland. Her father died in 1861 and she moved with her mother to Yorkshire and then attended finishing school in London. In 1871 she married David Chambers McFall, an army surgeon and widower with two sons; her own son was born the same year. She spent several years in South and East Asia with her husband, who retired in 1881 in Lancashire. In 1890 she left him to pursue her career as an author, adopting the name Sarah Grand in 1893. In 1920 she moved to Bath, where she served six years as Mayoress, and met her friend and biographer, Gladys Singers-Bigger. She had begun writing quite early in her life, but without much success until *The*

Heavenly Twins in 1893, which attacked the sexual double standard. Other major works include *The Beth Book* (1897), *Babs the Impossible* (1901), *Adnam's Orchard* (1912), and *The Winged Victory* (1916). She is credited with coining the term 'New Woman' in 1894, and she toured America as well as England lecturing on women's suffrage. After Bath was bombed in 1942, Grand moved to The Grange, Calne, where she died the next year.

Vernon Lee (*Violet Paget*) (1856–1935) was born in France near Boulogne. For financial reasons, her family moved frequently throughout Germany until 1866, when they were persuaded to accompany Mary Singer Sargent and her son John to Rome. There she pursued her education and began to write under Mrs Sargent's tutelage. Her first article, published when she was fourteen, dealt with ancient coins. She took the pen name Vernon Lee in 1878 because she believed that 'a woman's writing on art, history or aesthetics' would never be taken seriously. *Studies of the Eighteenth Century in Italy* (1880) established her reputation in literary and artistic circles in London. She published numerous novels, many with carefully researched historical settings, such as *Ottilie* (1883), *Penelope Brandling* (1903), and *Louis Norbert* (1914); other fiction included the satirical *Miss Brown* (1884), the fantasy *A Phantom Lover* (1886), and a collection of stories, *Hauntings* (1890). Lee also wrote travel books, including *Genius Loci* (1899), *The Spirit of Rome* (1906), and *The Sentimental Treveller* (1908). Her works on aesthetics were well received, especially *The Beautiful* (1913), which she co-authored with Kit Anstruther-Thomason, and *The Handling of Words* (1923), applying the ideas to literary texts.

Ada (Beddington) Leverson (1862–1933) was born in London. Her wealthy family was able to give her a sound education at home, emphasising French, German, and the Classics. At the age of nineteen, she married Ernest Leverson without her father's consent. It proved an unhappy union: their son died while still a boy, her husband suffered financial troubles, and by 1905 he had left her without financial support and gone to Canada. She met Oscar Wilde in 1892; he dubbed her 'The Sphinx.' Later she assisted him during his trials. She was also a friend of Edith Sitwell and Violet Hunt. Leverson's early works were parodies published in *Punch*, including one of Wilde called 'An Afternoon Party' (1893), in which Lady Windermere, Salome, and Nora (from Ibsen) get together. She also did pastiches of Kipling and Beerbohm. Her novels, often partly autobiographical, included *The Twelfth Hour* (1907); *Love's Shadow* (1908), about an egotistical husband and his long-suffering wife; *Tenterhooks* (1912), about an illicit love affair; and *Love at Second Sight* (1916), in which the heroine discovers happiness after her husband departs for the United States. Leverson also wrote a book on astrology in 1915, a tribute to her old friend Wilde in 1926, and left a comedy, *The Triflers*, incomplete at her death.

Charlotte Mew (1869–1928) was born in London, where she attended a girls' school; she also took some classes at University College, London. Her father's death in 1898, however, left the family in dire circumstances; she had six siblings, of whom two were in institutions for the mentally disturbed. Mew published her story 'Passed' in *The Yellow Book* in 1894 and wrote prose and poetry for magazines in order to support herself until the First World War. May Sinclair and Alida Monro helped her publish her poetry in *The Egoist* and in a volume of her own entitled *The Farmer's Bride* (1916). She also wrote about her private life, the social problems of the day, women's history, and literary criticism. Mew's mother died after a long illness in 1923, and her last surviving sister died in 1927, again after a long illness. Less than a year later, Mew took her own life in a nursing home, by drinking disinfectant.

Olive (Emily Albertina) Schreiner (1855–1920) was born in Cape Colony, now part of South Africa, the ninth child of a poor missionary living on an isolated farm. Her harsh upbringing instilled in her a lifelong sympathy for the oppressed. From 1870 to 1881 she worked as a governess, writing in her spare time. In 1881 she moved to London, where she joined the Fellowship of the New Life, a society founded by Havelock Ellis and other intellectuals to promote socialism and sexual equality. She returned to South Africa in 1889 and married Samuel Cronwright, who shared her political views and agreed to take the name Cronwright–Schreiner. Schreiner devoted herself to working against the racist and imperialist policies of the South African government, and to campaigning for women's rights organisations and trade unions; during the Boer War she was imprisoned. Her career was launched with the immediate success of the autobiographical *The Story of an African Farm* (1883); other major works include *Women and Labour* (1911), hailed as the 'Bible of the Women's Movement.' She returned to England in 1913, in ill health, but went home to South Africa alone in 1920, where she died the same year.

Edith Newbold (Jones) Wharton (1862-1937) was born in New York, of wealthy and socially prominent parents. She spent much of her childhood in Europe and although she received little formal education, she developed an early taste for the arts. In 1885 she married Edward Robbins Wharton, a wealthy banker thirteen years her senior. After several years of relative idleness and depression, she turned to writing; her first book, *The Decoration of Houses* (1897), was based on her work remodeling a newly purchased house. She moved permanently to Paris in 1906; she had a passionate affair with a journalist, Morton Fullerton, and divorced her husband in 1913. By that time Wharton had become famous as a novelist, and frequented a cosmopolitan society of writers and intellectuals, including most notably Henry James. She worked to aid victims of World War I and was decorated by the French and Belgian governments for her contributions. She achieved great renown with the publication of *The House of Mirth* (1905); other well known novels include *Ethan Frome* (1911), *The Custom of the Country* (1913), and *The Age of Innocence* (1921), for which she was awarded the Pulitzer Prize. She returned only once to the United States, to accept an honorary degree from Yale in 1923. Wharton died in surburban Paris, of an apoplectic stroke, leaving an unfinished novel, *The Buccaneers* (1938).

Constance Fenimore Woolson (1840–1894) was born in New Hampshire, and grew up in Cleveland, Ohio. Her mother was a niece of James Fenimore Cooper. She attended schools in Cleveland and finishing school in New York. Hew family vacationed regularly on Mackinac Island in Lake Michigan. After her father's death in 1869, Constance travelled extensively in the eastern and southern

United States with her mother. Both the family holidays and the later trips provided material for Woolson's first publications, a series of travel sketches. On her mother's death in 1879, she moved abroad, settling mainly in England but also touring frequently on the Continent; she was a close and longterm friend of Henry James. Her works include two volumes of sketches, *Castle Nowhere: Lake Country Sketches* (1875) and *Rodman the Keeper: Southern Sketches* (1880); several novels, including *Anne* (1882, serialised in 1879), *For the Major* (1883), *East Angels* (1886), *Jupiter Lights* (1889), and *Horace Chase* (1894), the last four of which were accounts of the pioneer life; and the posthumous collections of stories and sketches, *The Front Yard, and Other Italian Stories* (1895), *Dorothy, and Other Italian Stories* (1896), and *Mentone, Cairo, and Corfu* (1896). Ill with influenza and typhoid, and depressed, she died in Venice by falling from a window, possibly a suicide.

Mabel Emily Wotton was born in 1863 in the London borough of Lambeth. She never married, and little is known of her early life. Her novel, *A Girl Diplomatist* (1892), met with such disparaging criticism that Wotton nursed a lingering bitterness throughout her life towards the world of books and bookmen. This anger surfaced in *Day–Books*, a set of stories published in 1896 in the 'Keynote Series' of the Bodley Head, edited by John Lane. The stories depicted the pains of everyday life, including the trials and moral dilemmas of authorship. She published several other collections of stories, including *A Pretty Radical and other stories* (1889) and *On Music's Wings* (1898). She published no new books of fiction after 1900 and died at her home in London in 1927.

Also by Elaine Showalter

THE NEW FEMINIST CRITICISM

Essays on Women, Literature and Theory

'A chorus of insistent, eloquent voices proving . . . that women's writing and feminist criticism are diverse, vital, flourishing' *Elizabeth Wilson*

Together, these eighteen essays, by such well-known critics as Rosalind Coward, Sandra Gilbert, Susan Gubar, Carolyn Heilbrun and Annette Kolodny, offer a much-needed overview of feminist critical theory and practice. They explore the intellectual and political issues that have emerged with the development of feminist literary theory, looking closely at the relationship of women's writing to ethnicity, separatism, and feminism itself. And they ask how women's writing differs from men's in its recurrent images, symbols, themes, plots and styles. From the Brontës to modern romance, the poetry of Emily Dickinson to the novels of Toni Morrison, these lively, provocative essays call upon a wide range of authors of different nationalities and generations. Complete with a comprehensive bibliography of feminist literary theory, this is an indispensable contribution to one of the most important intellectual movements of recent time.

A LITERATURE OF THEIR OWN

From Charlotte Brontë to Doris Lessing

'Elaine Showalter's proceedings in this book, both as historian and as literary critic, are sane, illuminating, fascinating and wise'
A. S. Byatt

In this brilliant study of British women novelists, Elaine Showalter traces the development of their fiction from the 1800s onwards. This original, refreshing and sometimes controversial book not only includes assessments of famous writers such as the Brontës, George Eliot, Virginia Woolf, Margaret Drabble and Doris Lessing, but also presents critical appraisals of Mary Braddon, Rhoda Broughton and Sarah Grand – to name but a few of those prolific and successful novelists – once household names, now largely forgotten.

The result is an invaluable record of generations of women writers and the way in which their work reflects the social changes of their time.

THE FEMALE MALADY

Women, Madness and English Culture, 1830–1980

'She writes with penetration, precision, and passion. This book is essential reading, for all those concerned with what psychiatry has done to women, and what a new psychiatry could do for them'
Roy Porter, Wellcome Institute for the History of Medicine

In this informative, timely and often harrowing study, Elaine Showalter demonstrates how cultural ideas about 'proper' feminine behaviour have shaped the definition and treatment of female insanity for 150 years, and given mental disorder in women a specifically sexual connotation. Along with vivid portraits of the men who dominated psychiatry, and descriptions of the therapeutic practices that were used to bring women to their senses, she draws on diaries and narratives by inmates, and fiction from Mary Wollstonecraft to Doris Lessing, to supply a cultural perspective usually missing from studies of mental illness.

Highly original and beautifully written, *The Female Malady* is a vital counter-interpretation of madness in women, showing how it is a consequence of, rather than a deviation from, the traditional female role.

THE END OF THE NOVEL OF LOVE

Vivian Gornick

In this book of new and collected critical essays, Vivian Gornick examines a century of novels of love-in-the-western-world in which authors have portrayed romantic love as an emblem of the search for self-understanding and self-discovery.

However, today, Gornick argues, love as a literary metaphor is no longer apt – such has the nature of love and romance and marriage changed. Gornick traces this progress of realisation through the lives and works of celebrated authors such as Willa Cather, Jean Rhys, Christian Stead, Grace Paley, Raymond Carver, and others, and shows us how novels have increasingly questioned the inevitability of tender romantic love and marriage as the path to self-knowledge and fulfilment.

Today, love as metaphor is an act of nostalgia, not of discovery.

Also of Interest

BLOOMSBURY PIE

The story of the Bloomsbury revival

Regina Marler

'Shrewd and stimulating' *Guardian*

'Fascinating' *Independent on Sunday*

We hotly debate their work, film their obscure love affairs, name pubs after them, buy coffee mugs painted with their images . . . Why, almost eighty years after the emergence of the best-documented literary and artistic coterie in twentieth-century Britain, are we still fascinated by the 'Bloomsberries'?

Regina Marler chronicles the story of the Bloomsbury boom – its scholars, collectors and fanatics – and explores the industry it has spawned among writers, publishers and art dealers. In the process she creates an impressive social history of a tenacious and unwieldy cultural phenomenon.